THE ANSWER YOU ARE LOOKING FOR IS YES

Olivie Blake

ALSO *by* OLIVIE BLAKE:

Masters of Death

Lovely Tangled Vices

One For My Enemy

La Petite Mort

The Atlas Six

Alone With You in the Ether

Fairytales of the Macabre (Fairytale Collections, Vol. I)

Midsummer Night Dreams (Fairytale Collections, Vol. II)

The Lovers Grim (Fairytale Collections, Vol. III)

By OLIVIE BLAKE *and*
LITTLE CHMURA:

Alpha

Alpha, Vol. II: Rising

WITCH WAY
PUBLISHING

First Edition, 2020

Witch Way Publishing
9090 Skillman St, #182-A/203
Dallas, TX 75243
www.witchwaypublishing.com

Editor: Tonya Brown
Cover Designer: Olivie Blake

Printed in the United States of America

ISBN 978-0-578-5552-01

for my mother and mother figures,
the cult of (inclusive) femininity,
and Swedish electro-pop duo Icona Pop.

I don't care, I love it.

TABLE *of* CONTENTS

STONE'S THROW (JANUARY-MARCH 2020)

WHEN ARTIST JENNY LI agrees to help Dr. Salim Amrani with his research on global practices of witchcraft, she's mostly looking for a paycheck. The two never meet in person, but when the professor suddenly disappears without warning, Jenny's instincts tell her that something more troubling might be at play. Seeking the compensation she's owed, Jenny goes after Salim, intent on recovering her lost income.

What Jenny doesn't know is that Salim has a secret that might consume them both.

PART I: MYSTICAL ANTHROPOLOGY

She first heard his voice on a podcast about mythology from the so-called Ancient World. It was something she was trying out, podcasts. New Year's resolutions and all that, with the general aim of educating herself beyond her little bubble of creativity, though she didn't expect to stick with it. What had interested her wasn't so much the subject at hand (something about the lost library of Carthage) but the way he spoke, and specifically, his title. Dr. Salim Amrani was what he had dubbed a "mystical anthropologist," ostensibly meaning he studied the effects of the paranormal, the supernatural, and the spiritual on various cultures in the world. He had the credentials of someone much less eccentric—raised among London's elite, Eton and Cambridge educated, currently at Oxford and on loan to Harvard—and a measured, deliberate pattern of speech that made him sound perfectly scholarly, and therefore undoubtedly academic.

Also, he was looking for witches.

This interested Jenny, of course. The way Dr. Amrani spoke about his research on the subject of mysticism in the modern world was less cinematic or romanticized than it was simple curiosity: If there were rituals, where did the rituals come from? Who had passed them down? Were Western witches different from Eastern witches? All interesting questions, though to this day Jenny remained unsure what compelled her to email him. She supposed his podcast summons for someone with experience in what he called, "occultism, the metaphysical, or other related spells and rituals" had hit her while she was feeling particularly visionary (blame her Aquarius moon).

The interesting thing about being the daughter of immigrants, she wrote, *is that I have experience in both worlds. Chinese medicine, Celtic runes, all that. I learned from my family on both sides. (The influence of the moon, interestingly enough, is pretty much the same no matter how you slice it.) Overall it's not as exciting as you'd think— I can't fly on a broomstick or anything, but I make a lot of my own herbal remedies. It's a lot of fae superstition, astrological intuition, that sort of thing. I design tarot decks for a living.*

His response had been ruthlessly direct. *Would you consider collaborating with me on a book I'm writing? It's something I'm doing for a Harvard syndicate. The university will pay.*

Jenny certainly wasn't an academician, but her career (if you could call it that) wasn't going particularly well at present. She was teaching yoga part time to supplement the income she wasn't making on her tarot decks. Social media was a performative drain, and this seemed… interesting. Promising. At least a lifetime of lessons and stories from her Chinese grandmother and her Irish mother could be put to use for something.

How much work are you expecting? she wrote.

He replied immediately with his stipulations: about twenty hours a week for the next two months, which took some time away from her art, but he offered a shocking amount more than she made at the studio. Part of her wondered whether it was a scam, but the contract seemed clear enough (there was mention of a 1099 tax form) and for the first three weeks she was paid with such committed regularity it seemed borderline religious. She had never met Dr. Amrani, as his work was based in Boston and she was currently living in Berkeley, but came to understand the fundamentals of his personality quite quickly. Namely, that he didn't care much about her or her feelings, but he was heedlessly devoted to his work.

Then week four came along. *I'm expecting to make some real progress before we move into the next chapter*, wrote Dr. Amrani. *Please send over a list of celestial fertility runes at your earliest convenience. End of day Wednesday if possible.*

She did, though it was difficult to complete on his timetable, and she was moderately annoyed at losing half her workweek to the whims of a man who made no effort to be friendly. She waited, grumbling, for the inevitable response; the next "actionable item," as he liked to say. When it didn't arrive within ten minutes, she wandered away from her computer, relieved she might have some time to properly eat lunch. When an hour passed, she checked her watch expectantly, thinking it might be fair to spend the afternoon working on her subscriber newsletter. When she hadn't heard from him by that evening, she grew a little concerned, but was mostly relieved. In the morning, when there was still no response, she cheerfully took herself to coffee, contentedly buckling down with Illustrator on her iPad and not checking her phone for the entire day as she worked.

By that evening, though, she grew impatient. She had never had to wait longer than an hour for a response from him; even when he had faculty meetings, he usually sent a perfunctory email that said something to the extent of "We'll discuss this further in forty-five minutes." And then, forty-five minutes later, a response, like clockwork. This sort of silence was not only inconvenient, it was distinctly odd.

When Jenny didn't receive her direct deposit as she usually did, she progressed to annoyed. *Following up!* was her too-cheerful reply to her unanswered email, the exclamation point included to prevent herself from sounding as irritated as she felt.

The weekend came and went without reply.

By Tuesday she was feeling significantly off. *Proof of life, please?* she wrote, only to realize that if he *had* died, Harvard might easily overlook the task of informing her. After all, he was a visiting fellow, as far as she knew. He wasn't actually a tenured professor, so maybe they wouldn't have access to all his projects.

She googled his name, just to see, and after sifting through people who *weren't* him and finding no evidence of an obituary, she realized he was much younger than she'd thought. The British accent she'd heard on the podcast was obviously misleading; according to his very sparse university bio, he could have only been in his early or mid-thirties at the oldest. He was unmarried, did not have children, and the personal information from his previous books stated only that he lived in London, no mention of pets or friends. He didn't have an Instagram, and his Twitter feed contained nothing of his own voice, only re-Tweets of colleagues and other academics.

"Whatever happened with that book you were writing with that professor?" asked one of her friends at brunch, which was not something Jenny should have even had time for. Also, it was something she should have had another two weeks of hourly wages to pay for, if only the professor in question had not gone missing.

"I think he might be dead," said Jenny, only half-joking.

By the time three weeks had passed, she had progressed from annoyed to concerned to angry. By then he had cost her half a rent payment in unpaid wages without even the decency to reply to a single email. She called his office, left a message, and then called his department head. They hadn't heard from him, they said.

After a month, she was boiling over. Really, who behaved like this? She was drumming her fingers to the sound of her own agitation when the studio owner tapped her on the shoulder, saying something had come in for her.

"What is it?"

"A fax."

"A *fax*? What is this, 1986?"

"Don't ask me," said Maria, shrugging and walking away, as Jenny was left to glance down at the strangest message she'd ever seen.

Jenny, he needs your help.

It was the off-season. Tickets were cheap. Besides, she had never been to Boston. Jenny ran through her more reasonable explanations in her head, ticking them off slowly, comfortingly.

In reality, her more pressing reasons were irrational to the point of nonsense: she had pulled the moon card from her deck. A full read had told her something was waiting for her; not waiting, actually. More like looming. The fool, the eight of cups. The knight of wands, upended. She wanted to chalk that up to bullshit, only she was the one who had designed the deck, so that was a tough call. She knew what these cards meant down to her bones, and besides, her witch's intuition meant alarm bells had long been ringing. Something was wrong, and it wasn't like she was going to get paid if she didn't find out.

Rent wasn't cheap in the Bay Area. At the very least, she was owed an explanation.

"I'm looking for Dr. Amrani," she said to someone in Harvard's anthropology department, who shrugged with apparent lack of recognition. "Is there anyone who could track him down for me?"

"That asshole?"

She turned in time to catch the sound of the passing voice.

"Jesus, thought he finally OD'd or something. Hasn't been by in weeks," said someone Jenny assumed was a T.A., a young-looking blond who happened to overhear as he was walking by. "Are you here to pick up his shit?" he asked before Jenny could clarify whether the man she worked for was or wasn't on drugs (which might explain things, albeit not satisfactorily). "The office is starting to get a weird smell."

"No, I'm—" She considered it, deciding it was probably better not to get into what she really was to Dr. Amrani, which was essentially a stranger. "Well, sure," she amended. "I locked myself out of my apartment, so I thought he might keep a spare set of keys here."

"Oh. Are you like, his girlfriend?" asked the T.A., looking bewildered. "That seems unlikely."

"Thanks," said Jenny, opting to take that as a compliment. "Keys?"

The T.A. led her to Dr. Amrani's office, which he shared with two other untenured professors. "That's his desk," said the T.A., remarking something again about the smell before turning to the door to make 'a shitload of copies.' "If you ever want to date someone normal, look me up," he added in underwhelming conclusion, and then he disappeared.

It was unclear where the drug suspicion came from at first glance. Dr. Salim Amrani was extremely neat, his possessions potentially sparse to the point of being secretive, but unlikely. The smell in question was mundane enough, coming from what turned out to be a Greek salad left in one of the bottom drawers. In the top drawer, Jenny located a pad of sticky notes, a keyring with two identical keys, one office key, and one mail key (spares from the super, she guessed) and a small tin of paper clips. If he kept his notes somewhere, they weren't here. There wasn't even a thumb drive anywhere in sight, nor was there any proof he did any real work here. She picked up the keys and buttered up the student working in the department's main office, procuring his address from his university contact form. (This time, she didn't lie. "He owes me money," she said in flatlined explanation. "Oh god, what an asshole. You should call the police," said the redheaded sophomore, pursing her lips conspiratorially.)

Calling the police and reporting him missing was probably a more reasonable idea than breaking into his house, but she'd already come this far. Jenny let herself into his apartment (bottom floor in a small complex) and discovered immediately that this, unlike his office, was where he *actually* did his work. The place was undecorated but absolutely littered with notes to himself; she counted six whiteboards, none of them hung on the walls, all of them covered in incomprehensible scribbles. Handwritten notes were everywhere, flung around amid a maelstrom of heavily piled books. He had one sofa, ten empty water bottles, and a coat rack with a single double-breasted Burberry coat. His phone was sitting on top of the kitchen counter, dead.

Jenny picked it up with a grimace, plugging it into the nearest outlet to charge, and then continued making her way through his apartment. There were two bedrooms; one contained a bed with one side fastidiously made, the other rumpled and untucked. A pair of reading glasses sat beside the bed above a book called *Lost Wonders of the Ancient World*. The nightstand also did not contain drugs, much to Jenny's relief; a brief glance produced a handful of condoms (normal) and then, much to her surprise, one of her own tarot decks. She slid one of the cards loose, glancing down at the familiar knight of cups and fingering the edge of her art: part celestial runes, part sophisticated minimalism. Or so the online distributer touted on her behalf.

She plucked the card from the nightstand and paused, frowning, when she heard a sound from the kitchen. His cell phone, most likely. It went off once, then twice, and then several times in succession, and she wandered back into the kitchen, tarot card still in hand.

Aside from the expected bursts of confusion from senders blandly labeled *Dad* and *Department Head*, the messages were mostly from an unknown number. Disregarding the series of frantic *where are u are u dead* messages, Jenny scrolled up, looking to identify the source. *Tell me if it works*, had been a recent one, and *price is steep my man*, and then before that, *u sure u want to try it alone?*

The earliest message was this: *Yo, I think I found that key.*

Jenny hit call, dialing the number. It rang with no answer, and then, abruptly, the call failed.

"Weird," she said aloud.

The one thing that was missing—that she was *sure* he needed, drugs or otherwise—was a computer. The second bedroom, she reasoned, must have been his office. She set the phone down and headed for the other room, distracted for a moment by her reflection from the bathroom.

Well, she looked insane. There was no doubt about that. She was in a stranger's house poking around in his things, half afraid he might walk in at any moment. A normal person might have done as the office assistant suggested and call the cops.

But then what? Explain that she'd come here because of… a *feeling?*

She sighed, turning away. Too late now. Something had obviously happened to him, and if this room contained a flash drive or something, then maybe she'd at least have an answer to her questions. After all, that was what she'd come here for, wasn't it?

So she set her hand on the knob, pushing it open.

Salim Amrani had been convinced from the age of six that his older brother was not actually his brother, but in fact some sort of faerie changeling. This is a fact that eventually came to define his life. When Hasan Amrani was found dead of an overdose at twenty-one, Salim had not wept at the funeral. *Whatever that thing was, they weren't of this world,* he had said to his grieving parents, earning himself a hard slap across the face. He had been fifteen at the time.

Salim had come to realize long before then that there were certain things he ought to keep to himself; like, for example, the belief that his brother had been stolen one night and replaced by a thing designed to do nothing but mindlessly consume. Hasan was "troubled," according to Salim's mother and father. An alcoholic, a drug addict, a sex addict. Troubled.

Therapy didn't help, and pharmaceuticals certainly didn't. Salim knew the thing that had replaced his brother had dead eyes and a carnivorous mouth where his heart should be, but there was no convincing anyone else. Only he could see it.

Salim's parents had always considered him overly imaginative, too bookish. Hasan, while he'd still been Hasan, had been the opposite:

brightly illuminative, charming, and athletic, with a smile that made their aunties exclaim things about how he'd drive the girls wild one day. He did, though not in a normal way, because again, that wasn't Hasan. Whatever it was, it was destructive and cruel even while it was handsome. It treated flattery like a noose and wielded poison like a blade.

Knowing that he shared a house with a monster, Salim had taken to reading. Portals, he learned, were very real. There were other dimensions, other creatures. This new not-Hasan was one of those, though he didn't know which one. He read and read and read to find out.

Then the thing that wasn't Hasan died, and Salim started reading different books. How to summon things from other realms. How to ward his house from malevolent spirits. Which places in the world were most known for paranormal activities. He became obsessed with cultures that personified death. He grew enamored with concepts of spirituality and mysticism; anything that suggested there was something *beyond*. Whether that was astronomy or astrology or physics or crystals, Salim didn't care. He just wanted to know whether any other humans had ever found an answer to the question of where things went when they mysteriously disappeared.

This led him to history, then to sociology, then to anthropology. He made a career on fairly normal things—Muslim contributions to philosophies of naturalism during the golden age of antiquity—and then branched out quietly from there. His official work, the things he got paid for, were almost always about comparative cross-cultural studies, like his latest project concerning lunar rituals across hemispheres.

His private work, when his papers were written and his books were published and his expertise as an anthropologist was done being prodded and poked, was different. The same work, intellectually speaking, but deeply different, because as Salim had learned from an early age, there were some things too outlandish for others to believe. His paychecks didn't come from searching for ley lines and portals.

What did Salim believe in? Everything. Witches. Ghosts. Fairies, though after what he'd gone through with not-Hasan, he doubted they were all sparkly wings and pretty wishes. Demons. Jinni and prophets and portent and doors. The tarot artist, Jenny Li, was a lucky find, considering she was both a diligent researcher and an excellent source of insight. He knew very little about her aside from her art, which did have a certain uncanny quality to it, and her capacity as a witch, which by contrast was mostly mundane. She didn't seem especially eccentric, but then again, probably neither did he.

Salim didn't bother to know many people in Boston, though he did make a point to find a drug dealer very quickly. He didn't do any drugs himself, obviously, having watched the changeling thing that had been his brother fall prey to their destructive qualities, but people who distributed them were often ideal sources for information. Illicit activity shared the commonality of secrecy, which meant that if Salim wanted to find out what sort of oddities were happening in his latest place of residence, it was always best to have a dealer around.

This one was particularly fruitful.

"Doors are easy to find," Salim had explained while Alcott, the dealer, smoked quietly on his couch. "They're always centers of paranormal activity. Or electromagnetic forces. Or weather. Or time of year. The point is, a door's no good without a key," he said. "My brother must have found a key. Or something else found it for him."

Given their vocations, dealers usually did not respond negatively to this sort of bullshittery. Predictably, Alcott did not. "I think I know a guy like that," he said. "Claims he saw through space."

"What was he on?"

"Nothing habitual," said Alcott. "Now, though." A shrug. "Now it's like he's just trying to kill whatever it was he saw."

"Who was it?" Salim asked.

"Boyfriend," said Alcott. "Ex. Obviously."

"Are you on good terms? Communicable ones, at least."

"Why?"

"Because," Salim said, thinking it was obvious. "I want to see the key."

There was only one way to traverse the laws of time and space: Cognitive dissonance. Ancient physicists and astronomers understood that, even if they hadn't known how to use it. Only the difficult-to-reach portions of the mind could do it. Doorways, as Salim had long suspected, had to be conjured within the mind. They had to be imagined, powerfully so, which almost no adult could do properly. Most things a human could imagine were only variations on things they'd seen in the realm they physically occupied.

"It's a pill," Alcott said over the phone.

"Of course it is," muttered Salim. They came to an agreement on the price, which was exorbitant. If it failed, Salim would have to write another book this year and offer several more guest lectures just to make up for it. If it succeeded, on the other hand, the money didn't mean a damn thing.

Presumably there were other ways to do it. After all, Hasan was certainly not taking pills at the age of eleven, if it had indeed been he who opened the door. What humans lacked in waking imagination they possessed only in dreams, in the twisted nature of their subconscious. But a pill would work in a jam.

Salim took the pill in his kitchen and began tasting sound immediately. His brain was rejecting the constraints of reality, and there was something yawning nearby. He turned to it, finding a zipper, then a series of musical notes to be played in a very specific order, which he obligingly performed. Then he licked the color pink and felt little seeds of azure burst between his teeth. Outside, the sun swallowed up the sky. His phone buzzed incessantly, merciless, so he put it on the counter and walked into his office, where his computer winked at him suggestively and reached out to stroke his thigh. Salim mumbled something about boundaries and the computer smiled its pornographic smile, and then he turned his head, spotting a cavernous piece of sky. He tore it down like wallpaper, and behind it was a flock of birds that burst into bits of marshmallow down, and then he tumbled backwards for thirty years, landing beside a tree. He spoke to it in owl-language and then in Arabic and then he wept profusely, prodigiously, and whispered, "Hasan."

Then he pushed into empty space and plucked a harp string, and suddenly there was a doorway. A portal.

An entrance.

He could not truthfully say he walked inside. More like he was pulled, and then he thought oh no, I need to close the door behind me, but he didn't because something was pulling him, twisting in his chest and dragging him in two directions like a breath he hadn't fully caught. He knew he was somewhere he didn't belong—he was a not-thing, a nothing, like the thing who had taken his brother's place—and he wanted a burrito and also he wanted to lie down, but he took several careening steps forward until reality ripped and he fell through the tear in the page, landing on something soft.

When he woke, his hands were bound, and something with keen eyes and sharp teeth smiled at him.

"English?" it asked.

"Yes," Salim managed to croak. Everything was bright and blinding.

"Excellent. And what is your offering?"

His mouth was dry. "Offering?"

"You cannot arrive without a gift. Surely you know that."

The dazzle of brightness soothed a little, gradually. It was gold and crystal, mostly. Everything that could be gold was very, very gold. Everything that could be crystal was very, very sharp.

"I'm looking for my brother," said Salim. "I've been looking for him a long time."

"You do have a look of perpetuity," commented the thing Salim was now fairly sure was person-shaped, though not an actual person. "But I'm afraid the prince will find you quite dull without a gift. Have you any talents?"

Yes. He could fall through worlds. "Such as?"

"The prince cares only for beauty. Or for ugliness which is beauty. Or for beauty which is profoundly ugly."

"I'm an anthropologist," Salim said.

"Meaning?"

"I study culture. Humans."

He could see immediately he'd made a mistake. "Humans are not interesting," said the thing, "without gifts."

"Could I come back with a gift?"

"You are already here. You have already failed." A pair of fingers snapped. "Take him away."

"Wait—"

That was days ago, or perhaps not. Whatever this place was, it seemed to have a moon so bright it was an alternate sun. Either night or day was unending, or he was being tricked with the concept of time. A very good trick, really. A common psychological tool meant to subjugate its victims. To lose control of one's mind was a dangerous thing indeed.

"Dr. Amrani?"

A face appeared above him, prettily concerned.

"You're not him, are you?" she asked, and this time, she was a she. The rest of this world was unidentifiable, murky. She, however, was a definite she. Her eyes were brown and did not hurt to look at. Her voice reminded him of the candies his grandmother kept in her purse. "You're not what I thought you would be," she said, and her hair was black and kinder to his vision than the ebonies of laughing shadows that filled his cell.

It was difficult to speak after so much silence. It had been silence that made his lungs hurt, his chest burn. "How did you find me?"

Then he remembered: *I left the door open.*

"We have to run," he said, struggling to sit up, but she was bending over him, pressing her hand to his temple as if he had a fever. She wasn't moving, wasn't running, and suddenly he understood.

The door is closed now, and we are inside it.

"Don't let them take you," he said deliriously, and then he collapsed into nothing again, sliding between the incisors of empty, open space.

Jenny understood where she was almost immediately, though her sense of understanding was old and misshapen. Suddenly she was a child again, her grandmother telling her about the many kinds of fairies, all with different names. Many would inflict harm upon humans; spirits of the dead, or little devils. Others were nature-spirits, inoffensive. Some were more like the fae of her mother's childhood, for whom they had always left out a bit of cream, just in case.

Mostly, though, she knew she had walked through an open door.

It hadn't felt like something she'd done on purpose. The moment she'd turned the door to Dr. Amrani's office, she had been consumed against her will by whatever was inside. Well, more accurately, her will had had nothing to do with it. No decisions were made, no observations had. It was difficult to explain; colorless and without details, like how no one ever remembered falling asleep. They simply knew they had done it when they arrived back to a state of waking in the morning.

Whether Jenny had closed the door behind her or whether she had swallowed up the door by virtue of opening it was unclear. What *was* clear was that she could not reverse her steps.

Wherever she was now, it felt like a mix of past and future things. There was a palatial feel to it, but the architecture did not belong to any time periods she recognized. Instead it was eclectic, like a collection of dreamt things. Clocks that didn't appear to tell time. Paintings of impossible pigments, blackest blacks and pinkest pinks. The archway that led to the room with the throne was industrial and oppressive, shining with dullness. Her mind recognized the paradoxes and filed them dutifully. She craved the sight of something familiar, but even the air was tinted differently. It smelled and tasted like rose thorns.

"What is your gift?" asked the guard, or what seemed to be a guard.

Jenny had nothing, of course. Her phone, when she pulled it out, was cracked, as if the pressure of transitioning from one state of reality to another had shattered it from the inside out. There was only one other item in her pockets: the card. Her tarot card. It wouldn't mean much to a human, but then again, this wasn't a human. She thanked her inadvisable snooping for probably saving her life, or at least her sanity.

"I'm an artist," she said. Fae liked artists and musicians. They liked beauty. She knew that from the stories. "I have this," she said, pulling the card free. "It's optimism. Good news. Portent," she added, seeing the guard's brow furrow with interest. "This is the gift of future blessing."

The guard reached for it, obviously intrigued, but she held it at bay.

"First you have to take me to Dr. Amrani," she said. "Is he here?"

"There is a human here," confirmed the guard, warily. Jenny could feel the weight of his answer and knew it had been taken from the value of her gift. Quite a lot of effort for an answer to her email, her rational mind scolded her.

"I'd like to see him," she said. She was still not convinced it wasn't a dream.

The man who was Dr. Salim Amrani was a pitiful mess, his black curls overlong and wild enough to cover his face. He had not been treated well, and the cost of being a thing which did not belong there was obvious. He didn't seem to recognize her or anything, though she felt a mix of frustration and pity at the sight of him. He had opened the door, dragged her inside it. Had he known what he was doing? According to the messages from the unknown number, he had done it on purpose.

But surely this had not been the outcome he'd wanted.

"Don't let them take you," Dr. Amrani said, obviously weak and delirious, and it added a bit more value to Jenny's card, replacing what the guard had taken from it for answering her question. The professor's suffering meant she was owed something more now, and she used it to her advantage.

"The card in exchange for our lives," she said. "You let us go."

"It is only one card," said the guard dismissively. "Only one life."

"What do you want with him? He's obviously not doing you any good in a cell."

"He can't go back," the guard said. "Nobody goes back."

That was probably true.

"Fine. The card's value in exchange for privilege," Jenny said. "We're… guests." That sounded right. "We should be treated as guests. We request an audience with the—" Clearly a monarchy, though she didn't want to guess which kind. "Whoever's in charge."

"Good fortune for good fortune," the guard acknowledged unwillingly; offer and acceptance. "I'll be back when I've spoken to the prince."

Then he left, leaving the door open to Dr. Amrani's cell.

Jenny looked down at the professor, feeling the strange second-hand embarrassment of seeing someone partially exposed. She took off the sweater she had worn on the plane and draped it around him, covering him as best she could. He slumbered heavily, only partially conscious, and she sighed, kicking herself a bit. This, for a paycheck? Now they were both trapped, and for what?

Her fury battled her empathy. This was the first time she was seeing him outside of the unsmiling university portrait, and to her distress, he looked unfairly young. Boyish. He had three freckles beside his closed eyes, a cosmological dusting of stars. She ought to have been thinking about his emails—the tone of "I only have so much time for you or anything" that was her only insight to his mind—but instead, she remained chronologically untethered.

Only people with terrible longing find their way to a fairy realm, her grandmother said in her thoughts, and Jenny sighed, trapped from every direction.

So she had an answer, then.

This was not what she had signed up for when she took the researcher job.

PART II: RELUCTANT DIPLOMACY

Jenny, he needs your help.

Fright was a fairly childish emotion—Jenny could scarcely remember the last time she'd been *frightened*—but something about being wherever she was now as a result of that bizarre fax was like the persistence of memory. Chronological disembodiment, melting clocks. Surrealism; a brush through the dampness of her certainty to draw old feelings to the surface, the sum of her parts. She was distantly aware of it, the sense of unknowing. As an adult, fear was so often the consequence of worst imaginings, stories on the news, women getting their Achilles tendons sliced from beneath their vehicles at the mall. Only truly childish fears ended with the confusion of not being able to predict the outcome; everything else was already dismally known.

Her mind was buzzing with a fruitless effort to understand the details of her environment. Foggy memories of art history and medieval architecture told her it was closer to a palace than a castle, given what seemed to be a lack of defensive walls. Other instincts told her it felt like a bank, the austerity and the general concept of money, the existence of some commodity or another. She was led to a bedroom, the professor's footsteps unsteady beside her like a man waking slowly; emerging only to wobble from a foot cramp or a powerful, disembodying dream.

Inside the room were hard geometric lines of gold, blinding contrasts of light and dark to create the existence of invisible things. There were jewels, too, embedded in something recognizable as a bed frame, a chest of drawers, a vanity, but they were like bruises, purple gems shadowed with tiny sparks of something opaquely black. The space itself was oppressive, with towering ceilings and a window that faced an impenetrable grey, indicative of neither day nor night. A thin fog hung outside the windows like gauze, from which branches shivered on the exhale of a breeze.

"Is he yours?"

Jenny jumped, surprised to find herself addressed from just beside her shoulder while she'd been staring numbly around the room. The steward, who was surely more steward than guard, was waiting expectantly, nearly hanging on her answer, while Dr. Amrani had taken a seat in silence, leaning with palpable exhaustion against the post of the bed.

"I beg your pardon?" Jenny said slowly, perhaps too slowly, and the steward or butler or whoever it was that had led them into the room cleared his throat with what Jenny thought was embarrassment, possibly at the prospect of having asked such a strange question. "I'm sorry," she amended, clarifying, "I just… don't know what you mean."

"Is he yours?" the steward repeated, appearing to pretend she'd said nothing.

"He's—" Jenny paused. Of course he was talking about the professor, but how to respond? She and Dr. Amrani were little more than strangers, but that didn't seem worth telling anyone here. "He owes me a debt," she answered privately, and then, after a pause to consider not only the missed paychecks but also the fact that chasing after him (a feat which itself had cost a transatlantic plane flight, plus the accommodations for which she would not be able to check in) had also led her here, to a place she could ostensibly not escape, she clarified, "Several debts."

"Interesting," said the steward, appearing to find it interesting indeed. His eyes widened bloodlessly. "Very interesting. Is that all, then?"

So there were no adjoining suites, no extra beds. Even the privilege she'd bought them with her tarot card had its limits, which Jenny supposed was fair. A hotel room like this one would cost significantly more than her entire deck, much less a single card.

"That's all," Jenny confirmed, wondering if the steward expected any sort of tip.

There was a ripple in the murkily perfumed air and the steward was gone, leaving Dr. Amrani and Jenny alone in the room together. She opened her mouth to say something, anything, but he spoke first into empty air. "You shouldn't beg."

"What?" slipped brusquely from Jenny's lips, unpreventable.

"You begged his pardon." Dr. Amrani turned to face her, the hollow area below his cheeks sucked in with either strain or thought, or possibly both. "The fae commonly regard obligation as a burden akin to profanity, according to my research. I believe you may as well have shouted vulgarities at him."

"Vulgarities?" That was nonsensical, even alongside everything else. "Are you saying you know where we are, then?"

"Not entirely. I have guesses, though I might have made a similar mistake myself had I not observed his reaction to your efforts at decorum. I am an anthropologist," he said, as if he were willing it to still be true. "Cultures, behavior patterns, these are my areas of expertise."

Now that he was fully conscious, she could see that his lips were full, almost effeminate. She thought of the dusting of freckles beside his eyes, which were invisible to her now. The canvas of him from this distance was poised and defined, rather than the blur of unfamiliar details it had been up close. He was still wearing the oversized cardigan she had slung around his shoulders like a blanket, though aside from his mouth, it was the only thing in the room that appeared to have any softness. Dr. Amrani's gaze was fixed on hers so intently she might have mistaken it for hard-edged and sharp if she had not realized upon closer inspection that it was dazed, unclarified longing in his desperate search for resolution.

"You are Jenny," he said, which was a fact more than it was a question. "I take it you've… arranged something?"

She considered the card in her pocket, which now seemed to crest heavily above the fabric as if she'd drawn it forth mid-thought. "Yes. Sort of. I think." It seemed worth qualifying now that he'd essentially reminded them they were strangers, and that in fact he was her employer. *Is he yours?* Perhaps the more correct answer was *no I am his*, but it felt deeply unnerving to acknowledge. "I… my mother said," Jenny began, and cleared her throat. "The fae like artists. So I offered—" She withdrew the card from her pocket and Dr. Amrani blinked. "I'm supposed to give it to the prince at dinner," she concluded without any real enthusiasm. "As for what it will buy us—"

"You should leave me," he said.

"—I'm not entirely sure I should—" She stopped, belatedly registering his interjection. "I'm sorry. What?"

"Don't apologize. They won't like that either." He pulled himself upright, turning to face her. At his full height, Jenny had the sudden sensation of being dwarfed, though he had a fluidity to his movements that reminded her of the fae themselves. "I wasn't entirely forthcoming with you about my work," he said. "Though in fairness, it was extracurricular and irrelevant."

He paused.

"You should leave me behind if you are able," he said. "I apologize for my part in bringing you here, though I can't imagine what it might have been."

He stopped expectantly, purposefully this time, and Jenny blinked, realizing it was an unsubtle invitation for an explanation for her presence there. She supposed she hadn't really given any thought to what might happen once she had found him. She had been so consumed by the idea that he was dead or abducted or lost or ill that she hadn't considered he might eventually ask her how she, a person he had never met and who, by all accounts, lived well across the country, might have come upon the open door in his home office.

She opened her mouth, then closed it. "Why," she decided, "would I leave you here?"

His brow furrowed slightly, recognizing her sidestep of an answer, and appeared to accept it. (Gratitude for being out of his cell might buy her some compliance, or at least keep them from discussing anything they both already knew or could assume, such as her flagrant disregard for his privacy.)

"My brother was a changeling," he said, before amending with a series of rapid blinks, "or in any case he was abducted, with something else left in his place. I have spent my career searching for evidence of where he might have gone."

And now that I'm here, Jenny translated in silence, *I will not leave without an answer*. Her grandmother's words echoed again in her head: *Only people with terrible longing find their way to a fairy realm.*

"Well, I wish I'd known that before I bargained with the guard," Jenny said stiffly, feeling a sense of unfunny Shakespearean miscommunication. "But somehow, Professor, I didn't think it would sit well with my conscience for me to leave you there."

"You don't think I'm—?" He stopped, amending the direction of his thought. "No, I suppose it wouldn't." His attention grew foggy, drifting to the view outside her window, which swirled like the blizzard inside a snow globe. Perhaps the sensation of captivity struck them both in the same moment, because he added, "Fairies, aliens, angels. Everyone has a word for the same concept of a beyond. They want to imagine it is only good or only bad, but in reality it is simply other."

He turned his dark eyes back to her, adding tangentially, "Call me Salim."

"So then I should call you by your name and leave you behind?" slipped out inadvisably with a scoff. "They always say to not give names to strays."

"Well, I was wrong, I think. I misunderstood, or forgot. You are right that you cannot leave me behind, and for me to pretend otherwise is to violate a moral code that we in all likelihood share." His voice droned like a carbon copy of his emails, which Jenny realized must have been the cadence of his thought process. A rhythm that was predictable, steady, secure. Strange to think he was her only trace of the familiar in this room.

"Forgive me," he said, "my judgment is… clouded."

It occurred to Jenny that the professor, Salim, had not expected her to believe him—perhaps he had never been believed before—and she felt a little upsurge of sympathy for him. There was little reason to deny it now. "How long ago did your brother disappear?"

"Nearly thirty years," he said, and Jenny frowned. "Yes, a long time, I know," he confirmed, correctly reading her skepticism. "I suppose there is no urgency now. I am surely only looking for fossils, traces of a man." He glanced at his hands with a quiet, prodigious emptiness, and her first instinct was to poke holes in the stifling atmosphere of their container, securing some relief.

"Assuming this is the place he fell," Jenny said, and Salim looked up. "Well, if there's one door," she clarified with a reference around the room, "surely there are others. The existence of one other world means multiple other worlds, doesn't it? So maybe he's here, maybe he isn't. In the event you don't find him, that is," she added hurriedly. It was meant to be helpful, though she wasn't sure if it was.

He tilted his head, processing. "Logically there is a fallacy to the presumption there must necessarily be others. Dualities do exist in nature, yin and yang. But the presumption there are *not* others is erroneous on my part, I agree." He kept his eyes on her, wary. "Thank you."

Jenny was growing increasingly certain there was more to Salim Amrani than even his choice of career suggested. The T.A. she'd run into at his university wasn't wrong that there was something inherently strange about him, but he wasn't a drug addict.

He was an addict, definitely. But not to drugs.

She opened her mouth to reply, but before she could, there was a little ripple in the air, the parting of an invisible seam, from which a voice emerged, full-bodied.

"Dinner is served," it said, and with it, an intangible urging to comply.

Salim had not heard what the artist's reply had been to the fae who had asked if he was hers. Absently, he toyed with it from an anthropologist's eye: the single bed they were given, and the question which had no implication of spouse or partner, but merely hinted at ownership. Where did sex factor into the workings of this society? Biologically speaking, reproduction was always a necessity, but was copulation? Perhaps not, or perhaps it was paramount to all else. Perhaps the fae did not pair off the way humans did; marriage was an unconventional practice for most other species, and fidelity even less so. Look at most mammals, or the gods.

His mind ached indiscriminately. He suspected he was dehydrated as much as he was confused, and certainly he was stressed by his own confusion. Cortisol. Glucose in the bloodstream. Muscle weakness. Chest pain, meaning possible infection. Or maybe just pain.

"Salim?" asked Jenny quietly.

He blinked from his seat at the table, realizing they were being summoned to their feet.

"The Prince," announced the herald, and from within the cocoon of double doors burst a flurry of fabric, rustling like petals on the wind. The ruffled exoskeleton of a gown flooded the room with color like juices dripping, the eruption of sweetness that gushed from the flesh of a plum, carnivorous and overripe.

The Prince, Salim observed with surprise at first glance, was a woman, or at the very least presented as one. Their eyes were a malicious pale pink, which could have been brown with another notch of pigment. Their hair was pulled tightly back before cascading with unruly subterfuge down their back into rivulets of sand-colored braids, and atop their head was a single luminous band of gold.

"Sit down," they said in a melodic command, seemingly bored by the fanfare until perking up at the sight of Jenny, who had been given an astonishingly repulsive gown for the occasion. It was gossamer in an innately displeasing way, like a spider-spun web that clung to the shape of her hips, lasciviously draping around them. Salim, likewise, had been given breeches of velvet so thick and grainy it reminded him of a dog's tongue.

"Are you surprised?" the Prince asked Jenny, whom Salim observed did not hurry to nod. She was taking everything in slowly, bracing against the possible errors of her preconceived notions. "I will inherit and that makes me a Prince," sniffed their host, waving a hand and collapsing into a chair like a seed into the ground, neatly sowed. "And you've brought me…?"

The Prince held out a hand, expectant, and Jenny produced the card from where it sat tightly clutched in her palm. She slid a glance to Salim and he thought it again: *I'm sorry*. She didn't seem to notice, nor did she appear scared, but he could tell that she had anchored herself to him invisibly. He had the sense that if he suddenly lifted a hand—if he burst riotously into song or ran for cover—she would, too. Purely out of reflex.

He could conclude with certainty now that Jenny Li was attractive in an uncontroversial way; everyone would agree with the way her hair formed a sleek river over her shoulders, or the shape her eyes took, wide and lovely, or the pert end of her delicate nose. She wasn't unaware of it, exactly. She seemed to carry the knowledge of her beauty like an emergency credit card, unacknowledged by her conscious mind but clung to, just in case.

"Good fortune," said Jenny, holding up the card: the knight of cups. She had a distinctly Californian voice. No vocal fry, but certainly traces of suburban sensibilities. Markers of a comfortable childhood, probably middle class, suitably eloquent but not overtly educated. Nothing outwardly bohemian.

"Future blessing," she clarified, and the Prince's eyes narrowed.

"No," said the Prince.

"What?" said Jenny.

"You said he had debts." Here the Prince's eyes shifted to Salim, who was jolted from his silent observation. "How many debts?"

Ah, so that was what Jenny had told the steward. An interesting choice of words from someone who claimed to have some knowledge of the fae. No, he corrected himself inwardly, not claimed. She was guarded, not enraptured. She knew where she was, and therefore she must have understood where she was not.

"I owe her two debts," confirmed Salim before Jenny could decide on a response. "Financial and moral."

"Moral," echoed the Prince, with a hollow moan. "Fascinating."

"The card was an exchange for our privilege as your guests," inserted Jenny, her eyes darting from Salim to the Prince. Salim could see the quickness there, the piecing together of a constantly evolving plan. "The card is already yours. I don't mean to be crass, but we do owe it," she said quickly, noting the derision Salim had already told her to expect at the concept of obligation. "If there's something else you want, Your Highness, it will require another deal."

Salim made a mental note that foreign dinner parties were an excellent way to gauge comprehension of social practices. Already Jenny had learned how not to commit a crucial error, and even better, how to leverage a custom to her benefit. If he ever returned to earth, he would have to note it for final exams.

"What do you want?" asked the Prince.

"A door," said Salim, as Jenny said, "Out."

Surely neither had been specific enough. "My debt cannot be paid here," Salim said quickly, as the Prince's judicious eyes fell on him. He had the sensation of overcrowding, like Shaftesbury Avenue at peak high.

"It is not the debt I want, but the bond." The Prince licked their lips accordingly. "It is unusual to encounter."

"The bond of owing?" asked Jenny. "As opposed to…?"

"Opposed to? No little monster, there is nothing to oppose, there is nothing else. There is only having and wanting and owing and nothing else." The Prince looked lustful with the idea of it, the monogamy of obligation. Salim supposed it was their world's equivalent of true love, soulmates. Short of feeling it, there was nothing but tales to prove it true. Probably copulation was about only the transaction of sex, then, or the outcome of reproduction.

No. No, there could be no reproduction for the species, or what would be the point of changelings?

"There is also pleasure," Salim guessed aloud.

The Prince looked up, leering. Their host's suspicion was a door left ajar, and Salim considered it: Doors. Portals that could form the shape of a person's private imagination. Already his was being stretched to its outer limits, punished for its insufficiencies, but surely his mind had never been more pliable. If a drug had opened one door for him before, this state of waning reality could easily open another. A little pulse of mindlessness might do it, and there was nothing more mindless and powerful as pleasure, elation, rapture.

Ecstasy. It came in many forms. Maybe the thing that was not his brother had only been trying to find its way back the same way it had arrived, and that was what had killed it in the end.

"What is it you're offering, debtorling?" mused the Prince, leaning toward Salim with salivation; a spider having found its next meal.

Surely Jenny wouldn't like it, Salim thought. Perhaps she would not agree, given the implications of their own social practices. That was the trouble when cultures treasured something that another thought commonplace; it was one thing to embrace unexpected value, but another entirely to leap a crevasse of long-established decency.

"It's not what I'm offering you," he said to the Prince, and then turned to Jenny, whose clever eyes went brilliantly wide.

"It's quite simple," said Salim, leaning over to speak in Jenny's ear. "The Prince clearly would like to watch us."

"Watch us what?" asked Jenny, hoping Salim might clear his throat or shift his feet, expressing discomfort more similar to hers. She waited for a tic of hesitation, anything. An um, a hint of anxiety, a pause. Anything.

Around them, conversation continued unhindered by anything but the food and wine, the point of which appeared to be consumption without any refinement of palate. There was no obvious curation to the meal, no complementing of one dish to another. The idea seemed to be to have as much as possible—as much flavor, as many distinct sensations—as a marker of prowess, or perhaps significance. Compared to the Prince's other guests, Salim and Jenny were insubstantial to the point of being skeletal; mere slivers of beings.

"Foreign emissaries typically indulge a spectacle of sorts," Salim said, lifting his glass for a sip. In her head, Jenny heard phrases from his emails, his educational podcast episode: *Cultures and communities are not books to be read, but worlds to be experienced.* "A dance from our home culture might be expected, or a favored cuisine, gifts of jewels or novelties. Unfortunately, as unrehearsed diplomats we have only one thing this realm does not, whereas they have only one method of observing it." His dark eyes flicked from her own to the fairy Prince, who was waiting like a child in line to see the penguins at the zoo. "If you agree," said Salim, leaning so close it half-melted into the skin below her ear, "I can get us out."

The offer was tempting, even if the request was not. "Agree to…?" She was almost afraid to ask.

"Sex." Helplessly, she winced. "Ritualistic, I'm guessing. Purely physical." His eyes slid over the occupants at the table, judicial. "I wouldn't be surprised if polyamory is a common after dinner social activity, not unlike the Victorian practice of gentlemen withdrawing for conversation and cigars."

Melting clocks, registered Jenny with panic. The persistence of memory. Her father saying *boys only want one thing!* interspersed with her mother's lectures about lubrication and condoms.

"But how—?"

"You'd have to trust me, I'm afraid. But if I were to succeed, I would at least repay one debt." Salim's lips curled up in something Jenny suspected of being a rare smile. "When in Rome," he added as an afterthought, and smoothed his hands over his nauseating velvet breeches as if he were clearing them of something as unremarkable as lint.

The irony of the professor becoming increasingly more handsome as the evening went on began to strike at Jenny's sensibilities like nonexistent church bells: the slender knuckles on his immaculate hands. That feminine mouth, its perfect shade of raspberry from the vibrancy of the food, the probably exquisite tongue. There was a succulence to his manners, the way he absorbed his environment and became one with it, an artist of mimicry. How convenient, Jenny thought with inward loathing for her own attraction. Maybe there were aphrodisiacs in the food, the wine. Maybe it was a strange, unrelenting dream. What was she willing to do to escape it?

More than this, probably.

"You may stay as long as you like," announced the Prince with a timely glimmer of malevolent delight. Again, Jenny became aware of her cage, gilded and invisible and still, somehow, lit ferociously by candlelight. She and Salim were oddities for them, amusements. They would be kept in pristine condition, but they would almost certainly be kept. Her cobwebbed gown tightened around her neck like a noose, and Jenny swallowed.

"Fine. I'll do it," she said to Salim quietly. "But it had better work."

He seemed unsurprised. "It would be best if you could climax." A stray glaze of wine had bled from his lips, which he dabbed carefully with a napkin. It tasted distinctly crimson, neither sweet nor sour but an explosive amalgam of both. Jenny's senses had awoken to the presence on her tongue, her instincts jarred. "Multiple times, if possible."

Every culture, including this one, suggested it would be ungainly to gape at him.

She did it anyway. "Can you *bring* me to climax multiple times?" left her lips with a disbelieving splutter, and across the table, the fae Prince looked greedily up at them, overhearing the subject of their discussion and appearing suddenly wide-eyed with longing. The sort of eagerness tainted with fear, hovering along the precipice of having or having not.

Salim replaced the napkin on his lap, pausing with deliberation.

"Yes," he said, plucking his fork from the table and arranging it carefully between his teeth. He seemed to have taken her stunned silence for an answer, so Jenny reached for her glass, draining it in one long sip alongside the blanketing weirdness of her acceptance. Both had crept in silently, stealing away her more rational thoughts like changelings. The only trace of her foregone reality was the foggy realization that it had been at least four days since she'd shaved her legs.

She was starting to understand certain things about mythology. Ambrosia, nectar of the gods, that sort of thing; that collective imagination was possibly not imagined at all. She was beginning to come to terms with the idea that she and the professor she hardly knew were probably not the first to fall into this world, which bolstered her enough to think they could indeed fall out of it. Surely artists, poets, musicians had all arrived here at some point and then brought it back in stories, in verse and song. The wine that flowed unhindered, the enrapturing quality of honeysuckle air, the unique form of drowning; it was literary, musical, painted. She had never noticed so acutely the way intoxication was sluggish and heavy, but it made sense to her now. She imagined pulling taffy, the slow tears of maple from a tap. Thickly saccharine, her body pulsing in tune with a slow, decomposing current.

Salim's palm crept up the side of her waist, the heel of his hand a long distance from anything of consequence, which Jenny couldn't decide through her haze of prickling sensation whether she found comforting or enthralling. Maybe she was beginning to ease into the seduction of unfamiliarity, or unfamiliarity itself was so omnipresent and full of continued fright that this was somehow more reassuring. This was Odysseus and Circe in a way; a clever plot against some mystical enchantress. This was the adult content left out of her grandmother's tales when she had tried explaining to Jenny why some people chose not to return. Impossible not to conflate the two ideas, magic and sex. Certainly impossible not to conflate *now*, when the idea had already been planted and was beginning to flower like the sensation of premonition in her belly, blooming unwisely to bear tiny twin fruits of tension and thrill.

"I teach yoga," she told the professor nonsensically. "I don't know if you knew that. Body awareness is important. Connection. Breathing. Important for stress relief."

"That's good," said Salim. She was suddenly aware of his accent, the heating effect of his voice. Her daze grew more lethargic, sweat pooling at her lower back. "Helpful. Very healthy."

"Yes," she said, and swayed towards him, resting her head briefly on the line of his shoulder. The weight of her drowsiness was suddenly too much, and obligingly, he shifted her fully into his arms. Whether he was more or less or equally intoxicated was a brief and fleeting concern, and then Jenny reached up to touch his mouth, parting his lips experimentally.

"Does it help your art?" he asked. "Yoga." The words were soft beneath her fingertips.

"Sometimes." She had never thought about it in those terms but yes, her art was best when she was most in tune with herself, and there was no quicker way to feel *out* of sync than when she was stressed. Then she could feel her tension in her calves, like an itch. The need to create was like a tightness in her muscles, knots in her shoulders. "Or maybe always." She leaned forward, tasting an inhale from his lips, which was bitterly molasses. Like bourbon vanilla.

"I'm going to touch you. Can I do that?" he said quietly. She mumbled a yes, and the dress fell away from his fingers like grains of sugar. "Do you want me to talk?"

The sudden knowledge of what they were about to do swept over her. Somewhere overhead the Prince was watching, observing their 'bond,' whatever that meant, with the curiosity of a lion for its prey.

"Tell me about your brother?" she asked.

It came away quietly, girlish. This is a secret, she wanted to tell him urgently. This, what you're doing with me, for girls this is a secret. You need to give me a secret so that I don't feel so naked, even if I am. Even if I'm not. Either way, you need to be naked, too.

He seemed to understand that, though he glanced up warily before speaking, lowering his voice. "I was six when he was replaced with something else," he said. "I knew it wasn't him, but my parents didn't believe me."

The Irish were more suspicious of changelings, it seemed. Jenny's mother always said it was an excuse for developmental disabilities or inexplicable disorders, but maybe it wasn't. Maybe sometimes it wasn't.

"What was his name?"

"Hasan." It left Salim's lips like a sigh. "He was my parents' favorite. And mine."

"Even after?"

"For me, no. He wasn't mine anymore." A pause. "For them, yes. Even after."

Her sympathy for him unfolded, a blossom from a bud. "You've been looking for such a long time," she said, which was meant to be *I am so terribly sad for you* and sounded instead like *touch me*.

Rousingly, he complied. His kiss, when it met hers, was fragrant with gratitude, lush with it. He opened for her as she had for him, and suddenly she thought she understood it. Portals and passage. She pulled him closer the way she would have sprinted towards something unmissable, a train leaving the station. She pried open the doors of his reservations and in response he was alight, whisking her off the platform. She felt the edges of herself blur with his, his sadness becoming hers, his loneliness cloaking her shoulders. She bled her hope into his mouth, her art, her practiced hand at beauty. She poured the meditation of her entire being into his soul.

In practical terms he clearly knew what he was doing, slipping away to run his tongue along the curves of her thighs, and she half-remembered the past vestiges of them: the cardigan she'd worn on the plane, the condoms in his nightstand. Did he belong to someone else back home? No, he was hers, she'd told the fairies that much and they'd understood it, and if he would belong to someone else later… but he wouldn't, Jenny realized, remembering the cards she'd drawn that led her to him. There was a moon here, whispering of prophecy: change. Secrets subsiding. A stream that runs to an ocean.

Hazily, her body awash in pulses of sudden clarity, Jenny thought she saw a door.

She pulled Salim closer, circling him in every way she knew how, enveloping him entirely. Consuming him, thinking of runes, the way humanity and time were reproduced in cycles, in waves. Absent beginnings and ends, perpetually receding only to return, higher and higher tides. She smiled to an empty void, coaxing it nearer, feeling herself fill. She mumbled her secrets to Salim's ear, burying her nails in the blades of his shoulders. *I stole a lip balm when I was fourteen, yesterday I broke into your house.* His response was a rumble, a little masculine tremor of a groan, and Jenny laughed in painstaking silence, answering with a roll of her hips. *The secret is the witch is me.*

She gradually forgot the Prince, though she grew distantly aware of anger, paralysis and outrage, and Salim was urging her with his touch, *keep going.* The glimpse beside them grew less faint, indicating entry. Instinctively Jenny knew it was a door, and she reached for it. Her legs shook with desperation, her muscles tightening, every piece of her gritted and coiled and tightly wrenched.

Nearly there, she thought, and then—

The door opened with a burst of darkness, devouring them in a rush of shadow, sharp teeth belonging to empty space. It was pain unquestionably, euphoria unmistakably. It was crashing helpless to her knees, ascending beyond her limits. This, Jenny thought, is what it was to exult.

Behind the door was his face, beautiful and hand-carved, only older, brighter, illuminated by the gold of his clothing instead of clouded by darkness and loss. The celestial markings, the constellation of freckles to dot the plane of his face, those were Salim's alone, his little mystic scars, his Orion's belt of quiet contemplation. This was someone clamorous with experience, a life that reverberated beyond their world. This was someone empty of scars, an identical chest of drawers with nothing left inside.

This was someone else.

"Hasan," Jenny whispered with wonder, and tumbled backwards from the force of Salim's cry of relief, agony intermingling with excruciating joy.

Jenny, he needs your help.

PART III: VESTIGIAL BIOLOGY

Instinct could be a powerful thing, as Jenny's grandmother used to tell her. Senses were rarely wrong. They could be informed, of course—improved and advanced with sufficient time and wisdom—but even without experience to develop them, they could mean the difference between life and death, love and loss, missed connections. *If I had not been there, if I had made this choice instead, if I had been a minute later, even a moment delayed.* It could feel like a matter of fate if a person wasn't careful, but even as a girl Jenny had been warned not to be fooled. Instincts existed for a reason, each one tailored with her survival in mind. By contrast, fate was merely some apathetic god descended from machines. It did not care in what ways a person might be trampled.

"Salim," said the man who must have been Hasan, Salim's missing brother, as Jenny and Salim tumbled forward, a door falling shut in their wake. "Finally," Hasan murmured gladly, pulling Salim into his arms. "Finally, you found me."

Jenny, left in a state of undress from the unforeseen consequence of their transfer between realms, hardly bothered to flush at her exposure, capable of little more than staring while a numbly speechless Salim melted into the shape of his brother. From her vantage point, the two men, already so alike in stature, melted easily into one being.

Delineations between them were made possible only by the finery of Hasan's clothing, the glint of his crown against the smooth, dark canvas of Salim's bare skin.

"Come," said Hasan, taking his brother's face in both hands. "I have been waiting a long time to have you as my guests."

With a flutter of his fingers Hasan had dressed them both, outfitting Jenny in a loose, gold-embroidered caftan in a berry-bitten red while Salim wore a similar garment in a deep blue-grey, like the crests of a tempestuous sea. The sleeves of Salim's caftan were stitched in silver that twinkled like jewelry, giving him an air of luxury that was still within reach of Jenny's finer imaginations. This, unlike the fae Prince's palace, was a recognizable form of excess.

In many ways, this world was similar to the one they'd come from, though markedly less claustrophobic in its exorbitance. Hasan had taken care to shape the inconstancy of fae predilection, molding it recognizably into the shapes of his own memories, his earthly desires. Here, the clocks didn't melt, but they were still extravagant—alive, as if time itself could twine like ivy. The halls of Hasan's palace were ornate but not austere, not nearly so unfeeling. His decadence was a thing to be admired, and certainly to be envied, but not to pose a lethal threat, as the Prince's palace had done. The intent here was not to suffocate the viewer, but to smile down at them, benevolence incarnate.

"Are you a prince, too?" Salim was asking Hasan. Jenny hurried after them, realizing she had been staring at her surroundings while the brothers had begun to walk.

"Me, stop at prince? Clearly we've been apart too long," laughed Hasan, leading them from the glittering halls to the lushly fragrant courtyard. This place, less bright than the palace corridors, could only be described as a Garden of Eden; lined with fruit trees, embraced by tendrils of orchids and vines, kissed by afternoon sun. An intimate and painstakingly laid table sat low to the ground, surrounded by plush velvet pillows.

"Sit, sit," Hasan urged, beckoning Salim with a glance. A wave of Hasan's hand prompted food to materialize on gleaming platters, every inch piled high with color and light while a cerulean canopy flowered generously overhead. "I've been trying to reach you since I learned you'd crossed the threshold."

"Have you?" asked Salim, dazed.

Hasan gave an unburdened laugh, delighted by his brother's obvious wonder. "Have a drink and I'll tell you the whole story," Hasan assured Salim, clapping a hand around his shoulder before turning fleetingly away, towards Jenny.

It was not until Hasan's gaze met hers that Jenny realized she had not yet been acknowledged by him as an entity separate from Salim. The moment she rose up in the center of Hasan's attention, she felt a chill of something idle down her spine, like the slender line of a crooking finger. It could have been a breeze, as the afternoon here was cool and still but not stifling, or possibly the phantom coaxing of a nearby branch. She was uncannily certain, though, that it was something recognizable only to her; a smallness so fragile that even she could not prove its existence, spoken in a language she only faintly understood.

Instinct.

"You must be Jenny," said Hasan, smiling broadly as he gestured her into the chair across from his own. He positioned her to Salim's left, himself to Salim's right. "Welcome."

She had the brief sense that she should run, but knew that if she did, Salim wouldn't follow. He had searched too long for this, and she could see on his face that he was blinded, crippled the way only happiness could wound. His brother had been gone since he was six years old, and now, finally reunited, Salim was a child again, trusting and sure. His joy was juvenile, innocent, precious. Oblivious.

There was no leaving him behind. Not now.

Jenny settled in, adjusting her caftan while she took her seat. "Thank you for your hospitality," she said, holding Hasan's gaze while she said it, and he smiled back thinly, the translation clear. "I think I'd like to hear that story, if you don't mind."

As a child, Salim had always found his older brother to be the source of the best games, the funniest jokes, the most enrapturing stories. In that, little had changed.

Hasan's tale of his rise through the fae was like a maze of golden rays. He had been brought here long ago, stolen and afraid, and after finding there was no escape, he had worked his way up gradually. There was an entire nursery of changelings, Hasan explained, children taken from their world and raised as students or servants, put to work in the palace to make their way up the ranks if they were worthy. Hasan had been singing a folk song taught to him by their mother when the previous King had found him, purchased him, and raised him with the intent to make him something of a minstrel, but Hasan had been clever, finding allies and patrons until he was no longer a changeling, but an heir. He had fought against the rival Princes, displacing the others who would vie for his throne. The day Hasan had become King, finally having access to the palace's best magic, he had begun searching for Salim—and imagine his relief when Salim had been only a stone's throw away, just on the other side of a door.

"You will have every luxury here," Hasan told Salim affectionately, placing a hand around the back of his head the way he had done when they were boys. "You are my brother, my most honored guest."

It was like a dream, too-perfect, rosy and unblemished. His brother was alive, Hasan was King of some strange alternate realm, and of course he was! How foolish Salim had been to ever question that his brother, who had always been larger than life to him, would not be the prisoner of another dimension, but the chosen one instead. Of course Salim had wasted away the moment he'd left his world behind, but Hasan had always been better, always brighter. Salim took a sip of his wine, this one sweet and refreshing, and then another. He could feel himself shrinking, but not unpleasantly. It was as if his own relief was so vast he needed to curl inside it, embraced by the warmth of hard-fought resolution. The mystery he had so long sought had ended with satisfaction; with joy.

Salim, too breathless to speak as Hasan began regaling them with stories from his days as a fae countess's lover, raised his glass to his lips and took another hearty swallow in lieu of contributing, turning to look at Jenny. She was more withdrawn than usual, merely moving her food around on her plate and watching Hasan through beautiful, studious eyes. She couldn't seem to look away from Hasan, as if she were looking for something, some piece of a puzzle on his face. Understandable, Salim thought, only suffering a moment's worth of envy over it. Hasan was difficult to look away from, and by contrast Salim was like a shadow: darker, slimmer, easily forgotten between cracks of light. He was a friendless academician, an exacting professor, a humorless scholar who'd dragged her here by virtue of getting heedlessly lost. Now Salim's life's work was complete, and though he had proven the impossible, it was Hasan who already ruled it. It was Hasan who commanded magic and riches; who had stolen his way to divine.

But still, helplessly, Jenny was a beacon for Salim now, an anchor. He was indebted to her, endlessly, and therefore understood what the fae Prince had meant: having and wanting and owing. Salim had not repaid a debt by finding his way here with her—he had created a new one by virtue of their joining, and now it would be irreparable, lifelong. Maybe he was simply a person designed for eternality, the constancy of searching. He had found his brother, and now his body, accustomed to the ache of unfulfillment, was looking elsewhere for something newly unrequited. Was it still only sex, even when it was the kind that opened portals to the unbearable decadence of other, impossible worlds?

Jenny looked up, catching his eye as Salim drank what remained of his wine, and the corners of her lips flicked upwards, helpless to a smile. He could feel himself smiling broadly at her in return, everything suddenly dulling to singular, undeniable clarity. *I understand,* he wanted to say, *I understand now what it means to search,* and he reached out, taking her hand and observing the way surprise registered on her face.

He found when he opened his mouth that the words didn't come, not the way he planned them. His lips parted and something spilled out, clumsy syllables beside the ones belonging to her name. He laughed, the sensation of it steeping momentarily in his chest before blooming from his tongue, alight like the wings of a bird. Petals fell instead of language, frothing up from night to dawn, and nothing, nothing was wrong, nor would ever be wrong again.

Bliss was this world's intoxication. Salim closed his eyes, taking flight, and in a moment of soaring exultation he felt the ground give way beneath him. He would not notice the way Jenny's fingers fell from his, slowly, when he sank instead into restful slumber, bathed in the warmth of his brother's golden light.

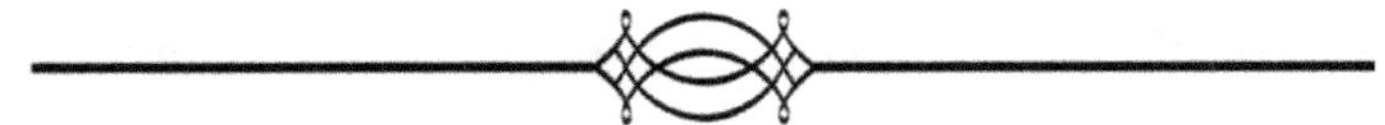

Salim collapsed backwards, his hand slipping from hers, and Jenny leapt instantly towards him, gasping aloud. Hasan had already waved a hand, producing a huddle of Grecian-draped handmaids that materialized from nowhere, drawn from the folds of the canopy's drapes. They were each bronzed and bright like Hasan himself, portraits designed to flatter his image. Jenny had the feeling she could ask each of them anything she liked and still, only Hasan's voice, his thoughts, would come through.

"Let him go," Hasan advised Jenny, beckoning with his chin for the handmaids to come forward. They swept Salim up without effort, the hand that had clutched Jenny's falling limply at his side while the others levitated him into the air, his head supported by an ample bosom. "He can sleep it off in his room," Hasan advised, flicking his wrist once more to instruct the others as they went.

"But—" Jenny tried to follow in Salim's wake, concerned he might have somehow fallen ill, but Hasan rose soundlessly from his seat, slender fingers wrapping her wrist to pause her in place.

"Not everyone can handle so much at first," he said, releasing her when she turned to him with a startled glance. "He'll get used to it eventually."

Then Hasan resumed his seat, gesturing for her to take hers. Jenny complied, albeit warily, and glanced at Salim's goblet, which was empty. She had not even touched her own.

"Did you drug us both, or just him?" she asked quietly.

Hasan arched a brow. "You think I would ever harm my brother? Or you, for that matter?" He seemed to find the prospect laughable, reaching across the table to take a sip from her glass for show. He slid his tongue between his lips, coating them with the jewel-colored liquid, and then drained the glass of its contents. "How very suspicious you are," he murmured, "when I have done nothing but welcome you into my home."

"I thought it worth asking, given the circumstances," she said flatly. "I've been led to believe the fae do not lie—except by omission," she pointed out, "and you haven't answered the question."

Hasan eyed the empty goblet in his hand for a moment before locking eyes with her. "What makes you think I am beholden to the laws of the fae?"

"I saw your face when I thanked you," she said, recalling Salim's anthropological lesson when she had inadvertently begged one of the fae's pardon upon arrival: *gratitude is a vulgarity to them*. "You're one of them now, aren't you?"

Without Salim, the atmosphere around them had changed. Jenny wasn't entirely sure how long they had been there, but the sun-drenched afternoon had turned quickly to early twilight. Stars were beginning to surface against the darkening sky, mimicking the freckles beside Salim's eyes, and Hasan's glow had dimmed, growing bluer.

"I tell you my story of triumph and now you think I'm a monster?" asked Hasan. He leaned back in his chair, scrutinizing her. "Impolite," he murmured, before refilling her glass with wine and raising it to his lips. The air, Jenny thought with a sudden chill, was now perceptibly colder.

She didn't consider the question worth answering. "You were the one who called me here, didn't you? You sent the fax." She remembered the words, feeling the same thing then that she felt now: *Jenny, he needs your help.*

"Time is an odd thing here," replied Hasan blandly. "I wasn't sure how much of it had passed."

"Not many people have fax machines. You might not have found me."

"Perhaps not. But, then again," said Hasan, sipping his wine, "you are not the important thing."

Jenny thought back through Hasan's story, formulating her suspicions into theories. She thought of how he had been one of many changelings, children stolen by a previous King. How he had positioned himself close to inheritance, weaving himself into the fabric.

"I don't believe you ever tried to go home," she said. "But you want Salim to believe you did, don't you?"

"You think I could have found my way back?" Hasan scoffed, irritated. "Perhaps you've failed to notice, but this world is not so free with its prisoners."

"Maybe not," she permitted. "I just don't think you actually bothered trying."

"Whatever gives you that impression?"

"I know stories," Jenny said. She thought of her grandmother's stories, her mother's. She thought of Salim and his story of searching. "I know that your story is about ambition," she said, "not desperation."

Hasan's lips curled up thinly. Amused, but not scathingly. "Is that so wrong?"

No, it wasn't wrong, but there was something there, something important. Some evidence for why he sought Salim out now, when anyone so intent on making himself King would have otherwise forgotten he'd ever had a brother to forget. She thought of the fae Prince's words—*I will inherit, therefore I am a Prince.*

"You need an heir," she realized aloud, "don't you?"

Salim had been the one to point out that this world likely could not reproduce. They stole children when they couldn't make them. Hasan must somehow straddle the line between species; human in origin, fae in deeds. He would remember the need to make an heir even if he had lost the ability to produce one, and he had fought other Princes to arrive at the head of this court. Surely his legacy would matter to him.

"It's obvious Salim wants you," Hasan said in lieu of answering, though that was answer enough. He was sitting upright now, having begun his negotiation. "Would it really be so terrible? You did it once," he pointed out. "And unlike my captors, I would let you go if you wished it. Once your service was complete, that is."

That was one way to think of childbirth, Jenny thought bitterly. The fairytales were all accurate to some extent, then. Just hand over your firstborn and everything would be fine. "What about Salim?"

"He is free to go if he chooses," said Hasan, shrugging. "But he won't."

"How can you be so sure?"

"I left a door open in Salim," he said plainly. "He will always long for me."

Again, Jenny's grandmother's words echoed again in her head: *Only people with terrible longing find their way to a fairy realm.*

"He'll be happy here," Hasan assured her. "Everyone is happy here, because nothing else exists to prevent it. He will have everything he could ever want, everything he could possibly dream. Every child taken here finds a place, a home. It's not as insidious as you seem to think."

"You mean that everyone finds pleasure here," she told him. "But that isn't happiness, even if no other option exists."

Hasan said nothing, merely swirling the wine in his glass, and in his silence, Jenny thought again of Salim, of the words he'd mumbled to her just before the effects of the wine had taken him. *Jenny*, he slurred, fingers tightly entwining with hers, *I found my brother, now I'll find you.*

"How did you find the door?" Jenny asked Hasan, setting her jaw. "Salim took a drug that cost a small fortune just to produce it, and he still wound up in a prison cell when he arrived. You were nine years old and by all means empty-handed. How could you possibly have gotten here?"

Hasan gave her a tight-lipped smile, finishing his glass and rising to his feet.

"The world has a way of showing you where you belong," said the fae king who was once Hasan Amrani.

Then he summoned more of his handmaids from the dew kissing fragrant grass, showing Jenny to her room before retiring wordlessly to his own.

Sleep was not an option. Jenny let her restless feet carry her elsewhere, to the only place she felt even remotely recognizable as herself.

Safety would have been the sensation of choice, but the scope of things had to be limited.

By the time she had crept across the floor from the threshold of Salim's room to the bed where he lay serenely above the covers, he had already begun to stir. He raised one hand to his head, pressing his fingers into his temples, and glanced at her with something like confusion mixed with ordinary, commonplace humiliation—like coworkers at a holiday party who'd drunkenly made out.

"I don't usually overindulge," he said with a wince. "Though I suppose on occasion indulgence may be warranted."

Despite being properly dark outside now, the moon's light was so potent it shone reflectively from every angle of the gleaming white walls. Even the stars themselves were piercingly bright; against the sky's pitch of iridescent navy, Jenny could still see every feature of Salim's face clearly. She was quietly pleased to witness the way Salim's eyes slid over her lips, briefly, before flicking gravely back to hers.

His chambers were larger than hers, grander. Hers was a guest room, designed for temporary occupancy, and his was a princely suite. She didn't say anything about it, choosing instead to let the slippers Hasan had conjured for her slide to the floor as she climbed onto Salim's bed, stretching out beside him.

"Does he seem lonely to you?" murmured Salim. "In need of a consort, maybe."

She watched him moisten his lips, resolutely not looking at her.

"No," she said. "No, I think your brother's loneliness is something very different from the usual kind."

They lay in silence for a moment while Jenny again recounted the familiar. The recognizable sky, the moon, the transitive quality of

Hasan's palace versus the Prince's. Hasan had recreated things he had once seen or wanted rather than inventing newness. Jenny understood now what it was to want with limitations, to pursue meaning rather than empty grandeur. She suspected that Hasan, for all his wealth, was finding it all to be quite colorless, without taste. He would always be lonely and therefore he would instill it elsewhere, infecting others with pieces of himself. It was why his servants were only vacant reflections of him; he was a man with magic who could not create life.

Everyone has doors, Jenny thought, reaching out to brush the knuckles on Salim's right hand and thinking of his longing, his desperation, his loss. Mystically speaking, they were all just trying to walk through something; striving to find something else on the other side.

Only people with terrible longing find their way to a fairy realm.

Jenny felt Salim's chest hitch at her touch, his sharp inhale errantly mislaid. "I didn't expect it," he said hoarsely, apologetically, and she knew he meant *I didn't think we would be like this, two threads through the eye of one needle.* She knew he meant: *I would have liked to have offered you less, to have asked for nothing in return.* Sex and magic, that strange conversion, energy that could not be lost. Of course it would never be simple—or maybe it was actually so primal and miraculous they could never understand how simple it actually was.

She slid her fingers from his wrist to his inner arm, a meandering touch to mirror his wandering thoughts. It was a little game of tag, her palm chasing his skin as he turned towards her, gradually igniting. His hesitation, a matter of questioning, was only a momentary lag until he faced her fully, his hands finding the edge of her thin caftan and drawing it up past her leg, to her hip. Jenny wondered if they would have an audience this time, like the first time, and assumed there must have been.

This palace and everything in it were an extension of Hasan, and she doubted she could have found her way to this room if he hadn't expressly wanted her to.

She wondered if Salim knew his brother's less-noble intentions, or if he suspected them at all. She had a feeling he did but was ignoring his better judgment, pushing it aside as an unwelcome obstacle to his long-fought joy. He was here, finally, a lonely man who had once been a boy in mourning. Surely if he wished to question his place here, he would know where to look for flaws, but she didn't blame him for not pursuing them. He had an open door inside him, with decades of longing to solder the hinge. In the war between reason and hope, any mistrust Salim may have felt for his brother could never possibly win.

Jenny thought back to their research, the book, the miles she had traveled; to the person she had been, and the card she had drawn from his deck: the knight of cups, a message from the heart, purity and passion and light. Absolution and arrival, exultation in the form of release. She pulled Salim closer, asking and answering both, as if fate were currently held between her palms. She let him swell over her like the roll of a tide, exhaling a penitent sigh. To them both, she promised the same as the card: *the answer you are looking for is yes.*

This time it was less inhibited, more desperate, like he was counting on his fingers how many times he had left to touch her and every moment it was less, less, less. His hands tangled in her hair, woven through it, and her legs were cast around his waist, her gasp floating between his lips. Somewhere, Hasan was probably laughing, smiling to himself over their silly human longings. What fools these mortals be.

What was the difference between this world and that? Why could some worlds create life when others couldn't? Maybe it was the fragility of it, the delicate divide, the powerlessness of existing only in small bursts; the helpless clinging to base sensations. Maybe it was because they didn't have magic that this was how they kept themselves alive.

A flame ignited in her chest and leapt to his tongue and this was their tranquil ordinariness, the meager wildness of their existence. This was what had so awed the Prince—what Hasan had gone to such strange lengths to get. That two people who were virtually strangers would feel so obligated to each other, so immutably entwined, was a marvel in its way. It was a spectacle, spectacular, not unlike the flavors and colors and the grotesque sort of beauty this world kept like a pet. It was the finest of all their world's offerings, with the volume set on high.

Jenny had opened a door with Salim's help before and this time was no different, even if it was. True, this was more her choice than the last time had been, but that was what allowed her to take her time, to slow down, to find what she was looking for. Everyone had doors, more of them than just the biggest ones, the most obvious. There were doors to private lives, past experiences. Doors that were shared only in moments of intimacy, and now that she knew they could be found, she took the time to be selective. She panted in Salim's ear, *wait, slower, deeper,* he bled the words *yes yes yes* numbly into her shoulder. The two of them dragged time by the shoulders, digging their heels into that nameless, mounting ache.

Still, friction was friction. "Did you mean what you said?" Jenny rasped to Salim, who by that time had balanced them both on his haunches. She twisted around, finding his mouth, waiting for his answer to slip from his tongue to hers. "Will you find me?" she said, only it was a demand, sharp and urgent.

His expression was uncertain, but undaunted. "Yes."

"Good," she said, and gasped.

Like before there was a door—several doors—only this time, she found the one she was looking for: dull and empty, colorless and vacant. It was only some distant sense, some nameless intuition that told her she had found it, the right place, the most fitting, and that she would be doing him a kindness even if it would seem, at first, terribly, selfishly cruel. She could feel him resisting, pulling away, but she held him fast, taking him with her. Come with me, take my hand, don't let go. If you can trust nothing else, then trust me.

She felt his acquiescence like a sigh of relief, his euphoria matching itself to hers, and she knew, distantly, that Hasan was there; that he wasn't going to allow this to happen without a fight. She shoved Salim through the door alone and she, caught in the middle, had only one spare moment, only a breath, to wrest herself free from Hasan's grip on her hand.

She felt Salim leave her, his touch erasing from hers like a ghost, and then she heard Hasan laugh, his voice gleeful and furious and strangely, diabolically magical. It was the Prince's strident beauty, the discord of existence. The persistence of memory, the ugliness of beauty, the immaculate peril of rapturous descent. Synthetic, unnatural, the ambition of an empty vessel. *That* kind of magical—born from nothing, deluded that it could ever be more.

"It's over, it's over, he found me once and he can find me again!"

But what remained as Jenny's body gave its final ebbing convulsions was the strength to pull the door shut behind her, Hasan's laughter drowning to a scream as she faded into black.

Salim may have had an open door, she thought while drifting slowly into nothing, but she was an anchor, and that would be enough to save them both.

Dr. Salim Amrani opened his eyes to find himself seated at his desk, facing the black screen of his sleeping laptop. He blinked himself back into focus, unsure how long he may have drifted off, and pressed the space key, waking the screen. From there, his gaze slid lethargically to the notification of an unopened email.

Dear Dr. Amrani,

I suppose you might find this a bit odd, but I was listening to you speak on a recent podcast episode and thought I might offer my assistance.

His attention dragged through the rest of the email to find her parting benedictions and her email signature, specifying the name Jenny Li along with a link to her tarot art. Ah, so she wasn't an academic, then. He moved the cursor to close out of the email but paused, re-reading. She said she had a background in both Irish and Chinese witchcraft, which was interesting. Not that Harvard would pay for it. But it was interesting.

He clicked the link to her art, browsing the explanations for her tarot deck. She seemed to have a strong understanding of mythology; a grasp of the intersect of mysticism and art. Each of her cards, as far as he could see, had been painstakingly rendered based on her connection to her heritage. He clicked back to the email, re-reading the section she'd written about her background.

The interesting thing about being the daughter of immigrants is that I have experience in both worlds. Chinese medicine, Celtic runes, all that. I learned from my family on both sides. (The influence of the moon, interestingly enough, is pretty much the same no matter how you slice it.) Overall it's not as exciting as you'd think—I can't fly on a broomstick or anything, but I make a lot of my own herbal remedies. It's a lot of fae superstition, astrological intuition, that sort of thing.

He had the inexplicable sensation he ought to reply to her. Maybe she had caught him at a strange time of day, or his blood sugar was low.

His phone vibrated in his pocket and he reached for it mindlessly, glancing down at the screen. *Yo I think I found that key*, from Alcott, the drug dealer, whose number Salim had still not programmed into his phone.

It occurred to Salim to be excited by the news—to leap to respond—only something odd was happening. Usually when he thought about the possibility of getting close to his brother it was like something took over him, burying him with the sudden magnitude of his need. Instead, he turned his attention back to the email, reading it a second time, and then a third.

Would you consider collaborating with me on a book I'm writing? he wrote. *It's something I'm doing for a Harvard syndicate.* He paused, considering it, and then added, *The university will pay.*

He got up to make a cup of coffee, planning to work through the night. The message from Alcott sat on his phone screen, unanswered. For a moment Salim contemplated replying, curiosity nudging at him to give the aforementioned key a try, but then his computer dinged with the sound of a new email.

I think it's best if we met in person first, the tarot artist, Jenny Li, had written in response to his offer. *I like to know who I'm working with.*

That was probably wise. He was fairly sure she had said she was working in Berkeley, which was very well across the world from him as far as he was concerned, but considering his brother had once been stolen by fairies, there were further distances to travel.

Again, Salim had the strange sensation that he carried some vestigial need within him, an old reflex accompanying any thoughts of Hasan. He waited for desperation, searching for former feelings of urgency and despair, but they didn't come. It was as if he had managed to cross a threshold, no longer only a fragment of himself without Hasan.

His phone buzzed again from Alcott. *Maybe I'll try it if you won't.*

Well, that was certainly one way to find out if a thing worked. *Do it, then*, Salim replied, closing the book on the conversation for the night before turning his attention back to his email.

Jenny roused from a place of groggy half-consciousness, having recently suffered the sensation of walking through a door. Whether she had closed the door behind her or whether she had been swallowed up the door by virtue of opening it was unclear. What *was* clear was only that she could not reverse her steps. It was difficult to explain; colorless and without details, like how no one ever remembered falling asleep. They simply knew they had done it when they arrived back to a state of waking in the morning, and it was from that precise place that Jenny had found herself pulling open Gmail on her computer.

Since then, the evening had carried on as normal. The professor, Dr. Amrani, agreed that Jenny should come to Boston and arranged to supplement the funding for her trip. She glanced from his reply down to her cards, fingering the worn edges and wondering what had come over her to send the email in the first place. It wasn't like they needed to meet in person in order for her to do a few hours of research virtually, but something had told her she ought to make an effort.

Instinct or something, she guessed. Witch's intuition.

The knight of cups slid out from the deck as she aimlessly shuffled, the card leaping headlong into her hand, and Jenny chuckled to herself when she looked at the familiar design, shaking her head. There were some things too obvious to be taken blindly; some signs so on the nose that they seemed almost laughable to accept, even if they were vastly more foolish to ignore. This was a romantic card, a gift of future blessing. If she didn't take it as a sign, she was either an idiot or a cynic, and she had been raised quite specifically to not be either of those.

So, despite working on her second deck—despite her yoga teaching schedule and despite the exorbitant rent that she'd still have to pay upon her return—Jenny wrote back to the professor, Salim Amrani, that she could be available to meet him whenever he found it convenient. The day before she left, there had been another oddity.

A fax containing only three words: *Fine. You win.*

It was hard to explain what happened when she met Salim. She took one look at his face, far younger than she'd expected, and felt something she could only call a sensation; another sign. Some intangible sense of purpose, of destiny and satisfaction, absolution and relief. She looked at Salim Amrani and knew, somehow, that the answer to her question was yes.

They dated slowly, of course. Reasonably. They were inseparable for the weekend she was with him in Boston (regrettably she went to bed with him the first night, but she'd done worse to far less satisfactory results before) and after that they communicated over email about the book, about his search for his brother, about the drug dealer he casually knew who'd gone missing. About how her new deck contained colors she didn't know how to name but they were flowing out of her, as if from a dream she'd once had.

She convinced Salim to reposition his book as a compilation of research about his brother from over the years. Tales of people who had fallen through worlds, or claimed to. Some were literary, some were mythological, some were anecdotal. All were the result of a lifelong search, with such surprise commercial success that Salim was later approached for a film adaptation. He declined, stating that his research was more suited to a documentary, for which he eventually served as writer and producer. Jenny was asked to participate, having recently moved to London to be with Salim, but she demurred, opting to focus on her art instead. She had been named an artist on the rise and later published a book of surrealist illustrations she called *Banquets with the Fae*.

The introduction to the film *Stone's Throw*, filling the international festival hall on the night Salim planned to propose to Jenny, was hailed as an instant triumph by critics, later quoted in bold type in the official *New York Times* review:

"We are always only a stone's throw from collapsing into another form of ourselves, in versions of lives we cannot relinquish. Luckily, the world has a way of showing us where we belong."

SAINTS AND LIARS (NOVEMBER 2018-JANUARY 2019)

CECILY AYERS HAS NO INTEREST in coming back to her tiny Midwestern hometown after a successful decade spent living in Los Angeles, but when her grandmother and family matriarch falls ill, Cecily's mother summons her home to secure the inheritance of her family grimoire. Porter Callahan hasn't seen or heard from Cecily in seven years, but when he runs into her in their town's only bar, Cecily asks him for a favor: Date her, at least in public, to get her mother off her back.

Unbeknownst to Cecily, Porter has an agenda of his own.

PART I: HOMECOMING

Saint Sturm High School
Saint Sturm, Iowa
March 2011

Cecily Ayers was the rare overlap of desirable school-aged qualities, falling centrally on the Venn diagram of pretty girls, smart girls, and sporty girls. She got good grades, generally knew how to wear her hair, and didn't have too much acne-related trauma—*plus* she was a setter on the varsity volleyball team. Her cocktail of qualifications was enough to secure her early acceptance to UCLA, which she not-so-subtly reminded people by wandering the halls of Saint Sturm High in her grey hoodie with its powder blue letters. She was popular, but not a snob. She was involved, but not overwhelmingly. In general, she was the sort of girl most boys found themselves fantasizing about at least once during their adolescence; not untouchable, but not exactly within reach, either.

It was probably also worth mentioning that Cecily Ayers was a witch, which was more specifically what accounted for her considerable significance to Porter Callahan. Needless to say, there weren't too many witches in northern Iowa, so their families had been fairly insistent they spend time together at events that ranged from festive coven gatherings to mortal track meets. Before Cecily's father had passed away their sophomore year, Porter had seen her almost every week as a result of cross-familial obligations. Now it was once a month or so, on the increasingly rare occasions that Porter's mother Maggie could convince

Cecily's mother Evelyn to join her at whatever seance or book club she was up to that week. Maggie Ellis Callahan was aggressively social, much to Porter's dismay, and forcefully extroverted. He didn't blame Evelyn for decreasing their visits, though it had come at a price of drifting further from Cecily.

"Hey," Porter said, wandering over to Cecily's locker. "Got a second?"

She shoved a book into her backpack and looked up. "Sure. Although," she sighed, "if this is about the picnic your mother's planning, could you find a nice way to tell her that my mother would rather die? I mean, I'll go, assuming I don't have to be in L.A. for orientation," she concluded, to which Porter hastily shook his head.

"No, it's—I mean sure, I'll tell her, but it's not about that. I was actually wondering if maybe you'd, um. Want to go to prom with me?" he posed in what he hoped was a reasonably disaffected way.

In answer, though, Cecily gave him something of a long-suffering grimace.

"Porter, listen, it's really nice of you to ask, but we both know why you're doing this," she said, exhausted beyond the wealth of her teenage experience. "Maggie would kill you if you didn't, and my mother would kill me if I said no, but can't we just… *not* do this, for once?"

"Uh," Porter said, noticing as she spoke that some of the chatter around them had stopped. A few heads had swiveled towards them, curiously speculating in a way that made his stomach lurch.

Sometimes he really hated living in such a small town.

"It's just getting really out of hand," Cecily continued, smoothing her ponytail over her shoulder before pulling on one strap of her backpack; behind her, Jennifer Saltzmann halted in place, eyes widening as she registered the tone of the conversation. "I mean I get it, you're a Callahan boy and I'm an Ayers girl, blah blah," Cecily said, rolling her eyes, "but like, I'm *leaving*, you know? So, I don't know." She chewed her lip. "I don't think I'm gonna do the prom thing."

Porter tore his attention from the troubling way that Jennifer had begun whispering to her tyrannical friend Emily and blinked down again at Cecily. "You're not going at all?"

"No, I mean... *why*, right? Spend a ton of money on some dress that I'll just regret in five years, all so some dudes I've known since I was in diapers can try to dry-hump me in the dark until Principal Marsden shines a flashlight in our faces and tells us to leave room for Jesus? No, thanks." Cecily slammed her locker shut, shrugging. "I know Maggie's probably on the prom committee, so at least this way you can go with someone who, you know. You actually like."

"Oh." Porter cleared his throat. "Yeah, um. Thanks."

"Of course," Cecily replied, and paused a moment, her brow furrowing slightly as if the thought was just occurring to her that perhaps Porter wasn't savoring this process of pseudo-public rejection. "You get it, right? I mean, I'm certainly not sticking around here forever," she said, shuddering theatrically at the thought, "so I'd rather just stay home and spend some time with my mom before I leave. She's going to have a really tough time when I'm gone, you know? So, I don't know. Prom just doesn't seem like a priority."

"Right, totally," Porter said, forcing a nod as Jennifer grabbed Luke Emerson's arm across the hallway, yanking him to a stop and gesturing to Porter and Cecily. "Yeah, I... get it. Of course."

Maybe if their conversation hadn't had such voyeuristic appeal, Porter would have told Cecily that Evelyn Ayers wasn't the only one who would miss her when she was gone. Considering there was no getting around their audience, though, it was what it was.

"Cool, well, good luck," Cecily said, shrugging. "See you in physics, I guess."

Good luck, see you in physics I guess. Porter was pretty sure that was going to follow him around in his nightmares for a while.

"Yeah, later," he said, and she slipped past him into the corridor, appearing not to notice that anyone had overheard.

In Cecily's absence, Jennifer Saltzmann's unfortunate crowd of onlookers bore similar expressions: a mix of teen horror and abject hilarity.

"Callahan, tough luck, bro," Luke managed, spoken as if he weren't shaking with laughter. "*Ouch.*"

Internally, Porter sighed. They'd never let him live this down, and unlike Cecily, he wasn't exactly going anywhere.

"Whatever, man," he forced out, shrugging. "Her loss."

Two months later, Cecily Ayers went to Los Angeles for freshmen orientation and never came back.

She didn't say goodbye.

SEVEN YEARS LATER
Los Angeles
December 2018

"Hi, Mom," Cecily said, picking up the phone before it rang. It was one of her particular talents, along with not needing to check the caller ID, though it could have just as easily been a guess. Her mother called for fifteen minutes or so several times a week—usually out of boredom, Cecily suspected. "What's up?"

"Sweetie, you need to come home," Evelyn said, which wasn't new, though she did sound abnormally agitated. Normally she called to complain about the rest of the Ayers family, or to fill Cecily in on the latest in Saint Sturm gossip. Occasionally it was about baking, sometimes about witchery, but it was rarely anything serious. Evelyn had recently given up on trying to coax Cecily home, opting instead for an annual trip to California when the Iowa winters got too dreary and hinting, usually with a thin veil of passive-aggression, that a return to Saint Sturm might be a novel twist.

"I mean it this time," Evelyn added, correctly anticipating Cecily's thoughts.

"Mom, I already told you, I can't. Ansel and I are leaving tomorrow, remember? The tickets have been booked for months."

"It's your grandmother, Cecily, or you know I wouldn't ask," Evelyn said, to which Cecily blinked, and blinked again. She supposed her grandmother was getting on in years, but she hadn't considered that anything might ever be wrong with her. "I'm afraid she doesn't have much time," Evelyn said, using the delicate voice she sometimes adopted when delivering bad news. "Or so she seems to think, anyway."

Cecily sat up in bed, frowning. "Wait. Grandma Eleanor's sick?"

"Yes, so it seems," Evelyn said, and then, musingly, "I really believed she'd outlive us all on spite alone, so I'm finding it all quite difficult to process myself, to tell you the truth."

"But it's…" Cecily broke off, still unable to process this. "It's serious?"

"Yes. She's summoned all the cousins. It's a whole production."

"But," Cecily attempted, and stopped. "But Grandma Eleanor never gets sick."

"I know, hon," Evelyn sighed. "But in typical Eleanor Ayers fashion, she's asked for everyone to be there, so you know what that means."

"But I'm supposed to leave tomorrow," Cecily said, dismayed. Beside her, Ansel rolled over in bed, throwing an arm around her waist with a low, soft snore. "I'm supposed to be gone for two weeks, Mom."

It had taken ages for Ansel to even convince her to go, given her work schedule. She'd pushed everything aside and only recently finished with all the relevant pre-beach wax appointments, so to now consider all of that a waste was pushing in on her already compromised thought process.

"Well, you'll have to change your tickets," Evelyn said with an audible shrug. "I'd make your excuses for you, sweetheart, but truth be told, you really do have to be here. That grimoire should be yours"—*This again*, Cecily thought glumly—"and you know your grandmother loathes me too much to give it to me without you there. It's hard enough with her suspecting I've kept you away *on purpose*," Evelyn muttered under her breath, "just like it's somehow *my* fault your father had a stroke—"

"Mom," Cecily cut in, "this isn't about my inheritance."

"Maybe for you it isn't," Evelyn said matter-of-factly, "but your father would come back to life and *drag* you back home if he knew it might go to that idiot Adria—or worse, Rosabella," Evelyn said with palpable displeasure, "who, by the way, has just about birthed her own personal coven in the time you've been away—"

"But—" Cecily glanced down at Ansel, feeling a rush of disappointment. She'd never tell her mother, of course, considering how little Evelyn already approved of him, but something had been off between them for weeks. She'd been secretly hoping the vacation might set things right, reinstating the ease they'd had together at the beginning of the relationship, back when she'd worked less and he'd… cared more. Not that he didn't, of course! He'd been the one to insist they go away together, after all, even if their holiday plans did involve his family rather than hers.

But while the urgency might revolve around the Ayers family spellbook for her mother, for Cecily, this was about Eleanor. She did love her grandmother, despite that love being mostly expressed from a distance, and would be heartbroken if something happened while she wasn't there.

"But I *hate* Iowa in the winter," Cecily concluded, grumbling it under her breath.

"We all do, sweetheart," Evelyn said evenly. "So, will I see you tomorrow?"

Ansel rolled onto his back, yawning stiffly as Cecily stared down at him with brutal indecision. "What's up, babe?" he mumbled, and she sighed, shaking her head as he reached up to toy with her hair.

"Yeah, Mom," she grudgingly said. "I'll look up flights right n-" She broke off as her phone vibrated in her hand. "You already emailed them to me, didn't you?"

"Maybe," Evelyn said. "Thanks, sweetie. It won't be too bad, I promise."

"Doubt that. Love you, Mom."

"Love you too, Cecily. See you soon."

She hung up with a groan, falling back in bed. "I have to go to Iowa tomorrow instead of Mexico," she said, turning to face Ansel. "My grandmother's sick."

"Oof, bummer," Ansel said, stifling another yawn. "Want me to come with? Could change my tickets, meet up with the fam later."

Thank god he'd offered. Maybe they'd be fine after all.

"No, you go," Cecily assured him. "Your family is expecting you. They won't miss me."

That, and her grandmother would probably die on impact if she knew Cecily was dating a non-witch. She didn't need her mother bugging her about it to know that for certain, and besides, Evelyn had done plenty of lecturing anyway. *All your cousins have nice witch husbands and cute little witch babies,* Evelyn regularly wailed, *and all I have is a giant empty house and a mother-in-law who's probably poisoning me!*

Ah, the irony, Cecily thought, sighing.

"You good, babe?" Ansel asked, kissing her shoulder.

She opened her email and clicked the first link, figuring that would be fine. Her mother would have picked out the best flight. It was the destination that was the problem.

"Yeah," Cecily said, relieved that they, at least, seemed to be headed for a nice morning, which they didn't always have these days. "I'm fine."

Paradise Bar,
Saint Sturm, Iowa

"You won't fuckin' believe who's here," Luke said without preamble, shoving Porter over to make room in the booth and slamming a beer down in front of him as Ben Parish took the opposite bench. "Feeling especially rejected this evening, Cali?"

Porter rolled his eyes, picking up the beer. "Sure."

Not at all, in fact. Last night's yoga instructor had been… well, enlightening, to say the least. He could hardly call himself wanting, but still, even after seven years, the jokes never stopped.

This, Porter thought, was the problem with living somewhere like Saint Sturm. Sure, you always knew who to ask when the recipe called for more sugar, but also, you couldn't go a day without someone mentioning how you'd been chewed up and spat back out *seven fucking years ago*.

But there was something about the glint in Ben's eye that felt more specific than previous episodes of historical abuse.

"No prom-posals coming to mind?" mused Ben.

Alright, this had better be a joke.

"No," Porter said, the beer paused halfway to his lips.

"Yes," Luke countered smugly. "She's over at the bar."

Cecily Ayers, the one who got away. *Good luck, see you in physics I guess—that* Cecily. Didn't say goodbye Cecily. Bailed without a single word and never came back Cecily. Cecily, the girl his mother still couldn't stop talking about, but who couldn't spare an ounce of interest for him.

It took everything in Porter's power not to look.

"Weird," Porter finally managed, shrugging. High school, he reminded himself, was a long time ago, so he dragged the bottle upwards for a sip he only half-tasted.

"What's it been, seven years?" Luke said, conveniently managing to process this information for the first time in their collective lives, "and this is the first time anyone's seen her." He took a swig from his bottle, shaking his head. "She is *hot*, man. L.A.'s been plenty good to her."

"Good for her," Porter said impassively.

"Come on," Ben said, kicking Porter's foot under the table. "The first and last person to ever say no to the great Porter Callahan is in the building and you don't have a *single* curiosity about her?"

"It was high school," Porter reminded him. "Things have changed."

"They haven't changed *that* much," Luke said with a laugh, looking over at Cecily again.

Porter swallowed, the beer still tasteless, but said nothing.

"Come *on*," Ben said again. "Go talk to her. Win her over," he suggested with a wink. "Sweep her off her feet."

"Stop," Porter warned.

"I'm telling you, Parish, he *can't*," Luke said obnoxiously to Ben. "I mean, one rejection is fine," he said with a bark of a laugh, "but *two*—"

Porter caught a glimpse of her then, the way she'd shifted slightly into his periphery by the bar, and allowed himself a moment's speculation. She was wearing black jeans and a coat that was definitely too thin, especially considering how unseasonable the cold already was. It was windy, supposed to snow that evening. Her hair slid from her shoulders to her back as she turned slightly, offering him a fuller view of her silhouette. Same nose, same lips, slightly shorter hair. One of those fashionable haircuts that every Instagram model seemed to have these days. She was tapping her nails idly against a glass of *wine*, which was hardly the bar's specialty.

She glanced over her shoulder and caught him looking—for which he kicked himself, furious. She frowned for a second, surprised, and then gave a tentative wave.

"Oh, shit," Luke said with a laugh. "Spotted."

Porter slid a glare at him, wishing he'd stayed home that night. "Just get up, would you?"

"Oh, my pleasure," Luke said, slinking out of the booth and gesturing grandly for Porter to walk by. "Try not to strike out again, Cali."

"Good luck," Ben called after him, and Porter shook him off, wandering over to Cecily.

"Hey," he said, and she gave him a broad smile.

"Porter," she said warmly, hopping off her stool to give him a hug. "It's seriously *so good* to see you."

"Is it?" he asked, and she leaned back with a broad grin.

"Of course," she said. No emails, no calls, no texts, not even a Facebook follow, and yet here she was—so yeah, sure, *of course*.

"You're exactly the person I needed to see," she added in relief.

"Am I?" News to him.

"God, yeah. My mother's driving me crazy." She beckoned to the stools, gesturing for him to sit beside her. "I'm in town because my grandmother's sick."

"Oh, I'm sorry to hear that," Porter said, having already heard as much. There was very little he didn't hear living in such a small town, and his mother had been *remarkably* quick to tell him Eleanor Ayers would soon be passing down the Ayers grimoire—though he hadn't really made the connection to Cecily at the time.

"Yeah, well, my mother's taking the opportunity to make this completely about her," Cecily grumbled. "Or about how I'm failing her, I guess. She's bugging me about absolutely everything and, I don't know, I just needed to get away."

"Relatable," Porter said. His mother was a similar case of helpless smothering, as Cecily would know perfectly well. Predictably, she passed him a conspiratorial grimace.

She was, to his dismay, much lovelier than he remembered, though his memories of her had not been lacking by any means.

"Anyway, I was sitting here thinking about how perfect it would be for someone to get her off my case, and then you show up. Kismet, right? Magic or something," she said with a laugh.

Porter frowned. "Sorry, what?"

"Look, could I ask you a favor?" Cecily said, twisting to face him. "My mother really hates my boyfriend." Boyfriend. Of course she had one. "Do you think you could like, be his stand-in for a bit?" she posed hopefully, as Porter stared at her in disbelief. "I'd really appreciate it. I just… I need some relief, you know? If she saw me spending time with you, I don't know." She shrugged. "Might get her off my case, at least until I leave."

"Are you serious?" Porter asked her, and she looked up.

"What? Yeah," she said, and then blinked. "Oh gosh, sorry, are you seeing someone? Or married? Jesus," she exhaled, "I didn't even consider that you might be."

He wasn't, obviously—hence the ongoing jokes from Ben and Luke, married to their high school sweethearts for four years and two, respectively—but that wasn't the point. Seven years of silence and she managed to act like nothing had happened.

"I'm not," he said, ruffled, "but still, Cecily, I'm not an escort."

"What? No, oh god, you're right," she said with a laugh. "Sorry, I shouldn't have asked." She glanced down at her glass of wine as if it had been her co-conspirator, which he supposed it probably was. "I guess I was just looking for something that might make it a little easier, that's all. I've got Midwinter at my Grandma Eleanor's house and, I don't know, I was just thinking that if I brought *you*, then—"

She broke off.

"Never mind." She drained the rest of her glass, setting it down on the bar. "I'd better just head back, anyway."

He eyed her too-thin jacket again. That, and her lack of keys.

"How'd you get here?" Porter asked.

"Walked," Cecily said.

"That's a two-mile walk."

"I know," she said, shrugging. "So? Used to do it all the time in high school."

"Yeah, but—" He growled with frustration. "It's supposed to snow tonight, Cecily. Have you forgotten how cold it gets here?"

"Whatever, I'll be fine." She tossed a couple of bills down on the bar and slid off the stool. She was wearing a pair of suede boots that definitely weren't weather appropriate; even if she conjured a charm for them, it'd be a lot of work to keep her feet warm *and* dry, and she'd been drinking. "Okay, well, it was good to see you, Porter, but—"

"I'll drive you," fell out of his mouth for reasons he couldn't explain, and she looked up, brow furrowed. "Just… don't ask me to be your fake boyfriend again, okay?" he told her irritably. "We don't like it, FYI. Not very flattering."

"The royal we?" she echoed, half-laughing.

"Yes, the royal we. Me and the king."

"She's a queen, and I can walk," Cecily said, but he cut her off with a shake of his head.

"That old prince guy, then, and wait here," he told her, heading back to the booth and reaching for his coat. "Hey," he said to Luke, "toss me my jacket, I'm just—"

"Oh, I know what you're *just* doing," Luke agreed with a sly grin, picking the jacket up from the booth while pointedly withholding it from Porter's reach. "Make sure to close the deal this time, eh Callahan?"

"Luke—" Porter reached for the coat and Luke pulled it back. "Seriously, just *give* it—"

"Coats are for closers, Cali," Luke told him, to which Porter rolled his eyes, snatching the jacket from his hand. "Don't let us down, bro. Time to even the scales."

"That," Ben laughed into his beer, "or wallow another seven years, either or."

"You done?" Porter said, waiting until Luke had pantomimed a mirthful zip of his lips before jogging back over to Cecily. "You ready?"

"Is that Luke Emerson?" Cecily asked, frowning over his shoulder to where Ben and Luke toasted her from afar. "Jesus, I haven't thought about him in *years*."

We get it, Porter thought gruffly. None of us ever mattered.

"Let's just go," he muttered, ushering her out the door.

The moment Cecily had set foot in her childhood home—even before dragging her suitcase up to her bedroom, which was, as far as she could tell, still a shrine to her teenage self—Evelyn had been on the offensive, chattering slyly about engagements the entire drive from the airport and then forging ahead once it was clear there would be no escape.

"You do realize that Camille just got married," Evelyn informed Cecily, ignoring her attempt to close the bedroom door. Locks, as Cecily had always known, weren't particularly useful when one's mother happened to be a witch. "She married a witch from Minnesota who, okay, made an excellent cocktail for the wedding but still, he's nothing terribly impressive. Rosabella's got her brood, as you know, and Adria's husband just got promoted, so she's pregnant again—and oh god, *Miriam*, Miriam is *the worst*," Evelyn continued, apparently failing to notice that Cecily now held a pillow over her ears. "She's the one who just married cousin Jonathan and she's constantly—and I do mean *constantly*—sucking up to Eleanor. She's not even from here, so I mean honestly, as far as whether she's an *Ayers*—"

"You're not an Ayers, Mom," Cecily sighed. "And you're from Michigan."

"Yes, but this isn't about me," Evelyn said, sniffing with disapproval and appearing to miss the irony of that particular defense. "Listen, this Ansel of yours is pretty enough but he isn't a *witch*, sweetheart. Do you really want our line to die out? Because it *will*, you know—"

"It *might*," Cecily corrected her, "and anyway, Ansel and I aren't getting married any time soon, okay? We're just, you know. Hanging out."

Not entirely true. She *had* been planning to spend part of their Christmas holiday with his family, but she was under the impression that drinking cocktails with his mother on a beach wasn't exactly a relationship rite of passage. And true, an engagement was far off, but they were more than casual.

At least she hoped they were.

"*Do not* let your grandmother hear you say that," Evelyn admonished firmly, and then shook her head, reconsidering. "Well, never mind. Better to believe you're single than to hear you're 'just hanging out' with a mortal, so if it's a choice between the two—"

"Mom," Cecily groaned. "Can you ease up for a second? I was supposed to be drinking mojitos on a beach right now." She glanced at her phone screen for the time, realizing that Ansel would probably text soon to say he'd landed. "And at least I'm here, aren't I?"

Based on her mother's expression, it seemed that wasn't quite enough.

"You know, it wasn't exactly my dream to have a monster for a mother-in-law *and* a daughter who resents me for bringing her home, but here we are," Evelyn bemoaned dramatically, which had been approximately the time Cecily had made an excuse about meeting an old high school friend (none of whom she still had phone numbers for) at the only bar in town.

"IF THAT OLD WITCH GIVES THE GRIMOIRE TO MIRIAM I WILL KILL YOU MYSELF," Eleanor had called after Cecily when she left, which certainly wasn't helpful. In fact, the whole nonsensical debacle was now living unhelpfully in Cecily's head as she sat in Porter Callahan's car, staring out at the too-familiar flatness of the Iowa landscape and the snow that was starting to dust the roofs of the houses nearby.

"I'd forgotten how quiet it got around here," Cecily said. Minus the wind. And minus her mother's nagging. Even the noise in the bar had been different from L.A. noise; it felt stagnant and unwelcoming. People had been staring, which she hated, and which had been half the reason she'd left. Anonymity was a gift requiring a few million people, not a small town of barely a thousand.

"Yeah," Porter said, and she turned to look at him.

He looked different than she remembered. He'd always had that clean-cut jock look, ever the All-American athlete, though by now he'd grown into it a little. His sandy hair was a little messy, with a bit of darkened stubble to shadow his cheeks and chin, and he was dressed in light-wash jeans and a flannel shirt that were *actually* worn, not just fashionably altered.

He was pretty good looking, Cecily admitted to herself, though not at all her type. Ansel was, and it didn't hurt that he was also an artist. He wore tight black plants that made his ass look incredible and tied his long hair back with a spare bit of repurposed leather from an installation he'd done in NoHo, a detail that somehow managed to reflect carelessness and thoughtfulness all at once. Ansel Westcott painted politically charged murals on the sides of coffee shops. Porter Callahan looked like he probably still played touch football on the weekends, which was definitely *one* type. It just wasn't hers.

"It's weird to be home," Cecily said, and Porter glanced briefly at her before taking the right turn onto her street. "Feels like I just don't fit here anymore."

He paused a moment. "You never did, really."

"Hey," she said, feigning injury. "Real nice, Porter."

"It's true," he said, shrugging. "You were always trying to get out of here. Don't know if you've noticed, but that's not really the norm."

"Well, it used to feel like home, at least. Or like something familiar." She took a long look out the window, then turned back to him. "Now it just feels like, I don't know." There was nowhere useful to go with that, so she trailed off, redirecting her train of thought. "You seem different, too."

"Do I?"

"Well, yeah. I mean, I guess I remember you being kind of quiet, but now that I'm here, it's more like—" She hesitated. "Well, you know how some people are quiet because they have nothing to say? You seem like, I don't know. The opposite."

For a long moment, he proved her right with a heavy, implicating silence.

"You've been gone a long time," he said eventually, slowing down as they reached her house. The car came smoothly to a stop as the snowfall began to increase, blanketing the front yard and burying the tomato vines Evelyn was so enamored with. She texted Cecily pictures of her prized tomatoes at least once a week, which Cecily realized with a pang might have been for lack of anything else to nurture.

She stared out at the house for a few seconds, thinking about her mother, before registering that Porter was waiting for her to get out of his car. "Oh, right," she said with a laugh, unbuckling her seatbelt. "Okay, well. See you around, I guess. Maybe in another seven years or something."

She reached for the door, about to venture into the snow (which she was now very certain that her shoes would *not* have outlasted) when Porter's hand unexpectedly shot out, catching the inside of her arm and pausing her in place.

"Midwinter," he said. "Tomorrow. When should I pick you up?"

She blinked, surprised. "What? But I thought you said—"

"I know what I said. What time?" he asked, waiting, and she stared at him, wondering what had possibly changed his mind.

"Six-fifteen," she said eventually. "Dinner's at six-thirty at my grandma's house."

He nodded, releasing her. "Fine. See you at six-fifteen. Should I wear anything specific?"

"No," she said, slightly dazed. "I mean, whatever you think is best."

"Great. See you then."

She stepped out of his car with a mix of confusion and relief, twisting to pass him a parting wave before heading up to her front door. She reflexively reached for keys before remembering she didn't need those here; no thefts. Nobody ever bothered to lock their doors.

She opened the front door and Evelyn shot up from the couch.

"I was worried I'd have to come get you," she said in a motherly tone of accusation. "You left the house without a scarf! Though, speaking of scarves," she continued before Cecily could manage an apology, "Rosabella made your grandmother a *hideous* one th-"

"Porter drove me home," Cecily cut in, and Evelyn stopped mid-sentence, thunderstruck.

"Porter," she echoed faintly. "Porter Callahan?"

"Yes, the only Porter in this town, Mother," Cecily sighed, rolling her eyes. "Oh, and he's coming with me to Grandma Eleanor's tomorrow."

"He's… he is?" Evelyn asked, cheeks flushing pink with delight. "Really?"

Clearly her plan was already working. "Yes, really," Cecily sighed, aiming herself up the stairs. "So is that enough lecturing for the day, then?"

"Is he still cute?" Evelyn called after her.

Cecily paused, considering it.

"Yeah, he's, you know. The same," she yelled back.

"Oh," said Evelyn, sounding positively enamored with the thought.

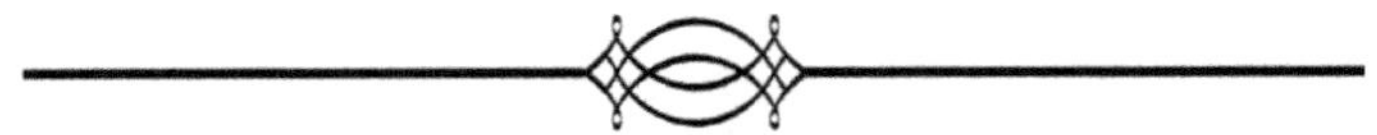

Porter had absolutely no plans to attend any sort of event with Cecily Ayers, solstice-adjacent or not, until she'd said the worst thing she could possibly have said: *See you around, I guess.*

As if he hadn't had those words echoing around in his brain for almost the last decade. He certainly wasn't going to let it happen again. This time, he reasoned, *he* was going to be the one saying it. *Good luck, I guess,* he imagined telling her as she set off back for Los Angeles.

He trudged through the snow that lined the path to her front door and raised a hand to knock, though it opened before he could.

"Hi," Cecily said, breathless, and then, noting the placement of his hand, her cheeks flushed slightly. "Sorry. I usually know when someone's about to knock, but then I forget whether or not it actually happened, so—"

"Not a problem," he assured her. Be charming, he reminded himself, because the plan was very simple. It was exactly two steps, neither of which were very complicated.

Step one: Convince Cecily Ayers to fall in love with him.

Step two: Let her spend the rest of her life wondering why he never said goodbye.

Easy. Straightforward. Highly doable, as was he.

"My mother had to pick something up," Cecily said as she closed the door behind her, "so she'll meet us there."

Was she nervous? That was a promising sign. She seemed to be babbling a little bit, he noted, and gestured her towards his car, making a point to open the passenger side door for her before ushering her into it.

The drive was both familiar and not very long. Around here, twenty miles usually meant fifteen minutes or less, but in the snow it was something requiring his full attention. Porter built and maintained his own engines (read: improved them with a few charms here and there) but the elements were never very reliable, even with magic. He was fine with letting Cecily chatter nervously to herself, eyeing her hands.

"The thing is, I love my grandmother," she was saying, "so this is hard enough, but then add in the issue of the grimoire, and—I don't know. It's a mess." She slid a glance at him. "What do you do now, by the way?"

"I teach," he said. "You?"

"Oh, I run the marketing department for a line of boutique hotels, but—wait," she registered, frowning slightly with surprise, "what do you teach?"

"School," he said, and then, "Marketing, really?"

He wondered if she could hear his real question, which was something along the lines of: you went all the way there just to convince rich people to stay in hotels?

"The line is incredibly sustainable," she said "They use organic products, all the ingredients in the kitchen are locally sourced, the facility uses renewable energy and recycled water, and—"

"You're a witch," Porter noted, drumming his fingers against the steering wheel. "What's fun about a marketing job?"

"Well, um." She smiled a little to herself. "There's some magic involved. I do run some very… *persuasive* ad campaigns, I guess you could say."

He glanced over at her, arching a brow. "You cheat?"

"Only to help the good guys win," she insisted, shrugging. "Some of these bigger luxury hotels are more concerned with their profit margin. I'm just trying to give the little guys a leg up, that's all."

"Interesting," he said, just before they pulled up to her grandmother's house.

The Ayers' matriarch lived on a farm out in the country, which was even more remote than the small town of Saint Sturm. The house was a large Victorian with a barn, silo, and series of sheds, all of which were practically invisible amid the surrounding fields of corn and soybeans. (This, Porter noted, was a soybean year for the Ayers' farm.)

Porter only went there once a year or so, always with his mother, for coven meetings. Their coven was the largest one in Iowa, spanning almost fifteen counties, and the Ayers family—specifically Eleanor Ayers, once her husband had passed—were the heads of it. They had the most expansive line of witches in the Midwest, so it was no surprise to Porter that there were so many vehicles already in the driveway. Eleanor Ayers had had five children, the eldest of which was Cecily's father, and the others had been quick to reproduce in spades.

The inside of the house was packed with people, all of whom seemed completely unconcerned with Porter's entry to the house until they did a double take at Cecily, noting the prodigal daughter's return. The first of these observers was a woman Porter had seen around but couldn't name, though she clearly recognized Cecily. He watched her eyes narrow with scrutiny, the baby on her hip staring with an equal sense of doubtful consideration.

"Hi, Rosie," said Cecily, obviously putting some effort into warmth. "Nice to see you."

"It's Rosabella," corrected the woman who was apparently Rosabella, shifting her baby from one hip to the other, "and I didn't think we'd be seeing you, Cecily. How lovely," she added, Midwesternly false. Then she turned to Porter, half-frowning. "You look familiar."

"Porter Callahan," he supplied, opting to shake hands with the baby, who then eyed him with wide-eyed rapture.

"Callahan?" echoed someone else, a blur of auburn hair materializing into a girl who looked precisely like Rosabella, though her own baby (less skeptical, more bored) was strapped to her chest while resting above an obvious pregnancy bump. "Of *the* Callahans, you mean?"

If the Ayers were the most significant witch family in the coven, the Callahans were a close second. Porter was the third son of the third son, hence his name, which was a take on 'portent.'

"My mother would want me to assure you I'm equally an Ellis witch," Porter said, "but yes, I am one of *the* Callahans."

"What on earth are you doing here?" asked the girl, glancing stiffly at Cecily. "Oh, hi Cecily."

"Hi, Adria," Cecily replied, equally unenthused.

Porter, who had in the past seven years become the sort of man who'd learned to seize a moment when it arrived, slid an arm around her waist. "I'm here with Cecily," he explained, and though Cecily stiffened in apprehension, Adria and Rosabella exchanged a glance that told him, in no uncertain terms, that he'd made the right choice. They did not care for this news, which indicated he'd played his cards correctly.

He was precisely the ace that Cecily needed, and if she didn't appreciate that now, she would soon.

"Evelyn didn't say you were dating a Callahan," Rosabella said suspiciously to Cecily. "Is this new?"

Cecily shot Porter a glare, and he smiled.

"Yes," Cecily muttered, "*very* new. One might even call it news to me."

"Very funny," he remarked, leaning in to brush his lips near her cheek. "Just play along," he advised in her ear, and though she gave him a disapproving glance, she certainly didn't argue.

"But Cecily's never home," Adria said, patently bewildered.

"Well, when you know, you know," Porter replied, pulling Cecily in closer. "So, shall we say hello to your grandmother?"

"Yes, I think we should," Cecily said, gruffly taking hold of his hand and yanking him into the next room. "What are you doing?" she demanded in a little whisper-shout, spinning to face him the moment her cousins were out of sight. "I just wanted you to, you know—*be* here," she said with a touch of frustration, apparently failing to notice that she hadn't released him yet. "I never told you to lie to my *family*—"

"If you want the grimoire, you're going to need to make a better case than the one you've got," Porter reminded her, as she grimaced, cutting her gaze away for reasons he wasn't entirely sure he understood. "You saw your cousins," he pointed out. "They're threatened by you. You're the eldest of the eldest, so once you add in a Callahan to sweeten the pot—"

"Yes, yes, I get it," Cecily said through her teeth. "It's precisely why our parents wanted us to date to begin with."

"Which, of course, we never would," he assured her smoothly, giving the hand that was still holding hers a delicate, ever-so-gentle pulse of pressure. "Would we?"

She yanked free from his grasp, shaking her head. "Don't," she warned. "This is just… *pretend*, okay? I have a boyfriend."

"You certainly do," Porter agreed, aiming her toward the crowd of elderly witches that meant Eleanor Ayers was surely among them. "Do you want the grimoire or don't you?" he murmured again in her ear, and she turned to protest but was quickly cut off by the motion of the small crowd parting.

"Cecily?" called Eleanor, who was sitting beneath a pile of charmed blankets in an armchair that may as well have been a throne, accommodating her peerless glance of scrutiny. She wore her silver hair in a long braid down one shoulder, not a speck of makeup evident on her face. Matriarch or not, she was a farmer's daughter and a farmer's wife, never one for fripperies or fuss.

"Hi, Grandma Eleanor," Cecily said with relief, stepping forward. Porter noted that one of the women who seemed to be waiting on Eleanor hand and foot had faltered at the sound of Cecily's voice, backstepping slightly. He was pretty sure she was Miriam Braddock, newly married into the Ayers family, and he caught her sneaking a glance at him, eyes widening.

"How are you?" Cecily tentatively asked her grandmother, bending to kiss her cheek. Eleanor's cool glance fell slowly on Porter, her head tilting curiously as she gave Cecily's hand a slight pulse of pressure.

"Fine, dear, though I prefer not to discuss the tedium of my mortality. I see you've brought one of the Callahan boys," Eleanor noted, and Cecily turned over her shoulder, passing him something of a half-desperate, half-pleading grimace.

"Yes, Grandma," Cecily said. "You don't mind, do you?"

"Of course not," Eleanor assured her, beckoning to Porter. "Come here and let me look at you. Porter, isn't it?"

"Yes," Porter confirmed, stepping forward. He noted that the two women they'd met earlier, Adria and Rosabella, had handed off their babies in order to step closer to the unfolding scene. "I hope you don't mind my intrusion on a family event, but I thought it was best that Cecily not be alone. She's been so worried about you," he said, reaching for Cecily's waist again. This time, he noted, she didn't stiffen in protest, and her grandmother's mouth visibly twitched with approval. "Is there anything I can get you, Eleanor?"

"Please, call me Grandma Eleanor," she assured him, weakly summoning two chairs (one of which had contained Miriam's husband Jonathan until he'd stumbled to his feet, displaced by the slow-motion scraping of the chair) beside her. "Join me for a moment, would you? Tell me all about your life," she said to Cecily, beckoning for her to sit. "And how you two came to meet again, of course."

Cecily glanced uncertainly at Porter, who gestured to the chair. "Shall we tell her?" he prompted, and she returned his look blankly, flushed with either mortification or panic. "Oh don't worry, I'll start. Here, sweetheart, sit down," he said, giving her a pointed nudge before taking the chair beside her. "It's not a very exciting story, I'm afraid. We reconnected via the internet. Facebook, actually."

Eleanor arched a brow, glancing at Cecily. "Oh?"

"Um, yes," Cecily confirmed. "Porter found me and we… started talking. There's, you know. Not much to tell," she said quickly. "It's very early still, so, you know. Don't want to get ahead of ourselves, but—"

"She's being modest. Truth is I completely embarrassed myself for her," Porter said, draping an arm around her shoulders and finding that an absurdly easy half-truth. "I hate to say it, but she brings out the romantic in me. If you'd asked me seven years ago whether I thought I'd be writing love notes in the middle of the day, I'd have told you you were crazy. Turns out all it takes is the right girl," he said, lightly brushing his thumb over her cheek when she slid him an impatient glare.

Corny, she mouthed. He smiled back, unperturbed.

"Love notes?" Eleanor asked, glancing with curiosity between them. "Cecily's grandfather was quite the fan of those as well."

"Well, you should see Porter's poetry," Cecily said, reaching up to remove his hand from her cheek before lacing her fingers with his, sitting it firmly in the space between them. "Totally humiliating," she added with a saccharine glance, "or it would have been, if not for being so *charming*, of course."

"True," Porter said, cheerfully playing along. "Not too much rhymes with Cecily, but you can't blame me for trying."

"I'd love to hear some of this poetry," Eleanor remarked with a chuckle, missing the motion of Cecily kicking Porter's foot. "Maybe after dinner?"

"Ah, it's for her ears only," Porter said, "but who knows, maybe inspiration will strike. She does look awfully pretty tonight, doesn't she?" he said, giving Cecily a long look that was met with more furtive glaring, though Eleanor, who seemed more than pleased by the coupling, smiled warmly.

"Well, I for one am glad to hear it," she announced, prompting some of the cousins around the room to begin whispering to each other as Eleanor stretched out a weakened hand, laying her fingers approvingly on Cecily's knee. "A Callahan witch is an excellent choice, Cecily. Is your mother pleased?"

"Pleased about what?" asked a breathless Evelyn, bustling in with snow on her coat and freezing at the sight of her daughter in the coveted spot beside Eleanor, her fingers still laced with Porter's.

"I can't believe you didn't tell me, Evie," Eleanor chided her, but rather than blanching at the comment, Evelyn couldn't seem to prevent her joy at seeing Cecily beside Porter.

"Well, why ruin the surprise," Evelyn exclaimed with delight, and Porter, seeing that Cecily could clearly find no fault in her family's approval of him, leaned in to speak to her once more.

"Secret's out," he murmured, and Cecily shook her head.

"I'm going to *kill* you," she whispered firmly, for which he had no problem sparing an unburdened laugh.

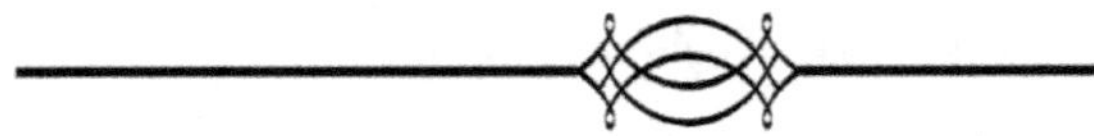

Whatever Porter was up to, it was certainly working. Grandma Eleanor was enamored with him, her mother was infatuated, and even Cecily couldn't deny that his presence made them the focus of the family's Midwinter dinner, causing her cousins a mix of confusion and distress. By the time Eleanor invited Porter to the annual Ayers Christmas party—an invitation he accepted with a perfectly earnest politeness, frustrating Cecily even further—Rosabella had let out an inadvertent squeak of dismay, exchanging a glance with her cousins

Camille and Adria. Clearly, all of them had noted what even Cecily instinctively understood: An invitation to a family event, from Eleanor Ayers herself, was coveted. It meant acceptance to the Ayers tier of prestige within the coven, and *that* meant the act was cemented.

There was no getting around it; Porter Callahan was her fake boyfriend for the remainder of the holiday, precisely as Cecily had tipsily asked him to be.

Be careful what you wish for, she reminded herself with a groan.

Porter, much to Cecily's dismay, was completely charming. He was funny, warm, utterly immune to embarrassment, fully capable of showing affection without thinking twice about it—he even offered to clean up after dinner and instructed all the women to stay seated, he'd take care of it, *like some kind of mutant*—and Cecily couldn't help wondering if any of it was real, given how little he'd wanted to come with her in the first place.

He had to be doing all of this on purpose, but if that was the case, then why?

Porter's mystifying behavior aside, it was impossible for Cecily not to notice the extent that her grandmother had aged. Eleanor's charms were noticeably weaker, and though she shoved most everyone away (especially Miriam, who was about as underfoot as a small, overexcited terrier) it was clearly a strain on her health. Cecily, who hadn't noticed anything like it the last time she'd been home, realized just how long she'd been gone with a pang of guilt, eventually excusing herself to make a phone call.

She dialed Ansel's number, holding her phone to her ear.

My grandma's gotten older and I've been gone, she wanted to tell him. *I missed everything. I hardly recognize all these new faces, all these new babies and husbands and wives. My mother looks older and I've missed it, she's been here all alone and honestly, I'm just so sad, I wish I'd come home sooner—*

"This is Ansel, leave a message," said his voicemail, and Cecily shook her head, pausing a moment in frustration before heading back inside. He was never very good at answering his phone, which was unfortunate. She could really use someone to talk to right now.

She paused beside the door to the kitchen on her way back to the dining room, catching the motion of Porter summoning a dish towel and buffing a spot on one of the plates. Behind him, the dishes were washing themselves, the counters being sponged down and cleaned, the trash neatly sorting itself. She half-smiled for a second, watching him hum to himself as he worked, and then she swallowed in surprise when he turned to notice her in the doorway.

"Hey you," he said, tossing the dish towel over his shoulder and leaning against the counter. She wandered in further, reluctantly joining him. "You okay?"

She opened her mouth, about to say something, and then shook her head.

No use complaining. Not to him. He made no sense.

"Yeah, thanks," she said instead, clearing her throat. "You're a real hit," she informed him drily, gesturing over her shoulder to where the women remained in the dining room. "I can't believe you actually told my grandmother to put her feet up."

His smile quirked slightly. "My mother often complains she isn't told that enough. I listen on occasion."

"Sure," Cecily said, shaking her head. She slid a hand around the back of her neck, feeling a little self-conscious. "Listen," she said quietly, "I appreciate you doing this for me and everything, but I just want to make sure you know this isn't…" She trailed off. "It's not like this is, you know. A real thing. Because I have someone, and—"

"Something's bothering you," Porter noted, and Cecily balked, tripping over her words and into a stumbled halt.

"What? I wasn't—I was just—"

"It must be hard." Porter leaned forward, resting his elbows on the counter beside her. "Seeing your grandmother like this," he clarified, and Cecily blinked.

"Oh. Yes. Yeah," she said, clearing her throat. "It is, actually. I just—"

She broke off, shaking her head.

"You don't want to hear this," she said, and he let his lips curl up in a smile before straightening, sliding his forearms towards her on the counter in a way that made her heart race just slightly; not enough to cause her any concern, but certainly enough to remind her it was there.

"Maybe I do," he said, glancing down at her.

His eyes were green-blue bursts, changing while he looked at her, little sparks of amber manifesting near the center of them. His sandy hair fell into his forehead and he slid it back, the line of his forearm shifting beneath the rolled-up sleeve of his sweater.

Cecily swallowed.

He wasn't her type, she reminded herself firmly. He was a Saint Sturm boy, Northern Iowa born and bred. He was precisely the type of person who made no sense to her, content with the same exact town he'd been born into, and therefore he *couldn't* be attractive—however muscled his forearm happened to be.

"It's nothing," she said, glancing askance. "I'm fine."

"Bullshit," he replied. "Your grandmother's sick. You love her, that's obvious. You're not fine."

"Porter—"

"Cecily."

She watched his mouth form a little half-smile and bristled.

"Listen, Porter—"

"Yes, Cecily?" he mused in reply.

He was impossible. Had he always been that way?

"*Porter*," she growled, half a warning, and his smile twitched.

"Cecily," he murmured, tutting softly in disapproval, "it won't actually hurt you to tell me the truth, you know."

She wasn't so sure about that.

Still, she *had* wanted to talk about it, and besides, she was starting to feel her cheeks heat. She wanted very badly for him to stop… *looking* at her. Like that, at least. She needed a reason to look away, and honesty seemed a fine enough excuse.

"I do feel sad," she mumbled in concession, glancing at anything else but his face. "And guilty, too. I've been gone for so long. I guess I just always thought time stopped around here, but obviously it doesn't. I don't know." She eyed her hands. "I feel selfish for being upset but it's… hard."

"You're allowed to have some sort of conflict about it," Porter said, shifting his stance again. With his entire body angled towards her, it was difficult not to notice how fully she had his attention; he wasn't thinking about the road, like he'd been while he was driving. He wasn't toying with any percolating thoughts about an art installation. He was entirely focused on her, and it was both liberating and constricting to be the thing that he was looking at.

Listening to. Thinking about.

"And maybe," Porter continued, "you shouldn't bother feeling guilty. You're here now," he pointed out. "Why waste this time with her worrying about the things you could have done? Just… I don't know." He shrugged. "*Be* here. You know?"

It occurred to her that what he was saying made sense.

He made sense, so she exhaled slowly, nodding.

"You're right," she agreed, though she heard a set of footsteps come to a sudden halt behind her and immediately fought a groan.

This house, honestly. This *town*.

"Who is it?" she murmured to him, exasperated.

He glanced up at whoever it was, then back at her. "Miriam."

Of course it was. "My mom was right," Cecily muttered under her breath. "She is the *worst*, and—"

Porter cut her off, taking her face in both hands and giving her a long, searching look.

"Don't feel sad about time lost," he said to her. "Just don't waste a moment."

She stared up at him, temporarily unglued from being looked at this way, so… intensely.

"I," she attempted, and faltered. "Right, I just—"

He smiled, and she stopped talking.

He leaned forward.

Her lips parted.

She'd known he was going to kiss her, hadn't she? She *had* to have known, and yet it still took her by surprise. He tasted like the traditional spiced mead her mother always made for Midwinter, and she felt her heart flutter up to her throat and lodge itself there, her fingers going rigid around the jut of his hips where they pressed firmly into hers. It couldn't have been long—it was a fairly chaste kiss, all things considered—and it ended the moment she heard Miriam's footsteps retreating—probably to report to Rosabella what she'd seen—so it should have been nothing—but still, it seemed to go on for hours, to last for days, lingering on her lips even when the taste of him should have already been long gone.

She pushed him away, shaking her head.

"I have a boyfriend," she reminded him.

"Miriam was watching. And given how close you're currently standing to me," he added, flicking a glance at the minimal distance between them, "it wouldn't make sense if I didn't."

"Still," she protested, taking a lengthy step back, "you can't just— you didn't need t-"

"You're not worried about falling for me, Cecily," Porter asked neutrally, "are you?"

She felt something coil up and tighten in her chest.

"Just... don't keep doing that, okay?" she said. "Touching me and stuff."

He pointedly held up his hands. "I'm not touching you."

He wasn't. But still, she thought.

Still. Too close. He was still holding her, even if he wasn't. She could see it on his face. He was holding her captive with a look.

"You should finish the dishes," she told him, clearing her throat and spinning on her heel. "Make sure you get all the spots." She needed to get out of there, and quickly. The air in the room was stifling, something uncomfortable burning sticky-hot in her throat.

"Cecily," Porter called after her, and she paused against her will, going rigid as he took a step towards her. "It's just pretend," he said in a low voice, the words curving smoothly around the back of her neck and slipping down her spine until they seemed to hook around her waist, filling up her ribs, collecting in her lungs.

How dare he, honestly?

"I know that," she snapped, exiting the room without another glance.

PART II: STORM

Cecily hung up the phone, shaking her head as the call once again went unanswered. Ansel had never been especially reliable with his phone, but that had always been more of fun, whimsical detail about him until recently. He was an Artist in an almost archaic sense, never tied down by technology or social media, and though he'd always been somewhat communication-challenged as far as boyfriends went, she'd never minded on account of their habitual proximity. However, now that Cecily was about to go to yet another family event with a fake boyfriend who wasn't him—plus the fact that her grandmother was ill, *and* that said not-boyfriend had kissed her the last time they'd seen each other—she was looking for a little bit of emotional reassurance.

She wasn't particularly thrilled Ansel was so difficult to track down. She'd tried emailing him, wondering if maybe cell service was a problem, but that had been met with very little; only a few sentences' reply about his day of wine tasting and a conclusion of *talk soon, ily*.

"Are you coming?" her mother shouted up the stairs. "I'm leaving now if you are!"

"No," Cecily called back, grumbling as she tossed her phone aside. "Porter's picking me up in an hour."

"Well, tell him to be careful," Evelyn yelled, predictably thrilled. "It's supposed to snow!"

"We're witches, Mom," Cecily barked. "I think we can handle it."

She heard the sound of footsteps coming up the stairs, followed by the bursting of Evelyn Ayers through her bedroom door.

"Cecily," Evelyn said, a little breathless, "try not to sulk so much, would you? He's doing you a favor. Besides, it's not *so* bad, is it?"

No, it wasn't, and that was really the worst part. Porter Callahan was supposed to have kept her family off her back, not given her mother unreasonable hopes that they might spontaneously elope on their way to the Ayers Christmas party. He'd been all Evelyn could talk about since the solstice dinner, and Cecily could see perfectly well that her grandmother loved him, too. It made the situation that much worse, actually, to know that if Cecily truly wanted her family to be happy, all she had to do was…

Well, be with Porter *for real*, only there was no way that would possibly work. For one thing, she couldn't, and for another, she didn't want to.

"Just… don't get your hopes up," Cecily warned her mother. "I still have a boyfriend, Mom. Porter and I are just spending time together, that's all. He's helping me to, you know—"

"Get the grimoire you so rightfully deserve?" Evelyn supplied.

"Yes, that," Cecily said, rolling her eyes. "So I'm doing what you asked, aren't I?"

To that, Evelyn beamed. "Yes, you are," she agreed, warmed by a resurgence of maternal satisfaction. "Though, that being said, wear the red dress, would you?"

"Mom," Cecily groaned. "Isn't the red dress a little much?"

"Do you want the grimoire or not?" Evelyn demanded.

"That," Cecily said, "has nothing to do with the grimoire. You just want me to look better than Rosabella."

"*Everything* has to do with the grimoire," Evelyn corrected, "and so what if I do? Porter will like it, and red's your color."

"It doesn't matter what Porter likes," Cecily said firmly, "because it's not real, Mom. Porter is my friend, he's doing me a favor, end of story."

"Well, if you insist on missing the obvious," Evelyn sniffed, "then so be it."

"*Mom—*"

"I know you kissed him," Evelyn said with a wicked grin. "Miriam told just about everyone who would listen, so don't pretend there's nothing there, darling. I didn't raise you to be so heinously oblivious."

That kiss. Never mind everything Cecily had thought before; upon further reflection, *that* was the actual worst of the situation. The fact that Porter Callahan had kissed her with such undeniable success was bewildering at best, debilitating at worst. It made Cecily's fingers twitch to call Ansel again.

You're not worried about falling for me, Cecily—are you?

She shoved Porter's voice from her mind, returning to the task of dispatching her mother.

"Better get going, Mom," Cecily said. "We'll see you at Grandma Eleanor's, okay?"

The strategic use of the word *we* sent Evelyn right to a fit of euphoria. "Oh, alright," she said cheerfully, practically skipping from the room as Cecily wandered over to the red dress and sighed, contemplating it. Behind her, her phone buzzed, and she turned quickly, expecting to see Ansel's name and instead finding a message from Porter.

I'll bring some of my mother's absinthe as a gift for your grandmother. Is there anything else you need?

Yes. For him to stop being so attentive.

No, thank you, Cecily said, and then, grudgingly, *That's very thoughtful of you. Thank you for asking.*

She watched the response bubble appear, indicating he was typing, and then it stopped.

Started again.

Stopped.

I'm looking forward to seeing you, eventually buzzed in her hand.

She swallowed, locking her phone, and tossed it onto her bed.

Red dress it is, Cecily thought, wandering into the bathroom to fix her hair.

"Here," Maggie said, handing Porter a small bottle of her best batch of absinthe. She was a fair hand at draughts; her brew of choice was brandy steeped in wormwood, and this particular bottle had a few basic healing elements, too.

"I wish you weren't missing Christmas Eve with us," Maggie lamented, briskly depositing the absinthe in Porter's hand, "but at least try to make sure you make a good impression on whoever inherits the Ayers coven next. Especially if that's going to be Cecily," she added, and Porter grimaced.

"I'm starting to think she doesn't actually want it. You know she hates it here." He eyed the bottle, which had his mother's personal seal burned into the cork: an E for Ellis intertwined with a C for Callahan. "But I'll be back this evening, probably. Not too late, I don't think."

"Well, Sayer says there's going to be a storm," Maggie said, referencing her firstborn son and Porter's oldest brother. Sayer had always been intuitive about weather, which served them especially well in rural Iowa. Knox, the second Callahan son, was good with animals, and Porter had always had a way with fixing or improving things; machines, mostly. "You be careful out there, Port."

"I built the engine myself, Mom," Porter reminded her. "I'll be fine."

She smiled dotingly at him. "I know you will," she said, before busying herself in the kitchen. Everyone in the Callahan family had very practical forms of witchery, and Maggie's was mostly chemical, which meant she was often put in charge of Christmas dinner. Porter assumed she'd be fussing over him more if she weren't so busy cooking, so he was relieved at the fortuitous timing. "Did Evelyn say anything to you, by the way?" Maggie asked, chopping an onion. Her strokes were perfectly clean and even, no fumes wafting to irritate their eyes. "I keep trying to reach out to her, but ever since Cecily left she's just impossible to get ahold of."

Porter had always liked Cecily's mother, despite the fact (or possibly because) she was everything Maggie Callahan wasn't. Among large groups of people, Evelyn Ayers was a bit introverted, even skittish; it was a behavior pattern that felt familiar to Porter, who generally preferred to observe rather than be observed.

"Well, not everyone's as social as you are, Mom," he said, rising to his feet. "Need help with anything?"

Maggie paused to smile at him, shaking her head. "Nah. You go get ready," she said, gesturing to the stairs.

"I was going to shower at my place," he reminded her, and in response, she gave a none-too-innocent shrug.

"Stay, would you? I put a cologne in the bathroom for you," she said, and he groaned.

"Mom, please, if you're trying to magic Cecily into something—"

"Oh no, I can't make pheromones," Maggie reminded him with a sigh, "much as I try. No, unfortunately this is purely something to make you smell nice." She leaned over as he passed, pausing expectantly for a kiss, and he rolled his eyes but conceded to touch his lips to her cheek. "It's blackcurrant, sap, fir, cedarwood—"

"No need to spill all your secrets, Mom," Porter assured her, loping up the stairs of their family farmhouse and checking his phone. There'd been no response from Cecily, but that was to be expected. He was beginning to learn the more silent she was, the more effectively he was swaying her. He tucked his phone into his pocket, rifling through the clothes he had at home and picking out a blue shirt he'd been told (by women other than his mother, though Maggie had said so as well) made his eyes look nice.

Porter had always been his mother's favorite, the one who came home most often, though he supposed that was for lack of replacing her with some other woman, unlike her other sons. Sayer was married with kids and Knox had one on the way, but Porter, who worked closest to home, was still willing (and possessing the free time) to see Maggie from time to time for something unrelated to free childcare.

"You're putting more effort than usual into this thing with Cecily," Maggie had remarked after Porter returned from solstice dinner with the Ayers family, which was an occasion that had been haunting him slightly. "I've never known you to try so hard for a girl."

"Well, it'll be good for us, gaining a foothold with the Ayers family," Porter reminded her, pointedly leaving out that this, his long-term shot at retribution, required much more effort than any meager romantic tryst. "I just want to make a good impression, that's all."

"On Eleanor Ayers?" Maggie asked doubtfully, "or on Cecily?"

He shrugged. "Both," he'd said, because his mother wouldn't understand. It was probably best she didn't think of him as the sort of person who'd lure a girl into falling for him, which he was fairly sure he was accomplishing. He'd seen the look on Cecily's face right before he kissed her, and she'd definitely kissed him back.

She'd *definitely* kissed him, her lips soft and tentative; her chin had tilted up, eyes bright, and her cheeks had held a flush of wonder and surprise.

He shivered slightly at the memory, heading into the bathroom.

All the kiss proved was that his efforts were working, he reminded himself. All he had to do was win Cecily over with one more afternoon, and then he could leave her to spend the rest of her life in Los Angeles, haunting her fantasies of what they could have had if he hadn't told her goodbye.

Easy, he reminded himself, sniffing at the cologne his mother had made him.

Just one more afternoon.

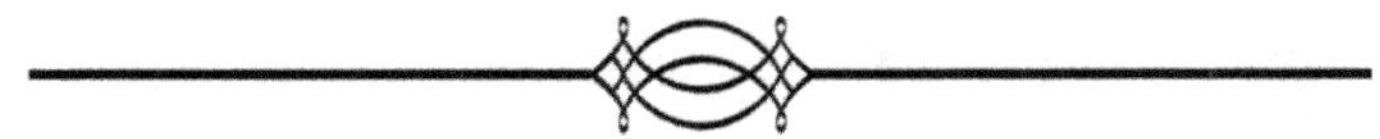

Snow was falling when Porter arrived at her front door. Cecily pulled it open before he could knock, yet again, and she watched him swallow a little, gaze falling openly over the shape of her dress before he quickly dragged it back up.

"Ready?" he asked her.

"Just a sec—grabbing my coat," she said, snatching it from the coat hanger, and he paused her, taking it from her hands.

"Let me," he said, holding it out for her, and she stepped warily towards him, slipping one arm through and then the other. That close to him, she could smell the faint hint of cologne he was wearing; it was woodsy, a little smoky, but fresh and clean, and she had to fight the urge to lean in closer, inhaling another noseful of what smelled precisely like a contemplative walk through a quiet wood.

"Thanks," she said instead, checking her phone for the thirtieth time. Ansel had sent a message saying he'd call that afternoon, but nothing yet. Porter motioned to the front door and she nodded, briskly passing him to make her way to his truck. "Is the snow picking up?" she asked, watching it swirl on a blustery wind, and he frowned.

"A bit," he said, "but we should be fine."

She nodded, letting him close the passenger door after she'd clambered inside. It was only a short drive, thank goodness, and hopefully not too long of an afternoon overall. A breeze, all things considered.

She glanced at Porter, who despite already having climbed into the driver's seat, had paused to frown with a bit of concern at the road.

"What?" she asked, and he shook his head.

"Nothing," he said, and then glanced at her. "You look nice."

Outrageously, she felt her cheeks heat. "Thanks."

He nodded, and they said nothing else, Porter adjusting the vent for her before pulling into the road. They drove in silence for a few minutes, the snow starting to fall more heavily as they made their way to the two-lane interstate. It never failed to awe Cecily, who was accustomed by then to the complex freeway system of Los Angeles, that this was how people in Iowa got around. Just... two lanes, covered in snow, no lines to be seen. Nothing but flat land and cornfields for miles.

She pulled out her phone, checking it again.

"Expecting a call?" Porter asked.

"From my boyfriend," Cecily said, grateful for the opportunity to use the word, if only to remind both of them she had one. She tucked the phone back into her coat pocket, fidgeting. "He's in Mexico."

"And he's going to call?"

"Well, Skype call, probably. But yes." She cleared her throat. "He's going to call."

He gave her a sidelong glance, half-smiling.

"What?" she demanded, instantly irritated.

"Nothing," he told her smoothly, his fingers tapping the wheel.

"I have a boyfriend," she said again. "His name is Ansel. He's an artist."

"That's great," Porter replied lazily. "What kind of art does he do?"

"Murals, mostly. Street art."

"Ah."

"'Ah'?" she echoed, turning sharply to him. "What's that supposed to mean?"

"It's just a sound, Cecily," Porter said. "It typically indicates acknowledgement."

"Oh, *stop*," she grumbled, rolling her eyes. "You totally did it with a… a thing."

"A thing?"

"Yes, you did a *thing*, you had an… *inflection*—"

"Do you want me to have an inflection?"

She glared at him, watching his mouth quirk with suppressed laughter.

"What do you do?" she demanded.

"I told you," he reminded her. "I teach."

"Yes, fine, but *what* do you teach?"

He turned slowly onto the interstate, careful not to slip out as they drove out of town. There were no cars on the road, save for one coming towards them.

"Physics," he said, and she blinked.

"You… teach physics," she echoed slowly, and he arched a brow.

"You sound surprised."

"I am," she said, and she was. "I wasn't expecting, you know. Science."

He shrugged. "I like it. It's practical."

"Practical? You're a witch."

"So?" He glanced at her, then back at the road. The oncoming car was closer now, its high beams somewhat obnoxiously left on. "I work on cars, sometimes farm equipment. I learned to fix up my brother's tractors a few years ago and now it's something of a hobby."

"A hobby? But—"

"Shit," Porter said, blinking, and Cecily frowned, feeling the car come slowly to a stop.

"What are you doing?" she asked.

"That car," Porter said, pointing to it, and she squinted, watching it swerve across the lanes. "The driver's lost control."

"So you're… you're just…" She inhaled sharply, realizing it was heading straight towards them. "You're just *stopping*? But—"

"I can't do anything," he told her, shaking his head. "If we're lucky, the car will have slowed down a little before it—"

"OH MY GOD," she shrieked, shutting her eyes just before the opposite car slammed into them, the driver swerving into the ditch and screeching back onto the road just after an impact that nearly shook her lungs free from the inside of her ribcage. The impact of being hit ricocheted through her, her hand shooting out impulsively, and she felt Porter catch her fingers, shifting in his seat to face her.

"Are you okay?" he asked, scanning her for injury, and she cracked one eye to find him shaken up, but mostly unharmed. She'd forgotten how common car accidents were in the snow; her own pulse was flaring wildly with panic. "Cecily," he said, and she inhaled sharply, trying to slow her breathing. "Can you hear me?"

"Yes, I'm—" She swallowed. "I'm fine, I just—"

"You're okay. We're okay." His fingers had laced tightly with hers. "Can you breathe? Anything hurting?"

"No, no, I'm—" She shuddered, then pulled free of him. The heat from the vents had stopped, cold air starting to fill his truck. "Porter, the car—"

"I'll check it," he said. "Let me go take a look and then I'll be back, okay?"

She shivered, her fingers already going numb.

"Okay," she said, though in reality, she had a slowly sinking feeling, suddenly not so sure it was going to be a brief afternoon after all.

"Fuck," Porter muttered to himself, shutting the hood of his truck.

Not even magic was going to fix this.

He glanced up at where Cecily was shivering in the passenger seat and grimaced. The other driver, wherever they'd ended up, was going to be waiting for a tow truck, but Porter wasn't interested in the prospect of

Cecily freezing to death before it arrived. There was no way they'd be getting here anytime soon; it was Christmas Eve, not to mention that snow was falling harder now. If he and Cecily didn't leave soon themselves, they'd be trapped in the middle of the road for the duration of an oncoming blizzard.

"Fuck," he sighed again, making his way to the passenger side and opening the door to a startled Cecily. "Do you have any sort of spell on those shoes?"

"Shoes?" she echoed, blinking at him, and he glanced down, grimacing again. Of course she was wearing stiletto heels.

"We have to walk about a quarter mile," he said.

"No," she said instantly, and he rubbed his temple.

"It's that or stay here," he said, "in the cold."

She made a face.

"Hold on," he said, making his way to the bed of his truck and finding a pair of work boots, digging them out and then coming back around to hand them to her. "Put these on."

"We're going to be late," she said inanely, chewing her lip.

"Yes," Porter said, "but we don't have to die, unless you want to."

She glared at him, but conceded to put the boots on. Grumpily. With a lot of noise and opposition and strife, as if this had been his idea of a marvelous way to pass the time. Porter, meanwhile, fought a growl of annoyance.

"Come on," he said, holding out his hand, which she shoved away.

"I'm fine," she said, stepping out into the snow, and then promptly slipped. He caught her around the waist, one of her hands flying out to grip his shoulder, and he glanced down with a shake of his head.

"Next time," he said, "just accept help when it's offered, would you?"

She narrowed her eyes at him, yanking free and tugging her coat in closer. "Where are we going?"

"Somewhere warm," he said, and gave her arm a nudge, leading her down the road.

It didn't stop her from arguing. "You're just going to leave your truck here?"

"Yes," he said. "Can't exactly drive it."

"I thought you said—"

"I know what I said. But I'd need more than a few minutes to fix it, which I can't currently do without freezing to death, so we're going somewhere warm."

It was too cold to speak for the rest of the walk, which was probably best. On the outskirts of Saint Sturm there was very little outside of the church (not ideal), the cemetery (not helpful), and the town library, which Porter happened to have a key to. Though, if he hadn't, he doubted he'd even need one; it wasn't as if doors in Saint Sturm were ever locked, and particularly not for a witch.

"Where are we going?" Cecily asked, her teeth chattering, and he led her through the side door.

"In here," he said, gesturing her inside, and she darted into the mostly-heated building as he toyed with the light switch. "Power's out."

She was looking at her phone again, which made him bristle a little with impatience, at least until she looked up. "No service."

"Figures." He gave her a quick, scrutinizing glance, watching her tug her coat tighter around her as she wandered through the shelves. "You sure you're not hurt?"

She paused to look over her shoulder. "I'm not. Are you?"

He shook his head and she returned to her wandering, making her way through the room. It wasn't a very expansive library, owing to the very, very small population of the town, and it didn't have much.

Porter bent down near the old Wi-Fi router, eyeing it. "I could see if it's something I can fix," he said, and she paused her meandering to look at him. "Would take me a while, but I guess we've got time."

"Guess so," she muttered, irritably tugging her coat tighter. "Are there candles?"

"Probably in the office," he said, pointing to it, and she nodded, heading briskly inside.

When she returned, she had a single votive candle in her hand.

"That's it?" he asked, unimpressed, and she narrowed her eyes at him, setting it down in the approximate center of the room.

"Oh ye of little faith," she said impatiently, and added, "Watch and learn."

She settled herself across from it, holding out her hands, and closed her eyes.

A second ticked by, and then the flame of the candle lit.

"Well, that's all well and g-"

"Shhh," Cecily said, cracking one eye. "Quiet."

He rolled his eyes. "Fine, but—"

All at once, the room was doused in light and warmth. It was as if Cecily had created an echo of sorts, magnifying the candle's heat until it filled the room, abruptly fogging the windows and creating a flickering, crackling sensation of being before a fire.

"Better," she said, and slid her coat from her shoulders, exhaling onto her hands as Porter cleared his throat, trying not to stare.

Cecily was wearing a red dress that had clearly been designed to hold men—and women, probably—entirely captive, featuring a rounded neckline that showed off the delicate lines of her clavicle and shoulders. The waist was tapered to fit like a glove, flaring gently out to a demure but hardly unimaginative skirt, and the color gave her an ethereal sort of glow. For a moment, she was impossible to look away from—though he certainly tried, catching the twitch of her lips when she caught his eye.

"Something wrong?" she asked, with all the knowing pretense of a beautiful woman in a nice dress.

"Nothing." He looked down at the unresponsive router. "The problem is with the network signal, so I can't really repair it from here."

She grimaced. "I guess we'll have to wait it out," she said, and shrugged. "At least it's warm in here."

It was *quite* warm. Porter tugged at the buttons of his coat, slipping it off, and to his greatly vindicated pleasure, her gaze had followed his motions. The candle's light doused them both in a hazy, golden glow, the snow continuing to fall in horizontal sheets outside.

They marinated in a bit of awkward silence as she averted her gaze from his, both of them equally uncertain. It wasn't as if he could conceivably offer her anything as far as alternate solutions; cell towers were hardly something he could fix from here. He searched his brain for something, anything, to ease the situation, but thankfully, she spoke first.

"Think there's anything to drink?" she asked, glancing around, and abruptly, he recalled the small bottle of absinthe he'd placed into the pocket of his coat.

"Yes," he said, relieved.

At least there was one thing they could do while they waited for the storm to pass.

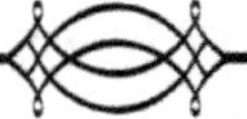

"This," Cecily pronounced, "is *delicious*."

It was also extremely potent, though that didn't seem worth mentioning. Maggie Callahan had always had a way with alcoholic beverages; Cecily remember her parents had nearly always come back from Callahan dinner parties a few miles past tipsy back when Cecily's father had been alive.

"It's the Maggie special," Porter agreed, taking the bottle back to indulge another dizzying sip. "Like my mother always says: if she can't make the time fun, she can at least make it hard to remember."

"Does she still have those dinner parties?" Cecily asked, and Porter made a face mid-sip.

"Oh, always. Your mother came to one a few years ago," he added, and then chuckled to himself. "She was hiding for most of it."

Cecily felt her face fall slightly. Her father, Nathaniel, had always been the more social of the two. Once he'd fallen ill, Cecily had always suspected Evelyn would have a harder time venturing out. It was one thing to do it with family, but women like Maggie had always been a little too much for Evelyn to handle.

"You okay?" Porter asked, offering her the bottle, and Cecily shook her head.

"Fine, just… missing my dad. Worrying about my mom." She accepted the bottle from him, taking a sip. "I don't think she does much anymore."

Porter shook his head. "I don't see her often. I always got the feeling she was strong, though," he said, and Cecily paused, her lips pressed to the bottle's opening. "I don't know. I guess I see a lot of her in you, so I always figured she was fine. She just…" He shrugged. "She's one of those people who doesn't need a lot."

"Yeah, but my dad was, you know. The social one." She took a small swig, letting the black licorice flavor marinate on her tongue for a moment. "He was the one who pushed her, got her out of her comfort zone, all that."

"What's wrong with comfort zones?" Porter asked. "Some people like to be comfortable."

Cecily eyed him for a moment, squinting slightly.

"Why'd you stay?" she asked him, and he frowned.

"What?"

"Why'd you stay in Saint Sturm?" At his shrug of dismissal, she leaned forward. "You're smart, Porter. You always were. And you're… you know." She felt her cheeks flush slightly as his brow arched. "You know what I mean!"

"I don't, actually," he said, though she had the distinct feeling he was toying with her.

"Alright, *fine*. You're good-looking," she muttered, and he smiled with a palpable sense of triumph. "What, come on! You *know* that—"

She gave his shoulder a shove, knocking indelicately into him, and he gave her a little pressure in response, the two of them leaning on each other where they sat on the floor, in front of the flickering candle.

"Well, to answer your question," Porter said, carefully taking the bottle from her with a barely-there brush against her fingers, "my whole family lives here. My dad and Sayer have the farm, Knox is just a few towns over with his vet practice—"

"And you're at Saint Sturm High?" Cecily asked.

"Yep." Porter took a sip from the bottle. "It's fine."

She slid him a glance. "Fine?"

"Well, yeah." He cleared his throat, and she pursed her lips knowingly.

"Ah, I see," she said. "So it's not what you *want* to be doing, is it?"

He gave her a look of impatience. "You're exhausting," he said. "All this dream-chasing in Los Angeles, it's clearly corrupted you—"

"Come on, Porter," she said, swinging her legs around to face him. "Tell me the truth. If you could do anything," she pressed him, "what would you do?"

He shook his head, taking another sip. "I'm already doing it, Cecily."

"Oh *come on*, seriously?"

"Seriously."

"*Porter*—"

"Yes, Cecily?"

He was definitely fucking with her.

"How about this," she countered, reaching out to grip his shoulders until he froze in place, half-swaying. "I'll tell you something, and then you tell me."

He looked skeptical, but mildly entertained. "What kind of something?"

"I'll, um." She thought about it. "I'll tell you a secret."

"Who says I want to know your secrets?"

She smacked his shoulder. "You dick. I'll tell you a secret about you," she clarified. "How about that?" She caught the flicker of interest in his gaze and snapped her fingers. "Aha! You want to know, don't you?" she teased, watching him grimace. "Look at you, Porter Callahan, you're *dying* to know—"

"You go first." In the candlelight, she caught faint flickers of a smile on his lips.

"Alright, fine." She inhaled deeply, then exhaled, "Remember when you asked me to the prom?"

He paused for a moment, the bottle halfway to his lips. "Yeah, it sounds familiar."

"Well, I…" She trailed off, embarrassed. "I sort of wanted to go with you. It was dumb," she said hastily, watching him blink with surprise, "but, you know. We were such good friends once, and you've always been… you know. But I knew Maggie was just making you go, so—"

"You thought I didn't actually want to go with you?" He sounded somewhere between incredulous and disbelieving, like he was pretty sure she was lying but would prefer it if she weren't. "Seriously? Why would I have asked you if I didn't?"

"Well, I don't know—look, it was a long time ago," Cecily said, shoving aside her humiliation and taking the bottle back from him. "Anyway, your turn. What would you be doing if you weren't here?"

"I—" He seemed to have to drag himself around to the subject. "Well, I build cars, like I said. Restore them, and—" He was fidgeting. "I like to invent things from time to time. Can't really build anything interesting here, you know," he added, "because of all the salt and rust. I just end up fixing things constantly, which is a headache. But anyway, about you wanting to go to the prom with me—"

"You could leave, you know," she told him. "You don't have to stay in this tiny town."

"You could have said yes," he replied, ignoring her. "I've got some moves."

She couldn't prevent a laugh. "I bet you do," she said, and he looked up, catching her gaze.

His shirt really brought out the blue-green of his eyes, she thought abruptly.

Then she instinctively glanced down, happy for the excuse to check her phone screen. Nothing, of course, seeing as there was no service, but truth be told, she hadn't really expected anything anyway.

"Why him?" Porter asked, gesturing to her phone. "What's so great about this guy?"

"He's—" *halfway out the door*, she thought glumly, though what she actually said was, "I don't have to defend him to you."

"No, you don't," Porter agreed, "but you could, if you wanted."

She glared at him, the warmth of the absinthe sweeping over her from head to toe as she watched the way the light bathed his features.

"We're not going to make it to my grandmother's Christmas party at this rate," she said, glancing down at the time and then up at the unceasing snowstorm. "My mother's going to be furious."

In answer, Porter merely slid the bottle from her hand, taking another deliberate sip, and she, to her dismay, couldn't not watch him. (Blame the absinthe, she thought, for whatever she'd say next.)

"What if you'd gotten out?" came courtesy of lowered inhibitions, and Porter let his eyes slide pointedly to hers.

"What if you'd stayed?" he countered, and she swallowed.

They sat in silence for a moment or so, her heart thudding and her mind racing, and then gradually, an actionable thought occurred to her.

"How far is the high school from here?" she asked, considering something. "Like another quarter mile, maybe? Surely something walkable."

"Yeah, I guess, if you like blizzards," he said, glancing at her. "Why?"

She smiled slowly, and he rolled his eyes.

"Oh, no," he said, vehemently shaking his head. "No way."

"Yes," she said, rising triumphantly to her feet. "Come on, Porter Callahan. I'm finally taking you to prom."

They were drunk enough to ignore the worst of the snow, which was probably stupid, but the benefit of being witches was that Porter could tuck Cecily under his jacket and shield them both from the brunt of the wind as they made their way to the high school. He let them in through the gym, both of them shivering and slightly delirious, and she pulled the candle out of her pocket, setting it down in the center of the gym floor and repeating the initial incandescence spell she'd used.

"There," she said, kicking off the boots he'd given her and tossing her jacket aside. "Come here."

"There's no music," he pointed out, slipping his coat from his shoulders, and she gave him a radiant smile in answer, her cheeks pink with cold and her hair tousled and damp from wind and snow. She looked like she'd blown right in with the storm, and he could have sworn she'd never looked so beautiful.

Which was a thought he promptly shoved away, coming towards her as she extended a hand for his.

"We don't need music," she said, taking his hands in hers. Her fingers were ice-cold and stiff; without thinking, he drew them to his lips, warming them with his breath, and she shivered a little, reaching out to tighten them in his collar. "What sort of song would they have been playing, anyway? Surely something shitty."

"Oh, you know," he murmured, setting his arms around her waist. "*All my life,*" he sang—badly, entirely out of tune, and only because absinthe had a way of influencing his decisions—as she giggled, pawing at him to stop.

"Who'd you end up going to the prom with?" she asked, gratifyingly interrupting his dismal serenade. "I can't remember."

"I didn't." The words slipped out without his permission; he'd had every intention to lie. She looked up at him, surprised, and he grimaced. "Well, you know. I'd already been shot down once, so with my sensitive ego…" She made a face. "Besides, you were right. I didn't actually want to go to the prom anyway."

Certainly not with anyone who wasn't her, he didn't add, though he had a feeling she'd heard the implication. She blinked, then shifted, resting her cheek against his chest as they swayed slowly in the center of the room.

"I just really wanted to be gone," she murmured, the sound of it muffled into his chest. "Everything here reminds me of my dad, you know? And it was just easier to cut ties. To not come back." Porter rested his chin on top of her head as he listened, nodding slowly, and she sniffled a little, adding, "I just wanted to rush through the end of high school and get out, you know what I mean?"

"Yeah." Her hair somehow managed to smell like rosewater and citrus and salt, like some sort of coastal breeze through an English garden. He doubted that even his mother, for all her talents with draughts, could bottle Cecily Ayers properly, and he took a deep breath of her, filling his lungs. "I think I understand, but still. It was—" He broke off. "Hard to watch you go."

He felt her stiffen for a moment.

Then she tightened her grip on him, one hand rising to rest on his chest beside her cheek.

"I should have said yes," she said, and he felt his pulse stutter and race, her fingertips brushing over the little rush of panic that rose up in his chest.

"Well," Porter said, clearing his throat, "it's nice that you came back eventually. Even if it's for, you know. Something hard, like your grandmother."

She sighed heavily, pulling away for a dual blow of relief and disappointment.

"Yeah, you're right." Her gaze flicked to her coat, and he fought a grimace, realizing she was probably contemplating checking her phone again. "I just… I hate the circumstances of all of it."

"Yeah." He cleared his throat, stepping away. "Yeah, understandable."

She looked smaller from where she was standing, even at the distance of a few feet away. She seemed a little lost, and a little lonely, and he realized with an abrupt wave of sympathy that *of course* she couldn't imagine a life in Saint Sturm—because to her, this town only brought her loss. He still had his entire family here, but for her, the town had only brought her sadness.

"Cecily," he said, registering all of this with a wave of remorse, and she looked up, a little caught off guard by his softened tone. "I'm sorry."

"For what?" she asked, frowning.

"For… everything." He grimaced, not sure how to put it all into words. "Your dad, your grandmother. I just…" He trailed off. "I just think you should know you're not alone, that's all. And don't worry about your mom. She loves you; she wants you to be happy." He swallowed carefully, adding, "And just because your version of happy and her version don't look the same doesn't mean you need to feel guilty about it."

Cecily blinked, staring at him.

Blinked again.

Then, before he could prepare himself for what was happening, she had barreled back into his chest, wrapping her arms around his waist and burying her face in his shirt, exhaling something that sounded like half a sob.

For a moment, he just stood there, unsure what to do, but when she didn't move, he let his arms fall around her, coming to rest atop her unfamiliar frame. He held her loosely, feeling her breath against him, and then tightly, providing the comfort she seemed to have wanted from someone—or maybe, as a tiny hopeful voice whispered unhelpfully in his mind, that she wanted specifically from *him*.

"Thank you," she managed to say into his shirt, and after what seemed like years of time—the smell of her perfume eternally delicate beneath his nose—she pulled away to look at him, something new filling up in her gaze.

Unhelpfully, Porter recalled at that moment how Cecily's kiss had tasted like every happy memory he'd ever experienced all compiled into one, limitless moment. She had been the warmth of familiar autumn spices and the heat of July all at once. She had been bright and crisp and tender and soft and he had been trying for days to forget, even for a moment, that nothing had ever passed his lips with such unshakable perfection as the breath he'd taken from that kiss with Cecily Ayers, who was now looking at him as if she were seeing him clearly for the first time.

Which, he reminded himself stiffly, had always been his goal.

"You should check your phone," he told her. "See if service has improved any. Your mom will be worried about you, and—" *your boyfriend*, he didn't say, and she nodded. She hastily disentangled herself from him, hurrying to her coat and pulling the phone from her pocket.

"Nothing," she said, and sighed, looking up. For a moment, she didn't move, staring into space, but then she angled her chin over her shoulder, looking at him. "Can I see your classroom?" she asked. "I'd like to see it. You. In your element, I suppose."

He nodded slowly as her voice rang in his ears: *See you in physics, I guess.*

"Well, you remember where the physics classroom is, don't you?" he prompted, and gestured to the corridor, letting her lead the way.

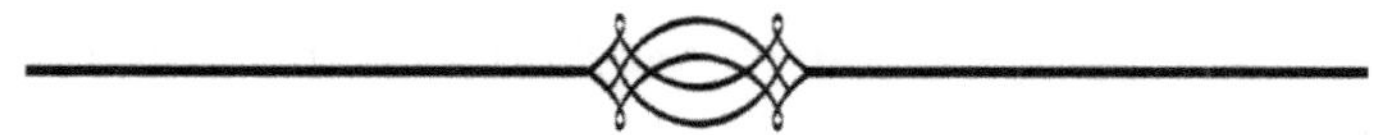

The words MR. CALLAHAN, PHYSICS were embossed on a small plaque outside the classroom door, and Cecily shook her head, entirely unable to make sense of it.

"Seriously?" she asked no one in particular.

She heard his footsteps come to a halt behind her.

"Seriously," he said, and she shivered a little, keenly aware of every inch between the placement of his chest and the notches of her spine. He leaned forward slightly, dropping his chin to speak in her ear.

"Cold?" he asked quietly.

He was truly the most impossible man she'd ever met.

Re-met.

Whatever.

"A little," she said, her tone unreasonably defensive.

"It's colder in the corridor," he agreed, and then, "Door's open."

She turned the handle and pushed it open, reflexively turning on the light switch and then, when nothing happened, reminding herself the power was off. "Oops."

"Habit," he offered with a shrug, gesturing her further inside. "Interested in learning about waves?" he joked. "Want to build a suspension bridge, or perhaps a Rube Goldberg machine?"

"Want to hear another secret?" she countered, and turned so sharply she barreled into his chest, accidentally letting out something suspiciously like a whimper when they touched. "Oops," she said again, and he steadied her with a laugh.

"What secret?"

"I cheated on my Rube Goldberg machine." She felt for the desk behind her, shifting to perch on top of it. "I'd been up late and it wasn't quite working right, so I used a *teeny* bit of magic to make sure it got the job done."

"Well, it's a good thing Mr. Daniels wasn't a witch," Porter said, admonishing her with a nudge. "Nobody's tried that with me yet," he added, "though I hope they will. That'll make for an enlightening conversation."

"I'll bet." She glanced down, running her fingers over the carved initials in the desk. "I can't remember which desk was mine," she said, frowning a little to herself.

"It was that one," he said, pointing to one in the second row. "I sat behind you."

"You did, didn't you?" she mused, looking down at the desk again. She watched Porter step closer, his feet coming towards her, and tried not to think about the way her heart pounded when he re-entered her space, enveloping her with that same woodsy, ethereal sensation. Being close to him was powerfully confusing, though she was pretty sure one thorough glance at him would remind her that he wasn't what she was looking for.

She looked up, finding his blue-green eyes on hers, and felt something in her stomach plummet to her knees before clambering back up her throat.

Maybe more than a glance, then.

"Um," she said, finding her mouth inconceivably dry, and his gaze fell to her lips.

The pace of her heart quickened. She didn't actually *want* him, did she?

"Yes?" he asked.

"I just, um. Thank you. You know, for helping me," she said. If he stepped closer, stepped between her legs, she could take hold of his hips. She could rest her chin in the hollow of his sternum and stare up at him, brushing the hair from his eyes. She could watch the shape of his mouth as it said her name, and she could breathe him in; could get lost in a breeze full of him.

None of which she wanted, of course. "And for trying to get me to this party, anyway."

"You're welcome," he said. "And we can still make it, maybe. Probably." He glanced out the window, and from his profile, she watched the bluish tint from the storm outside glinting along the lines of his cheekbones. "Snow's easing up. Once the power comes back, I can get in touch with my brother. Borrow his truck." He huffed a laugh under his breath. "And take something for sobriety."

"Right," Cecily said, exhaling. "Yeah, that'd be… good." Porter turned to look at her, and she looked hastily away. "Still feel kind of dizzy."

"Dizzy?" he echoed, and did the worst possible thing. He stepped closer, and she inhaled sharply.

"Yeah, I just, um—"

"Are you feeling okay, Cecily?"

He reached out, touching his thumb lightly to her chin and lifting her gaze to his.

She shivered again.

"Cecily," he murmured. It was a question of sorts, and one she desperately didn't want to answer, though she was starting to doubt she could refuse.

"Porter," she said, "I can't… I shouldn't, um—"

Suddenly, the lights overhead buzzed, returning to life with a crackle as power in the school resumed. Cecily blinked, tearing her gaze from Porter's, and hurried to reach for her phone from her coat pocket, grateful for the excuse to check the face of it. "Okay," she exhaled, fighting to calm her hurried pulse. "Yes, okay, I think I have some service, so—"

"Call him."

She blinked, looking up. "What?"

Porter was still looking at her. "Your boyfriend," he said. "Call him."

"Oh yeah? And say what?"

The corners of his mouth twitched at her calling his bluff, or so she thought.

"That it's over," he said, and she choked, caught off guard.

"Wh- why would I—"

"Tell him it's over," Porter said, stepping closer to her, "because he isn't there when you need him. Because he doesn't call when he says he will, or because you spend all your time waiting for him, or because he makes you feel stressed when you could be happy. Take your pick."

Her heart was thudding with a mix of apprehension and disbelief. "I can't just end things over the *phone*, Porter, I don't see why I would—"

"Or," Porter said, "tell him it's over because—" He leaned closer to her, tucking her hair behind one ear. "Because if you don't," he said softly, "I won't kiss you again."

She gaped at him.

He seemed entirely serious.

"Who says I want you to kiss me again?" she demanded, and he leaned forward.

She held her breath, feeling him come closer, and instinctively closed her eyes.

His nose brushed hers, carefully, and then—

And then he took her phone out of her hand, startling her, and selected Ansel's name, hitting dial and placing the phone back in her hand.

"It's ringing," he informed her.

"I see that," she said with a growl, "but you can't just—"

The phone rang once, then twice.

"Tell him you miss him, if you want," Porter suggested. "Tell him whatever's true. Tell him you love him, if that's how you feel. That, or tell him you'd rather someone else be the person whose calls you don't have to wait for."

Another ring.

"Tell him," Porter said quietly, "that you haven't stopped thinking about kissing me since I showed up at your door. Tell him you wore this dress specifically for me," he suggested, brushing his fingertips over the hem where it lingered above her knee, "because you wanted me to admire you, and I am. Tell him you're looking at me and wondering what it might be like," he murmured, leaning forward to place his hands on either side of the desk she was sitting on, "if I kissed more than just your lips."

Another ring. Surely there were only one or two more.

"Porter," she whispered, "I… I can't just—"

A familiar, tinny voice sprouted up from the phone speaker, garishly reminding her she was once again being ignored. "Hey, it's Ansel, leave a message."

Cecily closed her eyes.

Inhaled.

Exhaled.

Then she looked up at Porter Callahan, remembering the taste of him anew, and slowly drew the phone up to her ear.

"Ansel," she said, completely unable to believe what she was doing, "I just don't think this is working for me."

She didn't know what else to say, so she stopped.

Porter leaned forward, taking the phone from her hand, and hung up, placing it onto the chair beside her. He brushed his fingers against the fabric of her dress as he leaned over, and then, his breath skating lightly over the exposed skin of her clavicle, he straightened, looking down at her.

"Do you want me to call my brother?" he asked, and she shook her head numbly.

"No," she managed to say, "not… not yet."

His fingertips traced up the side of her thigh, drawing a meandering path higher and then pausing with a twitch of hesitation, his thumb stroking a line across the bone of her patella.

"What do you want?" he asked her, and this time, her shiver was undeniable.

"You, Porter," she whispered, and he took hold of her chin.

"Cecily," he said.

Then he lowered his head and kissed her, and everything but the sensation of him dimmed to nothing, cascading away on an unmistakable rush.

PART III: REVIVAL

"Oh good," said Evelyn Ayers, visibly relieved as she rushed to the door of the Ayers farmhouse. "You made it, thank god. I told you, Cecily, didn't I?" she said, reverting to maternal fretfulness. "That storm was nothing to gamble on—"

"We're fine, Mom," Cecily assured her, spotting her cousins Adria and Rosabella glancing up (disappointed, it seemed, that she hadn't been swept away in a blizzard, leaving them the coven and the grimoire) over her mother's shoulder. "Sorry it took us so long—"

"What on earth kept you?" Adria asked, sliding what was either a frown or her natural expression between Cecily and Porter, who had quietly materialized in the doorway behind her after parking his brother's truck. "You missed lunch *and* dinner."

"Well," Cecily said hesitantly, glancing at Porter, "we got in an accident, and then—"

"It's my fault," Porter explained, smoothly intervening. "I had some trouble with my brother's truck before we got here. Are you hungry?" he asked Cecily, turning to murmur to her. Rosabella, who was holding two children, looked enormously frustrated by Porter's attention to Cecily, glaring at her napping husband across the room. "I'll get you a plate while you greet the rest of your family, if you want."

His hand brushed delicately over her lower back, smoothing a thin trail of comfort down her spine that Cecily hoped no one else had seen. She nodded, suppressing a shiver.

"Thank you," she managed, catching her mother's close (and delighted) scrutiny and hurrying to step out of his reach, making her way to her grandmother.

To her dismay, Evelyn followed doggedly in her wake, catching Cecily's arm. "What happened?" Evelyn whispered in Cecily's ear, as Cecily rolled her eyes. "Don't you lie to me, Cecily Crescentia Ayers—"

"Nothing happened," Cecily told her, exasperated. "Don't get your hopes up, Mom. I told you, Porter and I are just friends. We ran into some trouble in the snow, that's all."

"Please, Cecily," Evelyn scoffed, "you called to tell me you were coming over an hour ago. Do you think I'm stup-"

"Grandma Eleanor," Cecily said loudly, reaching her grandmother's side at the table and bending to kiss her cheek, giving her mother's ankle a silencing kick as she moved. "I'm so sorry we're late."

Porter wandered the living room as Cecily made the rounds with her family, silently pondering the pictures on the mantle. Eleanor Ayers was, like all grandmothers, immensely proud of her family, displaying them all at various ages. He spotted a familiar picture of Cecily from their kindergarten Christmas production and followed a trail of maturing photographs, noting some familiar images from their shared adolescence and then very little afterwards. While the Ayers cousins all continued on with wedding photos and baby announcements, Cecily's little shrine—

which was the biggest of all of them from her youth, but then abruptly cut off—ended with a picture of her with her mother outside her dorm room in Los Angeles.

"Drat," came a low voice behind him, and Porter turned to find Eleanor Ayers struggling to move her arms from where she'd been swaddled in a blanket. "Miriam's done it too tight again, that silly witch—"

"Let me help you," Porter said quickly, setting his beer down and easing the folded corners out from the crevices of the armchair's cushions. "Better?" he asked, once they'd jointly managed to free her arms, and the Ayers matriarch looked up to give him a shrewd once-over.

"Porter Callahan," she said, which seemed to be more of an acknowledgement than a question. "I'm glad you've come." Her gaze slid over to Cecily, who was, at the moment, trying to avoid holding one of Rosabella's twins. "You make Cecily very happy."

"Oh, I don't know." He watched, stifling a laugh, as Cecily was unable to circumvent acceptance of the baby, and the child in her arms swiftly grabbed onto a clump of her hair.

He turned back to Eleanor with a suppressed smile, shaking his head. "I hope so."

To his surprise, Eleanor was giving him an unnerving smile. The sort that meant, as his mother Maggie would say, that the old bat knew something the rest of them didn't.

"You care about her," Eleanor noted, and Porter nodded, falling comfortably into his dutiful act.

"Oh, of course, she's—"

"She matters to you," Eleanor amended, and Porter blinked. That, by the sound of it, seemed to be a markedly different statement, and in response to his confusion Eleanor leaned forward, beckoning him closer. "Not just recently. Always," she informed him. "Everyone has a light. Yours is brighter around Cecily."

Figures, he thought, that the Ayers women would all be a little prophetic. Or at least be convinced that they were.

In considering his response, Porter glanced over his shoulder, watching Cecily from across the room. She'd adjusted to the holding of the baby, sort of. She seemed to be deep in conversation with it, anyway, though the baby still held her hair in one hand, staring vacantly at Cecily's moving lips.

Then Cecily caught his eye from afar, making a wry face and smiling at him. He smiled back, and then turned to Eleanor.

"Cecily makes everyone's light brighter," he said, but Eleanor was still watching him with that same unnerving look of certainty.

"Tell her," Eleanor said, and Porter blinked.

"Sorry, I don't—"

"Tell her," Eleanor repeated.

Okay, he thought resignedly, so maybe they were more than a little prophetic.

"She doesn't like to be told things," he murmured after a tick of hesitation, and immediately, Eleanor's smile turned soft.

"I'm sure you'll find a way," she advised, and then leaned her head back to close her eyes, seeming to find it an appropriate time to return to her armchair doze.

"Goodnight, Mrs. Ayers," Porter said at the front door, nodding politely to Evelyn. "Goodnight, Cecily. Merry Christmas," he called over his shoulder, making his way back to his brother's truck with a shiver from the snowy cold and climbing in, starting the engine as Cecily continued her efforts at shooing her mother away from the door.

"What *happened*?" Evelyn demanded, apparently not giving up her efforts at interrogation. "Cecily, please, you're killing me. Is this how you want your mother to die?"

"Nothing happened between us," Cecily said for the seventieth time, making her way up the stairs to her bedroom with a groan. "It just took a while to get through the snow, that's all. Don't get your hopes up, Mother, he's just a friend."

Evelyn followed after her, wailing a little in her distress. "But *Cecily*—"

"Mom," Cecily said with a sigh, turning to grip her mother's shoulders. "Don't be weird, okay? Porter's great. He's a friend. We're *friends*, and that's all. Okay? Stop planning our wedding in your head. I can see you doing it."

Evelyn withered slightly, pouting. "Are you sure?"

"Yes, I'm sure," Cecily said firmly. "Now, can we go to bed, please? It's late."

"Fine," Evelyn groaned, turning to her bedroom and sluggishly dragging her feet. "Take away my one thing to live for, why don't you—"

"Very funny, Mom," Cecily called back, slipping into her bathroom and listening for the telltale sounds of her mother preparing for bed. Evelyn was highly regimented; always had been, even when Cecily's father had been alive. Evelyn would wash her face, brush her teeth, read for exactly fifteen minutes, then shut off her light, asleep and snoring softly within an additional ten.

A forty-five-minute process, and at 12:46 a.m., Cecily's bedroom window slid open.

"Right on time," she said, rising to her feet and pulling Porter into her arms the moment he materialized with both feet on the ground.

He chuckled, nearly toppling with her onto the floor as she snaked her arms around his neck. "Missed me?" he said, hands floating under the cotton of her pajama top, and she shivered, shoving them back down.

"Your hands are cold," she admonished at a whisper, closing her window and pulling him with her onto her bed. "Take off your coat and stay awhile," she suggested, her own hands drifting to his jeans, and he sat up to shrug his shoulders free from his jacket, letting it fall to the floor before taking her in his arms.

"You know," he murmured, tilting her head to brush his lips lightly over the side of her neck, "you could have just come over to my place. We *are* adults, hard as it is to believe."

"And explain to my mother where I was going? No thank you," Cecily said, running her fingers over the planes of his stomach and digging her nails into the v-shaped line of muscle above his hips. "I don't want her to get her hopes up. This is just…" She exhaled, his lips finding a little spot of heat behind her ear before traveling down her jaw, silencing her with a kiss to her mouth. "I don't know what this is," she admitted, sighing it out as she kissed him. He let his fingers wander to the buttons of her top, carefully loosening each one at slow, measured intervals.

The last time he'd touched her like this they'd been quietly struggling for breath in the silence of his classroom, desperate and wanting and terrified in equal measures (at least for her). They'd both been dizzied by the absinthe and feeling a little too much like strangers, still learning he could touch her here and she could kiss him there and it could be something new and strange and exciting. Now, hours later, she was breathing him in like a gulp of something familiar, that woodsy smell of him filling her nose as she hurried to hold him, to be held by him, to press her mouth longingly to his.

I'm never going to be able to look at my desk the same way, he'd said when they were finished, her with her dress hiked up and yanked down and him with his shirt thrown open, stray violence from her nails scattered faintly across his chest. Then he'd wrapped his arms around her, syncopating their slowing pulses, and she'd known right then she was done for.

One time would never be enough.

"Take this off," she whispered, sliding her hands under his shirt, and he complied, letting her push him back against her pillows as she wiggled out of her bottoms, joining him under the covers of her duvet.

They hadn't discussed what would happen next, or what any of it would mean. Maybe being back in the town she'd gone to high school had rendered her a teenager again, thoughtless about the future while sneaking boys into her bedroom so her mother wouldn't see.

"Cecily," Porter said, his voice a gravelly rasp, and she looked up from where she'd been kissing her way down his torso, catching something telling in his voice.

"Porter?" she asked, waiting, but he only pulled her up to kiss her, fingers tangling in the dark mass of her hair as he rolled her onto her back, threading one of her legs through his.

It was only when she felt the comfort of knowing they were twined together at every possible axis of contact that she realized he'd been trying to pull her close, to keep her there, his lips finding her ear to say with painful gravity, "I missed you."

She shivered, burying her face in the crook of his neck and breathing him in.

She may not have missed him before, but oh, she thought with sudden anguish—oh, she would miss him now.

"Stay with me," she whispered, and felt his solemn nod before he drew her lips to his again, kissing her to mindless oblivion.

"Cecily, I was thinking about it, and—*oh*."

Porter's eyes snapped open, adjusting to the streaming light of daylight in an unfamiliar place, to find Evelyn Ayers in the doorway of her daughter's bedroom, one hand over her laughing mouth while Porter struggled to make sure he was fully covered. Cecily, who'd been sleeping with her head on his bare chest, gave a low groan at the sound of her mother's voice.

"Not now, Mom, it's too early," she said, brushing a sleepy, thoughtless kiss to Porter's chest, and then—having realized the incongruity of what she'd just done—she launched herself upright, turning to let out a whimper of, "MOM!"

Evelyn, Porter was distressed to note, was giggling quietly to herself, leaning with palpable relish against the door. "Well, Porter, I hope you know I'll have to tell your mother," she said, forcing a straight face. "I assume Maggie's going to ground you for at least three weeks."

"Mother," Cecily said in exasperation, attempting to disentangle herself from Porter without revealing either of them from under the covers. "Could you potentially not do this, please?"

"I'm so disappointed in you, Cecily Crescentia," Evelyn continued. "Disobeying the rules of my house, lying to my face about this being *nothing*—"

"MOM, CAN'T THIS WAIT?"

Porter, who was somewhere between entertained and mortified, watched with helpless amusement as Cecily finally managed to bully her mother out of the room before spelling her door shut. She slid out of bed, hunting around for her clothes, and tossed Porter his boxers, shaking her head. "Honestly, she's ridiculous, and now, of course," she sighed, as Porter rose to his feet, slipping out from beneath the duvet, "she won't be able to stop herself from bringing it u-"

Porter cut her off with a kiss, tucking her entire body against his and holding her until she relented, softening. She went slightly limp, curving into his embrace, and then finally ceased her agitated mumbling to give him a sheepish look of gratitude.

"Good morning," she said. "Sorry, I was just—"

"I don't want this to be nothing," he replied, and she blinked.

"What?"

"I'm happy to tell your mother the truth," he said, shrugging. "Let her say what she wants, I don't care. I want to be with you, Cecily," he informed her, having come to that conclusion at approximately the moment she'd asked him to stay.

It had been enlightening, to say the least, how quickly his entire being had wanted to say yes. Not the night. Not through the holidays. He'd wanted her to suffer his absence, yes, and he'd wanted to win—but he couldn't win, he realized, unless she was happy. Unless he was making her happy. He'd realized in that moment that if she wanted him in any measure, in any capacity, he would be helpless to refuse.

It had taken seven years of silence for him to admit it to himself, but there it was, unquestionably: He was, and perhaps had always been, in love with Cecily Ayers.

"Whatever it takes," he said, bending his forehead to hers as she stared up at him in silence. "If you want to do this long distance, I'll do it. If you want me to go with you to L.A., Cecily, I will. Once the school year is over I won't have any obligations here, and then we can do whatever you want—"

"Porter," she said, voice a little shaky with disbelief. "Are you… are you *sure*, it's only been… a *week*," she estimated, stunned. "I mean what if—what if we can't actually make it work, and then… and then you resent me, or I—what if—"

He watched her flounder, turning the idea over in her head. She looked dazed, a little lost, and he forced himself not to take it back. Not this time, he told himself firmly. He'd let her go once without saying a word, and he wouldn't do it again.

To his surprise, though, by the time she'd finished her mental calculations, she was looking up at him with a new expression on her face. Something wistful, or—if his imagination wasn't completely off-base—then possibly something tinged with wonder.

"Porter Callahan," she said slowly, her fingers drawing up the back of his neck, "are you telling me you don't want to pretend?"

He shook his head, flooded with certainty. "No, Cecily, I don't want to pretend."

"But then that means—"

"That means it's real," he told her, and the corners of her pretty lips tilted up, gifting him her radiant smile.

"So what do we do now, then?" she asked him, arching her hips against his, and he bent his head, rousingly compliant.

"CECILY," came Evelyn's voice from the other side of the door, startling them both. "JUST SO YOU KNOW, I THINK THIS IS A MARVELOUS IDEA."

"I guess we'll have breakfast with your mother," Porter said, and Cecily's laugh was boundless, leaving him with the sense that perhaps, after seven years, everything might finally be as it should.

Cecily felt drunker than she had on Maggie Callahan's absinthe for the entirety of breakfast. Porter had taken every opportunity he could to touch her—hands on her waist while she sliced some fruit, a wink while he flipped the pancakes, lips against her shoulder while she charmed the dishes clean, fingers floating up her spine as he handed her a plate—and all of it was positively intoxicating, equal parts excitement and joy.

This was it, wasn't it? This was what had been missing with Ansel, with every other person who'd never managed to fit into all the little spare parts of her life. They had all been the wrong shape, too saturated one way or another to blend with everything she was. There was something about Porter, some shade of him that seemed to complement every little hue of hers. He felt like home, and for the first time, that seemed boundless instead of limiting. For the first time since her father had passed away, Cecily found a place she belonged in Saint Sturm, and not even her mother's exuberance could ruin it.

Eventually, though, he had to go; he'd promised his mother he'd help her with something—it *was* Christmas, after all—and then he'd be back.

"You promise?" Cecily asked, and he smiled, kissing her forehead.

"I promise," he said, turning to his brother's truck.

She watched him go from the door, suddenly hating the view of his back. She shoved her feet into a pair of her mother's boots and darted out onto her snowy drive, catching him before he reached the handle.

"Porter, wait—"

She pulled him into her and he laughed, picking her up; kissing her wildly, inappropriately, in a way that would make most of her neighbors blush. Still, she wrapped her legs around his waist, running her fingers through his hair, and thought, *mine*.

Eventually he set her back on her feet, aiming her in the direction of her house. "Go," he said in her ear, adding a light smack to her rear. "It's cold, and I'll be back—"

"You'd better," she said, and then shivered, making her way back to her front door.

She was filled with blinding elation (stupidly, clumsily happy) when the bubble suddenly burst, someone's voice floating through the air behind her just before she re-entered her house.

"Finally closed the deal, eh, Callahan?" came the voice of Luke Emerson, one of their high school classmates whom Cecily had forgotten lived two houses down. "Only took you seven years," he said with a loud, disruptive laugh. "I really thought you couldn't do it, but hey, you proved me wrong."

Fuck. Cecily set her jaw, flooded with humiliation.

She'd forgotten, too, why she'd always hated living in a small town.

"Hey, Cecily," Luke called to her, prompting her to bristle. "Was he good? He's got plenty of practice by now. No one ever says no to the great Porter Callahan—do they, Cali?"

Abruptly, the little sheen of enchantment she'd been wearing since that morning broke. Her happiness shattered around her, crashing to her feet beside the grubby piles of snow.

"Luke," Porter said flatly, "would you just shut up?"

"Oh, come on, it's hilarious," Luke said, as Cecily resolutely refused to turn. "You've spent the last seven years hating her for humiliating you, and now you finally got to put it to bed. Put *her* to bed," he corrected himself, sounding perversely satisfied with his unclever joke. "I'm just saying, man, good job not pussying out this time—"

"Stop," Porter snapped. "Stop it. Cecily," he added, and she winced as she heard his footsteps approaching, suddenly feeling sick. "Cecily, don't listen to him, he doesn't know what the fuck he's talking about—"

He spun her towards him and she shrank away, folding her arms over her chest.

Suddenly, it all made sense. Of course he'd agreed to do this. She *had* humiliated him, hadn't she? And he'd decided to humiliate her back. He broke up her relationship. He *seduced* her, slept with her twice in the span of a day, and all of it had moved too quickly to be even remotely believable. Had she been totally steeped in delusion? Of course he wasn't going to leave Saint Sturm. This wasn't about her. This was about their history.

She wanted to vomit, or cry. She hated it here. All of it had gone too fast, sweeping her up and parting her from her better judgment, and now the impact of her idiocy struck her like whiplash. She had *always* hated it here, and she regretted every moment she'd let herself believe that she could let it feel like home.

"Just go," she said, and Porter blinked, shaking his head.

"Cecily, please, he isn't—"

"I have to go home," she said, stiffening. "This is… I was being stupid. I was sad about my grandmother and I let you take advantage of that, but we'd never work." She glanced up at him, shaking her head. "Just go, Porter."

He stared at her, clearly unable to make sense of what she was saying. "Cecily, you can't be serious, you don't actually believe that—"

"It doesn't matter, Porter, because I'm not staying, and this won't work," she said flatly, and then she turned, reaching for the door when she heard him following after her. "Don't," she shot at him, whipping around to face him. "Just let me go, Porter," she snapped, and then she yanked open her front door, leaving him to stare as she darted inside and let the door slam shut, her head falling back against the wood.

"Cecily," Evelyn said with a frown, materializing just as Cecily had begun to cry. "Honey, what happened?"

She opened her mouth, but no words would come. Not that it mattered. Her mother was half-psychic, anyway. She'd figure it out.

"I want to see Grandma Eleanor," Cecily said miserably, and for once, Evelyn didn't argue.

"Okay," she said, and brushed her thumb over Cecily's cheek. "Then I'll go get dressed."

"How was it?" Maggie asked, looking up as Porter entered the house. "Sorry to call you back here, I feel terrible—Evelyn texted me for the first time in *years*," she gushed, exhilarated. "Really, Port, I'm so pleased, you know I love Cecily, and—"

Just let me go, Porter.

See you in physics, I guess.

"Mom," Porter said, raising a hand to his mouth. "Can we just… *not*, right now, please?"

Maggie's face fell slightly, and then she nodded.

"Can I make you something?" she asked gently, gesturing to the pantry, which was her cupboard of witchery. After the prom debacle, she'd brewed him something that had tasted like frothy nutmeg; she'd called it hope, but he was pretty sure it had only ever been a latte.

"No, thanks," he said. "It's fine."

And it was. Or it would be.

He'd been fine before, anyway. He'd be fine again. He'd wake up one day—maybe tomorrow; probably tomorrow—to find Cecily gone, and he would adjust. The vacancy would fill. He would be fine.

Just let me go, Porter.

"Are you sure?" Maggie asked.

He could still smell her on his skin. That breeze of rosewater would haunt him for days, no matter how hard he scrubbed himself clean. But someday, some other day that wasn't today, it would be true.

Maybe.

"No, I'm not," he said, "but let's go. We've got things to do."

"Cecily," Eleanor said, struggling to sit upright when she entered. "Hello, sweetheart. I wasn't expecting you so early."

"I know, Grandma, but—" Cecily swallowed, perching at her grandmother's bedside and glancing around. "Miriam's not here, is she?" she asked tentatively, and Eleanor chuckled, shaking her head.

"No, not now," she said, "but try not to say her name too many times or she might spontaneously appear." She paused, considering Cecily, and frowned, reaching out for her. "Your heart," she murmured, "is it?"

Cecily glanced at her grandmother, tiny and frail, and felt flooded with guilt.

"I have to leave, Grandma Eleanor," she said, shaking her head and rushing it out. "I can't stay here. I know you wanted all of us to come, but it just… it hurts to be here," she said quietly, letting her chin fall. "I love you, Grandma, but I have to go back. Soon. Now, actually," she amended with a hiccupy laugh, "or at least very close to now."

"Cecily," Eleanor said, employing one of her sterner tones. "Are you running away?"

"I'm—" *Yes.* "No." *I have to, it hurts, I'm scared*—"I have a job there, Grandma. A life. I have to go back."

"A job is not a life, Cecily," Eleanor said, and Cecily sighed.

"Grandma, I know I'm never here," she said, "and I'm sorry I've missed so much, I really am. But I just wanted something bigger, I wanted *more* than this little town, and—"

"Oh, I know why you left," Eleanor cut in, giving Cecily an admonishing glance. "But do not fool yourself into thinking that why you left back then is the same reason you're leaving now." She paused, and then ventured, "Though, if you really must leave, then I suppose I should make a decision about the family grimoire."

Cecily let her chin fall, looking at her hands. "I don't expect to inherit it, Grandma, or the coven. I know you'd prefer to give it to someone who's here, and I understand."

"No, darling. You'll have it," Eleanor said, and Cecily blinked, looking up.

"I will?"

"Of course," Eleanor said, sounding as if this had never been up for debate, and Cecily wondered if somewhere out there, Adria and Rosabella had just let out a spontaneous scream. "You're the eldest of my eldest, Cecily. The grimoire is yours."

"But—"

"Not now, of course," Eleanor clarified gently. "When you're ready. When you've seen and done everything you want to see and do, Cecily, the grimoire will still be here. Your family, your roots, your coven—they will always be here for you to come home to."

Cecily blinked back a sudden rush of fresh tears. "But Grandma, I don't know how long—" She swallowed, shaking her head. "I don't know when I'll be ready."

"Well, there's no rush," Eleanor said with an air of scolding, as if Cecily were haplessly missing the point. "Evie will keep it until you decide it's time."

"Evie? Who's—" Cecily blinked. "You mean my mother?"

"Yes, of course," Eleanor said matter-of-factly. "She's the eldest daughter, a good wife to my son. She'll keep it, and the coven, until you're ready."

"She thinks you hate her," Cecily said with a frown, and Eleanor waved a hand, dismissive.

"Better she not get too comfortable," Eleanor said. "After all, she'll be the head of the coven when I'm gone," she said, evidently stating the obvious, "and she'll have to get used to being unpopular."

"But she can't do it alone," Cecily insisted. "She's not very social, and—"

"This is what I'm telling you, dear," Eleanor said. "She won't be alone. She has us, and you," she said, with a waving reference her house, "and she's stronger than you think. She'll be fine, as will we."

Cecily nodded, sobering a little at the reminder. "I'm sorry to disappoint you," she began, but her grandmother cut her off with a shake of her head.

"Go see the world, Cecily. Your happiness is all you owe me. I only ask that you remember where your heart is," she said, reaching for Cecily's hand. "So long as you follow where it leads, my dear, you can never disappoint me."

Cecily laced her fingers with Eleanor's, holding her grandmother's hand.

"That Callahan boy," Eleanor began, and Cecily sighed, about to argue until her grandmother shook her head. "No, Cecily, listen to me.

His name, his family," she sniffed, "whether he's a witch or he isn't—that means nothing to me." She looked up, fixing Cecily with her matriarchal look of authority. "But you should know, some people can't say things in ways you understand."

"I don't think," Cecily began, and withered. "I don't think it was ever real," she mumbled, and Eleanor scoffed.

"Child, you are the bone of my bone, and I know your intuition is better than that," she said, before startling Cecily completely, tossing her duvet aside with a sharp, abrupt motion. "Now, off we go," Eleanor said, planting her feet on the ground. "If you're looking to head back today, Cecily, we'd better get on the road before it gets too late."

"Grandma," Cecily said, shocked, as Eleanor rose to her feet, shuffling through her wardrobe for a coat. "What are you—I thought you were—" She sputtered, staring in disbelief. "I thought you were *dying*—"

"Hm, what? No, not especially," Eleanor said absently. "But you hadn't been home in a while, and frankly, it was getting dull around here. Now," she said, locating a scarf and winding it around her neck, "are we going, then? It'll take two hours to drive to Minneapolis, and Miriam's made a delightful soup I don't plan to miss—she's a pest," Eleanor said fondly, "but magic with a crockpot."

"Okay," Cecily said, rising to her feet, but then she stopped, something holding her back. "Can we just... do something first?" she asked, and Eleanor smiled knowingly.

"Oh, you know how slow Saint Sturm is, honey. I've got all day," Eleanor assured her, taking Cecily's arm and leading her to the door.

Porter climbed out of his truck, running his hand over the damage. It would take some time to fix cosmetically, but at least he'd have a project. The internal damage had been fixed, his brother's truck returned, and now he had… well. Certainly no better use of his time.

He shook his head, lamenting that he'd turned down a potion from his mother. She could have eased the melancholy, at least, so he wouldn't have to be pathetic *and* alone.

"Porter Callahan," came a voice behind him, and he tensed for a moment before turning slowly, surprised to find that he had not, in fact, imagined it.

Cecily Ayers stood there in something mildly winter appropriate, not that he focused on that. "I wanted to say something to you," she said, and he paused before answering, wondering how exactly to put into words *don't go* and *please, if you do, take me with you* but also *you can't honestly think so little of me, can you?*

Instead, he spread his hands, helpless. "I'm listening," he said.

Cecily took a step forward, chewing her lip in hesitation, and paused when they were face to face.

"I need to get my life together," she said. "Find out what I really want." She swallowed, and then added, "I have to go back to Los Angeles. There's no rush now that I know my grandmother's not actually dying," she added with half a laugh, and Porter frowned with confusion, but she shook her head. "Sorry. Long story, I just—the point is," she exhaled, "I can't stay here."

"I know," he said. "I never expected you to."

"Right, but I—" She fidgeted, eyeing her hands. "Last time," she confessed, "I should have said goodbye." She paused, not looking at him.

"You aren't nothing to me, Porter Callahan. You never were, and I shouldn't have let you believe it. I should have said goodbye." She looked up, dark gaze rising to meet his, and managed a tiny, gut-wrenching smile. "And," she added, her voice soft and hopeful, "if I come back, then maybe we could do this… slower. With less of me running away, anyway," she joked.

"I—" He stopped. "What?"

"Or not," she said quickly, sparing a nervous laugh. "I mean, maybe I misread things—"

"No," he said, taking a step towards her. "No, definitely not, that's what I was trying to tell you. Luke's an idiot, he doesn't know anything—"

"No, I know," she assured him, her smile trembling a little. "But maybe we could just… talk?" she asked, tilting her head. "I could come back for a long weekend, and maybe you can visit me for spring break, and then, I don't know, we can… talk about it. About us, or—"

Something monstrously optimistic reared up in his chest, roaring with warmth.

"You want to date me, Cecily Ayers?" he asked, and she made a face.

"Well, you're not worried about falling for me, are you, Porter Callahan?" she snottily replied, and in answer, he stepped closer, tucking her hair behind her ear and brushing a little warmth into her icy cheek.

No, he thought, he wasn't worried about it in the slightest.

Not when he'd fallen for her a long time ago.

"Well," he said, tilting her chin up. "Goodbye, then, Cecily," he said, and she gave him a teary smile, pressing her lips to the palm of his hand before reaching to wrap her arms around his neck.

"Goodbye, Porter," she said, raising her lips up for his, "and I'll see you very soon."

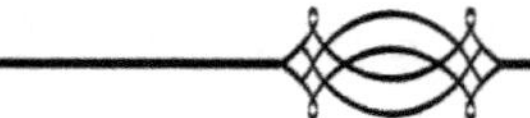

FIVE MONTHS LATER
Saint Sturm High School
Saint Sturm, Iowa
May 2019

"Alright, gimme that," Porter said, rolling his eyes as he reached for the water bottle in his students' hands. "You think I can't tell what's in that? *Behave*," he warned, corralling the group of seniors into the gym with a shake of his head. "Don't make me call your mother, Cleary," he shouted after them, sniffing at what was almost certainly cheap vodka before tucking it into his pocket.

"You clean up nice, Mr. Callahan," mused one of his students, wandering up to him with his arm around his date. "You're not chaperoning *alone*, are you? Lame," he judged, and Porter shrugged.

"Not the first time I've gone without a prom date," Porter said.

"Yikes," said the student. "Bummer."

"*Such* a bummer," agreed another voice, and immediately, Porter fought a smile, turning to find Cecily approaching, wearing his favorite red dress. "Sorry," she said when she reached him. "For being late, I mean," she clarified firmly. "I still think you should have expressly set me straight about your intentions the first time I wasn't there for prom."

"Yeah, yeah, I get it, I'm an idiot," he said, pulling her out of sight to make sure he could kiss her precisely the way he wanted to. "How was your flight?"

"Eh, fine, whatever. God, I missed you," she said, biting lightly on his lower lip as she kissed him once; then again, longer, and then a third time, her fingers trailing through his hair. "Is it summer yet?" she whispered, groaning with impatience.

They were going to spend it traveling. One step at a time, they'd agreed. The last five months had been full of flights back and forth between MSP and LAX, but it was worth it. Porter didn't need roots quite yet, and anyway, the frequent flyer miles meant they'd have one less thing to worry about.

"Almost," he said, savoring the taste of her on his tongue. He was certainly in no rush for summer; there were other things to do first. "Cecily Ayers," he said, disentangling himself long enough to offer her his elbow, "will you go to prom with me?"

She gave him another brilliant smile, looping her arm through his.

"Why, Porter Callahan," she mused, "I'm just so glad you finally asked."

THE GOLDEN AGE OF MONSTERS (JULY-OCTOBER 2018)

JOURNALIST AND SECRET WITCH Margo West arrives on the island of Avalon, a place nearly abandoned by the progress of time, to write what she assumes will be an innocuous article about historic waterfront mansions. However, after a visit to the island's casino (and an unpleasant meeting with its owner, Alec Del Mar), Margo accidentally wakes up a mysterious magical force within the island.

Soon after, Margo learns that nothing in Avalon is quite what it seems.

PART I: SUMMER SOLSTICE

June 18
Marina Costa, California

If someone had asked me to guess what my new writing assignment would be, even at my most cynical I wouldn't have gone with 'cast off to a literal island.' And yet! Here we are. Apparently Dan is still salty about the breakup, which… is unsurprising. I can't say I'm doing much better, but this is exactly why you shouldn't get involved with your higher-ups. Note to self: make a note of that for future reference. Add it to the List of Smart Behaviors, along with 'don't eat cereal directly from the box' and 'try to go for a run every now and then, would you?'

Ugh, who am I kidding. I'd lose the list immediately, even if it were stapled to my forehead. While it exists for the time being, though, add it to the minutes that I don't do well with water-based transportation. The ferry from the mainland is at least basically a ship (small boats are positively nauseating) but still, I don't particularly care for the constant motion under my feet.

Oof, pause. I have to look up for a second.

Okay, better. Anyway, of course Dan's chosen this unique form of punishment for me, because of course I stupidly mentioned to him my intention to never return to obscurity (or to another small town) again. How did he wind up with so much power over me, anyway? I thought surely someone would think to question why a journalist who just finished a celebrated exposé on toxic masculinity in Manhattan's art enclaves would suddenly be exiled to some tiny island to write about the preservation of historic waterfront mansions, but evidently not. I bet the rest of my department is too thrilled about my banishment to bother asking questions. They already act like characters from The Crucible when it comes to me, just like the kids I grew up around. And in this case, they don't even know how close to right they almost are.

Anyway, do I <u>want</u> to spend the summer touring the guest houses of rich divorcées? No, no I don't. Do I have a choice? Also no. I suppose it's as good a place to moodily traipse about as any other, and at least I won't run into any of our colleagues. Besides, maybe some time at the beach will do me some good. I'm not one for sand, but a little sun might be precisely what I need. At the very least I'll come back with a tan, and then Dan will remember why this happened in the first place.

I hope he does. I hope it haunts him.

After all, it's only fair.

"I'm sorry dear, remind me your name?"

"It's Margo. Margo West."

"Ah, yes, of course, here it is. Margo." The woman looked up with a smile, clicking a mouse and flashing Margo a look of rapturous welcome. "And you'll be with us for four weeks, then?"

God. "Yes." Margo shifted uncomfortably. "This is a lovely hotel," she offered, wondering if her general unwillingness to be there might be coming off as rudeness. It wasn't this woman's fault she'd been sent here, so lying seemed an acceptable way to ease the tension. In reality, the lobby was filled with those oceanic-themed pastels that Margo considered to be Of A Certain Age; the sort of thing a middle-aged homemaker might implement in her guest bathroom, complete with a decorative seashell atop the toilet.

"Oh, thank you, dear," the woman said, beaming. She had something of an island look to her, though not this particular island; Margo guessed she was Hawaiian or possibly even Puerto Rican, though that may have been Margo's own interpretation for missing her Brooklyn flat. "It's been in my family for quite a long time," the woman explained. "A bit more off the beaten path, so we get fewer tourists. Though, as far as tourists go, most of the visitors in Avalon are only here for the day."

"A day?" Margo echoed, surprised. "The ferry's not exactly an easy ride to come just for a day."

Marina Costa, the ship port the ferry docked from, had been about three hours from Avalon and two from Los Angeles. All in all, it wasn't exactly an easy trip, especially not from New York City.

"Well, most of the people who come here are on the cruises," the woman explained, gesturing vaguely out the window to where one such ship could be seen in the harbor. "They dock here in the morning and the passengers unload for the day until later in the evening. Hospitality on the island's seen better days." She smiled mournfully. "There used to be a time more people came for long, decadent holidays. Now I don't think people have the patience for it."

"Patience?"

"There isn't much to do here," the woman admitted, the corners of her smile drooping slightly. "Aside from the locals, there's the casino, the beach, and some restaurants, but that's about it. In its heyday, of course, Avalon was a bit more of a destination. Now it's just a stopover."

"Oh," Margo said, tucking that information (and the gloom of its pronouncement) away for later use; it seemed a suitable journalistic turn of phrase. Meanwhile, the woman finished checking her in, turning to pick up not a keycard, but an actual *key*, bronze and ornate, with a thin ribbon tied to the handle reading 221.

"Here you are," the woman said, holding it out to Margo. "Coffee and pastries are served at six in the morning, and you're welcome to alert me if you're interested in dinner in the evenings. I'm Cora, by the way," she added as an afterthought, as if she humbly doubted Margo would want to use it. "The shower's a bit finicky. Give it a minute before you step in, would you? And try not to flush the toilet simultaneously, you know. Old pipes." Her smile broadened. "Anything else?"

"No, I don't think so," Margo said, passing Cora something of a salute. "Thanks for your help."

"My pleasure," Cora said, and then, with a cheerful tone, she added, "Welcome to Avalon!"

June 19
Avalon, California

It's not as if I'm trying to be unpleasant, but it's hard to escape the knowledge of my reality, which is that having committed social treason, I'm now being subjected to premature convalescence. The pace of life on the island is extremely slow, which would be quaint, I imagine—if I were the sort of person who admired quaintness. My history of being the weird daughter of the weirdest person amid other, less isolated quaintness means that I am definitely not.

The mansions (which I have to continuously remind myself are the reason I'm even here) are suitably ostentatious, at least. I took some shots of the exteriors today, following the coastal path from the hotel and trying to sort out a satisfactory way in without alarming the occupants. This seems like the sort of place where people don't particularly want to talk to big city journalists, even if it's just about their houses.

Luckily, as with all small towns, people spend most of their time gossiping; unlike the "I saw Goody Proctor staying late in Dan's office" types I left behind, this can be useful when you're not the witch in question. I've come to observe from my early years of voyeuristic ostracization that three of the mansions (the three closest to Avalon's main street, and to my hotel) are occupied by women who meet regularly at a cafe to discuss… I don't know. How much they acquire in alimony, I imagine? They must be loaded. These mansions (which have all been restored at various points over the past couple of decades) would belong to Manhattanite gazillionaires if they were only located somewhere desirable, like the Hamptons.

Cora, who runs the ever-so-uniquely named Sea Breeze Inn, mentioned something about the casino on the island, which I noticed from the ferry ride in (when I wasn't busy trying not to puke my guts out, that is). It's a large, opulent building on one of the island's many hills, and while I can't quite figure out why an island like this would need a casino to begin with, I have to assume it's something to do with nostalgia. This seems like a place enamored with the past.

The divorcées, as Margo was beginning to call them in her head, were three petite women who could only be called *ladies*, each of them a forty-something carbon copy of the others clutching purses of whimsically shaped wicker and sipping fashionable afternoon lattes on the patio of a place called Cup o' Joe. Margo had initially wondered how she was going to approach them but discovered very quickly that there was no need to concern herself with a ploy; the divorcées themselves had smelled an outsider and hurried to make her acquaintance.

"Are you liking Avalon so far?" asked one of them; Faith, Margo remembered with effort, though it was difficult to tell the difference given that Faith, Sadie, and Amelia all had very similar aesthetics and voices. It seemed strange they would all blend so easily when, up close, they looked nothing alike (Faith was some sort of bottled blonde while Sadie had a vaguely Caribbean look to her, and Amelia had brown hair so shiny and neatly pulled back Margo could have seen her face in its reflection) but still, they ultimately lumped together in Margo's mind.

"New places can sometimes be a difficult adjustment," Faith added sympathetically.

"It's nice," Margo said, and when that seemed underwhelming, she hurried to add, "It's definitely peaceful."

"Oh, it's certainly that," Sadie agreed. Margo decided she would be Divorcée Number One, as she was the one who seemed to make the decisive statements. (Faith asked the questions; Amelia mostly nodded along, smiling.) "Though it can be a bit of fun, you know, if you let it. Today's quiet, of course," Sadie said with a palpable hint of boredom. "The cruise ships have already left, so the bustle is gone."

"Bustle?" Margo echoed.

"In the shops, the restaurants," Sadie explained, waving a hand. "The casino."

"The casino is fun," Amelia chimed in. "You should come!"

"I'm not much of a gambler," Margo said.

"Neither was my ex-husband," Amelia sighed.

"Have you ever done it?" Faith asked Margo. "It can be invigorating at times."

She said it the same way someone in New York might have spoken about Botox, or bone broth.

"Not really," Margo admitted. "I've played blackjack a few times at charity events and the like, but casinos have never really appealed to me."

"You should come with us, then," Sadie decided. "Tonight, maybe."

"Oh, I don't know," Margo demurred. "I'm a bit busy working." A lie, obviously. There was nothing to do here but scan Dan's Instagram and, at weaker moments, his Venmo feed.

"Well, think about it," Sadie advised. "You're missing quite a lot of what Avalon has to offer if you don't go, you know."

"I suppose," Margo permitted thinly, opting not to add that she wasn't exactly in a hurry to experience whatever it was Avalon offered to begin with. "I've still got four weeks, though. Can't very well get it all out in the first two days, can I?"

The three women exchanged glances.

"I suppose that's true," Sadie permitted, daintily lifting her mug to her lips.

June 20

This island really does revolve almost completely around tourists. The cruise ships dock early in the morning, materializing from the coastal fog, and then the people start to crawl up the shallow stretches of beach onto the shallower town paths, looking like little ants from where I watch them at my window. Why this would be a stopping point on any sort of cruise is a bit beyond me. I gather the boats are either going south to Mexico or north to Alaska, but either way, what in Avalon is even worth seeing? I suppose it must be amusing for a day, if you really want to see a place that hasn't changed since the 1950s. Like Disneyland's Main Street, but generally more boring and worse.

I've spent my first couple of days here doing research about the island itself, starting with a trusty Google search. Apparently Cora wasn't exaggerating when she said it used to be a vacation spot. Some of the mansions aren't mansions at all, but former hotels that were later bought and occupied by single wealthy owners. I'm not sure why single people would settle on this island, but there seem to be no families at all. Certainly no children, or none that I've seen. When the cruise ships leave, the island's as good as dead. The restaurants close at eight in the evening, which would be a travesty in New York. The shops close even earlier.

The only thing that stays open well into the night is, perhaps unsurprisingly, the casino. If I were to listen to my mother (which, generally speaking, I don't), she'd probably call that "portent." But even with her eccentricities, that's too interesting a concept to be true for anything in this town.

"How much for this?" Margo asked the cashier, holding up a postcard from where she stood near the door to the gift shop. GREETINGS FROM AVALON, the card said on the front, in retro-looking typography that was either intentionally faded or had become so from being placed on display for so long in the sun.

The cashier, a sandy-haired young man in his early twenties, looked up and eyed it.

"A dollar," he finally said, unconvincingly.

Margo raised a brow. "Did you just make that up?"

"Two dollars," he replied, and she sighed.

"Fine." She walked to the counter, searching in her purse for a pen. "Can I send it from here, too?"

"Have to buy a stamp."

Great. "And how much is a stamp?"

"Free," the cashier said, "but the postcard's three now. Supply and demand."

Exasperating.

"Fine." Margo scribbled three words on the postcard ('You win, dick') and addressed it to the editorial office. "Here," she said, sliding it across the counter to the cashier. "How long will it take to get there?"

"I'll send it out with the pony this afternoon," the cashier said, and Margo grimaced.

"Do you know what's open?" she asked, gesturing outside. "Somewhere that wouldn't be crowded with tourists, I mean."

"The place you're in," the cashier said.

Margo briefly entertained the idea of strangling him. "Is everyone in Avalon this difficult?"

"Some even more so," the cashier replied, unfazed. "I take it you haven't met Alec yet."

"Let me guess—he's even less helpful than you?"

"No, definitely more helpful," the cashier said, "but sometimes that isn't such a good thing."

"It is when you want to send a postcard," Margo informed him.

The cashier shrugged. "Can't have everything."

She supposed not.

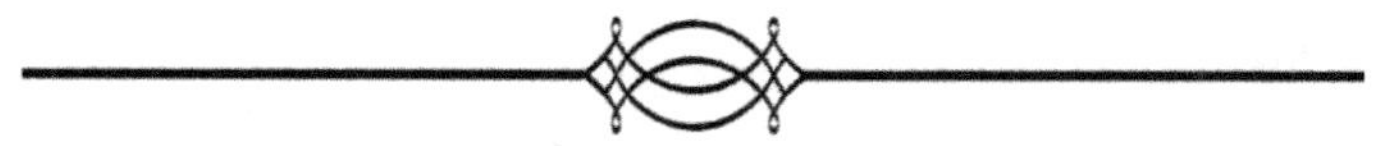

"You have a note," exclaimed Cora when Margo returned. "It's from Sadie. She stopped by looking for you."

"Oh?" Margo asked, bracing herself. She was about to ask how Sadie had known where she was staying, but then figured it probably wasn't hard to find out. It wasn't like there were too many other new people wandering around the island, and the Sea Breeze Inn was the most likely option. "Any idea what she wanted?"

"Read it and find out," Cora suggested, holding the envelope out for her.

Margo accepted, unfolding the letter inside. The letterhead was branded with a swirling, scripted S, which was surprising only in that it didn't include a full monogram, like the kind Margo would have expected to see on a Victorian hand towel.

"What does it say?" Cora asked, and Margo looked down.

Dearest Margo,

Please join us at the casino this evening. Henry tells me you've been wandering around aimlessly for days (Margo, figuring Henry was the recalcitrant cashier, sighed internally. For days? That was a bit of an overstatement.) *and I would be remiss if I didn't put a stop to it immediately. I simply won't take no for an answer. We'll see you this evening at eight.*

Sincerely, Sadie

P.S. if you don't have a gown, I'm sure Cora will lend you one.

"A gown?" Margo said aloud.

"Oh, did she ask you to the casino?" Cora asked, delighted. "That's a treat, you know."

Margo disagreed, but didn't particularly want to say so. "I didn't realize it would be so… formal," she said instead, grimacing down at the note. "I really only brought summer clothes and business things."

"Well, I do have some extras," Cora said, ripe with optimism. "Maybe it'll be fun!"

"Do you want to come?" Margo asked her, and Cora's cheeks flushed.

"Oh, I would, but… I don't know," she demurred. "I don't think Alec cares much for me."

"Who *is* this 'Alec' person?" Margo asked, frowning. "People seem awfully concerned with him around here."

"Hard not to be," Cora said, gesturing for Margo to follow her down the hall. "I'm sure I've got something," she said, and glanced over her shoulder, scrutinizing Margo from afar. "Might need to be taken in a bit, though," she mused, and sighed, shaking her head. "You city girls are always too thin."

June 22

Cora's collection of dresses is something that would make most of my friends weep with envy, even if I find it difficult to be too enthused about throwing dice at a table with a pack of divorcées. Though, if I'm going to do it at all, I might as well do it in a vintage gown. A beautiful, intricately beaded vintage gown. One that would cost a fortune if I bought it at Bergdorf's. I'm not sure why Cora has such a vast collection; she says she's just had them lying around for ages, but that seems crazy. Maybe Cora's just got a good eye?

Gambling aside, a long bath and a little introspection helps; now that I've come to terms with the fact that I may as well make the best of a repulsive situation, I'm not <u>not</u> looking forward to the night. I figure I may get a little inside information about Avalon, the divorcées, the casino… it might help set the scene for my article, or perhaps become something more interesting, a la Midnight in the Garden of Good and Evil (not *that I expect anyone to be murdered, although it would be a nice change of pace). I Googled this Alec person (whoever that is) since people seem to keep talking about him, but I couldn't find anything. Maybe that mystery will be solved tonight, too.*

And then after that… I don't know. I guess I'll just have sit back and see how the rest of the summer goes, assuming I don't waste away from boredom.

"Excellent," Sadie said approvingly, which Margo supposed was a comment on her dress, or possibly her general appearance. "Shall we, then?"

Margo had been prepared to trudge her way up to the hill upon which the casino was nestled, but it seemed the divorcées had another idea. They piled into a golf cart, which at first seemed a laughable method to get anywhere in formal wear, but it hadn't escaped Margo's attention that the roads were much too narrow for cars. Despite the mismatch of aesthetics, the golf cart was conceptually the best way to get around.

Faith was an excellent driver, albeit a bit of a speed demon, and before long they were pulling up to the horseshoe outside the casino, where (in a moment Margo found more than comical) Faith tossed the keys to a waiting attendant. Margo paused outside, taking in the casino's appearance; the exterior was made of Carrara marble—if not the real thing, then certainly something like it—and gleamed white against the setting sun, illuminated across the face of it. As far as she could tell, it was the newest building on the island.

"I can't believe it's still light out," Margo remarked, shading her eyes as she took in the sheen of the casino. It was rounded and almost temple-like, with pillars and arches that surrounded the outside. "Feels too early for debauchery."

"Well, it's the solstice," Amelia said. "Longest day of the year."

"Meaning the shortest night," Sadie pointedly remarked, impatient to get on with it.

"It's Midsummer, isn't it?" Margo mused, stepping toward the grand white arches. "I'd nearly forgotten. I always thought Midsummer was a bit of a fanciful time."

"The pagan rituals, you mean?" Sadie asked, glancing doubtfully at her.

"Well, just the concept of renewal in general," Margo said. "You know, life and fertility and whatnot. They say everything in nature has extra power around the time of any solstice," she said, surprised to find her mother's voice returning to her in such an odd moment.

"But you don't believe in all that nonsense, of course," Faith said, sounding a bit shocked.

"Oh, well, no," Margo replied quickly. The conversation halted as the four of them made their way through the lobby, a circular vestibule lined with paintings in austere bronze frames.

Here the locals gathered aplenty; even before they entered the casino itself, Margo could spot the crowds around the blackjack tables from afar. She strode forward to enter alongside Faith and Amelia when Sadie reached out, pausing her.

"Better you don't go on about any rituals," Sadie advised. "Alec won't like it."

"I wasn't—" Margo stopped short, glancing down at Sadie's hand on her arm. "Fine," she conceded, recognizing with a lurch of familiarity that she must have stepped over the invisible line separating 'different' from 'weird.' (Thanks again, Mom, Margo thought irritably.) "I didn't mean to upset you."

Sadie released her.

"You didn't," she said. "I'm just advising you. Shall we?"

Amelia frowned in curiosity at the delay while Faith doubled back, taking Margo's arm.

"Tonight's going to be fun," Faith murmured to her. Reassurance, Margo assumed.

"Of course," Margo said. Sadie, by then, had already taken the lead.

They passed into the casino's main room, their pretty gowns immediately swathed in cigarette smoke as their ears were doused with shouts from the craps table. It was the sort of scene that would have repulsed Margo if it had been anywhere in New York, but here, there was something comforting about finally seeing the familiar faces that drew her in. Henry, the cashier from the gift shop, was vigorously concentrating on a round of blackjack. She recognized the barista from the coffeeshop, and some of the people she'd seen at the beach. This was to be an evening spent with locals, and Margo, like all New York transplants, had been lacking a sense of place for many years. Perhaps it was silly, but it was nice to feel like part of the tapestry instead of always being the person watching from the outside.

That, and she'd already tired of all the books on her Kindle.

"Maybe it will be fun," Margo said to herself, warming up to the idea of giving it a try.

I don't know why I brought up Midsummer. Had I somehow forgotten what kind of place I was in? I shouldn't have been surprised to discover they found the whole thing stupid; I certainly found it stupid whenever my mother said the same thing, and I'm not even particularly small-minded. I probably should have guessed the divorcées would all be Episcopalians or something, so of course they'd find it more vulgar than whimsical. They're all about twenty years older than me, and probably set in their ways. I don't know why I said it.

I don't know why I did what I did next, either.

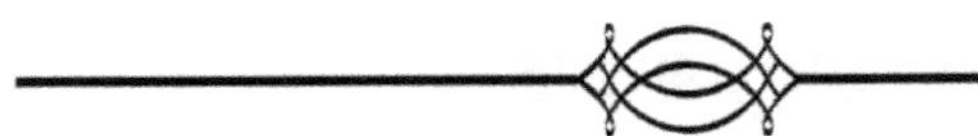

Craps was a hugely complicated dice game, or so Margo had always thought (it looked easy from afar, sure, but the tables themselves were cluttered with rules and nonsense), but it was clearly Sadie's favorite. She, Amelia, and Faith all made a beeline right for the craps tables, where it was apparent at once that they were regulars, with many of the others around the table shifting over to permit them places to play.

For a couple of rounds, Margo insisted on merely watching, sipping her martini in mild disinterest; she'd never understood what people got so riled up about, but eventually Amelia pulled her in, whispering instructions in her ear.

"You're betting on the outcome of the dice," Amelia explained, gesturing. "Of course, the bet itself can be somewhat more complicated—"

"Here," Sadie said loudly, reaching over to smack the dice into Margo's hand. "Throw 'em."

"Wh-" Margo almost choked on her swallow of gin. "But wait, I—"

"Place a bet first," Faith told her, nudging some chips into her hand. "Bad form to bet late."

"Sure," Margo permitted dizzily, "but—"

"Come point is eight," Sadie said in a perfunctory tone.

"But I—"

"Place the bet on the hard eight," Faith advised, pointing. "The whole table did. More fun that way."

Margo downed the rest of her drink, setting it down on the table ledge. "But is that—"

"Means a four and a four," Amelia said.

"But—"

"Throw," they commanded in unison.

Margo glanced around the table, about to protest further, only there was something hugely engaging about the way everyone was waiting for her to toss the dice. It was as if they were something of a community now, prepared to live and die together in their oddly fancy get-ups, and she found herself compelled to sigh and relent, finally permitting the roll.

It was bizarrely silent (as if the world had stopped) when she threw, and time itself seemed liquid, only to crash with some insistence once the dice hit the table. The first die landed on a four, and the table held its breath; the second, though, wobbled slightly, and Margo, reminded suddenly of a college game of flip-cup in which she'd glugged her beer too slowly, found herself rather unwilling to fail.

She twisted a finger out of sight; just one. The die *wanted* to come up four, she knew. Everyone at the table had compelled it, hadn't they? All she had to do was guide it, and that was easy enough. Someone pressed a new martini glass into her hand and she accepted, hiding her furtive motion from the table.

The moment the second set of four little dots appeared, the room burst into raucous applause. Beside Margo, Faith let out a quiet, girlish squeal, and Amelia gasped in delight, assuring her in a rapid-fire pronunciation of rambles that Margo had a magic touch.

"Oh, I'm sure it's just beginner's luck," Margo managed weakly, once Sadie had stopped furiously kissing her cheek.

Only it hadn't been luck at all.

I don't know why I did it. I almost never use my magic at all, because why would I? I always wanted to be a journalist more than I ever wanted to be a witch, and more than that, I've always wanted to be normal, urban. Generally not at all like the village loon I shared a house with for eighteen years.

Still, it's not like Mom would have let me get away with never learning how to do <u>some</u> *things. I suppose I was just having fun (or being nervous, which in my experience is sort of like having fun), and I didn't think it would hurt. I didn't think it would cause some sort of ripple in the universe, anyway, because again, why would it? I assumed it was a victimless crime, if you don't count the casino itself—and who does?*

Aside from the casino.

"Miss," came a voice behind her. "You have to go."

The table had won two more rounds by then. Hardly enough for anyone to be suspicious, and yet here he was, a tall man in a black suit and a badge marked Security.

"Why?" Margo insisted. The drinks that she and the divorcées had consumed thus far in the evening appeared to have gone to her head already, which was laughable, but she blamed the altitude (and, more quietly, her evening of popularity at the tables). "I haven't done anything."

"You have to come with me," the security guard insisted.

"She doesn't *have* to do anything," Sadie told him firmly, but the security guard gave her a stern look.

"Alec wants to talk to her," he said.

"Well," Margo scoffed, spurred on by Sadie's civil disobedience, "then tell Alec he can just go ahead and suck my lady ba-"

"You should go," Sadie told her abruptly. "We'll be here."

"What? But—"

"Just smile and nod," Faith suggested. "It'll get you out of there faster."

"But I wasn't—"

"Come on," the security guard said, nudging her gruffly toward the lobby.

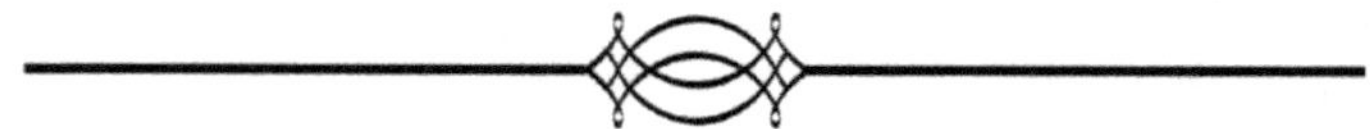

It seemed slightly outrageous to Margo that she should be marched up to some ornate, mahogany-filled office without so much as a word to why, like being summoned to the principal's office for a scolding. What had she really done, or more relevantly, how could anyone have known what she'd really done? It certainly couldn't be proven.

"You've got some nerve," she said hotly, and the man behind the desk looked up, staring at her.

No, not staring.

Glowering.

"Who are you?" he asked.

"I could say the same to you," she retorted.

He was younger than she thought he'd be, perhaps in his early thirties. He had one of those Greco-Italian-Hispanic looks to him, with wavy dark hair that swept back from his forehead and skin that looked like it had ripened on the vine. The kind of handsome that would be warm to the touch, like the sun itself, only his eyes were a little cold; brown, but hardly soft. He set his jaw and glared at her.

"You better not have done what I think you did," he said.

"Okay," Margo agreed. "I didn't."

His mouth tightened for a second.

"I don't permit witches at my casino," he said, and briefly, Margo's chest froze.

That can't have been what he meant. She'd spent a lifetime of being odd or weird or the daughter of a half-batty lesbian spinster, but nobody had ever called her *that*.

People never knew. They never even guessed.

"Who said I'm a witch?" she countered, forcing nonchalance.

"Please." He braced his forearms on the desk, irritated. "You think I don't know what comes in and out of this building? You're a witch. That's a given. My question is why you'd be stupid enough to use magic on the eve of the summer solstice. Did someone send you?" he asked. "Or are you just not a very good witch?"

Margo gaped at him, floundering.

"I beg your pardon?"

"Who sent you?"

"I… what? Nobody *sent* me, and I'm not a—"

"Do you really have no idea what you might have just done?" he cut in, and in her frustration, Margo averted her gaze to scrutinize the room. It was extremely clean, and aside from the nameplate on his desk that read Alexios Del Mar, it could have belonged to anyone. Or to no one.

"Are you listening?" he snapped.

"What?" Margo said.

Alec pressed his fingers to the bridge of his nose.

"You need to leave," he said. "Immediately."

"Fine." She bristled. "This place isn't that great, anyway. I was already getting bored."

"No, not—" He growled. "Not the casino. You need to leave. You need to get out of Avalon."

"Believe me, I'd be more than happy to—"

"Then go."

"I *can't*, obviously—"

"You can and you will. Now."

Okay, that was enough from him. "Just who do you think you are, asshole?" Margo demanded.

"It doesn't matter who I am," Alec replied. "What matters is that you used magic in this place, of all places, on *this night*, of all nights. Don't you know anything?"

Suddenly, Margo no longer cared how handsome she was. Rather than picturing his head on her pillow, she imagined smothering him with it.

"You," she said, brandishing a tipsy finger at him, "don't get to tell me what to do."

"No, I don't," he agreed, with what she considered a nasty glare. "But I can certainly advise it. You know nothing about this island or its inhabitants." He rose to his feet, which meant Margo gleaned the unfortunate knowledge that he was noticeably tall and street-style slender—something she would define as linear rather than simply lean. "Do not use magic here again. Certainly not until we know for sure what you've done."

"What I've done?" Margo demanded, irritated. "I've done nothing! And I'm not a witch, either," she added, lifting her chin. "I'm a journalist."

He turned, glaring at her again. "They're not mutually exclusive," he said obnoxiously. "Who are you?"

"Like I'd tell you," she scoffed. "Are we done here?"

"No, we aren't," he said crisply. "For one thing—"

"You can keep talking if you want to," she assured him, purposefully interrupting. For one thing, he'd done it to her first, and for another, if there was one thing she knew about men like him (and she knew many things about them), it was that they hated to be interrupted. "I, on the other hand, am leaving."

Alec, circumventing her exit, placed himself directly in her path. "The witches I know would never be so disrespectful," he said accusingly. "Or so careless."

"Then I advise you to meet more witches," Margo shot back. "What are _you_, anyway? Obviously you're not a witch," she noted with a scowl. "Are you fae or something?"

His eyes narrowed. "You would have no idea what I am even if I were to explain it to you. You have no idea what anyone is, for that matter. And I hope for your sake you don't find out."

For a second, Margo was silent, consumed by her own frustration and what it would feel like to slap Alexios Del Mar across his incredibly shapely mouth.

"I'm leaving," she informed him.

"Good," he replied.

And then, as promised, she left, and he didn't follow.

June 23

I woke up hungover, unsurprisingly. I didn't think I was out too long, but I suppose it's been generally proven that time moves faster in casinos. The darkness helps to further the vampire lifestyle, or so my mother would say. In reality they just don't have clocks.

Speaking of vampires (and other impossible things), I can't believe the nerve of that Alec. He's exactly the sort of person I'd run into in New York, but usually he'd be an editor or a CEO or the guy in front of me at Starbucks or something. What right does a casino owner have to drag me away and accuse me of witchcraft?? I'm half-convinced I dreamt it.

Maybe <u>he's</u> the real story here, not the mansions. I Googled him again today (easier now that I have more than simply 'Alec' to go on) and still didn't find much of anything, aside from development permits that must have been his father's or grandfather's. He certainly isn't old enough to have built the casino way back then. Maybe there's an organized crime aspect involved? He definitely has thugs, and 'Entire Island Run by Corrupt Casino Owner' doesn't seem nearly as far-fetched now, having met him. People definitely seem afraid of him, too.

Though, now that I think about it, they don't seem nearly as afraid of him as he seems of them.

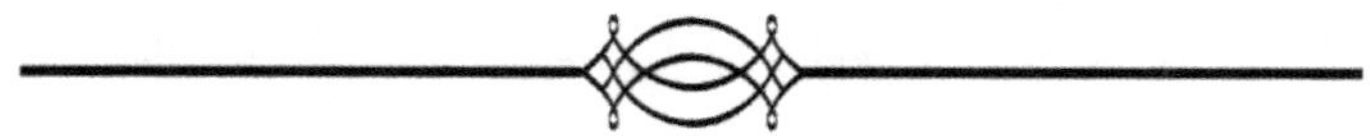

Margo was just about to head to one of the diners on Main Street when she nearly collided with someone just outside the hotel.

"Oh, I'm so sor- oh," she exhaled, looking up with annoyance. "It's you."

"Yes, though I believe we were not introduced. Alec Del Mar," said the man from the night before. He was wearing a navy suit (despite it being well over ninety degrees) and a pair of dark sunglasses. "And evidently you're Margo West, though that sounds like a nom de plume if I've ever heard one."

"Creepy," Margo muttered to herself, though it was loud enough for him to hear.

"Not that hard to figure out," he corrected. "Not hard to track down, either."

Margo bristled. "So now you're stalking me?"

"I'm doing you a favor," Alec said, just shy of an impatient snap. "I had to make sure nothing happened."

"Yes, well, I'm sure that's *very* gallant of you, but I don't need you t-"

"Not to you," Alec corrected stiffly. "To… to anyone. Have you seen Cora today?"

"No," Margo said, now equally irritated. "But I'm sure she's at the front desk if you want to talk to her."

"What about Sadie? Or Faith, or Amelia?"

"If you must know, I've been working in my room until just now," Margo informed him, "and I haven't eaten anything but a bagel all day, so if you could just *move aside*—"

"Cruise ship hasn't left yet," Alec noted with obvious displeasure, glancing over his shoulder to where the boat remained docked in the distance. "It's late."

"I'm sure it doesn't have to leave so early," Margo said, exasperated. "It'll be light out until almost nine. Now, if we're done here—"

"How much do you understand about the solstice? Midsummer. Do you know much about it?"

"I—" Margo grimaced. "Is this some kind of trick?"

"I have bigger things to worry about than tricking you," Alec replied impatiently. "I'm trying to get a sense of whether or not you know what you've caused, or at least might have caused. I haven't seen anything yet," he added, frowning at the cruise ship again, "but that doesn't mean—"

"What exactly are you so afraid of?" Margo demanded, drawing his attention unwillingly back to her. "It's not like I showed up here on my broomstick trying to collect eyeballs and drain people of their blood. I don't even *know* any other witches—"

"Let me stop you there. I have no problem with witches," Alec informed her, apparently insulted by her implication. "In fact, if everything *does* go south, one would be very useful to have around, which is entirely beside the point. I'm trying to explain to you what's wrong, and seeing as you clearly have no understanding what you've done—"

"Don't patronize me," Margo snapped.

He glared at her. "Wonderful. And now, since you're *refusing* to listen—"

"What exactly is your point?" She aimed for caustic and arrived somewhere near facetious, which was more than enough to agitate them both. "Let me guess, was there some sort of ancient magic hidden beneath the casino that I somehow managed to wake and now the whole world's going to hell?"

"It's not beneath the casino," Alec said, "it *is* the casino."

"And furthermore—Wait, what?" Margo asked, cutting herself off and blinking at him. "What did you just say?"

"I warned you that nobody here was what you thought they were," he reminded her briskly. "And believe me, it took quite a lot of work to make sure that was the case. Power like that, like what they are, it lives and dies, you know, just like anything else. It lived, and then it died. I killed it. But every solstice, there's always a chance that dead things can—"

He grimaced, and trailed off. "Look, suffice it to say this: magic that big requires sacrifice," he eventually said, "which is what the casino is for. Really, the more ancient stuff isn't too specific. Money sacrificed is as good as blood, at least where it comes to keeping things running smoothly. But if you woke them up—"

"Who?" Margo asked. "Woke who up?"

"Them," Alec said. "All of them."

"Who is *them*?" Margo demanded.

Alec fidgeted, glancing over his shoulder again. "Don't be out at night," he advised unhelpfully. "At least until we know for sure. Do you understand me?"

"I thought you wanted me to leave."

"I do," he said, not very politely. "But seeing as you didn't, it's a little late for that."

He was being maddeningly cryptic. Margo had never had any patience for cryptic men.

"I have to go," she said, shoving past him.

"Margo," he called after her. "Be back before the sun goes down, and be sure to lock your—"

"If you say so," she yelled back, not bothering to turn over her shoulder.

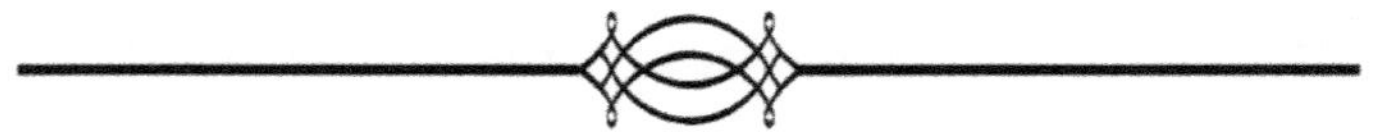

I hate to admit that Alec's fear is a bit infectious. Seeing as I <u>am</u>, in fact, a witch, I can't discount the possibility that he's telling the truth, and he does seem genuinely worried. But what exactly am I supposed to be afraid of? I've never been one to enjoy tales of things going bump in the night, and even if I did, it's not like I'm totally defenseless. I don't use magic often, but it at least protects me when I need it to. Mom always said it was like a muscle, or maybe a tendon. I may not always know the best way to pick something up, but my arm will still bend if I tell it to. I'm not exactly vulnerable.

Still, I'll probably lock my door before I go to sleep.

Better safe than sorry.

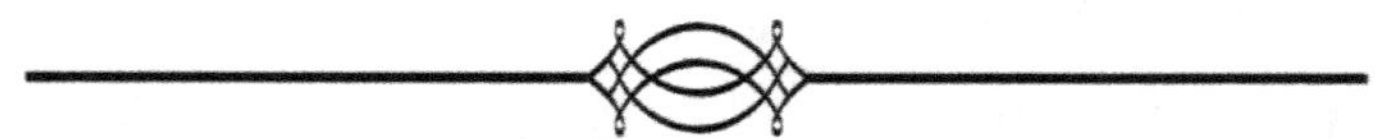

Margo woke with a start to a hand placed tightly over her mouth.

"Quiet," Alec mouthed, holding a finger to his lips, and she bolted upright, struggling.

"How did you get in here?" she hissed, pulling the sheets around her. Stalking was one thing, breaking and entering another. "What the hell are you trying t-"

"The cruise ship," Alec said, his voice low as he looked out from her hotel room's window. "Something's wrong. You should get somewhere safe."

"I *was* somewhere safe," she growled at him, gesturing to the door. "It was locked! And then you had to go and—"

She blinked.

The door was still locked.

"But if you're not a witch…" She frowned. "What are you, then?"

"Not likely to fight it for long," he muttered uneasily, and turned. "We should go," he said, beckoning for her to follow. "Come with me. My house will be safer than here."

"What? *No*," Margo seethed. "You can't just… just *burst* in here and—"

"I don't particularly want to do this, either," Alec said with a glare, "but things being what they are, I'm going to need you to listen to me. You have to get out of here, Margo, and quickly. If you come with me—"

"I don't even know you!" she snapped, and he held his finger to his lips again, shushing her.

"You have to calm down—you have to be *quiet*—"

"Or else what?" Margo demanded, though she didn't wait for the answer. Instead she stumbled to her feet, shoved her toes into a pair of flip-flops, and headed straight for the door, throwing it open. "CORA, HELP!"

"Are you insane?" Alec demanded, stumbling after Margo until she paused at the elevator, banging on the down button. "Listen to me! You need to sit still, you can't make a sound, not until I know for sure what's going on—"

Margo gave up on the elevator and ran for the stairs, shoving the door open and letting it smack in Alec's face as she descended the steps.

"Margo, for fuck's sake, would you just listen to me—"

She pulled the door shut behind her, locking it, and then made her way to the emergency exit at the back of the hotel, intent on slipping him. What sort of maniac came in babbling about things—about *nothing*—and then tried to abduct her? She shivered slightly (the island nights were far cooler than the days) and folded her arms over her chest before making her way down the path outside the hotel, catching sight of a familiar form down by the water.

"Sadie," she called, waving a hand, and Sadie straightened from where she'd been bent over something in the water. "Sadie, I need your help, where's—"

Margo broke off, gasping, as about three feet from where Sadie stood, Faith's bottle-blonde hair rose up from the water, her blue eyes suddenly a dark, viscous red. Faith smiled, something gruesome and crimson dribbling down her chin, and beside her, Amelia rose to her feet, holding what looked like a dangled intestine in her right hand.

"Amelia," Margo gasped, taking a step back. "Faith—"

Sadie looked up from what Margo could now see had been a body floating in the ocean, the last in a scarlet-tinged trail of floating shapes that led from the coast to the cruise ship, which had crashed against the rocks. It was surreal and almost childlike, as if someone had taken a bath toy and shoved it into the side of the island until the entire bough had collapsed.

"Hello, Margo," Sadie said.

At the sound of her voice, Margo's anxieties instantly eased, met instead with a peaceful serenity. Sadie would fix it, she thought. Sadie would fix everything. Margo stepped forward with one foot, and then another, each one coaxed further by the gentle humming from Sadie's lips. Relief, Sadie's smile promised. Sweet, blessed relief.

Margo reached out, fingertips straining. Nearly there now—

"Jesus, I told you!" Alec growled in her ear, grabbing Margo around the waist and yanking her back until she gasped, jarred back to consciousness by the sound of him panting in her ear. "They're sirens, Margo, don't listen to them—"

He clapped his hands over her ears, securing his palms firmly in place, and dragged her away as Sadie reached for her, still cooing a low, mournful melody from the vaults of her bloodied teeth. Margo shut her eyes, unsure if she were actually screaming aloud or if that was only in her head, until she and Alec turned the corner behind the hotel, successfully out of sight.

Alec removed his hands from her ears and dropped to the ground, tugging her down with him to hide behind a low cement barrier beside the Sea Breeze.

"Well, you did it," Alec muttered when they'd caught their breaths. "You woke it up."

"Woke *what* up?" Margo asked, and though she still wanted very badly to slap him, she realized she feared the answer even before he said it.

"Everything," he said grimly, and then turned away, pulling her along in his wake.

PART II: HEAT WAVE

June 23
Avalon, California

There's nothing quite like being woken up in the middle of the night by a handsome, consummately grouchy man insisting my life is in terrible danger. I say there's nothing like it because literally, there isn't—certainly nothing I can remember experiencing, and my mother had plenty of her own unpleasant quirks.

Still, this isn't Mom suggesting I howl at the moon with her when I'm supposed to be doing homework or insisting I help with some naked ritual bath that our neighbors will definitely see. This is the very unique sensation of discovering that a group of pastel-colored divorcées is actually some sort of bloodthirsty coven of sirens, for which I can say there's no conceivable preparation. I wish I could say that's the worst of it, but given how nervous Alec looked when he pulled me away from Sadie, I don't think it is.

I hate to say it, but I'm starting to think I should have listened when he told me to get out.

"Should we really be out in the middle of the street?" Margo asked, panting slightly as Alec sprint-walked her between two yellowing buildings to emerge onto an eerily vacant stretch of Main Street. "I mean, if there's other monsters around—"

"Not if," Alec corrected unhelpfully, not looking at her.

"*Fine*," Margo groaned, following again as Alec headed for one of the darkened jewelry stores, reaching into the pocket of his trousers. "*Considering* there are other monsters around—"

"Most of them won't be here," Alec said, fumbling through at least three dozen keys that varied in size, color, and metal before arriving at a sturdy cast-iron shape. "Creatures, that is. Not monsters. Well, maybe monsters. But either way, the island attracts them from the sea," he explained, struggling with the old latch before shoving his shoulder directly into the door, forcing it open. "Even if it's affecting everyone on the island, most of them will be heading for water," he concluded, beckoning for Margo to follow him inside. "In the meantime, we'll need a few things."

"Such as?" Margo asked, dazed, as Alec made straight for a vault she might have assumed (prior to that moment) was purely for decoration. It looked like one of those old-timey safes designed to keep robbers out of banks (usually without success, according to her limited experience with Westerns) only this one seemed to have an actual function, if Alec's urgency to open it was any indication. "And when you say *creatures*—"

"Hold this," he interrupted, having wrenched the safe open by then and smacked something that looked like quiver of arrows into her hand. "Be careful, though," he warned, sparing a narrowed glance at her before stringing an elaborate longbow around his shoulders, the wood strapped snugly to his back. "They're poisoned."

"They're—what?!" Margo demanded, nearly dropping the quiver on the floor. "What do you mean they're poisoned?"

"They're dipped in the blood of a hydra," Alec said matter-of-factly, "so watch your fingers. Also this," he added, digging around in the vault and removing what looked like a U-shaped harp, nudging it just enough to release a slightly clumsy (but surprisingly lovely) chord before depositing it onto Margo's tentatively outstretched arms. "We'll need this."

"Why," Margo said sarcastically, "to play music more beautiful than siren song?"

"Yes," Alec said.

Then he pulled a sword free from the vault, inspecting the edge before giving it a testing swing.

"Wait—" Margo groaned. "Alec, I was joking!"

"Hm?" he said, glancing at her. The sword had a little sickle-edged protrusion on the bottom, making it… not exactly Excalibur, to say the least. It was something that could do a lot more damage than that, though it wasn't nearly so sleek.

"Oh, right, well. It's not a joke. Hydra blood," Alec clarified, aiming the sword at the quiver of arrows, "comes courtesy of Heracles. No hydras here, thankfully, though regenerating water snakes in general are sort of common. You didn't meet Ed, did you? Doesn't matter, it could be worse. The lyre, as you pointed out, plays music more compelling than Sadie's song," he continued, "or even Faith's, who's really much more tempting. Can you play the lyre?" he asked neutrally, to which Margo slowly shook her head, dumbfounded. "Well, fine, give me that, then, and you take this—"

"I can't just *take that*," Margo said, gaping at him as he offered her the sword in his hand. "What the hell am I supposed to do with a sword?"

He waved it pointedly, slicing it again through the air for show, and she felt the blood drain from her face.

"You… you want me to kill them?" she realized hoarsely.

"What? No," Alec scoffed. "Don't be ridiculous. They won't die."

"I—*what?*" Margo demanded. "Then what—*how*—?"

"They're not going to die," Alec said again, slower. "They *don't* die. They're the children of gods," he added with an air of impatience. "Do you really think you can just bring them down with a mortal blade?"

Margo inhaled deeply, about to explode with frustration (*OF COURSE I thought that, seeing that in my experience a stab wound is a stab wound, YOU CROTCHETY PRICK*) when there was a loud sound of shattering glass from somewhere nearby. Margo immediately jumped, clutching the quiver of arrows as a shield, and Alec sighed, shaking his head.

"Look, I can explain this to you later," he said, "but seeing as you're very much mortal, you need something to defend yourself. You're the only thing on this island that won't regenerate in the morning if something happens to you."

She wondered for a moment if he was concerned for her safety; upon a second glance, though, she had the distinct feeling he was simply a glorified babysitter, currently tasked with more than he was capable of handling.

"Well, I can't use that bow," Margo said, grimacing. "I doubt I can lift that sword, and I certainly can't play the fucking *lyre*, so—"

"Ah," Alec said, and held up a finger for pause. "Right, well, hang on—"

He reached under the counter, feeling blindly for something and then nodding as his fingers closed around it.

"Here," he said, taking hold of it and offering it to her.

Margo looked down, choking slightly.

"A gun?" she managed.

"You can pull a trigger, can't you? I assume your dexterity is at least that good. Unless I'm wrong about that, too," he added drily, "seeing as you seem to feel you know best."

Just as he said it, something slammed against the glass of the jewelry store window and Margo let out a shriek, snatching the gun from Alec's hand in the same moment he shoved her behind him. It was an impossibly quick series of motions; he tossed the sword aside, took the quiver from her, drew an arrow, and strung the bow in less than a blink of an eye, aiming for the window. In response, the red-eyed nightmare horse that had appeared there made a snort of disdain, trotting off in the opposite direction.

Alec nodded firmly, slowly lowering the bow, and turned to look at Margo, whose finger was shaking around the trigger.

"Well," he exhaled, crouching down to pick up the sword again, "as I said, my house would be safer. For now," he assured her. "Sun'll be up in a couple of hours, and then you can go back to your hotel."

"Back?" Margo echoed hoarsely.

"If you want," Alec said, shrugging. "It'll only last the night, most likely, so. You coming?"

He headed for the door and Margo let out a muted yelp, hurrying after him.

"I'll take that as a yes," Alec muttered under his breath, restringing the bow and aiming it into the night.

I didn't want to follow him. I certainly didn't want to rely on him. Not for a second have I enjoyed being a damsel in distress, but, seeing as I have no hidden archery talents or any pressing desire to get eaten by something that lives on this island, I figured it was probably safest to do as I was told.

That, of course, and I have to admit… I was curious. What's a casino owner doing with arrows dipped in hydra blood?

Was he completely insane, or was I?

"So," Margo murmured as they paused, waiting for a group of tiny goblin-looking creatures to stumble down the street, "is this the gun Theseus used to kill Medusa or something?"

"Hm? No," Alec said, peering around the side of the building. "That's what the sword is. Theseus didn't have a gun."

"I—" Margo stifled a groan. "I was, once again, joking."

"Not really the time," Alec informed her, gruffly signaling for her to follow him into the street. "I'm sure you can joke plenty once you've gotten off the island tomorrow."

"Well, it's either make jokes or worry about dying," Margo muttered under her breath, slipping after him from the shadows.

"Considering one's much more useful to me," Alec said, "you might want to reconsider your choice."

"What are you so nervous about?" Margo demanded. "Don't you have some sort of powers? You said you killed the magic here."

He slid her a look of agitation. "Yes, well, that was something of a borrowed power. The gods put me here in order to keep an eye on their more… *recalcitrant* offspring, shall we say. Divine procreation can be something of a mixed bag," he finished, pivoting to aim the arrow at the flicker of motion between two buildings.

"So you really *are* a glorified babysitter," Margo realized once the danger had passed, wanting to laugh. "Is that it?"

"I'm a guardian appointed by the gods," Alec corrected.

"Yes," Margo agreed, "to watch their children, Alec. Literally, a live-in nanny."

Alec let out a frustrated scoff, lowering his bow and rounding on her. "You do realize *you're* the reason all of this is even happening, don't you?" he snarled. "Because of you, the gods are going to be furious with *me*. The best I can hope for is that I can reset the containment spell during the fall equinox, which is in *three months*—"

"Well, that's a fairly flawed system, isn't it?" Margo countered, stiffening. "If all I had to do was use one *tiny* bit of magic and now the whole island's gone mad, it seems like your *actual* problem is a faulty fucking spell—"

"See, this is the problem with modern witches," Alec muttered, to which Margo replied with a scoff. "None of you are taught any etiquette anymore. There's no codified understanding of behavior. You just run around casting spells as you please, not bothering to comprehend that on some nights it's really better if you just *stay home*."

The last part was said with a growl, which Margo firmly didn't appreciate. "You," she informed him, "are a patronizing asshole. As far as I can tell, you're the one who fucked this up," she added, watching his eyes narrow. "If your job is to watch this island, then *you* failed, not me. The fact that you can't accept any blame is completely not my probl-"

"Margo," Alec said.

"No, don't interrupt me!" she snapped. "You had your turn! You're the one who woke me up in the middle of the night with creepily unhelpful warnings! And *you're* the one permitting people to come here, aren't you? So it's hardly my fault if you failed to put an 'FYI, magic might make this entire island susceptible to monsters' sign in the casino window—"

"Margo," Alec said testily, "can this wait? Because—"

"Why? Because your opinion matters and mine doesn't?" Margo demanded. "Because I have to listen to you, but for *some reason*, you don't have to listen to me? I'm sure you're used to getting your way, Alec," she scoffed, "but considering that hasn't worked out so well for you so far, I think you're going to have to expand your horizons for fifteen goddamn minutes and—"

"Margo," Alec half-shouted, "stop talking and *turn around*!"

She spun, finding herself face to face with a translucent-skinned woman who dripped with water from head to toe. Her eyes were a haunted, pupil-less blue, she was naked, bony and scarred, and something was wrong; the closer the woman got, the more firmly Alec remained frozen, unmoving, even as his fingers wrapped tightly around the bow. The woman smiled, beginning to let her hips sway in a tender, sensual dance, and it was the moment her hand rose that Margo's own arm shot out, forcefully shoving Alec backwards.

She hadn't expected it; out of her palm came a flash of light, as fleeting as a bolt of lighting. It was the same sort of magic Margo had accidentally used as a girl—powerful but unrestrained, uncontrolled— and in response, the woman let out a shriek, clawing at her eyes and fleeing in the opposite direction as Margo pivoted swiftly to face Alec.

"They call them demons, or rusalka," he was mumbling to himself, or to her, though his eyes were still vaguely unfocused. "A different version of a siren. Rusalka can leave the water—obviously, you saw her—"

"For fuck's sake, shut *up*," Margo growled, taking hold of his shoulders and giving him a hasty, jolting shake. "Are you with me?"

"You're a witch," Alec said, dragging his gaze up to hers. "But you don't really know how to use your magic, do you? Not all of it."

No, she didn't. She had never wanted to know how.

"My mother was an herbal witch," Margo said. "She made things grow." And also drove away any possible friends that either of them might have had. "My aunt, she was a divinist, but—" She, too, grew old alone. "Small things," Margo clarified, clearing her throat. "I can do small things. I can turn a die, as you know. I can make a garden flourish, and sometimes my tea tells me what the traffic is like, but—"

"No," Alec said. "You've got more than that."

She stared at him.

And stared.

She was a bit closer to him than she'd anticipated. At the moment, her fingers were still wrapped around his shoulders.

"You should stay," he said neutrally.

"Oh, *fuck* no," fell out of her mouth.

"Yes," he insisted, and she took a hasty step back, recovering from her moment of… whatever that had been. "Look, you saw," Alec said, gesturing to where the female ghost-demon had been. "Some of these creatures aren't going to be stopped. Certainly not easily, and I can't just let everything go to hell and risk angering the gods." He paused, grimacing, and then continued, "You may be right, Margo, that I'm unfairly blaming you, but truth be told—" He exhaled, reluctantly confessing, "I really don't know if I can do this alone."

She recalled, then, her initial sensation that he seemed more afraid of the island's inhabitants than they seemed of him. If he was right about what existed here, then he certainly had a reason to be concerned.

Could she really stay here, though? True, she had nothing to return to in New York outside of a messy breakup and an editor intent on wasting her time, but if the alternative was fighting monsters…

She sighed. Truth be told, sirens were still more easily handled than her insufferably petty ex.

"Besides," Alec added, carefully restringing his bow, "you *did* help cause the problem, you know. It would be the least you could do to help solve it."

Immediately, her nebulous sympathy for him snapped. "Are you serious? You can't just—"

"Do you really want to wait out here for another creature to come and find us?" he interrupted, waving a hand to the empty street. "Or would you rather be somewhere safe until morning?"

He was by far the worst thing on this island.

"Fine," she said through gritted teeth. "Lead the way, then."

June 24

I obviously hadn't put a lot of thought into where Alec might live, but it would have surprised me if I'd discovered it any time before last night. It's something of an oddly modern building, almost fortress-like, and it's near the casino, close to the center of the island rather than along the coast. Now that I know what I know, this makes sense: it's strong enough to keep things out, centrally located, and as far away as Alec can get from the danger lurking on the shores. I stood in his bedroom and looked out the window at the sunken cruise ship for about ten minutes before I eventually fell asleep, exhaustion finally taking over.

When I woke up, he was downstairs, drinking a cup of coffee. His house is a lot like his office in that it doesn't look like anyone lives here. There's no art or pictures on the walls, and aside from a massive skylight that takes up most of the ceiling, the house has barely any features of interest. It's the home of someone who could pack up and leave at any moment, only he isn't that kind of person at all. It makes me wonder what he's really like—and what he really <u>is</u>. Assuming he's telling the truth about gods and myths, then what exactly could he be?

I guess I'll just have to find out.

"If you're planning to leave," Alec said when Margo entered the kitchen, "then you should get on the earliest ferry. I'll be canceling them for the rest of the summer."

Margo hesitated, lingering in the doorway before pulling out a chair across from him. "What about the cruise ships?" she asked, and Alec shrugged.

"I can petition to close the port," he said, "but outside of that, there's nothing I *can* do, really. I'm not king of the island," he reminded her, lowering his newspaper (which, she realized, was the *Los Angeles Times*) to look at her. "I still have to follow California maritime law. I can't prevent all ships from coming here if they need to dock, nor can I just casually advise they stay away."

Margo stared at him, aghast. "But you have to do something!"

"Like what? Tell the governor there are creatures living here? Warn the Coast Guard? Nobody would believe me," Alec pointed out, "and even if they did, they'd be in a lot more danger coming here to find out— at least until the equinox."

"But," Margo began, and withered. "But what if Sadie and the others lure another ship here?"

"Nothing I can do about that," Alec said, pointedly fixing her with a glance. "*I'm* not a witch."

"That's hardly fair," Margo argued. "I don't know how to keep them from coming, either."

"Not yet," he corrected.

"Not *at all*," she countered.

"Well, forgive me for thinking the possibility that you might figure it out is a better alternative than sitting back and marginally skirting disaster," he said curtly, to which Margo gritted her teeth in frustration.

"You know, if you want me to stay, you could be a little nicer."

"I *don't* want you to stay," he replied, which was maddeningly counterproductive. "I find it would benefit my safety, and probably that of most of mankind. But as for my personal feelings, I could do without the constant need to appease your fragile sensibilities."

"My 'fragile sensibilities'?" Margo echoed. Unbelievable. "You're impossible," she informed him, rising to her feet and storming in the direction she assumed the front door had been. "Now would be the time for a normal person to be *nice*, you know, but *no*, you only know how to be *difficult*—"

"Me, difficult?" Alec called after her. "Interesting assessment, considering you're the one storming out. Where are you even going?"

"Back to my hotel," Margo shot over her shoulder. "You said they're only like that at night, right?"

"Yes, but you still need to make a decis-"

She didn't hear the end of the sentence. She'd already yanked the door open and disappeared through it, intent on being gone.

To be honest, I'm not totally sure what I was expecting from Alec. Obviously he'd made it pretty clear what sort of person (or person-resembling thing) he was, so I guess I shouldn't have expected him to ask me to stay in any sort of sympathetic way. Why would anyone want to stay behind to fight monsters, anyway? I'd be crazy to want to, and I'm not crazy.

(At least I hope not. Morbidly curious, maybe, but not crazy.)

(I hope.)

It's strange, though. There's something about the island and the way the ocean gleams around it that makes you believe there's no possible way any harm could befall you so long as the sun is shining, which is probably why I never thought to wonder what would happen when I ventured back outside. Alec had been so insistent that everything would be fine in the morning I never really questioned whether 'fine' was, in fact, actually fine, or whether it meant something else entirely.

As it turns out? Fine is a mildly problematic statement.

"Margo, dear," came a voice, and Margo came to rigid halt from where she'd been hurrying back to her hotel. "Darling, where are you off to so early?"

Margo pivoted slowly to find Sadie, Faith, and Amelia all sitting at their usual table outside the coffeeshop. This morning, Sadie had chosen a butter-yellow dress with a boatneck collar that seemed increasingly absurd the more Margo considered that the woman had been wearing blood for lipstick the previous night.

"Um," Margo said, and took a tentative step towards them. "Are you," she began, and paused, hesitating. "Are you feeling alright?"

"Actually, now that you mention it, I do have the strangest headache," Sadie said, glancing at Amelia and Faith. "I was just telling these two that the humidity seems to have left me somewhat dehydrated. Avalon must be going through a heat wave," she lamented, fanning herself.

"Personally, I woke up with terrible dry mouth," Faith said, making a face before turning back to Margo. "Why do you ask?" she prompted kindly. "Are you perhaps feeling under the weather yourself, dear? Acclimating to a new climate can be a trial."

"Vitamin C," said Amelia with a firm nod. "Very important. A nice juice cleanse can do wonders, you know."

"Yes, and a plant-based diet," Faith agreed, as Margo struggled not to choke on the irony.

"You know, Margo," said Sadie, beckoning for Margo to sit beside her, "I have the oddest sensation I saw you last night," she mused, half to herself. "I must have had a dream about you. Isn't that funny?"

"Er ...yes," Margo said, slipping into the chair and frowning with confusion as she realized that none of the women had any idea what had happened the following night. "Did you three happen to see the cruise ship?"

"Cruise ship?" Faith echoed, shading her eyes to glance at the ocean. "None this morning."

"What about the one that was——"

Margo paused, glancing out into the rocks. Where she'd been expecting to find the remains of yesterday's cruise ship, though, there was nothing.

At around that moment, Margo's journalistic instincts kicked in.

"Tell me something," she ventured sharply, turning to Sadie. "Whatever happened to your husbands? And where exactly are you from? Before you moved to Avalon, I mean."

"Well, that's quite a personal subject," Sadie remarked, fanning herself. "I'm not used to being interrogated about my personal life over my first cup of coffee, you know."

"Right, sorry, it's just…" A different angle, then. "It's just that I'm getting over a breakup myself, you know," Margo determined. "So I, um. Just wondered how the three of you… recovered, I guess."

"This doesn't have anything to do with you coming home from Alec's house, does it?" Faith demurred, and though Margo had been the one attempting an interrogation, she immediately felt her cheeks burn.

"No, no, I was just… this is just, you know——"

"The trick is, Margo dear, that you have to move on," Sadie interrupted. "Cut ties entirely, I say. Look at us, for example. Where are we from? Who *cares*," she ruled, waving a hand. "We've put the past behind us. I for one barely remember my ex-husband's name."

"I certainly don't," Amelia agreed, frowning. "I couldn't even tell you what he looked like, come to think of it."

"Our exes are just a million men's faces mashed into one," Faith said with a little chuckle, as Margo hid a grimace at her choice of phrasing. "But we didn't grieve for long, did we girls?"

"Certainly not. Why would we?" Sadie prompted. "We have each other. And Avalon."

"And now you have Alec," Faith added spiritedly to Margo.

"I don't *have* Alec," Margo corrected with a sigh. "I just met him, and besides, I don't think he likes me very much."

"Cora told us he came around looking for you yesterday," Amelia informed her.

"Yes, and he asked me where you were, too," Sadie agreed with an omniscient sniff. "Does that seem like the behavior of someone who doesn't like you?"

"He was only looking for me to warn me about something," Margo said, treading carefully around any admissions. "I hardly think that counts as interest."

"Well, in that case, he clearly *does* like you. Personally, I never warn people I don't like," Sadie said smartly. "Why bother? Easier to simply let harm befall them. Cosmic balance," she explained, pursing her lips. "You know how it is."

"I suppose," Margo permitted before rising to her feet. "In any case, I should probably take a shower. The heat," she said, waving a hand, and Sadie nodded her solemn agreement.

"These heat waves can be positively murder," Sadie said, disapproving.

"So true," was what Margo settled on before hurrying swiftly away.

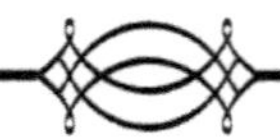

I fell asleep almost the instant I got out of the shower. I guess I'd forgotten that I'd essentially stayed up all night until my body remembered it was exhausted. By the time I woke up, I realized I'd inadvertently decided (by virtue of not deciding) to stay, and it struck me with a jolt that it was going to get dark soon.

Why hadn't I just left??

By coincidence, I glanced at my schedule just before dissolving in panic, and realized I was supposed to have written a draft of something intelligible about the mansions by now. Seems silly to ask myself why I couldn't leave—it's obvious now, isn't it? <u>This</u> is a real story! An island of creatures cast aside by gods? Maybe my curiosity was less morbid than it was journalistic. What writer could ever turn down something this big?

Still, there was the whole issue of getting out alive. I didn't exactly come to any useful conclusions while I was pulling on my most creature-resistant pair of shorts. The heat seems to have gotten worse throughout the day; it's positively sweltering as I try to sort out what to do next, even as the sun is getting lower.

What's the deal with nighttime, anyway? Oh, shit. How soon would the creatures start wandering the streets?

Maybe I should have gotten Alec's phone number, or at least tried not to piss him off.

Of course, the moment the thought occurred to me, I heard a knock at the door.

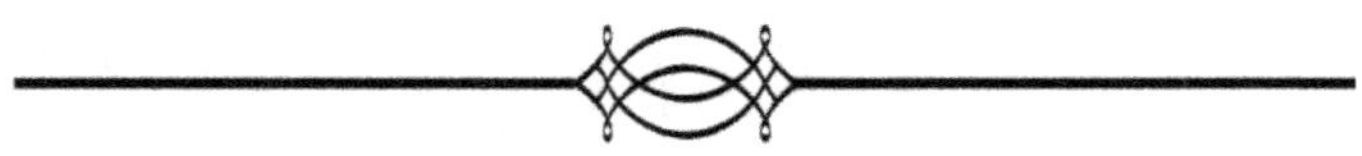

Margo pulled the hotel room door open to find Alec standing there, colorless and sweaty, as if he'd been pacing the corridor.

"Listen," he said before she could open her mouth, "this whole situation is a mess. It's not my finest moment. Or finest collections of moments."

She waited, figuring that was the polite thing to do, and he gave something of an irritable sigh.

"It seems like you want me to say something, or *do* something," he grumbled, "but look, I don't know what it is, okay? My job is to keep the creatures from killing each other. Or other people. Or me. Or each other."

"You said that already," Margo said.

"Well, it's twice as important," Alec said gruffly. "I'm supposed to keep them… you know. Safe. Protected." He grimaced. "And I didn't. But considering there's about a million ways that everything could still go completely fucking sideways, I'd really appreciate it if you'd consider not being so difficult."

Margo balked. "*I'm* being diff-"

"No, sorry, just—" Alec groaned. "Can you help me, please? Please," he repeated.

She set her jaw, not entirely ready to forgive him. "You said that already."

"It's twice as important," Alec replied stonily.

After a moment, Margo sighed.

"What do you want me to do?" she asked.

"Depends," he said, thinking. "How would you feel about learning the lyre?"

"Seems like that's a little too advanced," she said. "Got anything else?"

"Fine," he sighed. "You keep watch while *I* play the lyre. I'm worried Sadie and the others might try to lure in one of the passing boats," he clarified, "and if that's the case, then obviously I'm going to need a way to make sure the ships have *some* sort of distraction, which I can't *do* if there's more creatures coming after me—"

Margo fought a chuckle. "Are you asking me if I'll protect you, Alec?"

"I—" He grimaced. "Sure. Fine. If that's how you want to think of it, then yes."

She waited, folding her arms over her chest, and he sighed.

"Fine. *Please*," he muttered. "Please protect me, Margo, while I try to save people from being savagely consumed by sea creatures, and/or plummeting to their deaths."

"Well, when you put it like that," Margo said, which was for all intents and purposes a yes.

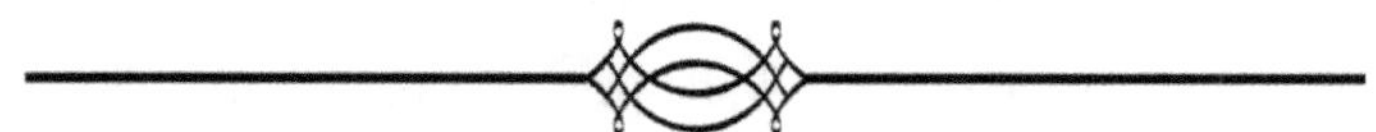

June 29

The first few nights doing something of a coastal patrol with Alec weren't nearly as bad as I thought they would be. He's careful to keep on land, which I appreciate (open water still isn't my favorite, and especially not with the carnivorous divorcées wandering around) and he's actually sort of helpful when it comes to using my magic. I never used it much before, as I told him, and especially not once I moved to the city. He seemed surprised until I explained that I'd never wanted to get caught—it was more important to me to be blend in the way my mother wouldn't, though I left that part out. I guess I never really knew what my magic was for until I needed it to do useful things, like scare away sirens or repel mermaids (Henry is one, actually, so maybe I should call them 'fin folk.' More politically correct).

I thought it was strange that everyone seems to wake up from all of this and remember nothing in the morning, but Alec says these things only happen at night because the moon and the sea are something like magnetic forces for each other, drawing out the magic in the other. Besides, not all the magic is gone, he says. Parts of it are keeping itself running during the day, like a backup generator.

I asked him what would happen if the generator itself ran out of power, and he got something of a queasy look on his face. Granted, he always looks a little displeased by everything, but that seemed to be a relatively new expression, even for him. He told me he hopes we don't have to find out.

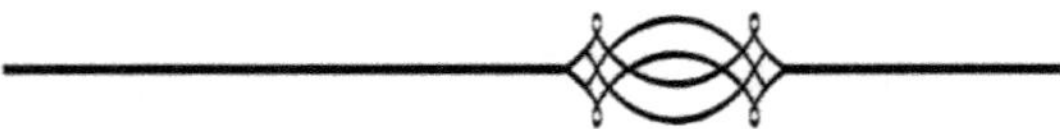

"Is it *ever* going to cool down?" Margo lamented, fanning herself, and Alec gave her one of his warning glares; this one was warning her to silence, but it wasn't too severe, so she pressed on. "It's unbelievably hot."

"Could be worse," he reminded her. "Better a heat wave than, you know. Serial deaths."

"Speaking of deaths—what's Cora?" asked Margo for the third time, as Alec gave a yawn that was also a wide groan, using the same general outstretch of displeasure to nudge her back from the coast.

"Cora is none of your concern, hopefully," he said once he'd recovered the ability to speak.

"Oh, come on, you've barely told me anything. What about the guy who works in the ice cream shop?" she pressed him. "What's he?"

"A kraken," Alec said.

Margo blinked, and then groaned.

"You're joking," she realized, and he gave her half a smile.

"Yes," he said. "Martin's a selkie."

"That's like a mermaid, right?"

"Yes, sort of. Scottish, though."

"But you work for the Greek gods?"

"They're different things to different cultures," he assured her. "It's all just different names for a variety of similar concepts. And they're not *all* children of gods," he added, "I just… I don't know." He kicked a pebble down the cliffside. "Seems like if we're making a home for *some* creatures, then why not all of them?"

"You're a creature," Margo guessed. "Aren't you?"

"I'm a guardian," Alec corrected, "and it's probably best if you don't ever see what I am."

"You keep saying that," Margo sighed, "but—"

"What about you?" Alec interrupted. "You're a witch, fine. Not a very well-trained one, obviously," he remarked, and she rolled her eyes. "So who are you really?"

"I'm Margo," she said. "I told you. I'm here to write about the mansions."

"You're not Margo. Margo West, really?" he said, with something of a scoffing laugh. "You don't actually think I believe that, do you?"

"Why wouldn't you?" she retorted, and his mouth curled into one of its three primary forms of amusement: the patronizing smirk, which was her least favorite behind 'surprised laughter' and 'humoring grimace of dismay.'

"What's your real name?" he said, leaning closer, and out of habit (or perhaps instinct), she took a step back. "It's not Margo. Something similar, though, probably. Margaret, maybe?"

"Margo's my name," she insisted. "Who cares if I gave it to myself? It's still mine."

"Well, sure, but since you keep asking about what everybody *actually* is," he reminded her, "I think it's only fair I know what your name is. And why you actually came here."

"I told you, I'm a wr-"

"You're a writer, yes, I know, but you would never deign to write about the mansions."

"Who says I wouldn't?"

"You haven't asked one question about them since you've been here." He slid her a doubtful glance. "You're a curious person who doesn't give a damn about architecture, so why did you come?"

She cast her glance at her feet. "I can't help where I'm assigned."

"Can't you?" Alec countered. "Look at the fuss you gave me when I was trying to save your *life*. I can't imagine someone had an easy time sending you here."

"I—" Margo squirmed. "I didn't have a choice."

He stepped closer again. "And why not?"

"Because—" She winced. "Because it was my fault."

He tipped her chin up, just once; gave it a tap. "Because?"

"Because…" She trailed off, and then sighed. "You're right," she conceded, sulking. "My name's Margaret, after my mother. Wexler," she clarified, making a face at the name she'd always hated, "but everyone called me 'Mad Maggie' until I went to Columbia for school. Then I was Margo."

"Was that so hard?" When she said nothing, he added, "For what it's worth, I have no intention of calling you Maggie, either. What you choose to be called is, of course, your choice."

"What's your name, then?" she challenged, lifting her chin to glare at him. "Alexios Del Mar doesn't sound real either, you know."

"I have a lot of names," Alec said, and prompted, "Why'd you come here?"

"Bad breakup," Margo shot back. "What's Cora?"

"A monster. How did the relationship end?"

"Badly, obviously. What kind of monster?"

"A terrible one. Badly in that you still have feelings?"

"No. He just… he thought I was using him, and he guessed correctly that I would hate it here. And terrible for you, or for everyone?"

"Both. *Were* you using him?"

"Not really. I mean, sort of, I guess. Is she a sea creature?"

"Sort of. Yes, but no. Are you sorry?"

"Sorry for what? And what does 'yes but no' mean?"

"Not every creature is relegated to one element or another, Margo. Not everything is so simple. And are you sorry you used him?"

Alec was standing very, very close to her now.

"No," she finally admitted. "I was young and hungry for a break. He was cute, funny, he paid attention to me. I didn't really *use* him," she clarified with a grimace. "I dated him. It was real, and I was a good girlfriend. I went to brunch with his mom once, for fuck's sake, so it's not like I was out here just trying to *take* everything—"

"But?" Alec prompted.

"But," Margo conceded with a sigh, "I wanted bigger stories. When he couldn't give them to me, I broke it off. He accused me of using him, and I didn't think I was, but…" She groaned. "It's just *stupid*, you know? It's not that I didn't like him. I miss him sometimes, when I'm able to forget what a dick he was at the end and remember the good things. But then I just… my mom passed," she mumbled, "and I think I realized that I didn't love him so much as I just wanted to be loved by someone. Anyone."

She exhaled, surprised she'd said so much so quickly, and then flinched in apprehension, dreading Alec's response. For someone who liked a good story, she wasn't terribly proud of her own.

"Well," Alec said, and paused. "Cora's a dragon."

"Wh- *what?*" Margo sputtered, taken completely by surprise.

"And you didn't use him," Alec said, shrugging and turning away before adding casually over his shoulder, "At least not any more than I'm using you, that is."

"Well, yeah, but that's different, and when you say *dragon*—"

"Is it?" he asked, pausing, and she nearly collided with his chest.

"What, different?" she asked, stepping warily back after he steadied her. "You and me? Of course. It's totally different than with Dan."

"Mm," said Alec. "Good to know." He turned away again, taking a few steps before sparing a glance at her. "Come on," he beckoned, pointing over the buildings to the opposite coast. "See that ship? Better get moving, unless you want Sadie to complain about how full she is over breakfast again."

"Alec," Margo said, though as always, he kept walking. "Alec," she growled after him, "what do you mean she's a *dragon?*"

But he only laughed, nearly disappearing from sight before Margo regained the presence of mind to follow.

July 4

Well, it's hard not to be extremely aware that everyone else I know is currently out having some sort of weekend in the Hamptons to celebrate the Fourth while I'm playing cards with the divorcées, blithely pretending I didn't magically fasten gags on them so they wouldn't lure any ships last night. I'm a little frustrated to be missing my usual fun, flashy Fourth, but actually, things aren't nearly as bad as I thought they would be.

For one thing, Alec and I have settled into something of a routine. I eat dinner, he picks me up at my hotel. Usually he'll teach me to play the lyre while the sun goes down, or sometimes how to use the bow or the harpe sword, or on occasion he suggests some drills for me to practice with my magic (tying knots with my eyes closed or turning the direction of a wave). Then, once it gets dark, we make our way around the island to keep an eye on the coasts. He avoids the Sea Breeze (and Cora), but sometimes he and I end the night early and he takes me back to his house. Nothing happens between us— it's not like that—but sometimes he'll have a drink with me, and it sort of feels… nice. Comfortable.

Is it stupid to say I don't hate it here? Maybe so long as the 'generator' of magic on the island stays functional, it won't actually be so bad to spend the summer here.

Hm. Knock on wood, I suppose.

"No, no, too much," Margo said, pulling the glass back as Alec poured. "I'm not going to be able to function in the morning if I drink as much as I did last night, and contrary to popular belief, I *do* have an actual job, you know."

"Don't tell me you're actually writing about those mansions," Alec said with a laughing look of disdain, setting the wine aside as Margo made an equally unflattering face at his tireless conceit. "Have you actually convinced your editor that it's going to take you three months to write it?"

"Well, I figured once he starts really making demands, I'll just take a sabbatical or something," she said, shrugging. "Cheers, by the way," she offered, holding up her glass.

"*Yiamas*," he replied, tapping the lip of his glass against hers, "though I didn't realize you'd be giving up your work to stay here."

Margo took a sip, grimacing. "Dan's only going to send me somewhere else terrible once I go back, so there's no point being in a hurry to leave. Maybe if I stay gone long enough, he'll forget me."

"Unlikely," Alec said. "I imagine he's wondering what that blissful silence is as we speak."

She flashed him a glare, and his mouth twisted. Her favorite form of his amusement: surprised laughter.

"Joking," he assured her, taking a sip of his wine. "Your chatter is wonderfully soothing."

"My *chatter*?" she echoed. "Please. I think you like my company, Alec."

"I like that there's less death because of it, yes. The rest I could give or take."

"You don't have to be so grumpy all the time, you know."

"True. There's so very little at stake, after all."

She sighed. "You're being difficult."

"According to you, I hardly know any other way," he assured her, nudging her foot with his. "Nor do you, I could add, but I won't. What have you learned about the mansions?" he added tangentially, and she shrugged.

"Actually, not too much that I can use, seeing as all the people who occupy them *should* be dead, but aren't. You included," she added into her glass.

"Well," Alec said, "the mansions have been here since the late nineteenth century, actually. I renovated them, but they were built to accommodate the wealthy. It's really not that interesting a story."

"Not as interesting as *your* story, no," Margo agreed. "You renovated them yourself?"

"Yes," Alec said, gesturing vaguely. "I'm the caretaker of the island."

"Did you want to be?"

"I," he began, and paused. "I just am, Margo."

He took a deliberate, pointed sip, and she frowned, leaning towards him.

"You're unhappy," she judged, and he coughed.

"Of course I'm unhappy," he said without expression. "A witch came and disrupted all the functions of my island. There's no money coming in, no tourists, no shipments of supplies from the mainland—"

"You were unhappy *before* I got here," she corrected him. "Is it because the gods put you here? What were you doing before?"

"I only do what the gods bid me," Alec said, "which, to be clear, is none of your business."

"But—"

"Margo. Please don't make me question my entire existence over a single glass of wine."

"I'm not trying to bring on some sort of existential crisis! I just want to know why you were put here. And who you are. Or who you... I don't know. Who you *were*. Is that so crazy?" she asked him, arching a brow. "You insisted on knowing why I came, didn't you?"

"You didn't have a choice," he supplied for her, and then shrugged. "Neither did I."

"No, but—" Margo groaned. He'd been the one to say she *had* had a choice, hadn't he? But if he was going to be difficult… "Fine. Forget it."

"Good." He took another grouchy sip. "Forgotten."

There was a long, stiff pause, and gradually, she let out a slow, lamenting sigh. He was staring down at his glass, watching the condensation with something that wasn't his usual frustration; something that was a little sad, or perhaps forlorn. She wondered if she might have pushed him too far that time.

"Alec," she said, and he glared at her.

"Margo," Alec grunted. "I promise, I'm not unhap-"

She cut him off with a kiss that she wasn't even aware she had wanted to give him until she suddenly decided she needed an effective way to shut him up, and this seemed to be the one her mouth wanted. Her hands landed with alarming certainty on either side of his face, her thumbs brushing the sharp bones of his cheeks, and he froze for a moment, every thread of him paralyzed with bemusement until his hands floated to rest on her arms, curling around the bends of her shoulders. He gave the slightest pressure—the tiniest brush of his lips against hers, like a little taste of honey—and ironically, that was enough to jolt her to reality. Margo sat back with a lurch, heart pounding, to wonder if she'd done something terrible as Alec's eyes widened in disbelief.

"I'm sorry," she said hastily, stumbling to her feet. "I just… it's late, I was… the wine, and I—"

"Margo," Alec said, blinking. "Margo, do you—"

"That was so stupid," she assured him, shoving the chair back and almost knocking into it. "I just—I don't know, I'm sorry. We're friends, that was dumb, I just—"

"Margo, wait," Alec said, reaching for her, but before his hand could close around her shoulder, he froze again, fingers jerking slightly as she turned to him, bewildered.

"Alec," she said, frowning. The look on his face was panicked, but not in a way she'd seen it before. "What's going on?"

He seemed to be struggling with something, though she couldn't tell what. His hands rose to his face, which momentarily seemed to… *warp*?

Margo stared, half-squinting, and Alec shook his head.

"Go," he said, forcing it out. "Go, *now*, Margo, *get out*—"

"What's happening?" she pressed, as he lurched away from her. "Alec, what's going o-"

"The generator," he choked out, the words frothing from his lips. "It's running out."

She gaped at him. "Alec, what does that *mean*—"

But he was already gone, stumbling down the stairs and darting swiftly out of sight.

PART III: HIGH TIDE

July 7
Avalon, California

It's been three days since I kissed Alec Del Mar.

It's been three horrible, awkward, humiliating days since I kissed Alec (LIKE AN IDIOT, I might add, but evidently self-destructive habits die hard) and, inconveniently, it's also been three days since I've seen him. He was in such a hurry to get rid of me that I can't help but run through the whole scenario over and over in my mind. I mean honestly, pulling away from a kiss is one thing, but saying 'the generator's running out' right before sending me back into the midst of a monster-infested island is a hugely inconsiderate thing to do, even for him.

I think the worst part about it (hard to calculate, really, considering there are so many bad parts in the running) is that he absolutely refuses to face me. After I fell into bed the next morning, I woke up to Cora bringing me a note—"I think we should split up the island," was all it said, with a map pointing out the places I should do my evening rounds and a package containing the sword and the lyre. For the last three nights, I've wandered the island by myself with no sign of Alec, and I'm rapidly spiraling from concerned to annoyed to furious.

It's about time I had an explanation.

"Hey," Margo called, spotting the familiar glint of dark hair as he collected his usual morning coffee from Cup o' Joe's. "Hey, Alec!"

He turned, obviously catching the sound of her voice but opting to duck his head, pressing through the shallow swarm of other customers until Margo stepped deliberately into his path.

"Stop trying to run away," she hissed, arms crossly folded. "This is an *island*, Alec. It only has one coffee shop!"

"So it would seem."

Honestly. "You don't actually think you can avoid me *forever*, do you?"

"I'm not avoiding you," Alec replied in what was clearly a flagrant lie, replacing his sunglasses on his face. "Not everything is about you, Margo," he added, to which she felt herself scowl, thoroughly unamused. "Now, if you'll excuse me, I really have t-"

"Is this because I—"

Mortified by the words she nearly said aloud, Margo immediately dropped her voice, gesturing him out the door. People were undoubtedly watching them with excess curiosity; the siren-divorcées in particular were eyeing her curiously from their usual table.

"Is this because I kissed you?" Margo demanded under her breath when they were out of earshot, and Alec slid her an impatient glare.

"Yes. And since we're both clear on that now, I really have t-"

"Because for the record, you definitely kissed me back." She launched in front of him again, apparently resorting to childish accusations.

The things he did to her. Truly, the mind reeled.

"Well, Margo, you didn't *invent* catastrophically poor judgment," Alec informed her, "you just perfected it. And like I said, I'm really very bus-"

"You're lying," Margo said flatly, which was either something she knew with iron certainty or something she felt with comparable staunchness *must* be certain, facts be damned. "Tell me the truth. This isn't about the kiss."

His eyes, unhelpfully, were unreadable beneath the sunglasses. Still, she caught the signs of his mouth tightening, which was the only confirmation she needed to unload seventy-two hours' worth of a full-fledged rant. "You said the generator was running out. What did that mean? And don't lie to me," Margo warned. "If you think this is me making life difficult for you, Alec, then you haven't even begun t-"

"Magic's running out," he muttered, and she opened her mouth to demand explanation, but he cut her off. "Yes, even with you here, it's running out. And we're running out of supplies, in case you haven't noticed. I have a lot on my plate without you chasing after me, Margo," he added irritably, "so if you could just let me——"

"You were the one who asked me to stay." She wondered if this, the ungluing of her chest and lungs, was closer to anger or pain. "You told me you needed my help, so I helped you. If you're just going to avoid me, then what's the point of me staying here?"

"Don't stay, then," Alec said gruffly, and Margo blinked, taken aback. "If you don't want to do this anymore, Margo, then don't. Just let me know if you want me to arrange passage back to Marina Costa and I'll be happy to take care of it. But leave a note with my office," he advised, his voice toneless. "I'm really quite busy right now."

This time, when he tried to leave, she didn't stop him.

She simply stared at his back, wondering how things had gone so wrong.

July 20

I don't know why I'm still here. I really don't. I think, at first, I just couldn't believe Alec would say those things to me. I was so sure he'd run back and apologize— beg me for forgiveness, like he did the first few times we fought. Then I started doing more research on the mansions (I do have an article to write, after all) and the more I learned about the work that went into restoring them, the more I couldn't stop seeing Alec everywhere. In the painstaking way they'd been renovated. In the little touches that had been added, giving them the island's signature color scheme and materials. The more I learned about the mansions, the more I felt I was reading about Alec himself, and now, over a week later, I'm still here.

I'm still here.

Why am I still here?

"He'll come to his senses," Faith said, watching Margo's eyes follow Alec's back as he slid into the coffeeshop and back out again. "Though, in the meantime, you could try washing your hair, dear," she mused, reaching out to toy with Margo's ponytail as she groaned, shoving Faith away.

"I don't care about Alec *or* his senses," Margo insisted, very politely not mentioning that Faith was, in fact, the reason she hadn't showered.

Hygiene was somewhat secondary after so much time spent wrangling Faith away from her attempts to lure an unsuspecting sailboat closer to shore.

Whatever the generator of magic 'running out' meant in the larger scheme of things, it certainly turned the sirens into their carnivorous iterations much closer to sunset. The same was true for the other creatures, too. Sometimes the sun wasn't even fully down before Henry's legs became a tail, and though Margo had tried to warn Alec about it, she found his house empty. She'd left a note in his office two days ago and still hadn't received a response, and by the time she'd spotted some weak spots in the layer of magic she'd learned to recognize in the air around the island, she'd given up on trying to reach him.

"I just think he should be more considerate," Margo continued, forcefully shoving him out of her head. "I had a business-related message for him and he *still* hasn't acknowledged my presence."

"Men," Sadie scoffed, ruthlessly tearing off a piece of her croissant, and though Margo knew she probably shouldn't agree (knowing, as she did, that the only distinction between Sadie's damaged pastry and actual human disembowelment was a few degrees of moonlight), she still found it highly relatable.

"Well, I still think he likes you," Amelia said kindly, patting Margo's hand. "Maybe he's just scared."

"Of what?" Margo demanded, before hastily amending, "It doesn't matter anyway, because we weren't anything worth discussing. I keep telling you, I don't like him. He doesn't like me. We're not twelve."

"Mm," Faith cheerfully agreed, which did not help.

Sadie, meanwhile, tilted her head, eyeing something over Margo's shoulder.

"Well. You know what I'd like?" Sadie remarked, nudging Amelia. "*That.*"

Amelia squinted, shading her eyes. "Oh, yes, quite so," she agreed. "Delicious."

"You guys really shouldn't say things like that," Margo said with a shudder, turning to find the source of Sadie's interest. It was a highly unwelcome sort of person, much to her distress, considering she felt a sweep of familiarity upon eyeing him head to toe. She qualified the pieces of him, taking grim inventory of things she once found attractive: old camel-colored loafers, a well-tailored pair of chinos, a relaxed white henley (an item of men's clothing she used to love), a chestnut swoop of hair that fell onto his forehead with a notable sense of ease. He wore sunglasses, but beneath them she imagined a familiar green gaze; something sharply familiar.

Whoever it was, Margo thought with a frown, he almost reminded her of…

"Oh, no, no, *no,*" Margo exhaled when he slid the glasses from his face, revealing precisely the gaze she'd been dreading. She rose to her feet without hesitation, her chair nearly collided with Faith's. "You three wait here!"

"Does she know *all* the eligible men on this island?" Amelia lamented ruefully as Margo hurried to the approaching idiot, curling a fist as she went.

"What are you *doing* here?" she demanded as her very handsome, *very* unwelcome editor and ex-boyfriend approached. "I sent in my article a couple of days ago, Dan! You hardly needed to come chase me down—"

"Nice to see you, too, Margs," he said, adjusting the weekender bag slung around his shoulders. "I got the article," he said, glancing down at her. "And I *also* got your request for a sabbatical."

Margo bristled. "So?"

"So you're not taking my calls. Or answering my emails."

"Of course not," Margo snapped. "You wanted me gone, Dan, so congratulations, I'm *gone*," she pointed out, flapping a hand around the scenery of Avalon before returning her arms to her chest, sparing him the most lethal glare she could conjure. "What are you even doing here?"

Much to her dismay, Dan's expression softened. "Look, I know you're upset, Margo," he said, "and I came to apologize. I shouldn't have sent you here, I understand that, but I just… I needed the distance. You hurt me, Margs, and I… I just didn't think I could stand to see you every day."

Men, Margo thought, silently fuming. It's either lure their ships and eat them or forever be at risk of them changing their stupid minds.

"But then you said you were staying," Dan continued, hoisting his bag further onto his shoulder, "and I realized I must have royally fucked up—"

"Yes," obviously, "you *did*, but that doesn't mean you were supposed to *come after me*. Jesus, Dan," Margo growled at him, "a voicemail might have sufficed! How did you even get here?" She was fairly certain that whatever else Alec had been up to without her, he'd successfully managed to keep the ports closed to non-emergency traffic. Something about a necessary viral quarantine, which Margo had once thought was clever until all thoughts of Alec had diminished to a vortex of ceaseless rage.

Dan waved a hand over his shoulder, gesturing somewhere. "There's a small airport on the island and I've got an amateur pilot friend who lives in L.A., so…" He trailed off with a shrug, turning back to her. "Look, Margo, I know I said some awful things," he said, reaching for her hand, which she let him take out of unwilling paralysis. "I was unfair and frankly, a total mess. But if you could just, I don't know. Have one more dinner with me, or—"

"No," Margo said instantly, and when his brow furrowed, she shook her head, ripping her hand free. "No, Dan, you have to *leave*, now. Immediately."

"I can't," he said, frowning. "My friend already flew back, and—"

"Dan, listen to me, you *have* to leave. You can't stay on this island."

"Why not?" he demanded.

"There's, you know, a virus."

"What?"

"A virus."

"What virus? I haven't heard anything."

"I don't know, it's… like, a flu. Contagious." Dan looked doubtful, and based on the way the divorcées were waving at him over her shoulder, Margo could see there was no way she could make this convincing. "There's no hotel rooms, Dan!" she shrilled, desperate.

"That's ridiculous," he said, and she kicked herself, because of course it was. "I already booked a room in your hotel."

"I… *Dan*," Margo growled. "You can't just *invade* my life like this—"

"Just have one dinner with me, Margo," Dan pleaded with her, pained, as Margo reminded herself to write an article on the uniquely male propaganda of never taking no for an answer. "Come on, Margs. I know you must be upset. You love your job," he pleaded, puppy-faced and disconsolate, "and I know you wouldn't still be here if I hadn't fucked this up. Please."

He fixed those green eyes she'd once found so compelling directly on hers, lowering his voice with obvious distress. "Just one dinner, Margo, and if I can't convince you to come back to New York with me—"

Christ. There was no getting around it.

"It'll have to be an early dinner," Margo warned. "Five o'clock. No," she amended hastily, "four thirty."

"Fine," Dan said, shrugging. "I can handle that."

"And you have to go home right after," she warned. "Make sure your friend can take you back."

"Fine," he said again, looking as though he only half-meant it. "But are we agreed, then?"

Over her shoulder, Margo caught Sadie passing Dan an outrageously unhelpful wink.

"Fine," she muttered, already certain it was going to be a long, unbearable day.

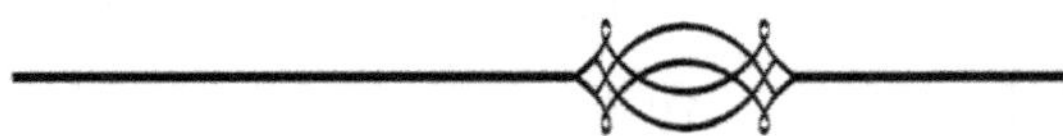

Dan is possibly the last person I wanted to see on this island, and what's worse, I can't even focus on the real reason I'm upset. He dumped me, basically demoted me and banished me, sent me to a fucking island so he wouldn't have to look at me, and now he shows up here without warning claiming to be sorry while I have to be concerned about saving his life? I wouldn't want to have dinner with him under normal circumstances, but now I have to do it to make sure nobody tries to rip out his esophagus or drown him?? That seems a little unfair, even with the notion of cosmic irony.

You know what else is unfair? That I had to send a note to Alec, which of course he didn't answer. Nothing sentimental, mind you, just a little, 'Hey, sorry my ex showed up on your island full of monsters, I'm handling it.—M.' It's four p.m. and still no response, of course.

What am I still doing here? Maybe I should just go back to New York with Dan. Assuming I don't strangle him first.

"I'm so glad you agreed to this, Margs," Dan said, smiling at her from across the table in Avalon's old diner, which was the least romantic place Margo could think of at the time. She'd even ordered a tuna melt, trying to make a point that apparently hadn't landed.

"You basically stalked me, Daniel," she reminded him, bringing a heavily ketchupped fry to her mouth and taking a moody bite. "I didn't really have a choice."

"Oh, come on, Margs," Dan sighed, reaching his hand across the table to nudge her forearm, as if this whole thing had been some playful disagreement. "Look, I get that I have a lot to make up for before we can even think about getting back to where we were—"

His delusion was absolutely unparalleled.

"Back to where we *were*? Is that a joke?"

"I know, I know, but if you could just give me a ch-"

"Excuse me," someone cut in. "Dan, is it?"

Margo immediately choked on her fry.

"Can we help you with something?" Dan asked, frowning up at Alec while Margo struggled to cough up rehydrated potato.

"Yes," Alec said, voice as clipped and impassive as ever. "You can leave."

"Excuse me?"

"Did you mishear?"

But Dan, unfortunately, was a New Yorker, and therefore accustomed to occasional effrontery by passersby. "Listen, buddy," he said, manspreading across his side of the booth, "you can't just order us to leave."

Alec pointed wordlessly to the usual sign about who or what could be removed from which establishments.

"Can," he said.

But Dan had been to Queens, and Long Island. And New Jersey.

"Alright," Dan said with forced patience, "look, whatever this is about—"

"I believe Margo has already informed you that she doesn't want you here?" Alec cut in, as Margo blinked in silence, unsure whether to contribute. After weeks of nothing, she wasn't entirely sure whose side Alec was on.

"Ergo," Alec concluded, "me saying it should hardly be necessary."

"Okay, listen," Dan said gruffly, rising to his feet, and for reasons that Margo planned to passionately deny to herself later, she was pleased to notice he had to tilt his chin up to meet Alec's lofty glance. "I don't know who you think you are, but—"

"Alexios Del Mar," Alec supplied, offering his hand. When Dan didn't take it, he merely shrugged, retracting it. "I trust we're in agreement, then? I expect you to leave this evening. Your belongings have already been removed from your room at the Sea Breeze and taken to the airport."

"What?" Dan demanded. "You can't do th-"

"I can, and I did." For a moment, it looked as though Alec had said as much as he came to, but he paused before turning away, clearing his throat. "For the record, Daniel," Alec informed him, "Margo is not in the same place you left her. If you wished her to stay, perhaps you shouldn't have told her to go." At that, Margo's breath caught in her throat, promptly taken by surprise. "She does not need you."

"And I take it you think *you're* what she needs?" Dan posed drily, drawing one hand to his belt loop in that very male, penis-measuring sort of way. (Silently, Margo drew one hand to her temple, repulsed.)

"Not remotely, no," Alec replied, to which Dan faltered, tactically outgunned. "But my concern for the moment is you, and more pressingly your departure. We appreciate your business here in Avalon and wish you a pleasant journey home," he finished with a curt nod.

Then Alec pivoted on his heel, heading for the door and leaving Dan to gape helplessly in his wake.

"Margo, do you know that guy? What is he even talking about—"

But she wasn't listening. "Alec," she called, stumbling to her feet and chasing after him to burst through the door, just managing to catch his arm. "Alec, come on, *wait*—"

"Yes, Margo?" he asked neutrally, turning to face her.

He didn't look particularly interested in whatever she planned to say, and she blinked, realizing now that she hadn't known, either.

"Thank you," she managed, and he nodded.

"You're welcome. Have a nice evening," he said, and turned away, leaving her to pull him back with a surprising urgency. The motion was so reflexive and forceful they both stumbled, colliding gracelessly on the sidewalk.

"Why," she blurted out once they'd caught themselves, both straightening. "Why do you care?"

To that, Alec made a face, exasperated. "I don't want him to get *eaten*, Margo, it's literally the basest form of human decency—"

"So you don't care about me?"

Alec met her eye, saying nothing, and Margo's defenses cracked.

"Say it," she suddenly spat, unopened again, leaking. "Just say it."

"Say what?"

"Just tell me you don't want me." Everyone else had always had the decency to tell her to her face how undesirable she was, how pointless. Mad Maggie. Get out of my office, go to Avalon, get lost.

"Just say it, Alec, just tell me."

Only then did a flicker of something pass over his face.

"What did I do?" she asked him, slightly humiliated by the undertone of pleading, and for once he showed evidence of remorse; he swallowed with uncertainty, gradually conceding to shake his head.

"Nothing," he said. "You didn't do anything."

"But—"

"Please," he exhaled. "Please. Just trust me, Margo."

She gave him what she hoped was a convincing look of challenge. "Alec," she said with the last reserves of her pride, "if you want me to stay, then don't tell me to go."

He stared grimly down at her, and her heart thudded in her chest. Once, twice. A third.

He opened his mouth to reply and she waited, breath suspended.

"Just make sure he leaves tonight," was all Alec finally said, and then he stepped away, aiming himself down the street and promptly out of sight.

There's something Alec isn't telling me. Something big. The whole mysterious "trust me" thing certainly made that clear enough. But why lie? He's no better than Dan at the rate he's going, and I really have my hands full, Dan-wise. I think Alec stopping by the diner only made things worse. Since he left, Dan won't stop chasing me everywhere with his useless apologies—he even tried following me into the bathroom! It'd be easier just to leave with him, I know, but I can't now. I mean, maybe I <u>could</u>, but I certainly don't want to. For whatever insane reason, I've started to like it here. I've gotten used to magic here, to life here. I like the island, I like the people in it. For the most part, I feel like myself here.

And as for Alec…

Okay, well, even if I factor him out of the equation entirely, I still don't want to go. But he's right—I don't exactly want Dan to get eaten, either. Nor do I want him to see anything that's on this island.

So how am I going to make sure Dan leaves by sunset?

(And what is Alec still trying to keep from me??)

"Margo! Margs, *please*—"

"Dan, I just, I really can't anymore, honestly." She rounded on him as he chased her down Main Street, finding herself quite close to losing her mind. "Could you just get to the airport, please? I'm not coming with you, I just… I'm just on vacation!" she half-shrieked, arms flailing. "Like a normal human being! Why is that so difficult to grasp?"

"Margs," Dan panted after her. "What's going to happen when you *do* come back? I'm willing to wait, but I just need to know if—"

"Are you saying this as my editor or my ex? Is my job at stake?"

It had better not be, she thought in vindictive silence. Not that she had any pressing desire to file a termination suit, but surely some of this disastrous day would have to count towards 'wrongful.'

"No, of course not, I just… Margs, come on—"

"Dan, for the love of god, we *broke up*," Margo snapped, gritting it through her teeth. "You *dumped* me, remember? You said I was using you, so congratulations, now I'm definitely not using you for anything."

"Fine, but you can't just—"

"You need to leave, Dan, seriously—"

"This isn't you," Dan insisted, pulling her back. "You *love* your job, Margo. You can't just stay on an island forever—"

"It's not forever," she corrected him stiffly. "It's just…" A swallow of hesitation. "I don't know. I don't know yet. But at least until the fall equinox."

"Oh sure, the fall equinox," Dan echoed, half-laughing until he saw her face. "Wait. You're serious?"

"Obviously!" she growled.

"But that's *weeks* from now—"

"Dan, seriously, can you just—"

But they both broke off, forcefully coming to a stop, as a heavy sound thudded out from somewhere behind them, sending a volatile tremor beneath their feet.

"What was that?" Dan asked, panicked.

Nothing good. Certainly nothing with a decent explanation.

"Earthquakes," she said weakly. "California. It happens."

"But—"

Another thudding footstep.

"Margo," Dan said.

"Quiet, Dan—"

"MARGO," Dan shouted, pointing over her shoulder, and Margo turned to discover that in her Dan-ignited fury, she'd been distracted enough to do the one thing Alec had repeatedly warned her about: she'd headed towards the Sea Breeze.

Behind her, a massive dragon stood guarding the hotel, coiled around it like a serpent and glinting red-gold streaks of color as the fading sun hit from above. It was impossible to tell where the dragon's head began and where its tail ended; the length of its body seemed to go on forever, the twisting barrel of its midsection rapidly in motion while it stared, unblinking, into Margo's eyes.

"Cora?" Margo asked tentatively.

And then, without warning, it lunged, snapping its teeth and slithering forward as Margo stumbled back with a stifled scream, dragging Dan by the collar.

"Fuck, fuck, *fuck*," Margo gritted out, waiting for the usual burst of power to coil up in her palm, cracking like a whip. She took hold of what remained of the island's magic—now weak in places from the island's power bankruptcy shortage, thinned like a patchy sky—and yanked it down, pulling it tightly over her and Dan like children hiding under the covers. "Get back," she warned an unmoving Dan, who was staring vacantly, paralyzed, at Cora. "Dan, listen to me, get *back*—"

But dragon-Cora lunged again, snapping at the reserves of Avalon's magic and crushing it between her teeth, crunching like the sound of bone. Margo pressed a hand against it, trying to seal it—a hopeless patch to a massive, cracking dam—but Cora lunged again.

And then stopped.

And then *howled.*

Margo exchanged an apprehensive glance with a pale-faced Dan. "What the—"

All at once, dragon-Cora was dragged backwards with a blood-curdling shriek of pain, her head whipping around to snap at something out of sight. "Come on," Margo urged at once, grabbing Dan's arm and yanking him up. Whatever it was that had attacked Cora, she wasn't waiting around to find out. "We have to get out of here *right now*—"

"What *is* that?" Dan asked hoarsely. "What did you…? Margo, what the fuck is going on?"

And then, in her attempt to force Dan to his feet, Margo saw it.

A second dragon, this one slightly smaller, had dragged Cora backwards, puncturing its teeth around her spine. This one had a dark line across its back, black jagged notches crossing in slashes along the vertebrae, but it shone a glowing, almost metallic brass. Cora thrashed around, aiming blindly for the other dragon, and momentarily it darted away, glancing briefly at Margo to fix her with a set of distinct—and distinctly *familiar*—brown eyes.

Go, the dragon's glare seemed to say, *and for heaven's sake, stop being difficult.*

"Alec?" Margo said, frozen in disbelief, but by then, Dan had finally come to his senses.

"RUN," he shouted, taking Margo's arm and tugging her in the opposite direction.

Holy crap. Did that really just—?

Wow. I can't believe it never occurred to me that with all the creatures on this island, Alec might be one, too.

Margo was already in his living room by the time the sun had come up. He stopped short in the doorway, blinking, and she rose to her feet slowly, having caught the telling sounds of his arrival.

"Sorry," she said, gesturing to the compromised latch on the front door. "But in fairness, you did it to me first."

Alec lingered near the threshold.

"I'm a touch more concerned about the unconscious man on my sofa, actually," he eventually said, and Margo turned, glancing down at Dan.

"Oh, him? He's fine." She turned back with a shrug. "I figured knocking him out would be easier than explaining things."

"That's probably true," Alec said.

For a second, neither of them moved.

Or spoke. Or appeared to breathe.

"So," Margo said, "what exactly… are you?"

Alec's mouth twisted. "I told you," he said. "I'm the island's guardian."

Margo arched a brow, expectant, and Alec sighed, stepping towards her in resignation.

"I was once the dragon assigned to guard the golden apples belonging to the gods," he explained. "After Heracles killed me, the gods put me in the stars. As the constellation Draco. Then they put me here. As a man, this time," he added, gesturing to himself with half a smile, "though I hardly remember my lives before. I just…" A heavy swallow. "I woke like this, and this is what I was. The guardian to an island that is slowly running out of magic, and now, without it, we're all turning back into what we once were, whether we remember or not. And honestly?" he added, suddenly ignited. "We're also running out of food, as if things weren't complicated enough already. We're really very close to fucked, which, believe me, is not a word I use lightly—"

"Alec," Margo cut in, sighing. "Why didn't you just *tell me* that?"

He fixed her with one of his exasperated glances. "Do you really think I wanted you to see me like that?" he countered, which was, Margo supposed, a fair-ish point. "I'm a cautionary tale, you know. In the stories, I'm reduced to the dangers of sea currents. I'm the guardian who failed—*twice*," he reminded her sourly, "and now I'm—"

"Not true," Margo cut in, taking a step towards him. "You protected me."

"I did, yes," he growled, "though once again, I wouldn't have had to if you'd simply learn to *do as you're told*. What did I say about Cora?" he demanded. "At least a dozen times, too—"

"You care about me," Margo noted, a smile pulling at her lips. "Just admit it."

"I care enough about you to prevent you from being eaten. Which, as I've already mentioned, is a base minimal standard."

"Oh, you *love* me," Margo teased, and he rolled his eyes.

"And I care enough to keep you away from me," he said firmly. "I wasn't sure if I'd know who you were when I was…" He fidgeted, falling back on resilient disdain. "Is it really such a crime to ensure that you not get murdered?" he muttered. "I already have to try so hard not to do it myself."

Another step, this one a taunt. "Listen to yourself. You're obsessed with me." At his scowl, Margo fought a laugh. "What else?"

"At this point, my main priority is getting rid of your ex-boyfriend." Alec gestured to Dan with disapproval as Margo finally stepped directly in front of him, looking up to meet his eye. "He'll be gone within the hour," Alec remarked darkly, "if I have to fly him there myself."

Men, honestly. "Sure. *And?*"

"And—" Alec glanced down at her, brown eyes locked on hers. "And what?"

She arched a brow, expectant, and gradually, he relented with a heavy sigh.

"And yes, fine, I kissed you back," he muttered under his breath, "though don't go getting any ideas. It's still very, very stupid," he informed her, ignoring the look of triumph on her face. "You still have to keep your distance, do you understand? And if I see you come near Cora again—"

"Alec," Margo said.

He looked at her.

She looked at him.

For a moment, nothing happened. They simply looked and looked and looked until something, everything, became quietly, bountifully clear.

"Whoa," said Dan, his groggy voice jolting Alec and Margo apart. "What the fuck happened last night?"

"Bad trip," Margo said over her shoulder. "You're fine."

"You're leaving," Alec added.

"I have a headache," Dan muttered, which privately, Margo thought was no less than he deserved.

In response, Alec gave a rare smile, reserving the warmth of it for Margo.

"Good," he said, reaching out to brush her cheek with his thumb. "Now get out of my house."

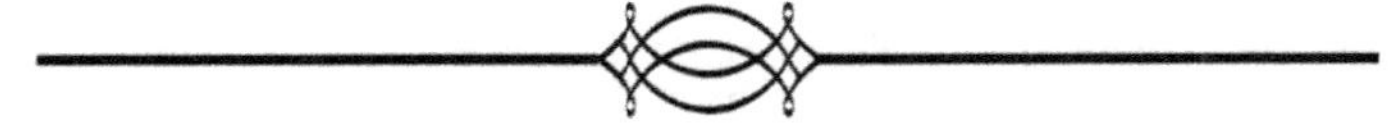

August 6

After Dan left, things didn't exactly go back to the way they were with Alec before. They can't, obviously, now that I know what I know. But now, instead of spending the evenings together, Alec and I have a few hours during the day. Nothing too remarkable, of course. Sometimes he sits with me and the divorcées in the morning instead of running away with his coffee. Sometimes I meet him at the casino, both of us trying (and mostly failing) to repair some of the holes in the magic surrounding the island, or trying to solve the problems he's having getting supplies. He teaches me the lyre before sunset now, and then sends me away when the colors of the sky start to turn. I hate to leave, but I understand his reasons. I leave without comment every time, even though I'd much rather stay.

We haven't done anything romantic, not really, though I think there are moments when we could. I guess he thinks it's strange, and maybe it is, though after coexisting with Henry and Cora and the divorcées, I'm starting to feel like the shapes they take at night are just different versions of normal. Different shades of who they really are. Maybe that's an insane thing to think, but hey, that's what a summer on Avalon has done to me. Until I came here, I'd never known what it was to live without the pressure to belong.

Besides, I think the term 'monster' might be relative. Aren't we all a little monstrous in our own ways?

I don't forget that no matter what form Alec takes, he still protects me. From the moment I set foot on this island, every form he's taken has been to keep me safe. Sometimes I look up to find him looking at me, and yes, I know it's crazy, but in those moments, I think I want something more.

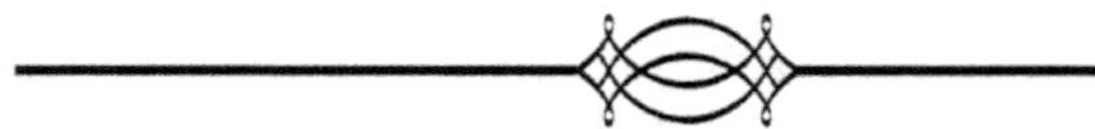

"Careful," Alec warned as Margo ventured into the waves. "High tide. Don't get swept out to sea."

"Oh, relax," Margo told him, rolling her eyes at where he stood on the edge of the sand. "I think I can handle ankle-deep water, Alec. You don't always have to be so gloomy."

"I told you," he said, shrugging. "I'm a cautionary tale. Or telling you to take caution, at least."

Margo sighed, turning to face the ocean and shading her eyes from the afternoon sun.

"You know, I used to hate open water," she said. "But I think I just didn't trust it."

Behind her, Alec gave an ironic-sounding laugh. "And you do now, after all this? Maybe you're not paying enough attention, Margo."

"No, I—" She turned to make a face at him, which he accepted with a shrug. "I just meant that not all mysteries are a bad thing. It's not so bad to face the unknown. Kind of beautiful, actually." She took a deep breath, letting the salty sea air lick her cheeks. "I think I love the way the water stretches on forever. But at the same time, I like the horizon, too. I like how it's steadying, in a way. It's like I can finally imagine a happy ending, because I know the water shines brightest right where it hits the sky." She hummed to herself for a second, content, and then sighed. "God, I sound like my mother."

When Alec didn't reply, Margo turned over her shoulder to look at him.

"What?" she asked him. Like his three primary forms of amusement, he also had different degrees of quietude; some were more vacant than others. This one was full of something.

"Nothing."

"Liar," she murmured, turning to walk towards him. Beneath her feet, the sand gave way against the tide, the ocean lapping at her ankles. "What is it?"

He looked down at her for a moment, considering her.

"You," he eventually said, "are going to make a very good witch."

"Oh, yeah?" she mused. "And how do you know so much about witches, Alec Del Mar?"

He shrugged. "I've known some." He reached out, gently touching her hair. "Anyway, the less afraid you are of the elements in magic, the better you'll be with them. That's just a fact."

She leaned into his touch. "Are you saying the water is magic?"

"Not exactly. I'm saying there's magic *in* water," he clarified. "And water in magic. And air, and fire, and earth. And sand. And stars. And dragons, I suppose." He smiled slightly. "And everything is connected, and so are you."

He curled her hair around her finger, releasing it.

"You're magic, Margo West," he said quietly, and she found herself catching his hand, holding it steady near her collarbone. He looked at her, and she looked back.

"I don't want to take caution," she told him, already a little breathless at the thought. "I *want* to get dragged under the current. I want to be pulled down to the depths." She watched his breath halt, motion rescinded. "I want to get swept away, Alec," she told him softly, and he bent his head with a shiver, taking her chin gently and holding her still.

"Margo," he said. "We've talked about these self-destructive impulses."

She tugged him down to her, laughing into his mouth.

"Believe me, I know," she murmured, and he kissed her anyway, molding himself to the shape of her as the ocean slid up to wash over their toes, the waves themselves sighing with satisfaction.

August 21

Okay. So maybe I know why I stayed.

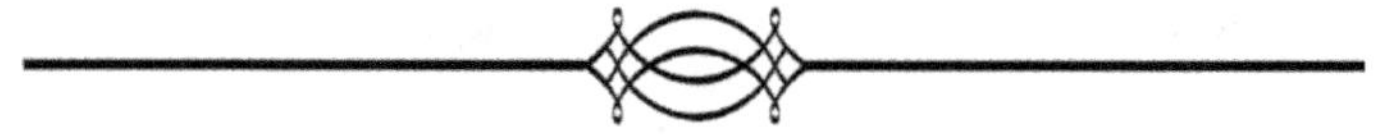

It had become Margo's custom to meet Alec in the mornings, letting herself into his house around sunrise and permitting herself a swift venture into the contents of his fridge, usually conjuring up something

252

resembling breakfast and then immediately falling asleep on his sofa only to wake up to him reading the newspaper somewhere beside her. The first time it happened, he'd been sitting in the armchair adjacent to the couch, one leg crossed idly over the other as he sipped a cup of coffee in silence. Then, gradually, he'd moved closer, fitting himself at her feet or, on one occasion, nudging her over in a state of drowsy half-sleep to serve as her very amenable pillow. The day before, she'd woken up to him sitting on the floor, and when she'd slid her leg out towards him—giving his shoulder a nudge to indicate her state of consciousness—he'd reached around and curled his fingers delicately across her calf, pressing a kiss lightly to her ankle.

She hadn't known something so innocent could be so… *decadent*, which was a word she'd mostly used ironically, or to describe cakes. Actually, Alec made her want to use a lot of words she'd never taken seriously, like *intimate*. It had been a description for humble brunch locales, not the feeling she got when she leaned over a man's shoulder to read the paper, until that man was him.

Alluring was a nail polish shade, or a halfway decent magazine purchase while buying cartons of ice cream, but certainly not the way a man looked at her—until that look was Alec's face.

And as for *excruciating*—well. That was a word meant for hot yoga or boredom, not the wait she was currently enduring in order to not push too hard with Alec. As wonderfully torturous as it was to take things slowly, it really wasn't Margo's style. Certainly not when the subject in question was an inordinately handsome man who also happened to be one of the only such men on the island, and *especially* not when she'd been starved of any bedroom activity for the last few months.

Which was why, this particular morning, Margo hadn't opted to fall asleep on Alec's couch before he got home from his foray into dragonhood. Instead, she made do with the minimal ingredients in his kitchen, fixing something of a suitable plate of eggs and placing them on the table in what she hoped was an artful display, just in time to watch him come in through his front door.

Naked.

"Oh, Margo," Alec said, instantly grabbing for a sofa pillow and holding it over his…

She swallowed, curling a hand around her mouth. *Not helpful.*

"You're, um. You're usually sleeping," he said.

She balked. "Does that mean you're usually naked?"

"My other forms don't necessitate trousers," Alec replied drily, his mouth curling up in her favorite of his expressions: the subtle laugh that meant she'd taken him by surprise. "Apologies, I didn't mean to, ah—" He coughed. "Offend you."

"I," she began, and swallowed. He was… impressive. Stately. *Majestic*, even. Again, words she might have used for the Grand Canyon and not for a man (particularly not one who was holding a couch cushion over his downstairs) until now.

"I'm not offended," she managed weakly, and was rewarded with another half-teasing smile.

"I'll just go put on some clothes," he offered, and turned to the stairs, permitting her a view of his backside. It was… *statuesque.* When had anyone ever used that word for something that wasn't featured somewhere in the Met?

At the sound of Margo's small cough, Alec turned, registering belatedly that he hadn't quite taken sufficient care with the rest of his exposure.

(*Exposed.* That was a word for film or something. Black and white photography, things of that nature. Definitely not this sensation of being out there, vulnerable, for him to refuse.)

"Alec," Margo attempted as he fumbled with the cushion, "you, um. You don't have to put clothes on," she managed. "If you don't want to, I mean."

He blinked. "Are you asking me to start a nudist colony? Because I know the island is unconventional, Margo, but finfolk are really much more conservative than you'd think—"

"Alec," Margo said, flustered, "stop. I'm saying I want to—" She paused, grimly addressing her feet. "I'm just trying to tell you that if you *want* to, I'm, um. I could—"

"Use your words," he advised, expressionless, and she threw up her hands, exasperated.

"Never mind," she growled, turning away. "You obviously know what I'm saying, so if you're not interested—"

"Margo." She could feel the underlying rumble of a laugh; it invaded her sense of well-being like a shot up her spine, a bolt of lighting.

(*Penetration.* Now there was a word she would have happily used in a more traditional sense.)

"Margo," Alec said, sighing as she turned away, "would you look at me, please?"

"Look, I'm being ridiculous," she muttered, only half-glancing at him. "This is all just—"

She broke off.

He'd returned the cushion to the couch, leaving himself open for scrutiny.

"I'm not uninterested," he assured her, and she gawked at him. The state of his interest was, in fact, virtually unmissable. She considered briefly that someone might observe it from space rather than miss it.

(*Astronomical.* Was there no end to her evolution in diction?)

"Margo," Alec ventured, stepping towards her. "This wasn't something I was going to push. But if you want to, then…"

He trailed off, arriving to glance down at her, his chest mere breaths from hers.

"I think it's pretty clear I'm on board," he said, and leaned forward.

He didn't kiss her like she thought he would; instead, he merely brushed his lips against the bare curve of her shoulder, slipping the strap of her tank top down her arm. She shivered, closing her eyes, and his other hand closed around the curve of her waist, pulling her closer.

"I'm going to need to hear something very specific," Alec said in her ear. "If you want to continue, that is."

"Oh?" Margo asked, mouth dry. His hand slid under the cotton of her tank top, brushing lightly over her navel until her entire stomach pebbled with longing. "And what do you need to hear?"

"Repeat after me." A kiss to the side of her neck. "'Alec, I want you.'"

She eased her head back, pulling him closer. "Alec," she murmured in agreement, "I want you."

"Good," he said. "There's a bit more, too. How about 'Alec, I want you to undress me slowly,'" he suggested, and she felt the air in her lungs suddenly falter, lodging tightly in her throat. "'I want you to really look at me, Alec,'" he said with the ghost of his breath along the hollow of her throat, "'and I *insist* that you take your time.'"

She swallowed, head spinning. "Undress me. Please."

"There's more to it."

"Well, I can't——" She gasped a little as his mouth traveled over her jaw, brushing her lips. "You added so many complex clauses, I can't possibly——"

"Alec," he continued neutrally, "I want you to put your lips on me carefully. I want you to taste me properly. I want to feel you, all of you, on my skin, and I want you to cover every spare inch of me before I feel you in my——"

"Oh *Jesus*," Margo exhaled, tightening her fingers in his hair as he chuckled again, arms tightening around her.

"And then I'll say, 'Margo, these are some very difficult demands,'" he mused as she tugged him towards the kitchen table, shoving her now-cold scrambled eggs aside. "And you'll say, 'listen, Alec, I want what I want,' and I'll say, 'well, Margo, you bossy little minx, if that's how you want me, then that's how it'll be'——"

"Oh god, Alec," Margo groaned, letting him hoist her onto the table as she slid her legs around his hips. "You're really not *helping*."

"Well," he said, bending his mouth to the lace of her bralette, "then I guess I'll just have to——"

"Ahem," said a voice, and they both froze, perilously compromised. "Normally I do hate to interrupt this sort of thing, but I'm afraid we have to have words, *Draconis*."

Alec stiffened, easing himself from what was obviously Margo's left breast to turn toward the voice in question. "You might have chosen another time to interrupt," he said irritably, and over his shoulder, an obscenely attractive man stepped into view, his shoulders gleaming golden.

Actually golden.

Like a—

"God," Margo said hoarsely, and slowly, the intruder smiled.

"Draconis, you have seriously fucked up," the god remarked to Alec, "which is really not a word I prefer to use in that context. But in my view, even an error this colossal isn't without some plausible fix. Let's just get to the leverage part of the discussion, shall we?" he asked, falling into a chair beside Margo.

Alec grimaced. "What do you want?" he asked after a tense moment of pause, and the god's grin in reply illuminated the apartment, rendering it sparkling from ceiling to floor.

"*Now* we're getting somewhere," said the god, at which point he picked up a fork, blithely helping himself to Margo's scrambled eggs.

PART IV: AUTUMN RISING

August 31
Avalon, California

Picture this: I'm finally about to have sex with the guy my hormonal bits have been clamoring for all summer, and despite a lifetime of catastrophically poor choices in this particular arena, he's not even disappointing. Turns out he's not just inconceivably hot (thus satisfying my cave-lady side, which definitely <u>does</u> exist and that's just plain science) but also, he's got plenty of material to make my brain go wild, too. Banter isn't the only thing his infuriating mouth is good at.

So, knowing this, imagine he's standing there—Alexios Del Mar, clearly designed to ruin me, head to freakin' toe—and he takes me in his arms, AND THEN—

An actual GOD interrupts.

Because of course he does.

If you thought gods had better things to do than interrupt pseudo-mortal coital pursuits, think again. Whatever else he is, the Divine Cockblock clearly possesses grand plans to throw a wrench in my (frankly, well-deserved) carnal urges.

"Who *are* you?" Margo demanded, and the god set down his forkful of eggs, swiping daintily at the corner of his mouth.

"Hermes, messenger god, son of Zeus and the nymph Maia, divine trickster, god of boundaries and all transgressions therein," he replied. "Patron of herdsmen, thieves, graves, and heralds. Also, conductor of souls, protector of roads and travelers—"

"I think that's enough," Alec cut in irritably, being that he was still quite naked. He looked about as uninterested as he was exposed, which was, in requisite proportions, quite a lot. "What do you want?"

"Oh, you know me. Just popping by to visit with the mutant cousins, as one does, and then I just *happened* to discover the marvelous oddity that is your spectacular mess. Whatever managed to go so terribly wrong here, Draconis?" Hermes mused. "I could feel the disturbances from the island nearly the moment I left Olympus."

"Just tell me how you'd like to exploit the situation, Hermes, and then we can all be on our way," said Alec, who seemed to Margo to be purposefully ignoring her.

"Well, now hang on," Hermes countered, attention darting between Alec and Margo. "Who's to say I *want* to be on my way? I did say I have an affinity for transgressions, didn't I?" he remarked to Margo, who made a face, crossing her arms tightly over her chest. "Maybe I'd like to stay and watch. Or participate." He shrugged. "I'm breezy. Totally up to you."

"No," Alec said flatly, and Hermes' smile broadened.

"Ah, so she's important to you, is she? Interesting." His gaze flicked to Margo again. "Then in exchange for my silence, Draconis, I want her."

"What?" Margo demanded at the same time Alec flinched, clearly having walked directly into some sort of trap. "I'm not leverage, first of all, and I'm certainly not for sale."

"Mm, right, yes," Hermes assured her, turning to Alec. "I take it you haven't discussed any potential matters of divine punishment? How the gods may unfavorably react, and so on? I can do so on your behalf, if you'd like."

"No," Alec said instantly. "It's… Margo," he sighed to her, "don't listen to him—"

"When the gods are displeased," Hermes cut in loudly, crossing one leg over the other to angle himself towards Margo, "they gain a rather gruesome stomach for punishment. Ever heard of Prometheus?" he posed in her general direction. "Bound to a rock in the ocean, where an eagle would tear out his liver and then it would grow back, you know, so as to carry on into perpetuity? And that was for giving mankind fire, not for letting their little monstrous offspring run loose, so imagine the consequences *here*—"

"What?" Margo asked, feeling the blood drain from her face as Hermes chuckled.

"Yes, well, seeing as Draconis has *clearly* committed errors of catastrophic proportions, I think you see my point. I hope you do, anyway," he said with a frown, "though modern mortal minds may be less sophisticated than I remember."

Margo blinked. "But Alec wasn't the one who—"

"You can't have Margo," Alec cut in bluntly to Hermes, taking hold of her elbow and digging his fingers into her inner arm. "Stop talking *now*," he warned in her ear, and Hermes arched a brow, catching the interaction.

"Well, surely you both realize that punishment by the gods is somewhat more *lasting* for a mortal—"

"She has nothing to do with this," Alec said again, and belatedly, Margo realized he was once again attempting to keep her out of trouble; protecting her, like usual, by denying that there was anything to protect. "She's a witch, Hermes. Her rules are different, and you know it."

"Oh, even better," Hermes said, exuberant. "I've always wanted a witch."

Margo balked. "Excuse me?"

"Hermes," Alec said, nudging Margo behind him, "she already said no, and you know perfectly well Zeus won't take kindly to abduction. It's been out of fashion for some millennia now," he warned. "Better not to chance it."

To Margo's relief, Hermes looked at least mildly convinced.

"Fine," Hermes said. "I want twenty-four hours with the witch, then."

"Done," Alec agreed, holding out a hand, and Margo felt her eyes widen.

"Wait a minute—"

"*If,*" Alec directed to Hermes, "you promise not to say a word about the island—and that's eternal, by the way," he clarified. "We have less than a month left, and then it'll be fixed. From now to forever, you'll stay silent?"

"Oh, certainly," Hermes jubilantly agreed, rising to his feet to clasp a gold-glowing hand around Alec's. "Anything else I should know?"

Margo's heart lurched in protest. "Alec—"

"Yes," Alec said. "If you harm Margo in any way, Hermes, I'm quite confident she'll cause you a sufficient amount of discomfort to ensure it never happens again. And then you'll have to deal with me." He took a step closer. "Is that clear?"

"You wouldn't harm me, Draconis," Hermes said with a laugh. "You couldn't, certainly not without consequence."

"Oh, I could," Alec said, his voice low as he muscled his way into Hermes' personal space. Margo, who forgot her misgivings long enough to become newly fascinated with the smooth lines of his back, swallowed heavily. "But again, it's not me you have to worry about."

Hermes gave a loaded sigh, then nodded.

"Fine," he said. "I won't. I wouldn't, anyway," he added, glaring at Alec. "I'm not Apollo. Or my father, for that matter."

"Yes," Alec said, "I know, but it doesn't hurt to leverage a threat or two every now and then, does it?"

For a moment, Hermes stared at him.

Then he broke into a smile.

"Very well," he said, turning to Margo. "Witch? You have a deal to fulfill."

She stared at him, prickly and furious, and contemplated the value of simply punching him in the face until Alec telegraphed for a moment of privacy, drawing her aside with the tilt of his head.

"I wasn't yours to barter with, Alec," she hissed to him when they were out of earshot.

"No," he agreed. "I'm sorry."

He said nothing else, and she frowned. "Is that all? You're sorry?"

"He won't hurt you, I promise. He's not…" Alec cleared his throat. "He won't. And actually, I hoped you might…" He trailed off again. "We could use his help, Margo," he admitted, and she blinked, surprised. "Magic on the island is draining faster each day. I thought maybe you could persuade him to help us."

"So you—?" She stared at him. "You actually *want* me to…?"

"What? No. No, certainly not… no." Alec's expression was battling itself. "I didn't say there was only one way to convince him. But he *is* a god," he mumbled, glancing over at an expectantly half-smiling Hermes. "So, if you like him—"

"Alec, *Jesus*," Margo exhaled, yanking herself away from him. "That's—how can you *possibly*—"

"Margo." He paused her with a hand on her inner arm, loose around her wrist. "At least you'll be safe," he told her quietly. "I know you'll be safe—Hermes isn't a threat. He's a young god, foolish. Only interested in being entertained." He kissed her forehead lightly. "I'm just saying, you owe me nothing. I'll see you tomorrow," he said, his voice hoarse, and then he gave her a nudge in Hermes' direction, urging her forward as she glanced over her shoulder at him, somewhere between bemused and betrayed.

"Come along, witch," Hermes beckoned spiritedly. "How do you feel about ambrosia?"

Alec had frequently told her never to eat anything offered by an immortal, god or otherwise, which up until now she'd found a pointless lesson. "How about pancakes?" she said instead, and Hermes' grin broadened. Behind her, she could have sworn she felt Alec's approving glance, though the last thing she wanted to do was to look at him.

"Pancakes it is," Hermes said, looping an arm through hers and spiriting them away.

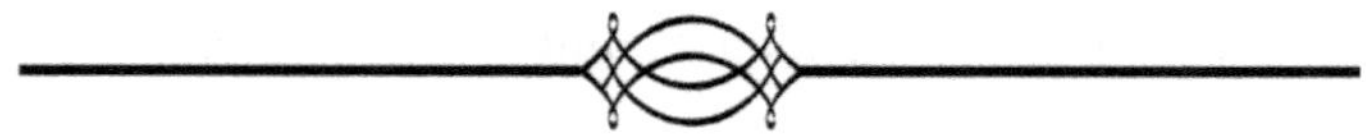

"You owe me nothing." I couldn't stop thinking about that. Was Alec honestly saying I should give Hermes, an actual Greek god, some sort of… shot at seduction? Did he really think my feelings about him were simply because he's my only viable option on the island? I guess I've said as much myself several times. Now that I think about it, maybe he's got a point. Not about seducing Hermes, obviously, but maybe he's

right about… this. About us. Maybe I don't owe him anything, and he doesn't owe me.

Was it possible that all of this, everything between us, was really just me getting horribly caught up in the moment? I've done it before, to some extent. Maybe Dan is proof of that. Maybe all I managed to learn from this summer of monsters was that I was always just another one of them.

By the time they made it to the diner, Hermes had crafted himself a set of normal clothes—or, more accurately, normal-adjacent: a short-sleeved Hawaiian shirt and a pair of boardshorts, his feet shoved into quintessential California flip-flops. Absurdly, even with the outfit, he remained a blinding level of handsome that everyone on the island seemed to notice.

"Need anything else?" asked the adoring waitress, a girl Margo happened to know was a harpy once the sun went down.

"Nothing, thanks," Hermes said, happily digging into his first bite. "So," he said with his mouth full, turning to Margo. "What sort of human men do you like?"

"I… what?" she asked, and Hermes swallowed, downing half his mimosa before returning to the question.

"What sort of human men do you like?" he repeated, and though she wanted to point out that her inability to understand him was *not*, in fact, the result of his mouth being full but rather that the question itself was somewhat impossible to answer, he merely continued on. "I can always change my appearance, you know, if you prefer. Blond?" he asked, and she didn't even see the transition. She merely looked at his blond hair and failed to remember what it had looked like before. "Dark-skinned?"

Again, she couldn't remember sitting across from a man who hadn't looked precisely like Idris Elba. "Do you like women?" asked a petite blonde who might have been Kristen Bell. "Or wait, no—"

"How's this?" asked a perfect replica of Alec Del Mar, only this version was smiling far too broadly to have been the real thing, and Margo blinked, startled.

"Please don't," she said, and the Alec across from her frowned.

"Why not?" he asked, shoveling another bite into his mouth.

Margo grimaced. "It's not… he's not. I don't," she finished lamely, and from the looks of it, unconvincingly as well.

"Well, that's probably best," Hermes agreed, now himself again, or something she assumed was himself. He glowed golden once more, his dark hair fading to sun- bleached strands like a water polo player who'd spent too much time in the pool. "Considering everything, that is."

"Considering… everything?"

Hermes shrugged, taking another large swallow of mimosa. "He's the island's guardian," he said, as if Margo hadn't heard that a million times before. "You, meanwhile, seem like a woman who wouldn't care for being trapped."

"Who says I'm trapped?" Margo echoed. "The only trap I've fallen into is having to spend the next twenty-three hours with you, which wasn't even my doing."

"Mm, that's a deal, not a trap," Hermes corrected her. "I meant the whole 'life on an island' thing. Doesn't seem to suit you." He paused, eyeing her. "What does a witch like you end up on an island for? Circe was on an island, sure, but she was the one trapping people, not *being* trapped." He wiped his mouth, frowning. "What's your story?"

"I—" She remembered Alec had advised her not to tell. "I just like it here."

"Mm, very well," Hermes said doubtfully. "Lies it is, then."

She opened her mouth, then closed it.

Let him think her a liar, she thought, so long as the hours passed quickly.

Alec was at least correct that Hermes wasn't a threat. If anything, he was a little bit amusing. He was fascinated by the most mundane parts of the island, like what the creatures were up to when they were imitating the behaviors of mortals rather than being their 'normal' selves. He had countless questions for Cora about the indoor plumbing of the hotel. He wanted to know everything about the ingredients in Sadie's perfume. He asked Faith about the orthopedic insoles she wore to keep her bunions from worsening.

Gradually, as the afternoon grew later and it occurred to Margo to wonder what Hermes might think about the concept of postcards, she took him to the general store to chat for a few minutes with Henry, the sulky mermaid she felt certain would keep Hermes immensely entertained.

"What's this?" Hermes asked, holding up a bottle opener in the shape of a beaver's mouth.

"A tool for dulling our miserable lives," Henry replied, and Hermes looked positively delighted, purchasing three of them and giving one to Margo as a gift, 'just in case.'

"I'm going to give him a try if things don't work out with you," Hermes remarked in reference to Henry, glancing over his shoulder at the back of Henry's neck as they exited the store. The potential object of his affection, meanwhile, returned to his usual work-hour nap.

"You still think I might sleep with you?" Margo echoed in disbelief, and Hermes looked at her, genuinely bewildered.

"You think I want *sex* from you? No, no," he said, now looking both insulted and plainly injured. "I mean, yes, of course, but that's hardly the important part." He picked up a rock, tossing it out onto the waves and watching it skip over them into the distance. "I hope that hits Poseidon," he murmured to himself, then turned to her with a smile. "Am I really so terrible, witch?"

"My name is Margo," she reminded him.

"Mm, yes, apologies. Margo," he corrected, and the sound dripped languorously from his mouth. "Am I so terrible?"

No, he wasn't, she thought grimly. In fact, he was inquisitive and funny and a bit of a cad, having stolen at least two caramels from Sadie's purse merely for the fun of it and, as he had with the bottle openers, offering one to Margo as a gift. Hermes was handsome, too, of course, and friendly. He was warm and playful. He was a god, and for some strange reason she'd probably never understand, he was enamored with her.

He must have noticed her opposition giving way. "Margo," he said, leaning forward, though before she gained the presence of mind to pull away, his lips were meeting hers with confidence; with a statement that gave way to a question as her breath caught in her mouth.

"I—" She swallowed, resisting. "I could use your help. With the island."

"Okay." He kissed her again, light this time. Like the sigh of the tide on her toes where they stood in the sand, feet buried. "What do you need?"

"I have to… fix some holes," she said dazedly. "Get some food."

"Done," he said. Another kiss, this time to her cheekbones, and then her eyes, which fluttered shut. He pulled her closer, his hands on her hips. He smelled like the earth after it rained and tasted like the sweetness of an old memory, faded with time and sun. "Whatever you need, consider it done."

"If—?" she asked, a little breathless. His hands were traveling over her spine. "What would you expect in return?"

"Nothing," he said. "You asked, so you'll have it."

He kissed her swiftly, with dizzying persuasion. "But—"

"That's how gods are, Margo. Don't you have any faith?" One arm curled around her waist, holding her tightly against him. "Not everything is tit-for-tat. Some things you need only to ask for."

She wondered if she should ask for more than this. If she *wanted* more than this. The little flames of her long-dormant appetite licked at her again, rising up and flooding her lungs until her pulse sped rapidly, the rest of her on the edge of giving in.

"I," she began. "Hermes, I, um—"

His hands traveled under her shirt in the same motion as the waves sliding over her feet, the tide changing, reaching up towards the sand. Abruptly, she stopped short, pulling back.

"I can't," she said bluntly, turning away.

I want to get swept away, Alec.

Yes, she was angry at him, but nothing had changed. No matter what Alec Del Mar did or said, somehow, he was always the one she wanted. It wasn't simply the thrill of the chase or the effect of having no other options. She wanted him, and only him.

Hermes watched her, looking amused. "Draconis?"

She shut her eyes. "Yes."

"Ah. A pity. For you, I mean. I already knew as much."

She cracked one eye. "What?"

"Well, it's one thing to inadvisably love a man, and quite another to love one that requires you to remain stuck on an island—"

"Who said anything about *love*?" she demanded, and Hermes rolled his eyes.

"Fine," he said. "I'd hoped you'd be above average mortal stupidity, but—"

"I don't love him." She couldn't. Hermes was right, after all. She'd be leaving as soon as the island was fixed. The equinox, she reminded herself. She had less than a month left here on Avalon. Alec couldn't leave. *She* could stay, but—

Well, she thought, frowning. She *could* stay, but…

"I don't love him," she insisted, and the ocean lapped at her toes, laughing at her. Hermes, too, half-smiled, arching a brow. "I couldn't, because that would mean—"

She blinked, and Hermes was wearing Alec's face again. Her heart leapt and lurched while she stood stock-still and torn.

Oh no. "What if I love him?" she wrenched out aloud, and Hermes changed back to himself, satisfied.

"How positively dreadful," he replied, giving her a sunny nudge as they made their way back toward Main Street.

September 1

I don't understand how this happened. He was so awful. I've never met anyone more irritating or more relentlessly, oppressively off-putting than Alec Del Mar. He constantly gets under my skin. He's vain, blunt, arrogant, manipulative, infuriating, selfish, maddening, clever, funny, and strangely kind…

He's not what I would have chosen for myself, but that's the worst part, isn't it?

He's nothing I ever knew I wanted, and somehow, he's everything I can't live without.

Alec looked around, toweling off from his shower and frowning curiously as he noticed there was no one else but her in the room. "Where's Hermes?"

"He's with Henry." Hermes had kissed her cheek and sent her off with his blessing even before the twenty-four hours were up, determining his pursuits better aimed elsewhere so long as she promised to still be his friend. Evidently the whole mermaid-tail thing was not much an issue when one was a god, though Margo really hadn't wanted to ask him questions about the details. "He said he'd help us with the island."

"Oh, good." Alec moved towards her, hesitating before sitting on the opposite corner of the bed. "How was it?" he asked, not quite looking at her.

She understood now that *you owe me nothing* had been only half the story. It was less *you owe me nothing* than it was *please, I hope you give me something, even if nothing is owed.*

"Not awesome," Margo said, and his brow knitted with apprehension. "He made me do something terrible."

Alec turned sharply. "What?"

"Oh, nothing really. Just the worst thing I could think of." She glanced up at Alec, whose face was unreadable and frozen. "He made me admit to myself that I might be in love with you," she clarified, and he blinked.

Inhaled sharply. Exhaled slowly.

"Margo," he said, clearing his throat. "I suspect you become a little more self-destructive every time we talk."

"Yes," she agreed. "That's almost certainly true."

"Margo." He shut his eyes. Then, more helplessly, "*Margo*."

She crept towards him, hearing something in his voice that compelled her closer, so she slid her legs on either side of his, holding him from behind to rest her cheek against his spine. "Alec."

"I can't—" He trailed off. "I shouldn't."

"Why not?"

"Because… because you can't stay. No matter how much I want you to."

She pulled back, surprised. "You want me to?"

"Margo, don't be ridiculous." His voice was edged with defensiveness, prickly and lined with doubt. "I've never wanted you to go. Isn't it obvious? But I can't keep you here. I couldn't, and it's not fair to—"

"You know what's not fair, Alec?" she asked, running her fingers over his bare chest. "That I've told you I love you, and you still haven't said anything in return."

She felt him give a ragged sigh. "Margo—"

She moved his arm and twisted into his lap until she'd slid around to face him, settling herself with her chest pressed against his. He held his breath, carefully not touching her, and she ran her fingers over his mouth, slowly.

"I want you, Alec," she whispered to him, and felt him shiver beneath her hands. "I want you to look at me, to take me in slowly, to take your time." His dark eyes rose to hers, the lids of them heavy with want, and she pulled his hands to her waist, up her ribs, to the curves of her breasts. "I want you to put your lips on me carefully," she teased, "and I want to you to feel me, all of me, before I feel you in my—"

"I love you," he choked out, and she froze, startled. "Margo West, impossible woman and disastrous witch, I'm inadvisably, inarticulately, implausibly in love you. I love you, with every strand of this form and with all of my others, and because of you—" He broke off, tightening his fingers in the mess that was her unwashed hair. "Because of you," he murmured, "I no longer hate this island. I no longer hate this job. I don't even hate the gods."

He kissed her, slow with gratitude, and pressed his forehead to hers.

"If I've been cruel to you," he began, but she shook her head.

"Alec," she murmured, drawing his hands below the fabric of her sundress. "Not now."

He slid his hands over her bare hips, absent the hindrance of underwear, and thankfully grasped her intentions, a carnivorous form of understanding manifesting on his face. "Are there any visiting gods I should be expecting?" he asked her, voice dry. "Any ex-boyfriends on their way, perhaps?"

She shook her head. "None."

He leaned her away, one hand on her lower back while the other crested between her shoulder blades, and brushed his lips carefully over the exposed skin of her neck, her shoulders, her breasts. His tongue slid out over thin cotton and she closed her eyes, submitting herself to his wanderings; ruled by the dominion of his lightly scraping teeth. When he'd committed every inch of her décolletage to reverence, he pulled her close again, lifting the dress from the frame of her shoulders and over her head as she tugged at the towel around his hips, leaving them both bare and waiting.

There were a lot of words that might have suited the occasion: *I want you, Alec. Make love to me, we've waited long enough. How do you want me, Alec? Take me. Have me. I'm yours.* Ultimately, though, she said nothing, and neither did he. In the end it was a wordless detente, and he lay her back against his bed and braced himself above her for a moment, something on the tip of his tongue as he gripped possessively at her hips.

It came out in nothing but a whispered sigh, though she was able to translate it perfectly. It was the sound of having waited a lifetime, several lifetimes; a breath of relief for which there were no words.

Later, she would learn there *was* a word for it in Greek: *nikhedonia.* Elation preceding victory. Anticipation. Exultation.

At last.

And then Alec Del Mar, whom she had loved nearly as much as she had loathed him, brought her to wordless feats of triumph—again, and again, and again.

September 7

With Hermes here to help with the fractures and cracks in the island's magic, we have most of the 'generator' repaired. I can have nights with Alec again, and believe me,

I've been taking advantage, though there isn't much to say about sex that wouldn't immediately sound like teen infatuation. If anything, sex is the least of it, even though it's easily the best I've ever had. He's… got stamina, I'll say that much. And talent. Normally I'd call it skill—talent is innate, I think, while skill is practiced, and I've always thought of myself as skilled—but what Alec has is almost certainly talent. Either that or we're just so good together it feels like instinct; like something brand new. He knows how to touch me in ways he can't have gotten from anyone else, and I am more myself in his arms than I have ever been. I no longer worry about being something so paltry as <u>normal</u>.

But still, it's more than sex. We've already been in the habit of staying up all night, so now, when we're done with our rounds on the island, we talk about everything, about little things, about nothing. He still argues with me, so irritatingly that I sometimes want to slap him. I still annoy him, to the point where he stomps out of the room and then returns immediately to kiss me with fury, telling me I'm impossible, that I'm terrible, that he loves me. Oh, he loves me, he says, sounding frustrated and resigned, and I kiss him back and tell him that I'm right, and oh yes, I love him, too.

Meanwhile, Dan's been sending a lot of emails over the last couple of days. I know he's got projects for me—things that admittedly sound very, very interesting—but I don't know what to do. I can't leave this behind.

How could I ever do anything but stay?

He'd been kissing his way down each individual vertebra while she drank her wine, which was… idyllic. Intoxicating. She was equally drunk on the beverage that she was pretty sure had been stolen from Dionysus as she was on the languidness of Alec's touch.

"What's the island like during the other seasons?" she murmured, and Alec chuckled against her skin.

"It's still California, Margo. There aren't really seasons."

"Well, *sure*, but—"

"The tourists will be back as soon as I fix everything." He'd begun to massage her lower back while she mewled her contentment, settling her cheek against his pillows. "The cruise ships, the casino, all of that. Things will be busy again."

"No time for spontaneous massages once the summer ends, then?" she sighed in disappointment, and he shook his head, leaning forward to kiss her shoulder.

"Believe me, I'd make time," he said, and seemed to consider saying something else, though he must have changed his mind.

"Well, I can help you with the casino," Margo told him after a moment of silence. "Maybe come up with some signs alerting witches not to accidentally cause any sort of major disruptions." He dug sharply into a knot on her upper back, and she turned with a growl. "*Alec*, you ass—"

He kissed the same spot, apologetic.

"Or I could hold some lyre concerts," Margo continued, resting her chin on her hands. "I'm getting really good. Sadie was furious I kept that little Coast Guard boat away last night."

"She was, wasn't she?" Alec agreed, though he didn't elaborate. Margo frowned a little, bemused. Normally he would have said something about her overestimating her lyre-related gifts.

"You sound weird," she said.

He was still avoiding something. She tried to turn onto her back to protest but he stopped her, removing the wine glass from her hand and setting it on the nightstand before easing her hips up, his hands tight on her thighs.

"Let autumn come when she wishes," he said. "I'm more concerned with you."

Margo opened her mouth to argue but then Alec's tongue had slid somewhere far more interesting, prompting her to a stifled yelp that smoothed to a moan, gradually transcending to whimpers.

"At some point we're going to have to talk about this," she told him, sighing.

He didn't reply. Not with words, anyway.

She, meanwhile, found distraction within minutes, forgetting the conversation entirely.

September 22

Strange how quickly time can pass. It seems like when I first arrived on Avalon, time positively crawled. Now, just when I've settled in and begun to really have a life here, it's the fall equinox already. Autumn is here and summer is over, just like that. I've been through so many summers before that it seems unlikely I'd be so sad to see one go, since they always return. This time, though, it does seem as if something golden is somehow fading.

Dan's emails have stopped, but I still look for them. I thought about writing my letter of resignation today, but I couldn't bring myself to do it.

Maybe too many things are ending. Maybe I just want one thing gold to stay.

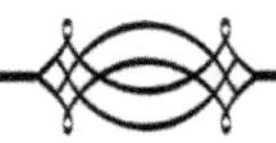

The day of the equinox was strangely reflective of the day of the solstice, when Margo had first met Alec Del Mar. "Come join us at the casino this evening," Sadie had said, and Margo had been quick to agree, not bothering to add she'd already planned on it for oh, give or take a quarter of the strangest year of her life.

"Sure," was all she said, as if the idea was newly resplendent.

"Will Alec be escorting you?" Faith asked hopefully, and though even a mere few weeks ago Margo would have opposed the suggestion, this time she only smiled into her morning cup of coffee, adding a nod that Amelia cooed over with helpless glee.

"Do you need a dress?" Cora had asked Margo later, and rather than deny it (or question the collection of oddly valuable formal gowns), she simply agreed. Cora was a dragon; of course she was compelled to hoard treasures. That she would lend one to Margo was a remarkably kind offering, knowing everything Margo now knew.

"Thanks, Cora," Margo said with as much sincerity as she could muster without over-explaining herself, eventually letting Amelia and Faith fix her hair and makeup while Cora offered her more jewelry. By the time she walked into the Avalon Casino, finding Alec waiting for her in his disastrously attractive tuxedo beside a broadly-grinning Hermes (and a smugly guilty Henry, which suggested they'd been up to something moments before), Margo felt a surge of joyful belonging that she hadn't felt in a long, long time.

"Hi," she said, taking Alec's arm, and he kissed her. She couldn't help it; she looped both arms around his neck and pulled him closer, refusing to let the kiss end until Sadie cleared her throat loudly, gaze flicking over the noticeable degrees Alec's hand had dropped in the direction of Margo's rear.

"Excuse me," Sadie sniffed tartly. "There's no need for that sort of show if we're not even invited to the denouement."

"Unless we *are* invited?" Hermes prompted, hopeful.

"Who are you again?" Faith said.

"Oh, no one, just a huge fan," Hermes replied as Alec rolled his eyes, leading Margo away from the casino's main floor and down a narrow staircase she'd never quite noticed was behind the grander marble one.

"Fixing the spell is fairly simple," Alec told her, one arm loosely around her waist as he led her down a labyrinthine series of corridors. "No incantations or anything, just a relatively simple binding. It won't feel like magic you've done before, though, because it isn't."

"Wait. Why am I doing it?" she asked, balking.

"Well, you created the problem," he said.

"Alec, for the millionth time—"

"I'm *joking*, Margo." He brushed his lips against her temple. "You've worked hard all summer. Don't you want to know what it's like to hold magic like that, from the very gods themselves? Consider it an honor, or at least… I don't know. Fun." He glanced at her. "I told you, Margo West, you're magic. More magic than I'll ever be."

"You're a dragon," she reminded him drily, and he shook his head.

"I'm a man who was a set of stars, and a dragon before that," he corrected her. "I have been at the bidding of the gods my entire life, Margo, so I'm slightly more capable than most of understanding what it means to take your destiny into your own hands." He paused beside a door, glancing at her, and then removed the vast ring of intricate keys, slipping one into the lock.

"Now it's your turn," he said, gesturing her inside.

He'd always described the tumor of disruptive, re-animated island power as something of a vault, which was definitely what this room looked like. An old bank vault, which didn't possess anything inside it but a pulsing, radiating form of energy she has only able to recognize from her months on the island. It was the same set of materials as the blanket of generated magic that had warped and reformed (with hers and Hermes' help) around the island. Margo could feel it like the fingertips of something familiar, but could also sense that the edges were unconnected somehow; like something that had been carelessly unplugged, only it wasn't just *one* cable, but many. Some strands were frayed but still connected, while others had snapped clean in half.

Even to Margo, who'd had so little training as a witch, the solution was obvious. She had to plug everything back in.

"That's it?" she asked aloud, doubtful of her own diagnosis, and Alec nodded.

"That's it," he confirmed. "If we'd come down here on any other night, you wouldn't have been able to see or feel it so clearly, but it's the equinox. Tonight, all the earth's power is yours to harness." He shifted her hair to one shoulder, kissing the back of her neck. "I'll be right here if you need me."

For a second she wanted to argue, to tell him she didn't want to do this alone, but it occurred to her that maybe she really could do this much more easily than he could. He'd had a certain amount of power granted to him by the gods to use, but this was about magic, not authority. This was the same force she had running through her blood, and her mother's. *This* and *her* and everything else in this world were made of the same materials, and she stepped close to the first of its wavering powerlines, pulling at opposite ends of a matching set and binding them together.

They fought her for a second, but then fell into place, quieting. Around her the other pieces hovered, waiting, and she stepped forward, fixing each little strand of magic, one by one. She could see now what had happened; the spell that colonized the island for the sake of its inhabitants had always belonged to the gods, passed to Alec to suppress the natural entropy of Avalon itself, the natural magic of earth and tides. His control had kept the island's power frozen, stable, and bound to the same unwavering force, but Margo had disrupted that when she used her own power—her own magic being more similar to earth, and Avalon, itself than the divine.

So, as much as she hated to admit it, Alec was right. She was the one who could, and *should*, put it back.

She knitted and wove, plugged and powered. It took her about an hour, but eventually she got to the last remaining thread, sliding a hand over it and soothing its frazzled edges, and then the lights in the building crackled cheerfully, settling to a low hum of resolution.

"Done," Margo said, stepping back with faint aches in her limbs, and Alec took her in his arms, exhaling with relief or gratitude or maybe… something she wasn't sure how to name. Sadness, she thought, frowning to herself, though when she pulled away to go upstairs—to play a magicless game of craps this time—he held on tightly, unrelenting.

"Alec," she said with a laugh, "what's going on?"

"I just—" His voice was hoarse. "I'm not ready to let you go yet."

"We can do this upstairs, you know," she reminded him. "Sure, Sadie will have comments, but Faith and Amelia will be pleased, so really it's a wash."

"I know, I know. Just…" He cleared his throat. "Just give me a minute."

He buried his face in the line of her neck, breathing her in. She tightened her fingers in his jacket, recognition dawning. Slowly, she calculated all the things over the last few weeks that he hadn't said, or that he had tried not to say. She pieced it together and found his sorrow.

The summer was over. Her job here was done.

That meant something different to him.

"I'm not leaving, Alec," she promised him quietly, and he shook his head.

"You are," he said. "You have to."

"Alec, I could stay."

"No. You can't."

"I *could*—"

"You can't. Please just… don't."

She quieted, unable to shove aside everything she'd been trying so desperately to ignore. Maybe she'd been hurting both of them by ever pretending he was anything but right.

"You could come with me?" she suggested. "You might like New York."

She felt him grimace.

"You're right," she sighed in agreement, "you'd hate it. But I could find a different editor, or a different publication, or I could freelance—"

"No, you shouldn't, and I can't—" Another pause. "I won't keep you from it. You've done enough for me."

"But Alec, I could stay for a while, at least—"

"And make it worse? No, Margo, you have to go. Please." He held her tighter, pulling her impossibly close. "Please, don't ever let me become the person who keeps you here, who traps you." There was that word again: trapped. "Don't let me be that for you, Margo, I couldn't stand it."

She could feel a horrible thickness rising in her throat. "But Alec—"

"Margo." He tilted her chin up, half-smiling tiredly at her. "Of all my lives, the one I had with you was the best one."

She understood that nothing she could say would make it better. She tried—oh, she tried, she kissed him fiercely in the hopes it would do either of them some good—but in the end, he had been the one to say it perfectly. Alexios Del Mar, master of having the last word, had done it once again. Sure, later she would tell him some other words—some classically important ones, like the near-voiceless *I love you* she would slip in his ear while he made love to her for the last time, or even the teary *are you hungry?* which would make him laugh, because she really couldn't cook for shit—but his would be the sentiment she remembered most.

Of all my lives—

"Alec," she said, fighting tears, and he suffered it too.

You were the best one.

"I know," he said, and tucked her hair behind her ear, wordlessly leading her back up the stairs.

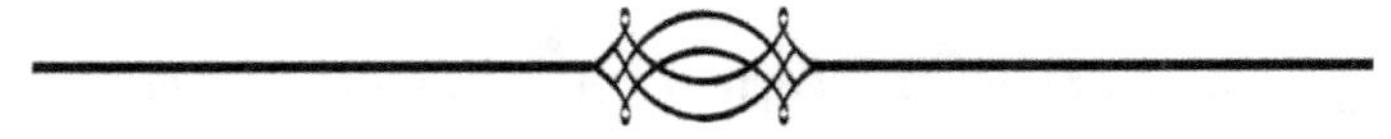

September 23

I've spent dozens of final nights with people in the past. Sometimes I knew what it was, sometimes I didn't. I used to think the surprises were the worst; the oblivious misconception that everything was fine only to wake up and find that it wasn't, hadn't been, that I'd missed it. This, with Alec, was the opposite. This was knowing perfectly well I wouldn't see him in the morning, but still being certain that even if it might hurt less, I couldn't be anywhere but here.

We slept for less than an hour. I left without waking him. I don't think he would have wanted something drawn out, or any repetition of all the things we'd already said. This is over, it has to be, and so I went.

I woke up and walked out the door, both devastatingly ready and crushingly unwilling to say goodbye to Alec, to Avalon, and to everything.

"I still hate that you're leaving, dear," Cora said wistfully, sighing as Margo finally checked out of the Sea Breeze. "It's the oddest feeling, but I really do suspect you're the only person in the world who's ever understood me."

"Well, who knows," Margo said, delicately not mentioning that was probably true, seeing as dragon-Cora wasn't safe to be around for anyone else. "Maybe now that the summer's over, some of the cruise ships will be back and you'll make new friends. You'll fill this hotel with more interesting people, or at least newer ones."

"That's true," Cora said, brightening. "New blood is always nice."

Margo, who had long ago learned not to shudder at such things, nodded. "Yes," she agreed. "A fresh start is always ideal."

"Well, don't be a stranger," Cora sighed. "Maybe you can come back next summer?"

"Maybe, yes." She'd make sure of it. Summer would never be summer again without Avalon, and besides, she'd gotten too damn good at the lyre to waste it on the unbearable humidity of Manhattan. "I think that can be arranged."

Cora stepped around the front desk, giving Margo a hug. "Safe travels, dear."

"Thanks, Cora." Margo returned the embrace and spared her a last, lingering glance. "By the way, I think you're totally fierce," she added, to which Cora blinked, surprised and delighted.

"Thank you," she said, gleaming a bit with pride, and Margo lifted the handle of her suitcase with a chuckle, making her way down to the port.

She spotted Sadie, Faith, and Amelia at the usual cafe. She was picking up her coffee to go, passing the divorcées as she left. They were deep in discussion about some new gossip, though Margo couldn't imagine what. Perhaps it was Henry's magnificently golden new girlfriend, 'Hermia.' Either way, Margo spared them a wave, and Sadie gave her a curt nod, immediately turning back to the conversation.

Margo, who had arrived on the island of Avalon furiously hating open water, gazed out onto the ocean and exhaled, the little undercurrent of magic she now knew to look for floating comfortingly under her palms.

"I know, I know," she said to it. "I'm going."

She boarded the ferry, choosing one of the open-air seats on top, and settled in for the two-hour ride. She put on her sunglasses and shaded her eyes, taking a last look at the island; at the casino, high on the hill, and the mansions, and the landscape that had changed her life.

Down on the docks, something glinted in the sun: dark hair and a pair of metallic-framed sunglasses. She waved, and he tilted his chin up, expressionless.

She paused for a moment, frowning, and at his lack of response she called up a wave, turning it slightly with a loop of her finger and conjuring it upwards on a salty breeze. It splashed near his face, prompting him to scowl, and he shook his head, glaring up at her.

"Say goodbye, asshole," she mouthed to him.

He lowered his sunglasses to look at her, pursing his lips. "Impossible witch," he mouthed back.

Then the ferry pulled away, setting off on the ocean, and she watched Alec Del Mar until he became a speck on the horizon; just another lovely thing on the island full of monsters she was leaving behind.

October 13
New York, New York

It's weird to be home. My apartment is totally disgusting, of course, and nobody will stop asking me where I've been, but it's also nice to be back to work. Dan tried asking me out again, but I shut that down right away. Miraculously, he didn't take it personally. He even promoted me, saying it was about time he'd recommended me for it. He's definitely right about that. I didn't even have to use any of my new fancy spells to punish him.

Sometimes I think about calling Alec, but I stop myself at the last second. We're not exactly good on the phone—or anywhere but Avalon, probably—and besides, I don't want to make things more difficult than they need to be. Maybe all we were meant to be was a summer. Maybe whatever we were, it was meant to fade, like seasons do.

Or maybe, somehow, when we're both ready, I'll find my way to him again.

The stars were hard enough to see in New York City, where the lights were at least twice as bright. It was cooling down now, and as much as she'd always loved autumn in the city, Margo desperately missed the salty Avalon air, the smell of the sea. She missed looking up at the stars and observing them clearly, stretching on for longer than her eye could see.

The blind date had gone terribly. Her friends, after pressing her about where she'd been all summer, thought getting out there again would be the best choice for getting back into the swing of things, but Margo could feel in her weary bones that it would be a long time before she ever took much pleasure in dating. Or relationships. Or other men.

Everything, she lamented, was so terribly normal.

At least this guy had taken her to a rooftop bar. At least she could feel the rush of city magic now, still a constant current in all her limbs now that she'd learned to recognize it. She'd developed a fondness for open space lately, and she was constantly looking upwards, missing that ocean view. She glanced again at the night sky, trying to find the constellation Draco. She seemed to keep missing it. Either that or it was hard to find.

She'd been staring for several minutes when she heard someone come up behind her.

"You're really not very good at this," noted someone derisively, and she froze.

Her fingers tightened around her glass.

That morning, she'd received a bizarre form of mail: a golden scroll, delivered to her office inbox. It had only contained two words: *You're welcome*, followed by an enormous letter *H*. She hadn't known what it meant, only that it had obviously come from a totally unsubtle Hermes and therefore must have been important. She'd been searching all day for signs, finding nothing.

Now, though, it made sense. Of course he'd wait to make an entrance. He was so very, very smug.

"Alec," she said, and turned to face him, already breathless.

He looked tan and toned and perfect, as sharply dressed as ever. "How was your night?" he asked casually. "Didn't happen to accidentally wake up some monsters this time, did you?"

God, he was the worst, she thought, and loved him fiercely for it.

Maybe Hermes had offered to take his place, at least temporarily. Gods were immortal, after all. Maybe Hermes had taken over the job of guarding the island long enough for Margo to have her successful career, or for Alec to share one mortal lifespan with her. It would feel like nothing to Hermes. Maybe not. Maybe Alec had snuck away. Maybe he'd simply cut and run. Maybe he was only here for one night, and that was all she would have.

She didn't care. He was here now, and he was hers.

"Hey, asshole," she said. "It's about time you showed up."

"You know, if you want me to stay," he advised, "you could try being a little nicer."

"True. I'd hate to upset your fragile sensibilities," she replied, and he took a step.

She matched it. Then another. Then one more.

"You're a dick," he said, and kissed her.

And with that, Margo West crashed into Alec Del Mar with the inevitability of the tide, breathing in the sea-salt taste of summer from his skin as she finally touched her fingers to him, to her own personal golden age, and to the undisputed glory of the horizon.

PARS FORTUNA (AUGUST-OCTOBER 2019)

LILY NASSER IS AN UP-AND-COMING politician; a Millennial who's had a startling rise to the top in advance of a narrow congressional race. Despite being widely considered the underdog, Lily firmly believes she's got a fighting chance. Why? If you ask her, it's because she's smart, she works hard, and she knows the game.

But when she meets preternaturally unlucky Sam, Lily's forced to question just how much of her success is in the hands of fortune.

PART I: LUCK PUSHER

"Lily, it's such a pleasure to host you this afternoon!"

"Oh, the pleasure's all mine," Lily replied, flipping her long black hair over one perpetually tanned shoulder and engaging the humbly enchanting beam she'd perfected after months of campaigning. This local talk show was one in a string of local talk shows that she doubted would be much different from the others—which was a good thing. She was practiced, not rehearsed, and it certainly didn't hurt her political ambitions that Lily, who even at her worst had never had a bad hair day in all her twenty-nine years of life, was such an appealing alternative to her opponent: a septuagenarian named Wallace Hart who'd sat in office unchallenged for nearly two decades.

"Now, Lily," said the host, Jackson Carter. "Many people question your qualifications for office, given your age and inexperience compared to Congressman Hart. True, you were top of your class at Georgetown Law," he conceded, sparing her a congratulatory nod, "but since then you've been working as a barista at a local café, haven't you? Not exactly the typical congressional career path."

"Well, I've never been very typical," Lily said, with the added sparkle of a confident smile. "The truth is, Jackson, that after leaving law school, I knew my heart wasn't in torts or contracts. No offense to the transactional enthusiasts of the world," she added, pausing for Jackson's predictable chuckle, "but, after working for a few months outside the razzle and dazzle of civil procedure, I started to realize that our politicians were deeply out of touch with their constituents. It was never about wanting to be a congresswoman," she added, always keen to make sure that much was clear. "I just wanted to do something good for my neighborhood, for my community, for my country. And you know what they say—" (This one always clinched it.) "If you want something done, do it yourself."

"If you want something done right, you mean?"

"Well, Jackson," Lily said, pausing to flash the camera a smile, "I'm so glad you agree."

The host laughed his delighted host laugh. "Always a charmer, Lily. So, with the election coming to a close next month, what are your plans moving forward?"

"I'm so glad you asked, Jackson, because *forward* is very much the goal. As you know, I've gone door to door for the entire summer trying to understand what people are looking for when it comes to social programs—"

"Yes, so admirable!"

"—Just part of the job, Jackson, really. It's all about public service, isn't it? Sure, my opponent prefers to spend his time schmoozing his corporate donors, but my team and I believe in real issues," Lily said, slyly dancing away from a deliberate smear, "and I'm happy to outline our five point plan for improving access to social services, continuing the fight for smart climate policy, and promoting economic growth among the middle class. You know, I represent so many disenchanted Millennial voters who no longer believe that a politician exists to stand for the things they consider important. And true, maybe there hasn't been one yet," Lily said, posing her usual question to Jackson, "but there should be, don't you think?"

"Couldn't agree more," Jackson declared, seducing the camera his own TV-worthy grin. "We'll be right back after the break with more details from congressional hopeful Lily Nasser!"

"Did you figure out how to watch the interview this morning, Grandma?"

"Yes, yes," Zaniah said, waving a hand at the computer that sat mostly unused in the corner, despite Lily teaching her how to use it at least a dozen times. "I had that nice boy from downstairs come do it for me. You know him?" she asked Lily, which was the sort of question that reminded her that while her grandmother was technically a medium, she was definitely still a grandmother.

"No, Grandma," she said, rolling her eyes. "I do not know the boy who lives in the apartment below you."

"You should meet him," Zaniah said firmly. "He's very polite, very nice. Well-mannered."

"Grandma, if all goes well, I'm about to be a congresswoman," Lily reminded her. "I don't really see the point in settling for 'nice' or 'polite.' Besides," she added with a scoff, removing the now-whistling kettle from the stove and pouring them two cups of tea, "even if I had the time to date, I doubt anyone would willingly subject themselves to my media circus right now."

"Hmph," said Zaniah, which appeared to be disgruntlement. "Your mother agrees with me that you should settle down with someone, you know."

This again. "You know, shockingly enough, even if Mom *were* an ever-present ghost who had nothing better to do than offer her opinion on the subject of my romantic life, I can't just take you at your word, Grandma," Lily said. "You're clearly biased."

"What? I'm paraphrasing, but fundamentally she agrees."

Lily spared a chuckle under her breath, sliding one cup across the table to her grandmother before seating herself with the other.

"Don't forget t-"

"I know, I know," Lily said. "Wait for Mom to read the leaves."

"Yes, that's right. She's slower now," Zaniah reminded Lily, waving a hand toward the ether, or possibly some other spiritual realm. "But still, she cares, you know."

"I know, Grandma." Alya, Lily's mother, had passed away after rapid deterioration from terminal cancer when Lily was a toddler. Lily had never been able to tell how real it was, Alya's communing with Zaniah, but there was no denying her grandmother had some sort of gift.

As had her mother, in fact. Both celestial witches, Alya and Zaniah had been extremely close, working the mystic industry as business partners for most of Alya's life. To Lily's understanding, Zaniah had been the quirky medium who communed with the dead while Alya was the pretty psychic who brought in passersby from the window. The two had rarely, if ever, argued; not even Alya's brief and sudden marriage to Lily's father, a mostly absent regional automotive salesman 'Nash' Nasser, had managed to tear mother and daughter apart. Lily had never known if it was sorrow or Zaniah's disappointment with her granddaughter's lack of magical ability that forced her to keep Alya's ghost alive.

Lily finished the rest of her tea, nudging it towards Zaniah and waiting perfunctorily. While her grandmother freely admitted she was never been able to read the leaves herself—"That was my daughter's talent, not mine," she used to say when people asked—she liked to conscript the more capable spirits do it for her. These days, Zaniah did the same work she always had, though it was mostly out of her living room and word of mouth rather than the aging storefront she'd once owned in the city's crumbling downtown. People still seemed to find her kitschy; in fact, the eclectic grandmother who could talk to ghosts was considered a 'fun fact' about Lily amid the personal minutiae of her congressional campaign.

"Hm," Zaniah said, closing her eyes. "My Alya tells me you will meet someone soon."

Zaniah usually said something along those lines, so that wasn't much of a surprise.

"Oh?" Lily said, humoring her.

"Yes," Zaniah confirmed, "though—" Briefly, her brow furrowed, and she turned with a little hint of surprise to whatever she was seeing that Lily couldn't. "You're sure?"

Lily glanced around the room, waiting.

"Well, that's trouble," Zaniah said, and turned back to Lily with a frown. "Maybe if we used the cards? Or no," she said, beginning her slow hobble towards her collection of unknowable mystic things, "the pendulum board should help—"

Oh no, not this. She'd be at it all day if they started now.

"Maybe another time, Grandma," Lily said quickly, scooping up her bag and rising to her feet. It was occasionally necessary to catch Zaniah before she started going full medium. "I have a few meetings with my team this afternoon, plus I have to draft a press release—blah blah, you know how it is."

"Right, right," Zaniah said faintly, accepting Lily's kiss on her cheek. "Okay, another time, then."

"See you tomorrow, love you!" Lily called over her shoulder, making her way to the corridor of her grandmother's apartment building just as her phone coincidentally began to ring.

Her daily visit to her grandmother over and done with, Lily got back to work, meeting her campaign manager at her apartment (the campaign office was well across town, and it had already been a long day) while scarfing down a spinach salad. Taj, the founder of the non-profit who'd first identified Lily as a viable candidate, was practically an installment at her kitchen counter now that he'd sorted out that his other candidacy bids were likely to fail. Out of every progressive candidate that Taj and his team had handpicked, only Lily still looked capable of winning the election in November.

"Right, so," Taj was saying, "I know we wanted to focus on small, incremental change, but I don't think that means we should ignore the big things."

"Of course not," Lily said through a mouthful of salad, gesturing for Taj to hand her the laptop. "I told you, we want to indicate that I *can* think big, even if we focus on small grassroots stuff. Otherwise, why run for congress when I could just run for city council?"

"Yes, good, same page, and als-"

They were cut off by a knock at the door as Lily frowned, glancing over her shoulder.

"Expecting someone?" Taj asked.

"Nope," Lily replied, hopping off the stool to peer through the peephole. "I never like a knock at the door," she muttered, shaking her head as an unfamiliar silhouette came into view. "Always so ominous these days unless someone's yelling UPS."

"Maybe we should say something about Millennials killing the doorbell industry," Taj said drily, and Lily briefly flipped him off before pulling open the door, revealing a youngish man whose shoulders and hair were very obviously damp.

"Hi," he said, in a tone that wasn't particularly friendly. He might have been moderately attractive if not for the tone, or for the look on his face, which indicated something like moody indignation. "Your bathtub is leaking."

"What? No it's not," said Lily.

The man seemed to take this exceedingly poorly. "Yes," he said, "it is."

Lily, more annoyed by his attitude than his request, folded her arms over her chest. "I haven't taken a bath since I was six. If something's leaking, it's not mine."

"Could be your washer. Got one in unit?"

She did, but she hadn't used it that day. Or had she? She was pretty sure she hadn't, and more importantly, she'd never be irresponsible enough to let one *leak*. "I told you, it's not my unit."

She moved to shut the door and the man's hand shot out, holding it open.

"Why don't you check?" he suggested, lips pressed thin. His patience, much like hers, had visibly strained.

"LILY," Taj yelled from the kitchen. "HURRY UP, WOULD YOU?"

"I'm very busy," Lily informed the man.

"Yeah, cool," he replied, "we're all busy. Luckily this shouldn't take long."

"Look," she said tightly, remembering that he probably lived in the building and was therefore an eligible voter, "I'm happy to help you figure out what's going on in about… I don't know, maybe an hour, but right now my campaign manager and I are—"

"Oh. You're that politician," the man registered, eyes narrowing. "I thought I recognized you."

"Yes, Lily Nasser," said Lily, giving the door another nudge, only to find that the man's palm was still flat against the wood. "Listen," she said. Voter or no voter, she was rapidly losing her will to be civil. "I'm trying to be reasonable, but—"

"You know, if you're really in such a hurry, then the five seconds it'll take to check should be the ideal length of time to end this," the man suggested, not budging.

"I'm not letting you into my apartment," Lily informed him.

"Fine," the man replied, shrugging. "Go look. I'll wait in the hallway."

"You could just leave," she reminded him. "I'm not going to find anything. I told you, it's not my leak."

"Well, forgive me if I don't take a politician's word as proof," he returned drily.

She scowled in unwilling concession, waiting for him to take his hand off the door. He did, pointedly holding it up for emphasis, and she let the door… not *slam*, exactly. But it wasn't her most polite door-closing maneuver, either.

She passed Taj on her way to the bathroom. "Don't eat that," she warned, catching him eyeing her salad, and he made a face.

"This? I wouldn't touch it with a ten-foot pole. Where are you going?"

"Nowhere," she called over her shoulder, checking the bathroom and determining that yes, as she suspected, the bathtub was perfectly fine. "Just off to prove my new neighbor a—"

She broke off, opening the door to her washer to discover that her feet were positively soaked.

"—liar," she finished, gaping a little at the flood that very definitely existed before hurrying to throw down some towels. "Holy—"

Damn. So she *had* used it, then, though she couldn't imagine what would have caused it to leak. She broke off, grimacing, as she realized she would now have to face the smug asshole waiting outside her door.

"One moment," she informed Taj upon emerging from her hallway, taking a deep, meditative breath before yanking the door open, forcing a smile.

The man, whoever he was, had leaned against the opposite wall of the corridor with his eyes closed, one of them snapping open once she resumed her position in the doorway.

"Washer or bathtub?" he said without preamble.

She opened her mouth, then closed it.

"Washer," she admitted tightly, and he shrugged.

"I'll get my tools," he said, turning away, and she balked, darting into the hallway after him.

"Excuse me?"

"I don't imagine you have any tools of your own," he said, pivoting around to face her. "You'll probably need more towels, too."

He turned away again as she gaped at him, furious for reasons she couldn't quite put into words. Something about his face, or his expression. Or his voice. Or his general demeanor, which was enormously male and hugely unwelcome.

"I'll just call someone," she half-shouted, then rapidly forced herself to cool down as he paused, heaved a burdensome sigh, and turned back to face her. "I'll call someone," she repeated, in a slightly more reasonable tone this time. "I have a good relationship with the landlord. It'll be taken care of this afternoon."

"Or," he replied, "I can take care of it now."

"I'm not letting you into my apartment."

He grimaced, then retreated a few rapid steps to where he'd been.

"I understand that I'm a stranger," he said, "and I've probably pissed you off, which is fair, because I can't exactly be my best self when there's water leaking into my apartment from all the cracks in my ceiling. But if you might consider some additional pertinent information," he added irritably, "then I would draw your attention to the fact that it is currently after five pm on a Friday."

Lily blinked, startled, and checked her watch. "It's that late?" Linear time wasn't exactly a huge consideration during campaign season.

"Yes," he confirmed. "Which means that not only is the landlord unlikely to answer your call, there won't be any plumbers willing to come until tomorrow, and when they do, they'll charge more, either for an emergency or for the weekend rate. Meanwhile," he ranted, "I actually know how to fix the problem. So would you like me to take care of it now, or would you like to deal with the mold that will inevitably make a home in your floorboards? Which, by the way," he added, "will eventually cave in my ceiling, all because you decided to put it off until later?"

Lily, who dealt with doomsday scenarios on a daily basis, narrowed her eyes in disagreement. Still, she supposed he was the one with the majority of the issue; she flicked a glance over his still-damp t-shirt and conceded, however grudgingly.

"I'm going to continue working," she informed him, deciding to set the terms.

"Fine."

"My campaign manager is here."

"Great."

"Please don't disrupt us."

"I find your work exceptionally boring and mostly pointless," he replied. "I can tell you right now that the intricacies of your washing machine are far and away more preferable to anything else I could possibly find in your apartment."

Lily bit her tongue on something snarky in return. "Fine. Lily Nasser," she said, extending a hand in forced politeness. "I suppose we should introduce ourselves."

"Sam Rainier," the man replied, accepting her grip with marked disinterest. "I'll be right back."

Then he turned on his heel and left, bypassing the elevator and taking the stairs.

Sam Rainier was many things, rude chief among them, but he'd at least kept his promise to stay out of the way. Lily hardly remembered he was there until after her meeting with Taj, which went on until close to nine. It wasn't until she'd ushered Taj out the door that she realized she should probably check on Sam's progress, returning to her washer to find him cleaning up the sodden towels on the floor.

"Good timing, just finished," he informed her, straightening, and Lily tried not to mention aloud that he was shirtless, his jeans slung below the nameless band of his black boxer briefs. "Sorry about this," he added, gesturing to the wet pile of towels in his hand and drawing her distracted gaze to something other than the slope of his abs. "Mind if I use your dryer? Mine's on the fritz."

Lily blinked, shaking herself. She supposed it was easier not to notice how attractive a guy was when he was being a dick. Specifically, when he was being a dick with his shirt on. She nodded absently, and Sam pulled open the door to her dryer, shoving the towels inside.

"Dryer sheets are right there," she blurted at him, remembering herself and then stepping closer, reaching for them on the high shelf. She toppled slightly, slipping on the still-damp floor, and Sam caught her hips, steadying her until they both registered the contact.

He released her, taking a lengthy step back.

"Thanks," Lily managed, putting two sheets in with the towels and hitting start, turning to face him. "I'm sorry, by the way. Not sure if I mentioned that yet."

"It's not your fault," he said, shrugging. "Washers leak sometimes, it's no big deal."

"No, I meant—" She chewed her lip. "I meant sorry for, you know. Being…"

"Unneighborly?" he guessed, and then, just as carelessly, "It's fine. Other people have handled it worse."

She felt her brow furrow. "How often has this happened to you?"

"Typically once a month or so," he said, and she blinked. "Usually something a little smaller, but I just moved in, so I expected something like this."

"Are you—" She broke off. "Are you a plumber, or…?"

"Me? No. Moved here for a startup," he said.

"Oh." Surprising. "Programmer?"

"Definitely not," he said, rifling his hair with a laugh. "I wanted to be one back in college, but I have a tendency to accumulate bugs." At her look of confusion, he clarified, "Software bugs. Code issues, whatever you want to call them."

Lily didn't know the first thing about code, but she figured that couldn't be a good thing for someone who worked in the tech industry. "So… what exactly do you do, then?"

"I run operations for venture capitalist firms," he said. "I handle risk management, mostly. When a new or risky startup gets an exorbitant valuation, VCs put someone like me around to put out fires. Means I tend to move around a lot," he added in explanation.

"Wow, that's—" She blinked, gesturing to the work he'd done on the dryer. "Sorry, I just assumed…"

"Understandable," he finished for her, highlighting the streaks tiger-striping his hands and forearms from toying with the washer's parts. "I just find it easier to handle most things myself. Faster, anyway." He untied his shirt from the loop of his belt, sniffing it and then frowning.

"This I'll deal with later," he muttered to himself, and then returned his attention to Lily, gesturing to the dryer. "Cool if I just come back?"

"Sure, yeah." Lily cleared her throat. "Should be done in about thirty minutes?"

"Great." Sam moved to pass her, pausing for a moment as he directed himself to the door, and then he turned back, pausing. "Listen," he said slowly, "I know I was a dick to you."

She made a face of yes, that's true.

"Rough day," he explained. "But I could've been nicer."

She gave him an arched brow of yep, also true.

"Don't feel like you have to," he said, "but I'm starving and I'm new to the area, so if you're hungry…"

He trailed off pointedly, and Lily blinked.

"Are you asking me to have dinner with you?" she said, surprised, and he shrugged.

"Think it over, I guess. See you in thirty minutes," he said, turning to leave just as her stomach let out a coincidental growl.

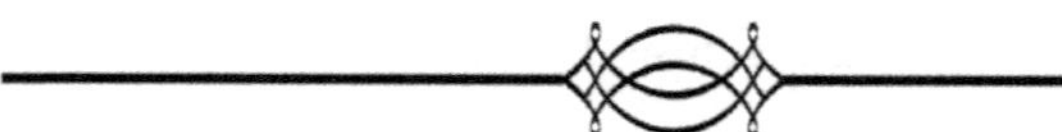

She met him at the door with a pile of folded towels, the strap of her purse already pulled over one shoulder. She'd worried briefly that she might appear overeager if she bothered to dress up any more than she already had, but having remembered that she was still running a highly visible campaign, she'd pulled on a nicer pair of jeans, thrown on some makeup, and selected the kind of casual blouse she wouldn't mind getting photographed in. He had done something similar, wearing a clean shirt and black jeans, and he now smelled a little like fresh pine and clean linen.

He did her the favor of not being too smug when she tacitly agreed to his dinner invitation, suggesting with as much nonchalance as she could summon that they go down the block for ramen. It was a new restaurant, hip and with some buzz, but not especially pricey. She'd still be in touch with her demographic, and hey, the owners were immigrants. All in all, a perfect choice.

"Soup, huh?" Sam asked. He pulled the door open for her, then pointed to the lip on the ground. "Watch out for the—"

She stumbled, missing it, and he caught her arm.

"—step," he finished with a laugh, propping her upright.

Lily felt her cheeks burn, taken aback at her awkwardness. What was that, twice now? She'd never stumbled before in her life. The clumsy romantic comedy heroine was one of her most tormenting pet peeves, as the whole thing always seemed completely unlikely. Women tripped and choked and spilled in movies, but not Lily. She knew how to walk, how to eat, how to hold a glass. She considered herself an expert in behaving like a functional human.

"Sorry," she said, and Sam gave her a puzzled half-frown.

"For what?"

"I… nothing," she amended, smoothing down her hair. "Hope I haven't lost your vote," she added, hoping a joke might salvage the moment of embarrassment.

"Oh, I've never voted," Sam replied, and Lily spun with dismay, knocking into someone as she turned to face him.

"Sorry, so sorry, I was just—What do you *mean* you've never voted?" she demanded, rounding on him. "Don't you care?"

"About… politics? No," Sam said, doubtful. "Not sure if you've noticed, but whoever the senator happens to be in whatever state I'm living in at the time doesn't have much of an impact on my life."

"That's—" She sputtered a little, trying not to use any overly aggressive words; it was *preposterous* was what it was, but that didn't seem like a fruitful jumping-off point for conversation. "You work for startups," she reminded him, hoping to appeal to his personal logic. "Don't you care about business legislation? Tech privacy laws? Taxes?"

"Sure," Sam said.

"But—"

"I just don't really see what one measly vote has to do with it," he told her, pulling up the menu on one of the iPads the restaurant used to take orders. "What's good here?"

"Democratic freedom," she told him sternly. "Our fiduciary duty as citizens to vote."

"Mm," he replied, not looking up. "And does that come with pork, or…?"

She groaned, and he glanced up, half-smiling.

"Fine," he said. "If I vote for you, will you tell me what's good here?"

"Don't just vote for *me*," she insisted, but seeing as it was probably not worth getting into at the moment, she sighed, pointing to one of the soups. "That one."

He hit the screen once, twice. No reaction.

"You try," he suggested, and she rolled her eyes, stepping in front of him to select it.

"Spice?"

"Medium, please."

She hit the respective buttons, ordering the same for herself.

"Split the bill?" she asked over her shoulder.

"Sure, if you want."

"I'm a modern woman, Sam."

"Well, there we go then. Do they take cash?"

"Oh, um—" That sounded like a headache. "I'll just pay," she assured him, and then, deciding to be a little bold, she added, "You can buy next time."

"Next time, huh?" His voice was a little softer when he was teasing her, she noticed. It made his brown eyes warmer, too. "Alright."

She dug out her debit card, sliding it when prompted and turning back to him. "Anyway, about you voting—"

He gestured over her shoulder with his chin. "Didn't work."

"What?" She turned, finding the error message on the screen. "Must not have swiped correctly or something." She slid it again, then resumed their conversation. "Anyway, listen, I get why you would think politicians are out of tou-"

"Still no," he said, pointing again, and she growled, turning to watch the message flash once again across the screen.

"Maybe it's just the strip or something." She dug another card out of her wallet, trying not to shiver when Sam's hands floated briefly over her waist. She paused, suffering a little tingle of excitement, before leaning back, letting her spine come into contact with his chest with the sort of deliberation that might have easily been mistaken for an accident. "I'll try this one," she said, narrating the transaction aloud as Sam's palm slid down to her hip. Even with how long it had been since her last romantic tryst, she couldn't believe how much her entire body thrilled from the tiny, insignificant brushes of contact.

She forgot about that, though, when the screen flashed with another error message. "*What* the—"

"This happens to me all the time," Sam said, unfazed. "Don't worry, I'll buy."

"No, no, you don't have to—"

"Hey," he said in her ear, leaning forward until the hint of his aftershave invaded the rest of her senses. "Relax, would you? You can buy the next one."

He leaned forward, hitting the button for 'pay in cash,' and Lily swallowed hard, finding it suddenly unacceptable that the detest she'd felt for him hours before had transmuted so helplessly to the reminder of him shirtless.

"This has never happened to me before," she admitted in apology when he finished paying, leading them over to two vacant counter stools.

"What, your card not going through?"

"Yeah." She made a face, pulling up her banking app. "It's probably just their machine, but—"

She broke off, blinking, as she noticed the PERILOUSLY LOW BALANCE message that popped up on her screen.

"I… what?" she said aloud, prompting Sam to glance over at her. "But… but I—"

"Well, there goes everything I thought about dirty politicians," he said, laughing to himself as she looked up with a glare.

"I'm not a *dirty politician*, asshole. I'm just someone who cares enough to run for office."

"I see that," he agreed, gesturing to the flashing message on her screen. "How exactly are you funding a congressional campaign, may I ask, if not with bribery and extortion?"

"Well, *I'm* not funding it, my campaign manager is… anyway, it doesn't matter," she said with a sigh, scrolling through her expenditures. "There must be a problem with a direct deposit from work, or something… Here, see?" she told him, holding up the screen and tapping it lightly. For some reason, it seemed crucially important to prove to him that she wasn't a total mess. "It just hasn't gone through yet. Weird," she muttered, shaking her head and sliding her phone back into her pocket. "Usually the check comes in just before I try to spend anything."

"Luck's a fickle mistress," Sam said. "It's why I carry cash."

"It's not *luck*," Lily informed him, making a face when he gave her a laughing glance. "What? It's not. I get paid, I spend money—it's the usual process of working for a living, not luck."

"Okay, sure, it's not luck. But sometimes it is," he said, and rotated his stool to face her. "Sometimes," he said, his mouth suddenly very present in her senses, "we get really lucky. Don't we?"

She crossed her legs tightly, one over the other. If her tongue happened to slip between her lips while she did it, well. That was just a consequence of dehydration.

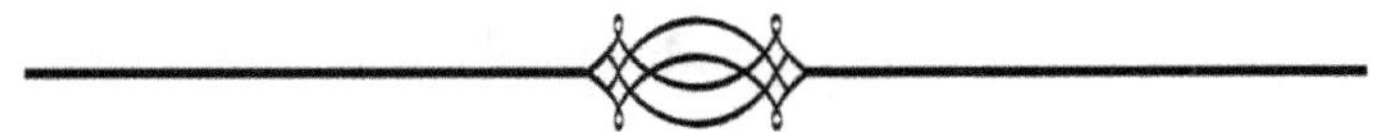

Sam was a meticulous eater, not that Lily minded. It meant the evening lasted until nearly eleven, by which point the kitchen had already closed and they were finishing their meal with a shot of sake each.

"Whoops," she said, licking the alcohol that had dripped onto her hand and then making a face. "I swear, I'm not usually such a disaster."

He laughed, giving his tiny porcelain glass a careful sip. "Oof," he said, shuddering. "That's a lot."

"You're not supposed to *sip* it," she told him with a groan. "This isn't fancy sake, okay? This is the kind you use to… you know, treat burns. Or kill brain cells." She shrugged.

"Hey, I'm not trying to be the guy who dies on a first date from choking," Sam told her, and to that, Lily paused, finding herself unable to repress a smile.

"First date, huh?"

Sam finished the rest of his glass, giving her a sly sidelong glance.

"What did you think it was?"

"Oh, I don't know." She flipped her hair over one shoulder, angling her stool to face his. Their knees touched as she moved, and she leaned forward. "A friendly hang?" she suggested blithely.

His palm slid over her thigh, fingers wrapping loosely around it.

"I could use a friend," he said.

"You sure could," she agreed. "You're an extremely off-putting neighbor."

He smiled. He had a nice smile, warm and filled with amusement whenever he chose to use it. The unshaven stubble around his cheeks accented the shape of his face perfectly, and after a certain amount of looking, Lily decided she'd done enough thinking about his mouth. Time to put it to use.

"Come on," Sam said, beckoning her to the door. "Let's get you home, Congresswoman."

His knuckles repeatedly brushed hers while they walked, the backs of their fingers meeting and departing in something of an anticipatory dance. They discussed a bunch of nothing—where they'd gone to school, the fact that he had three brothers who still lived back in Oklahoma, what her father had done for a living and how her grandmother had raised her—as they made their way back to their building.

"Stairs, really?" she asked, observing that he strode right past the elevator.

"Good exercise," he said. "Also, they don't get trapped."

"But what if the stairwell door locks?"

"I already checked," he assured her, gesturing her in as they traversed the four floors to her apartment.

Hers was closest to the stairwell door, and she paused while pulling out her keys, hesitating before things progressed.

"Listen," she said. "I don't really want to… rush this? But I'm honestly very busy," she told him firmly. "The election takes up a lot of my time, so—"

"Understood," he told her. "I'm in no rush."

"Right. Well." She swallowed hard, half-changing her mind. She wasn't normally a fuck-on-the-first-date kind of girl, but given how good he smelled and how stressful the campaign tended to be, she figured she could make exceptions. "I mean, I, um—"

"How about this." Sam stepped forward, taking her face in both hands. "I'll kiss you goodnight," he murmured, his mouth already disarmingly close to hers. "You'll say don't go, obviously," he mused, smoothing her hair behind one ear, "which I will definitely consider, and because I'm a gentleman, I'll kiss you again. Just one more time." He brushed his nose along her cheek, turning to finish in her ear, "Then I'll stay out here until the door closes. I'll send you a text that says 'that was fun,' and because you've got to play it cool, you'll wait to reply to me until the morning."

He leaned away, scrutinizing her face as her eyes fluttered shut, and then open.

"Sound good?" he said.

"Sounds perfect," she confessed, and he leaned forward, tipping her chin up to place his lips delicately on hers.

There was a jolt when they touched; an electric shock. "Whoa," Lily exhaled, the word escaping into his mouth, and Sam slid his hands into her hair in answer, pulling her closer to cup the back of her head with his palm.

Above them, the hallway light flickered and went out.

They both glanced up. "I should really have a talk with the landlord," she said, and then tightened her arms around him, pulling him closer. "And you," she murmured, "should really just come inside."

"Sorry," he told her, shaking his head. "Can't. I'm a gentleman."

She groaned. "You're an unhelpful prude is what you are."

"Eh, potato, potato." He slid his arms around her ribs, bending down for another kiss that was slower, deeper, more enthralling. This time, all the lights in the hallway buzzed and flickered, one of them sparking from afar.

"You'd better go," Sam said to her lips, "before I change my mind."

Lily nodded, breathless, and fumbled with her key, somehow managing to place it in the lock while Sam slid her hair from her shoulder, leaving the ghost of a kiss somewhere on the side of her neck.

"Goodnight," he told her, releasing her once the latch clicked. "Remember not to text me back until the morning. You're a busy woman," he reminded her, taking a step back. "Wouldn't want to give me the wrong impression."

"What impression would that be?"

"Oh, I don't know. That you like me or something."

She could feel her lips buzzing with the taste of him, rice wine and spices and the delicious promise of feeling like this all over again.

"Bye, Sam," she said, and he raised a hand in farewell, looking both identical and starkly different from when he'd leaned against her corridor wall that afternoon.

Once she closed the door, resting the back of her head against it, her phone buzzed from her pocket.

That was fun.

Lily smiled to herself, heart absurdly fluttering as she made her way to bed.

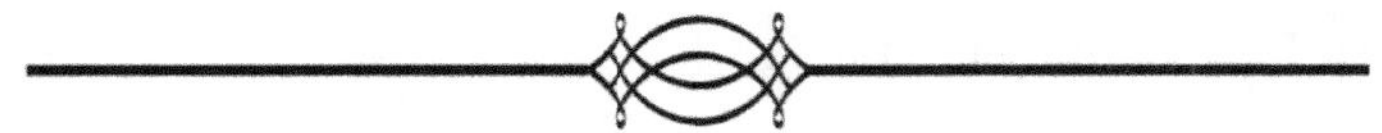

It wasn't every day that Lily was in a rush to see her grandmother, but she figured hey, who would possibly be happier to hear that she'd met someone than Zaniah, who never got tired of telling her to date? She sent Sam a text—*you're right, let's do it again sometime*—and replied to about forty campaign emails before hurrying to have breakfast with her grandmother, a brief reprieve from the canvassing that would occupy the rest of the day.

"Grandma," she said, bursting into the apartment. "I went on a date last night."

One of Zaniah's eyes snapped open from where she'd been meditating. "What?"

"I *know*," Lily agreed, removing her shoes and sitting cross-legged on the mat opposite her grandmother's. "It was amazing," she confessed, still floating a little from the memory of it. "Though, it was also a very weird night," she recalled, suddenly reminded that she needed to clear up the credit card issue with her bank.

Zaniah's brow furrowed. "Weird?"

"Mm, sort of. I mean, first of all, we only met because my washer flooded, which wasn't even a thing I realized washers could do. And I tripped a bunch, too," Lily sighed, "which, again, so stupid—"

"Hm." To Lily's dismay, her grandmother rose unsteadily to her feet, looking at one of the astrological charts on her wall. "Did you ask for his stars?"

She should have known her grandmother would want to know his astrological data before hearing anything else. "That's not exactly normal first date conversation, Grandma," she reminded Zaniah, not for the first time, "but I guess I can find out."

If there was one thing that had improved from Zaniah's day and age to Lily's, it was ascertaining personal information for purposes of astrology. Lily pulled up Sam's Instagram, his Twitter, and his—weirdly informative—LinkedIn account, finding his birthday and recalling the name of the town he'd said he spent most of his life. "Got his sun and moon," she told Zaniah, showing her the screen. "Ascending I still need the time of birth for, but—"

"You'll need to get it," Zaniah said. "Alya says it's important."

That wasn't exactly the sentiment Lily had been hoping for. "Grandma, I like him," she said, a little frustrated that Zaniah wasn't as excited as she'd hoped. "What does it matter if the stars say we're compatible?"

Zaniah hesitated, which was something she didn't often do. Not unless it was important. "Lily, there's… something we haven't told you.

Alya didn't want you to know," she admitted, "and I… well, I agreed with her at the time, but—"

"What is it?" Lily asked, mildly concerned.

"Your mother is clairvoyant, as you know," Zaniah said, "and I, of course, can speak to the dead."

That certainly wasn't new information. "Yeah, so?"

"You're not without gifts yourself, Lily."

"What? But I'm not—" She broke off, frowning. "But I can't do anything special."

"Actually," Zaniah said, and hesitated again, glancing at where she usually indicated Alya was standing, or floating. Whatever ghosts usually did. "You have quite a remarkable ability," Zaniah confessed. "One that your mother and I noticed when you were very young. A baby, even."

It wasn't like Zaniah to dance around her point. "Grandma. What is it?"

"Haven't you ever wondered why things have always been easy for you?" Zaniah asked, startling Lily with the unlikely question. "At every interview you've had, you've just *happened* to know the interviewer, or you've arrived just in time to meet someone important. And the store always has your size, doesn't it?" she asked, to which Lily blinked, unsure what she was being told. "Your train always arrives in the nick of time, sweetheart. And your campaign manager," she remarked, as Lily frowned again at the unexpected mention of Taj. "Didn't he walk into your cafe at the *exact* moment that you happened to be discussing politics?"

Zaniah was right—about Taj, and about everything—but still.

"What are you saying?" Lily asked, bemused. "Mom's a seer, you're a medium, and I'm…"

Could it really be so simple?

"I'm… lucky?"

It sounded like a joke, but Zaniah nodded gravely. "It is all a matter of our parts," she said, beckoning for Lily to look at her enormous book of astrological calculations. "Luck is little more than a convergence of fortunate probability," she explained, pointing to the patterns of stars that Lily had never fully understood. "Mastery, perhaps, of the likelihood that chance will lean your way. You have been blessed with the parts of fortune," Zaniah clarified, "but I'm afraid that, as with all stars, that alone is not a failsafe."

Lily looked up sharply. "What does that mean?"

She could see it on her grandmother's face even before she said the words.

"It means, my darling Lily," Zaniah said, "that even your luck may still run out."

PART II: STAR-CROSSED

The third floor was identical to the fourth, meaning it wasn't particularly difficult to find the apartment she was looking for. Lily knocked twice on the door, stepping back and waiting as she thought again about the conversation she'd had with her grandmother.

"Parts of fortune?" she'd echoed, doubtful, and Zaniah nodded grimly. "So what, because of the stars I was born under I'm somehow luckier than other people?"

"A bit more complicated than that," Zaniah said, exchanging a look with what was either the ghost of Lily's mother Alya or her own vibrant imagination. "You have our family magic in your blood, Lily, so it's not simply a matter of your stars. But it is certainly possible to be born under *unlucky* stars," she ruefully explained, "and for you, being near someone whose stars oppose yours could cause a warp to your abilities."

"But you said luck magic is just an increased likelihood that I get a favorable outcome." Having been raised with the impression that her mother and grandmother were the magical ones—as opposed to her, who had no such abilities—Lily found herself reluctant to believe what she was being told, even if she couldn't think of anything to refute it. "So how exactly would Sam's stars affect my luck?"

Zaniah gave her a small, sad smile. "A binary star is cursed to inevitable death, however spectacular," she said. "There's no telling what being around a person with opposing parts of fortune will do to the powers you were born with."

"But that doesn't mean his bad luck necessarily outweighs my good luck, does it? Surely it's not that simple." It certainly wasn't to Lily. For example, in her phone at that precise moment lived the text message from Sam that had brought her running breathless to her grandmother in the first place. "And why wouldn't you tell me that I had magic a long time ago?"

"Your mother didn't want you to know," Zaniah said again, looking wistful. "We argued over it, Lily, many times, about whether it would be better for you to be aware of it or not. In the end, she insisted that you deserved to live a life believing you had worked for everything you had."

It had never even occurred to Lily that any alternative might be true.

"Are you saying," Lily began, and swallowed hard. "Are you saying I haven't earned the life I have at all? Everything I've done—this *campaign*," she registered, suddenly dismayed. "It's all just... luck?"

"I'm simply saying that your experience has been, perhaps, easier than most," Zaniah corrected her gently. "But if this man has the stars I suspect he does, and if you continue to see him, then you may soon discover that life has a tendency to be otherwise."

The thought had plagued Lily all day, threatening to disrupt her focus throughout her meeting with her campaign manager, Taj, and the rest of her team. Fortunately or otherwise, it was getting close to election season now, so there wasn't much time to be distracted; all she had to do was ride the wave of momentum they'd built throughout the summer. No matter what her grandmother or her mother's ghost had to say about it, this campaign was about far more than Lily's luck. So long as she kept herself on track, there was nothing to worry about, so she put on her most reliable canvassing shoes and went to work, just as she had every day for the past year.

The moment Lily was alone, though, she hadn't been able to prevent herself from wondering again about the strange premonition her grandmother had revealed. If getting Sam's birth chart was all it took to prove her grandmother wrong, so be it. After a moment with her mirror to be sure she wasn't as covered in sweat as she had been earlier, Lily made her way down the stairs to Sam's apartment, knocking politely twice.

He was at the door in a matter of moments, pulling it open and giving her a surprised half-smile. By then, she'd only known him three ways: one, scowling at her with annoyance; two, coaxing her with humor; three, kissing her to breathless insanity.

Okay, so maybe this wasn't totally about Zaniah.

Lily gave a firm swallow as Sam leaned against the door, tie hanging half-undone below the buttons he'd freed around his throat. "Wasn't expecting to see you so soon," he remarked, though he certainly didn't look displeased. "Shouldn't you have hung me out to dry for a few more days?"

Lily noted a little bit of grease smeared on his cheek and forearms and fought a smile. They probably weren't at the stage where she could wipe it away, but lord almighty, she wanted recklessly to arrive there.

"I would have, but——" *But my grandmother says you're unlucky, so…* "But actually, I need something from you."

"Cup of sugar?" he guessed, and scrubbed at his cheek, looking equal parts handsome and irreverent. "Sorry," he added, gesturing to what she suddenly realized was a wrench in his hand. "I was working on fixing the dryer."

"You were working on it in… your suit?" she asked, making a face, and he chuckled.

"I own this exact shirt in about fifteen varieties, plus five versions of this tie. And I try not to get too attached to any articles of clothing. Want to come in?" he asked tangentially, gesturing behind him. "I'm not really settled yet, but it's probably better than chatting in the hallway."

Lily accepted with a little flutter of anticipation that made her feel stupid, girlish, and totally, freakishly enamored. "Sure," she said, adjusting her ponytail so her hair swam down the left side of her shoulder, boosting her confidence to something more befitting a normal, well-adjusted adult. "I guess I could have called first, but I just—"

She broke off as she stepped over his threshold, noticing that by 'not really settled,' he hadn't been exaggerating. "Do you even own *anything?*" she asked him, glancing around at the sparsity of items in his apartment, which amounted to… a brown leather sofa. A table lamp, which was sitting atop a small pile of books on the floor. A half-unpacked box of pots and pans, and an ironing board, the cord neatly curled around the iron itself at a considerable distance from any possible outlet.

Speaking of outlets, they had been… baby-proofed? Lily noted the plastic inserts and turned to face Sam with confusion.

"Exactly how unlucky *are* you?" she asked him, and he laughed, letting the door shut behind him.

"I mostly consider myself more realistic than other people," he said.

"So, very unlucky, then," Lily guessed, and he shrugged, still smiling.

"Things can go wrong, and they often do. It's not really a question of luck so much as probability."

An odd mirror of what Zaniah had said about Lily's luck. "Has it always been that way?"

"It's the way of the world, isn't it?" Sam asked, and while Lily contemplated an answer, he leaned against the counter; setting the wrench down carefully, as if it might destroy the granite below. "Anyway, you said you needed something?" he prompted, obviously ready to change the subject. "Surely you wouldn't be here so soon otherwise," he added, giving her a wry glance. "Since I know you're very busy and important."

"Well, you're going to think it's stupid," she assured him. "It's… pretty much nonsense, really, but I'm just going to need you to trust me."

"Is this about donating to your campaign?" Sam asked, feigning a sigh. "Fine, I'll give you five dollars, but don't expect me to be pleased about being on your email list."

"No, I just—" She rolled her eyes. "*No*," she informed him, silencing him with a glare while he smothered a laugh. "I just needed to know a weird bit of personal information."

"My mother's maiden name? My childhood pet? I knew it," Sam sighed. "Politicians *are* crooks."

"No, I—shut up. I just—" Oh, to hell with it. "I need to know what time you were born," Lily admitted, as Sam's face twitched with bemusement. "Okay, look," she said, before he could question her. "Fun fact about me? My grandmother is a spiritual medium."

"A what?"

"A… you know, a medium. She talks to the dead," Lily clarified, and at Sam's look of obvious amusement, she groaned, giving his arm a shove. "She *does*, okay? And my mom—well, my mom passed away," she admitted, and immediately, Sam's teasing expression faltered. "No, I'm

fine, don't worry, it was a long time ago. But my mom's a sort of…
psychic, I guess you could say. Or she was."

"Okay," Sam said uncertainly. "And you're close with… them? With
your grandmother, right?"

"She raised me," Lily confirmed. "Since my dad's never really been
in the picture, and my mom died when I was a kid." Sam gave her a look
like he might apologize or something, as if maybe he suspected it was an
area that caused her pain, but Lily quickly waved it away. She never
liked people feeling sorry for her. "Anyway, I know it's totally insane, but
my grandma loves doing these full astrological charts for people, and to
calculate someone's rising sign—which is like, the real you?" she said
thoughtfully, assuming he'd need an explanation. "Versus your sun sign,
which is your *best* you, but anyway I'm sure you don't believe in that,
which is fine, but the point is—"

"You told your grandmother about me?"

The moment the question left his lips, Lily kicked herself. Jesus, how
desperate *was* she? This was completely insane behavior, and she hadn't
even thought to consider how it would sound to him before bounding
obnoxiously into his home. "Well, no, I was just—"

She cut herself off, however, when Sam's hand shot out, tugging her
into his chest.

"Why, Lily Nasser," he murmured, one arm slipping around her
waist. "I think you've got a little crush on me."

"Oh my god, I do not." Oh, fuck, she really did. She glanced up at
his laughing brown eyes and squirmed a little, utterly dismayed with
herself. "I just… there's nothing else to talk about with her, okay? She's
obsessed with the idea of me dating, and—"

"And you wanted an excuse to see me again." He lifted her chin, playfully tutting with disapproval. "Lily, Lily, Lily. You like me so much you can barely stand it, can you?"

"Shut up." This time, the words were breathy and misleading, partially because she was resting her palms on his chest. "Look, I just came over to ask you one thing, and if you don't want to tell me—"

"Oh, I want to tell you." His lips brushed her cheek, then her nose. "I want very badly to tell you, Lily, though if you're going to leave after I do, then I suppose I should take my time about it, shouldn't I? Should probably consult my mother," he said, smoothing her hair back from her face, "and then, just to be sure, I should probably get in contact with the doctor who delivered me. Who, by the way, retired and moved to Aruba ten years ago, so really, it might be a few weeks—"

She cut him off with a growl, pulling his lips to hers, and within moments he had her bending back over the kitchen counter, his fingers tight on her hips. She reached behind her, trying to pull herself up, and knocked something to the ground; the wrench. Sam pulled her swiftly out of the way of its fall, setting her roughly atop the kitchen island and kicking the wrench out of reach from where it landed on the floor.

Having Sam's hands on her hips was bittersweet, and very nearly enough to distract her. "I do actually need an answer," she told him, panting a little bit. Either it would prove her grandmother wrong and she wouldn't have to worry about this anymore, or...

She didn't really want to think about the alternative. "Any way you can find out?"

He leaned a perfunctory distance away, sliding his phone from his pocket and, true to his word, texting his mother. "There," he said, turning back to Lily the moment the message had been sent. "She won't answer me for like, two days, though, so I guess this is where you live now," he said, tugging her forward by the back of her neck and kissing her so sweetly she half wanted to die right there on his tongue.

He plucked her up from the counter and set her on her feet, the two of them hastily making their way across the floor to his couch. She stumbled once, letting him catch her after he'd stepped not-particularly-gently on her toes, but when she tried to step away she heard a loud, inescapable ripping sound.

"What was that?"

Sam released her and she looked down, gaping, as the canvas of her shoes (her *canvassing* shoes, no pun intended) had somehow been torn from the rubber gum of the sole. "Oh *no*," she gasped, more dramatically than she'd intended to, and Sam quickly dropped to his knees, eyeing the shoe.

"Jesus," he said, nudging her back until she was sitting on the couch before taking her foot in one hand, eyeing the damage. "How have these not fallen apart before now? Lily, these are destroyed."

Yes, they *were* destroyed. Destroyed from a year's worth of effort. From knocking on doors and getting them slammed in her face. From walking all over her neighborhood—all over *every* neighborhood— listening and crying with people whose lives and happiness had come to mean everything to her. Conspiring and laughing with people who, conversely, made her feel like she was one of them. Going from business to business and collecting support, one by one. Talking and talking until her throat went sore and her tongue went weirdly numb.

Those shoes had been on her feet every day, the most reliable footwear she could find that were still pleasing to look at without giving her blisters. They were more than just good shoes. They were *great* shoes.

They had been with her through every hard-fought battle, and more than that, they were—

She swallowed.

They were her lucky shoes.

Briefly, she felt the sting behind her eyes that meant she was perilously close to tears, and Sam looked up, an expression of terrible remorse shadowing his face.

"I'm so sorry, Lily," he said quietly. "I can try to fix them, or I can find you another pair—"

"No, it's… it's fine." They're just shoes, she reminded herself, taking a steadying breath. Luck didn't mean anything. "They're just shoes, Sam."

"Are you sure? Because I mean it, if you want I can—"

"No, no, it's… don't worry, you're right. I just need a new pair." She sat upright, swallowing, and forced a smile. "Don't worry about it. It was bound to happen." Statistically speaking, they might have broken anyway.

Or, Zaniah's voice said in her head, *perhaps they might have never broken at all if you'd kept your distance like I suggested, Lily-girl.*

She tried to shove it away, reaching for Sam, but he hesitated.

"Let me do something," he said. "I can make you dinner?"

"What, here?" she asked, gesturing around his apartment with a grimace. "Sorry, I don't think so."

He rolled his eyes, kissing her forehead. "Tomorrow night, then," he said, "let's make dinner together, okay? Your apartment, if you want."

God, and didn't that sound blissfully normal. Normal, and really kind of sweet. She had a brief image of them cooking together while Norah Jones played from her tinny iPhone speakers. She'd wear shoes she didn't care about and a dress that didn't matter if it got stained and maybe he'd dance with her on the kitchen floor and she'd tell Zaniah, *See? It's not about luck.*

"Not tomorrow," Lily said, remembering at the last moment she had a fundraising dinner to attend, "but the day after?" She leaned forward, rubbing the grease from his cheek, and managed a smile. "Seven?"

It wasn't luck. She didn't need luck. She worked hard, and that was all that mattered.

He kissed her, and hell-on-earth, she absolutely melted. "Seven it is."

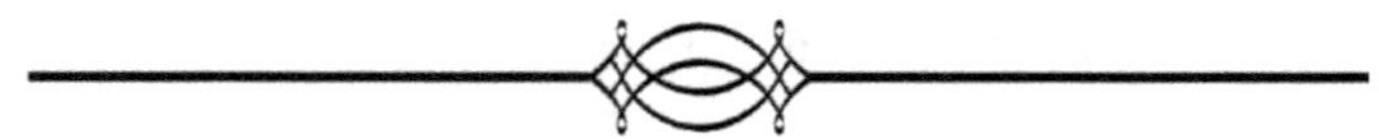

Ah, you're in luck, my mother remembered she owns a cell phone. I was born at 6:43 AM, and the hospital had a blackout five minutes later.

Lily looked up from her screen with a smile, setting down the curling iron she was using on her long black hair. It usually looked fine without help, but this was a special occasion. People were expecting to see her, so she tried to look as if she'd put in some effort.

Is that good? Sam asked, her phone buzzing again. *Did I pass?*

I don't know, Lily replied with a laugh. *My grandma's the celestial one, not me. I'll have to ask her when I stop by tomorrow.*

Try not to leave out my other good qualities. You know, my chivalrous manners and sparkling sense of humor. Plus I'm handy around the house. Grandmothers usually like that about me.

Lily wrapped a section of her hair around the barrel. *Anything else?*

Well, I'm also great with children and dogs. I know a lot of first aid procedures. I wanted to be a lifeguard when I was a kid, but my first day I drowned.

I'm sorry, what? Lily asked, releasing her hair with a giggle. *You… drowned??*

In my defense, I can still save other people from drowning. It wasn't my fault someone threw a football and knocked me into the side of the pool. Everyone knows that's not allowed.

You poor thing, Lily sighed, wrapping another section of hair around her curling iron as her phone buzzed again, this time with a message from Taj.

Lily, we have some damage control to take care of tonight. Please read ASAP.

Lily frowned, clicking on the link Taj had sent her. "Oh *shit*," she said aloud, scanning the page as quickly as she could even as her heart started pounding.

FATHER OF CONGRESSIONAL HOPEFUL LILY NASSER OUSTED IN SHOCKING EXPOSÉ, said the article, and Lily quickly leapt to Twitter, checking the trending tags. Yep, there it was,

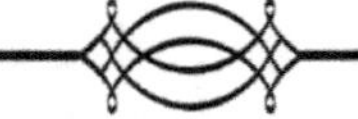

LilyNasser and below it, a horrifying headline: *Lily Nasser's father Nash Nasser revealed to be behind a string of used car scams.*

She clicked a short video clip, wincing as her opponent, Congressman Wallace Hart, spoke to a reporter. "Well, it shouldn't surprise anyone that Lily Nasser is the daughter of a crook," he said, shrugging. "She claims to represent the working class, doesn't she? But in reality all she's ever done is rob from them."

This isn't fair, Lily typed furiously to Taj. *I barely even know my father!*

His response was immediate. *We're drafting a press release right now. Sit tight.*

She noticed that in her haste she'd missed another message from Sam, though she could hardly focus long enough to read it. She was struggling to think how she was going to react to this in time; Congressman Hart was going to slaughter her. He used to have only her inexperience to hold against her—okay, and her race and her age and her gender—but now this, too? Hart's small-minded cult of supporters would smell blood in the water and spread it around fast; undecided voters didn't need to be informed about much of anything to understand something as clichéd as a used car scam. Lily hadn't known the details of her father's business and certainly hadn't profited from it, but it would take a lot of work to convince people of that.

Can't wait to see you tomorrow, read the text from Sam. Lily felt a little rush of something she absolutely didn't have time for. A resurgence of a crush that she *resolutely* couldn't think about right now. Thank goodness she was going to a public event. It would essentially be free publicity, and if she just drafted a response now, that would be easy enough. As soon as she finished getting ready—

Holy shit. She looked up with a gasp, realizing she'd left the curling iron on her hair for too long. How long *had* it been, exactly? She hastily pulled it away, letting the hair fall, and—

The long raven curl dropped away from the iron, breaking off with a sizzle and falling limply to the floor.

The moment her hair hit the ground, Lily screamed.

"Lily, great to have you on the show again," said the morning show host, Jackson Carter. "And sporting a new 'do, too—*so* chic! Care to tell us about your hair, Lily?"

Lily fought the urge to snap, forcing a smile. "Just time for a new look, that's all, Jackson."

"I'm told this is what's called a 'choppy lob,' isn't it? My wife absolutely loves it," Jackson said, as Lily fought the continued urge to shake him. "You know, normally when she goes on and on about this celebrity or that I can't say I have any idea what she's talking about, but even I think this look is quite the bold statement. A modern cut for modern times! Is that what you're hoping the voters perceive from you, Lily?"

"Just a haircut, Jackson," Lily said, wanting to scream. "Though, speaking of statements, thank you for having me on the show, as there is definitely one topic I'd like to addr-"

"Are you concerned that this departure from your usual look might be a little too edgy for your more conservative voters?" Jackson asked, handsomely concerned. "The haircut has been trending on Twitter since your appearance last night, and I have to say—"

"I think my voters are most concerned about the issues, Jackson, and to that, I have to take this opportunity to remind our constituents that I continue to be the candidate most willing to represent their interests. I know there has been some unflattering press about my father recently," Lily said, as Jackson gave a sympathetic nod. "And for that, I wanted to set the record straight."

"Yes, it's true that your father Nash Nasser has been accused of running quite an involved automobile scam over the last several decades. Nearly as long as you've been alive!" Jackson exclaimed. "What do you say to reports of his looming arrest?"

"Well, let me first say that law enforcement is currently investigating these rumors," Lily said carefully. "I'm sorry to say that my father and I are not particularly close, and therefore I can't comment on his involvement at this time. However—"

"Ah yes, you grew up with your grandmother, didn't you?" Jackson interrupted. "Zaniah Kazemi is… well, she's a fortune teller, isn't she?"

"My grandmother is a spiritual medium, yes," Lily said, her voice strained. "She is also a longtime business owner and a highly respected member of this city's vibrant mystical communit-"

"Well, sure," Jackson acknowledged, "but what do you have to say to those who accuse you of being raised by crooks and frauds, Lily? There's a tweet going viral right now—hang on, can we see that tweet, please? Yes, here we go: *'Of course Lily Nasser is running for Congress, it's the only scam left now that psychics and used car dealers are already covered'*—"

"My campaign is not a scam," Lily said, forcing a breath before her temper sparked. "My campaign is the result of months and months of listening to my constituents and drafting policies to meet their needs. There's nothing disingenuous about my run for Congress," she assured both Jackson and the camera, "contrary to what Congressman Hart's social media aides would have you believe. The truth is, Jackson, I think Congressman Hart is scared. He knows his record shows that he's done nothing but cater to corporations and interest groups during his time in Congress, and now he's resorting to cheap shots about my family. It may be a catchy tweet—it's funny, I'll give them that," she conceded, hoping she appeared gracious despite wanting to strangle the Hart team member who wrote it, "but this campaign is about more than a few characters and retweets. There is much more at stake than that."

It's not about luck, she reminded herself.

But even if it was, she wasn't taking any chances.

"Well said, Lily, well said. Lily Nasser, everybody!" Jackson said, smile glinting at the camera. "Up next, is gluten giving your child autism? Stay tuned as we find out after the break!"

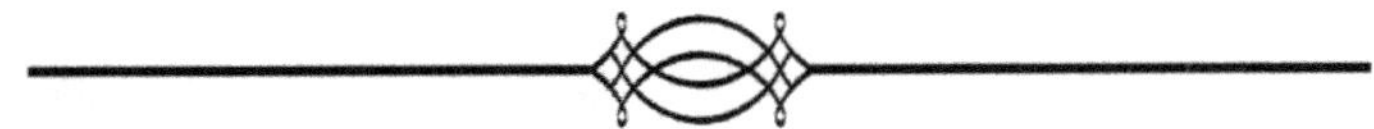

"I'm so sorry, my Lily-girl," Zaniah said, resting a soothing hand on Lily's shoulder as she glanced mournfully down at her tea leaves. "Sometimes that's just the way things happen, hm?"

Opposing stars. Who even knew that was a thing? Certainly not Lily.

Are you sure? she'd asked Sam hopefully. *Maybe your mom confused your birth time with one of your brothers?*

She checked my birth certificate, unfortunately, so I'm sorry to say that for once in my life, I am not being confused for Devin or Andrew or Rob.

Then: *Bummer you had to cancel dinner, but I get it, your campaign is the most important thing right now. Maybe this weekend?*

Then, a few hours later: *Listen, I just feel terrible about all this shit coming out about your dad.*

Are you sure you're okay?

She'd let the messages sit on read for hours, glancing up at the clock and resenting that she could have been with him right now if he'd just had the decency to be born under a more suitable celestial position.

"What about Dad?" Lily asked her grandmother, not looking up from the handle of her mug. "Did Mom know about him?"

Zaniah hesitated, glancing askance at Alya's absence. "I'm not sure," she said, frowning. "I've asked her myself, but she doesn't seem to want to discuss it."

A nice way to say yes, Lily thought. She supposed it wasn't her grandmother's fault; Zaniah had obviously never liked Nash, having spent most of Lily's life trying to keep him at a safe distance. He rarely did more than send a card for her birthday, usually getting it wrong by a week or so.

"I don't know what I'm going to do now," Lily sighed, leaning her head back against the chair. "Obviously I can't see Sam again, but what am I supposed to do if Dad gets arrested? The election is weeks away," she muttered, a little knot of fear tightening in her stomach. Had she really done all this for nothing? "Who knows what kind of stuff could come out in the investigation, and if it does, there's more than enough time for voters to change their minds about me."

"Perhaps it won't come to that, provided you keep your distance," Zaniah said, resting both hands on Lily's shoulders and gently kissing the top of her head. "You're lucky, my Lily. Perhaps without that young man of yours, luck will lean in your favor once again."

Lily closed her eyes, saying nothing. There was nothing *to* say, really. The irony of her grandmother being right was that what it might take for Lily to regain her luck currently felt like the unluckiest thing of all.

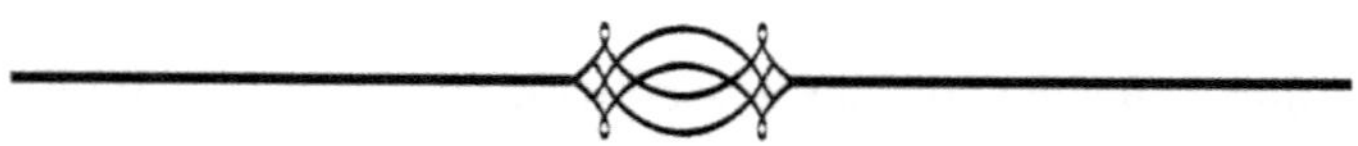

A week went by without incident. Twitter moved on. The news about her father calmed slightly, and Lily continued to keep her distance, not wanting to be associated with either Nash or his pending investigation. People continued to pester her about her haircut, but that was just one of the hazards of being female. Gradually, she fell back into the habit of focusing on work. She ordered a new pair of canvassing shoes.

Another week went by, and all was well.

After the first two unanswered messages, Sam only sent one more: *So that's it, huh?*

Lily hated that she was ignoring him, but there didn't seem to be a better answer. Maybe if she said nothing, he'd just think she was busy instead of entertaining the insane theory her grandmother had had about stars.

Worse, Lily hadn't forgotten what had happened the last time she'd been texting him. She ran her hand over the missing hair with a wistful sense of loss, feeling like a woefully defeated Samson without it.

It was a lucky thing Lily didn't have time to miss Sam. She was making multiple appearances per day now, at community events and local media outlets in addition to speaking at her own rallies and campaign fundraising efforts. The only time she thought of him was after the events were over, really, when she came home to her apartment and crashed on her bed, thinking of the way he tasted on her lips and the way his brow creased when he worried about her and the way he'd made her feel like maybe, just maybe, she could have normal things, like a relationship. Someone to laugh with. Someone to tangle up with at night and wake up to, smiling, in the morning.

But this campaign was more important, she reminded herself firmly. It was *the most* important thing she'd ever done, and she couldn't risk it being ruined. She couldn't leave all those peoples' lives to chance just so she could keep the giddy flutters she got from being near him.

No matter how much she may have missed him, she wasn't that kind of girl.

(Right?)

Whether fortune or mere coincidence, though, there was always the chance they'd run into each other, living in the same building as they did. She couldn't decide if that was just one of many possible consequences or the result of his bad luck warping hers again, but they both paused when they saw each other in the lobby, him giving her a long look as she gave a heavy swallow in return.

There was no hiding from him. They were alone in the building's foyer, with Lily hitting the up button on the elevator as he made for the stairwell. "Oh, hey Sam," she said, pitching her voice to something normal, as if running into him was casual instead of borderline apocalyptic. "Listen, I'm so sorry I haven't responded to your messages, but I've just been really busy and—"

"You know, believe it or not, Lily, you're not the first girl to 'get busy' when they've been around me too long." He sounded irritated again, like he had when they first met. Defensive, which made her flinch. "There's no need to explain yourself to me," he said gruffly. "You think I'm unlucky, and you're right."

"I—" She chewed her lip. It sounded really stupid when he said it. "It's not… Well," she attempted, "it's just that—"

"It's fine, Lily. I get it." He placed a hand on the door to the stairwell, pausing for a moment. "You know, I really thought you were the kind of girl who didn't need luck," he commented, not looking at her, for which she was grateful. She'd flinched again and was relieved he hadn't seen it.

He gave it a moment and then shrugged, finally meeting her gaze. "Too bad I was wrong," he said, and threw the door open, taking the stairs and disappearing as the elevator arrived, announcing its presence with a quiet ding.

Lily had always thought of happiness as an abstract thing. Making lives better for the faceless, the ones in her care who needed healthcare and sound policies and gun control. Things she could fight for. Things she believed in. But she'd never really considered what she might be doing to a very real, very disappointed-looking man who, for whatever reason, had actually started to matter to her.

The elevator doors shut. Lily shook herself of her temporary paralysis and sprinted up the stairs, arriving at the third floor just as Sam slid his key into the lock, gritting his teeth with frustration as it failed to turn.

"Sam," she said, huffing a little from the effort of running. "Wait, just… wait."

He turned at the sound of her voice, brown eyes registering confusion. Before she could think about how much she wanted to smooth the consternation from his brow, she was already taking the steps to reach him.

"Sam, I—"

"It's not my fault," he said, the muscle straining around his jaw by the time she reached him. He was staring down at the key, as if he were speaking to it instead of her. "The shoes, they were—"

"Old, I know." Holy balls, stairs were hard; Lily was completely, totally breathless. "That wasn't your fault, Sam."

That was enough for him to give her a long look, reaching out after a moment to brush his fingers beneath the cropped tips of her hair. "This is… different."

"It was me. I burned it." She shook her head. "I wasn't paying attention."

He glanced at his hands, swallowing.

"And your dad," he said, and she sighed.

"You obviously had nothing to do with that," she grumbled, feeling acutely idiotic. "That's clearly been going on for years. It's just…"

"Timing," he said. "I know. I get it."

She nodded, unsure what to say next. She glanced down at her feet, contemplating them in silence.

"Lily, I like you," Sam said, seeming to realize that she'd run out of things to say. "I want—" A pause. He shifted his stance, clearing his throat. "Look, it doesn't matter what I want. The point is if it's just a matter of timing, I can wait. You're allowed to ask me to wait," he informed her, "and I swear, I'll understand. If you want to just steer clear of me until the campaign's over, that's fine. But just be honest with me, please, because if you don't want my bad luck that's one thing, but if you don't want *me*—"

"No, Sam, stop." Lily winced, making the crucial error of looking up at Sam's face, directly at the way his eyes were fixed so impossibly on hers. "Sam, I…"

She trailed off, unsure how to put in words that she had missed him, in spite of everything. That in spite of her grandmother's warnings and all the work she'd done, she had spent most of it running on half-empty, wishing she could still have him.

Luckily, though, he didn't wait for an answer.

Sam pulled Lily close, dragging her flush against his chest, and before she could even think how badly she wanted to kiss him he was already kissing her, his hands tangled in the shorn absence of her hair. He slid the strands back from her face, stroking her cheeks, her jaw, his grip on her growing tighter and tighter until she realized she was clinging to him just as ferociously, arms snaked around his neck.

"Give me the keys," she whispered, and he gladly placed them in her waiting palm, hands on her hips while she fumbled to bring them inside, turning the key in the latch and then throwing the ring of them somewhere, she didn't care where. Something broke; probably the lamp. Sam didn't acknowledge it and neither did she, letting him half-stumble, half-carry her into his bedroom.

It was no different in here than it had been in the living room: a nightstand, a dresser, a bed on a box frame without a headboard. She tumbled backwards onto the mattress, pulling him with her, and when her fingers shimmied under his dress shirt he forced a pause, propping himself on his elbows.

"Are you—"

"—sure?" she guessed. "Yeah, Sam. Very."

"But—"

"I worked too hard to put all my faith in luck," she told him, and then corrected herself. "I *work* too hard to let the universe take credit for everything I've done."

He bent his forehead to hers, raggedly drawing a grateful breath.

"But just in case, use a condom," she whispered, and he laughed, reaching over for his nightstand and withdrawing one from the top drawer, tossing it aside.

"We'll get to that," he said, shimmying down her torso to rest on his knees at the edge of the bed. "We've got a long way to go before that."

"Meaning?" she asked, a little delirious with anticipation, but Sam shook his head, mouth already occupied with kissing his way to the lip of her jeans.

He flicked open the button. Lily let out a gasp. And then, his eyes on hers, Sam slid the denim slowly down her legs, patient and fastidiously careful as she congratulated herself on the fact that clearly, she was about to get very lucky indeed.

"Did you know your bathroom sink is clogged?" she asked, taking an appreciative look at Sam where he was tangled in the sheets before slinking back into bed with him, letting him wrap her in his arms.

"I was going to fix it tonight, but clearly I got sidetracked." He kissed the top of her head, toying with the collar of his shirt, which she was wearing. "Has the sky fallen, do you think?"

She grimaced. "I guess I should check," she sighed, reluctantly dragging herself away to search blindly for her phone. "Deep breath, here we go—"

Two email alerts. The first: *We're sorry! Your recent shoe order could not be completed, as the style has been discontinued.*

"Damn," Lily said under her breath. Sam's arms were painfully tight around her ribs; she had a feeling he was far more nervous than she was. She turned over her shoulder, giving him a quick, reassuring kiss, and then returned to her phone. "Whatever, really. I can always find a similar pair of—"

The word *arrested* caught her attention and she stiffened.

"What?" Sam asked, instantly on guard. "What is it?"

"I guess they must have finished my dad's investigation," Lily sighed, preparing herself before opening the email. "I thought it was going to take longer, but it's fine. It doesn't have anything to do with me, and anyway…"

She trailed off, eyes going wide as she opened the email.

A forwarded message. One of Taj's staffers, confusingly, had said: *Lily, call Ryan immediately! Do not speak to any press until we can brief you. Consider this a social media moratorium until the team decides how to move forward.*

Below that, the original email contents: *TAJ GARNER, FOUNDER OF POLITICAL ORGANIZATION* CONGRESS OF TOMORROW *AND LILY NASSER CAMPAIGN MANAGER HAS BEEN ARRESTED THIS EVENING ON CHARGES OF BRIBERY AND INSIDER DEALING.*

"What is it?" Sam asked, but only one thing came to mind.

"I'm fucked," Lily whispered, and it wasn't *at all* in the way she'd have liked.

PART III: FORTUNE'S FAVOR

The moment Lily found out her campaign manager had been arrested her entire body stopped functioning in any recognizable way. Suddenly she was hearing things as if she'd been fully submerged in water, the rush of blood deafening in her ears while she stumbled out of Sam's bedroom, hurrying to make the requested phone calls.

Her team, unfortunately, was no help at all.

"Look, I don't know what we're going to do," said a disgruntled-sounding Ryan, who had been Taj's right-hand man. "We're all being investigated, so I kind of don't have time to worry about your specific campaign. No offense."

Lily, however, had only one mode when it came to crises: undeterrable. "But if we can just prove these allegations are false, then—"

"Lily." Ryan's voice was agitated, impatient. "Did you honestly think the twenty-something female candidate of color ever had a shot at beating the undisputed incumbent *without* a leg up somewhere? That could have only been very careful cheating or a miracle," he said with an audible scoff, "and I can tell you right now which one it wasn't."

The cynical tone of his voice rang in her ears, momentarily debilitating.

"But," she began, breathless with disbelief. "But… all that canvassing. All the appearances," she stammered, "and all the *work*—"

"Helped," Ryan said bluntly. "No doubt it helped. But politics is dirty work, Lily, and most of what Taj handled wouldn't have been on anyone's radar if not for ending up in the wrong hands." Then he paused to laugh, of all things, before bitterly adding, "You're the only candidate who got this far, Lily. What did you think that was, dumb luck?"

She shut her eyes, forcing a swallow.

"Look, there's no way you can win now," he told her flatly. "All our accounts are frozen. There's no money, and unless you've got a magic wand that can turn back time, everyone who endorsed you is going to pull their support any moment now."

"But *Ryan*—"

"It was your job to stay ignorant," he said. "If you want to avoid prison time, that hasn't changed."

And that was that.

The idea that Lily's campaign was about to be torn apart and left in shreds was beyond disastrous. Her choices, though, were positively inconceivable. Continue campaigning on her own? She had no money, and certainly no time to win back whatever endorsements she was about to lose. Sure, if she stayed away from Sam, it was conceivably possible she might not lose any. Maybe one of her constituents would turn out to be independently wealthy? Maybe the final stretch of campaigning would magically pay for itself. If luck had saved her before—if it had made it so she never once worried about not getting the things she wanted—then maybe it would save her again now.

But if she wanted to capitalize on her luck, that meant no Sam. And the idea of not seeing Sam again, even for the next few weeks, felt like an unbearable betrayal.

I really thought you were the kind of girl who didn't need luck.

She crept back into his bedroom to spot him staring out the window, the duvet tossed aside with the glow of his bedside lamp illuminating the notches of his vertebrae. She supposed she hadn't noticed before the way his posture never really relaxed; he was constantly bracing for something. In this case, she was pretty sure the something in question was her.

"So," he said, catching the sound of her entry to the room. "How bad is it?"

"It's…" She sighed. "Pretty bleak."

He turned over his shoulder, looking fairly bleak himself, and beckoned her towards him. She considered resisting, reminding herself of her fairly contradictory options, but didn't. At the moment, her desperation for comfort outweighed her hovering fears that her maybe-boyfriend was some sort of magnetic force unintentionally warping her life.

She sat carefully beside him on the bed, contemplating his window's uninteresting view of the city street in silence.

"Maybe I was wrong about needing luck," Sam said, half-joking, and she turned to look at him.

"None of your girlfriends was unlucky enough to like, get randomly hit by a bus, right?" she asked, trying to lighten the mood, but she wasn't quite able to laugh like she'd intended. He didn't, either, which was just as well; she had a feeling his thoughts were elsewhere.

"Actually," he said, "nothing like this has ever happened to anyone I was dating. It's just me, usually. But, then again," he said, before clearing his throat and turning to her, reaching out to tuck the cropped strands of her hair behind her ear. "I always knew you were different."

Internally, Lily sighed; couldn't they have had normal problems? Maybe if he forgot her birthday or didn't call her back, then it'd be easier for her to put him safely in the rearview. Why wasn't he emotionally repressed, or just truly inept at sex? She hated that she couldn't even pretend that was a possibility.

All she wanted to do was fall back into bed with him; to lean into the palm of his hand and say hold me, Sam, until I forget; until today becomes tomorrow without me lifting a finger; until I no longer have to live in this place of uncertainty, because the stars already made up their minds for me.

Unfortunately, that probably wasn't the case.

"Sam," Lily sighed, and Sam shook his head.

"Don't," he said, "not yet," and tugged her closer, one hand sliding into her hair while the other stroked her cheek, drawing her lips up for something she felt was going to need a better name than *kiss*. Whatever this was between them was too full of sparks and certainty, too rare to be so common. With her lips on his, there was a moment when Lily could at least be sure of one thing in her life: that even if she abandoned her career in politics to devote a lifetime's vocation to nothing else but kissing men, none of them would ever make her feel like this. To her dismay, she clung to Sam despite her better judgment, digging her nails into his bare chest.

Outside, one of the streetlights sparked. She pulled away with a little shudder of a grimace, recalling the details of her situation and the immensity of her approaching doom.

"Just give me time," she pleaded, letting her hands fall guiltily away, and he gave a small nod of concession.

"Sure," he said, though he sounded like he didn't expect to see her again. She wanted to assure him otherwise, but, knowing that was a promise she wasn't sure she could keep, she figured it was best to say nothing.

He brought her hand to his lips, brushing a kiss across her knuckles. "For what it's worth," he said. "You changed my life, Lily Nasser."

She winced. "Did I, though?"

"You made me believe in something," he told her, "even if that something happens to be a political campaign."

In response, part of her wanted furiously to pry him open; to find their cosmic flaw and rearrange it. Stitch him back up and say *I solved it, we're fine now.*

Now, for the first time, Lily truly believed her grandmother was right; she had spent most of her life being lucky. Certainly luckier than she'd realized, because she was fairly sure that pulling away from Sam was the toughest thing she'd ever had to do.

What Lily needed now, more than she had ever needed it before, was to see the future. She had no idea what her luck had kept her from until today, and would it get worse? Was there more beyond a lost election? She needed to see what was coming; to understand what she should do next.

So she went to the one place where she knew someone who could.

"Hi, Lily-girl," said a somber Zaniah when she opened the door, giving Lily a look of sympathy. "Alya said you'd be coming by."

Not for the first time, Lily wished she could really believe that her grandmother meant it when she said that. As it was, she could only hope her grandmother's talents would lead to something helpful. "Can you ask Mom some questions for me, Grandma?"

"No, honey," Zaniah said, shaking her head, and Lily blinked, surprised. Rarely, if ever, had Zaniah ever said no, and certainly not when it came to Alya. "No," Zaniah clarified, catching Lily's expression of dismay and gesturing her to the dining room table, "because I think you should speak to her yourself."

"Oh." It seemed Zaniah intended Lily to speak to her mother via the ouija board, which felt more than a little absurd in the moment. Zaniah led Lily over to the table, seating her in her usual chair and placing her hands on the planchette.

"She's been waiting for you," Zaniah said, and though this was technically what Lily had come for, she wasn't sure this was the ideal scenario. It was always easier to talk to Zaniah, and besides, Lily's mother had passed when Lily was so young she could hardly remember her. Talking to a virtual stranger was just as difficult as talking to an occultist board.

"I don't know where to start," Lily began, turning to Zaniah, but already her fingers began to move, the planchette drifting towards the letters. She felt a little chill of discomfort but swallowed it down, reading the letters aloud as Zaniah wrote them on a legal pad.

ITS OK

Lily cleared her throat. "Um. Hi, Mom," she said, and again, the planchette tugged her hands.

HI BB

"She's just conserving letters," Zaniah offered in explanation, sliding the page over for Lily to see what she'd written. Lily gave a distracted nod, trying to get her thoughts in order.

"So," Lily said to the ghost of her mother, "I guess Grandma told you about what happened?"

YES

"Do you know what I should do next?"

A pause, and then, *YES.*

Lily waited, but then nothing. "Can you… tell me? Is there any chance I can win the election if I stay away from Sam?" She chewed her lip, uncertain. "Or am I just going to lose either way? Or, if I'm not, then is Sam worth losing the election for? Because if he's like, *the one*, then—"

"Too much," Zaniah said, resting a hand on Lily's forearm. "Slow down. One question at a time. Think of it like a real conversation you're having," she suggested with a softened smile, "but she can only answer in a text message."

Lily nodded, briefly closing her eyes.

"Mom," she said, trying to imagine what she could remember of Alya's face while she started from the beginning. "I met a boy."

The planchette gave another series of tugs.

IM V HAPPY

"Really?" Lily asked, surprised. "Even with, you know. His… parts of fortune and all that?"

UR V LUCKY

"But—"

"She's still going," Zaniah cautioned, pointing, and Lily glanced down.

UR V LUCKY 2 FIND LUV NOT EVRY1 DOES

Lily supposed she hadn't thought of it that way. Though, *love* seemed a stretch.

Unless there was something Alya knew that she didn't.

"But my campaign is also important, isn't it?" Lily said, chewing on the nail of her thumb. "It means everything to me."

I KNO

"So I guess…" She sighed. "I guess I just don't know what's more important. I mean, who's to say things will ever be different? I'll have to actually do things once I get elected, so maybe being with someone who makes me less lucky is a bad idea all around. Shouldn't I just find someone else? But if I did," she fretted aloud, "they wouldn't be *Sam*, and will I ever feel like this again? I just—"

"Lily," Zaniah said, reaching out to pause her again. "This is a lot of effort for her."

"Oh." Lily paused to reconsider her questions, contemplating them in silence. "Can you see what happens if I stay with Sam, Mom?"

YES

"And can you see what happens if I don't?"

YES

"And can you tell me…" Another pause for hesitation. "Which one is better?"

There was a pause.

Then, *NO.*

Lily's chest lurched with disappointment.

"She can't tell you what to do, honey," Zaniah said gently. "She can only help you see what's in your heart." She reached over to take Lily's face with one hand, smiling fondly at her. "Maybe what you really need to ask her is somewhere in there too, hm?"

Lily took a deep breath, forcing a disappointed nod, and closed her eyes again.

She remembered so little of her mother. Only glimpses; snapshots of feelings. She could feel Alya's presence like warmth, enfolding Lily in her memories, more clearly than she could actually see her face. Alya had been ill for most of the time Lily was old enough to remember her, often too tired to play, and for a long time it had been difficult for Lily to understand what was happening to her mother.

"Mom," Lily said without opening her eyes, "did you always know what was going to happen to you?"

YES

How strange that must have been, to have lived her life knowing all along how it would end.

"Couldn't you," Lily began, and stopped, hesitating again. "Couldn't you have prevented your death, somehow, if you saw it coming? Couldn't you have done something to change your fate?"

YES

There was more.

BUT THERE WAS GOOD 2

Was there? That was hard to believe. Alya had died young, younger even than Lily was now. If it were Lily, she would have searched around for a miracle cure, not wasted her time eloping with a used car salesman.

Speaking of. "Is it true about Dad?" Lily asked. "The scam and all that?"

She almost felt the planchette sigh.

IDK PRBLY

"Oh." It continued to be incredibly strange that Alya had ever chosen Lily's father to begin with. For one thing, Zaniah had never liked him, and by all accounts there was no way Alya would have done anything without Zaniah's approval. That, and Alya was the opposite of Nash, who had been hardly a figment in Lily's life. When Lily thought of her father, all she could see were distracted eyes, furrowed brows, as if he couldn't quite understand what she was doing there. He wasn't at all like her mother, who had always been smiling, even if she was in pain; even if that was the only motion she would manage for the day.

"Mom," Lily said. "If Dad was always… how he was," she determined with uncertainty, "then why even marry him at all?"

4 U BB

A pause, and then,

BCUZ I KNW I WLD HVE U

To Lily's dismay, her eyes filled with tears. She wasn't much of a crier; she regularly told people not to make a fuss when she'd mentioned her mother was dead. Now, though, she would have given anything to have Alya here, if only to tell her everything would be fine.

Not as a psychic. Just as a mother.

"What do I do now, Mama?" Lily asked quietly, and waited a long time while the planchette spelled out Alya's answer.

UR MY LUCKY STAR WTVR U CHOOSE IS THE RIGHT CHOICE

"Alya always knew best," Zaniah said, smiling at the place she always told Lily her mother was usually sitting.

And while it wasn't the answer Lily had initially come to get, she knew it was the only one she needed.

By the time Lily returned home, she wasn't any closer to knowing what to do about her campaign; luck or no luck, she didn't know what the reality of winning even was. But seeing as she had no one to answer to in the morning, giving herself the evening to try and think it through didn't seem like it would inconvenience anyone too greatly.

She turned on the television, which was set (as it always was) to political news. All those weeks obsessing over polls… it was hard not to think of them as wasted time. Lily pulled out a container of yogurt and hunted around for a clean spoon before hearing the name of her opponent, Congressman Wallace Hart, and coming to a rapid halt.

"Lily Nasser surrounds herself with thieves and liars," came Hart's voice, echoing from the footage of his press rally. "She can't be trusted with your interests, and she certainly can't be trusted with your vote!"

Typical. It hardly took an expensive spin team to nail the obvious, though Lily had no doubt Wallace Hart had paid for the best.

"Strangely," the anchor said, the picture cutting out to draw Lily's attention to the screen, "shortly afterwards, it appears the venue suffered some sort of wiring failure. According to some eyewitnesses, while Hart's team struggled to get him back on the air, one of the rally's attendants began to speak. One of the other audience members managed to capture this surprising expression of dissent via cell phone footage."

"Congressman Hart is telling you what to think as if you can't see his voting record for yourself!" came a barely audible voice, which still managed to startle Lily so intensely she dropped the container of yogurt. "At every opportunity, Congressman Hart has sided with his corporate donors and never once with his constituents. Lily Nasser, on the other hand, spends her time working for you, to make your lives better. Her policies don't reflect anyone's interests but yours." (Briefly, the unsteady camera jostled.) "And listen, we all know politics is corrupt. We know the people responsible for handling elections will take shortcuts if they can get them. That's why I've never voted, it's why I've never cared about politics at all, but if you think about it, that's exactly the kind of apathy the Wallace Harts of the world want from us. It keeps them in power until we're so disillusioned we no longer care what they do. Until we're willing to blindly believe what they tell us."

"If men like him had their way," continued the muffled audio of Sam Rainier's voice, "a barista without a family fortune would never have been able to run for office, much less come close to winning a seat. She's a threat to Congressman Hart's way of life, to his privilege. She has the power to change things, to disrupt them, and that's the worst thing that could possibly happen to him, because his life is perfectly fine the way it is. But is yours?"

There were some shouts of discord; a hurtled accusation of, "Who even *are* you?"

"Look, I'm nobody," Sam assured the crowd. "It's my job to deal with crises, to put out fires, and as far as I can see, politics right now has a hell of a bug. All I know is something has to change, and without Lily Nasser's vision for the world, we'll be exactly where we are now—left with a bunch of dispassionate, apathetic people like me, and a congress full of ineffective Wallace Harts!"

"The man was escorted out of the venue shortly after," the anchor said once the footage cut out, "but already the video has gone viral on Twitter. Both #LilyNasser and #IneffectiveWallaceHarts are trending nationwide, and—"

Lily did not stop to hear the end of her sentence. She left the yogurt on the floor and took to the hallway, racing down the stairs.

"So," was Sam's first word when he opened the door, "are you here to tell me you're moving to another apartment building to remain at a safer distance, or…?"

"How'd you tamper with the footage?" were hers.

"I didn't." He leaned against the frame, folding his arms over his chest. "I'm just… what was the word you used for it? Ah, right." A snap of his fingers, and a little half-smile. "Unlucky."

The idea that he could make light of the most important thing anyone had ever done for her was so destabilizing she hardly knew where to begin.

"Sam," Lily said breathlessly, "are you really so unlucky that power just… fails around you?"

"Yes," he said, seeming to have come to terms with it.

Guess there was no point skirting the issue. Better to actually know what she'd opened the door for the day her apartment leaked into his.

"Anything else?"

"My ad blockers are basically useless," he said. "I tend to contract a lot of malware. I almost never hit green lights, I miss my trains, and if I get a flu shot, I'll definitely get the flu." A pause. "Same if anyone around me sneezes."

"And?"

"And… sometimes things are more flammable than I suspect they are. And if I'm in the audience, my sports teams will definitely muff the punt or miss the free throw. I seem to be alright when it comes to natural disasters," he conceded thoughtfully, "but also, I do check to make sure the buildings I live and work in have passed their most recent inspections."

Truly, he was a disaster. At least it was mitigated. "What else?"

"I don't shop online. Half my packages end up lost in the mail. If there's any chance of rain, that means a 100% chance I'll get rained on. And I never," he sighed with weighty lamentation, "win raffles."

Her mouth twitched. "Never?"

"Never." He took a step forward; pausing right in front of her, until the two of them were mirror images straddling the threshold. "I'll never win you the big stuffed bear, Lily, but I will believe in you, I promise." At that, his brown eyes were softly imploring. "I know you're not going to quit this campaign."

She had already decided that much. She managed a nod, and he smiled.

"Good," he said. "It's too important."

"But," she said, and glanced tentatively at the space between them. "But if I want to win…"

"I understand," he assured her. "Take as much distance as you need. But if at the end you, I don't know, miss me, or—"

"No, Sam, I'm not—" She broke off. "Sam," she attempted slowly, "I don't want distance."

He blinked. "What? But I just told you I'm—"

"Unlucky, I know. I heard." She gave him a wistful smile. "But the thing is, I like you. And more importantly, I'm not the kind of girl who needs luck."

His relief melted like a sunray across his face, though he waited for her to finish. Which was ideal, as she didn't exactly want him to interrupt.

"What I *do* need, Sam," she continued, finally arriving at the crux of the matter, "is a campaign manager."

"I… what?" he said, bewildered. "Lily, I… you can't possibly want me anywhere near this campaign—"

"Why not?" She shrugged. "You've already proven you understand it perfectly. And you managed to condense my message into a single hashtag, didn't you? I'm here to shake things up," she reminded him, "so let's just shake it and see what happens."

"Lily, I have no experience with politics," Sam told her, as if she somehow hadn't noticed.

"You put out fires for a living, Sam, and what I am right now is one big fire. You said so yourself! And besides, I have nothing to lose," she reminded him, to which he gave a rather dubious scoff.

"May I remind you, Lily Nasser, that technically you have a *congressional election* to lose—"

"Yes, which I'm going to lose anyway if I don't have a team. You said you'd believe in me? I need that. I need you on my team, Sam, and more importantly I *want* you there." There. That was the truth, even if it was a reckless one. "And besides, if luck is just statistics, then there's still a chance I can win this election. And there's a chance I can do it with you. So," she concluded, leaning decisively into his side of the threshold, "will you take the job, Sam Rainier?"

He glanced down, observing the position she'd taken when she made her choice, and gave her a very suggestive sort of look. Namely, the sort suggesting he wouldn't allow her to regret it.

"Depends," he said, close enough now that she could taste the possibility. "Is there some sort of HR policy against dating?"

"Well, typically that sort of consorting would be poor form," Lily admitted, "but given the circumstances, there's a strong possibility the department is willing to look the other way."

"Politicians," Sam lamented with a shake of his head, curling one hand around her cheek. "I knew they were corrupt. You're manipulating me with sexual favors, aren't you?"

"Kind of," Lily said. "Only because I can't technically pay you in money."

"Wow. You're all in on this crime spree, aren't you?"

"I mean, if I'm going to be a crook, I'm going to be good at it."

"There's that winning spirit."

For a moment, smiling up at Sam, Lily wondered what Alya had seen of her future. She wondered if Alya had really believed Lily would make the right choice regardless, or if she had already seen that somehow, everything would turn out fine. Maybe she had known that Lily still had a shot; that Sam's social media nudge would be enough for her to scrape out a win from the district's highest voter turnout in history. Maybe she had seen that Sam would take to grassroots campaigning like a fish to water, abandoning his comfortable VC paychecks to help underdog candidates like Lily find their footing in local politics. Maybe Alya had seen Zaniah reading Sam's palm, or known that she would speak to him herself in something he'd brush off as a very weird dream someday. Maybe she had already watched Lily and Sam have a small autumn wedding at some hipster restaurant in D.C., where the lights would temporarily go out and they'd all cheerfully have dinner by the light of the candles that Sam had conveniently thought to bring.

Maybe Alya knew that Lily would be the start of a ripple effect, the first shatter in the glass soon to break; or maybe she'd seen only that her daughter, the bright spot in her short life, had fallen for someone who treated her like something precious, and Alya had found just the right time to tell Lily fuck the stars, live your life baby girl, and don't let a single thing stop you.

As if he could read her mind, Sam seemed to deem one additional form of caution necessary. "This could turn out to be a disaster," he warned, giving her one last chance to turn and run. Good sportsmanship, or something like it.

Overhead, the lights flickered, then abruptly went out. Someone groaned from their apartment, shouting something about finding a flashlight, but in the midst of the corridor's blanketing darkness, Lily had the good fortune of seeing things clearly enough.

"Well, who knows," she said, wrapping her arms around Sam's neck and drawing his lips down to hers. "Maybe we'll get lucky."

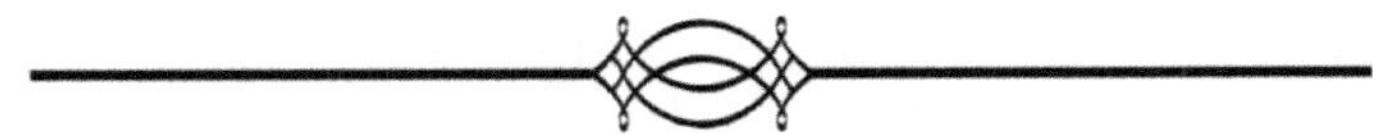

"Lily, it's such a pleasure to have you back on the show," said a characteristically gushing Jackson Carter. "Obviously you've had quite a whirlwind these past few weeks—"

"Oh, did something happen?" Lily asked, playfully light-hearted, and Jackson gave her a dutiful laugh.

"Well, let's see… shall I recap, or would you like to?"

"Oh, go ahead, Jackson, you do it so well."

"Well, where should we start? Presumably with the allegations brought against your former campaign manager, Taj Garner, just before the midterm elections," Jackson said, pairing it with a perfunctory grimace of sympathy. "I think most of us can probably agree the timing was—"

"Abysmal? Yes," Lily supplied, the tips of her hair skirting her clavicle as she leaned forward, indulging another conspiratorial laugh with Jackson.

"Right, right," Jackson agreed. "I think we all suspected you might drop out of the race, but of course that's not very Lily Nasser, is it?"

"No, Jackson, never. Like my grandmother always says, 'giving up means you're dead, and not even that stops most people,'" she quoted, finding that another 'yes, my grandmother is a spiritual medium, it's adorable and not at all about theft' reference was usually an endearing play. "My campaign was never about its manager, as you know," she said, sobering just enough to deliver the message sincerely. "It was always about the constituents, and I never stopped believing for a second that I had a better plan for serving them than my opponent."

"And you were able to find a new campaign manager, weren't you?"

"Yes, Sam Rainier was generous enough to help me during the weeks leading up to election day," Lily confirmed. "Of course, it doesn't hurt that a Hart staffer came forward shortly after Taj's arrest to reveal Wallace Hart's involvement in the efforts to discredit my campaign," she added pointedly. "It seems that some people really do prefer working for a candidate who focuses on the issues rather than systematically destroying their opponents."

"So true, so true. Still, quite a lucky break, wasn't it?" Jackson prompted cheerfully, and Lily demurred with a smile.

"Oh, Jackson, you don't really believe in luck, do you?" she asked, coy as ever. "Statistically speaking, you can really only act against your constituency's best interests for so many years before someone inevitably decides to speak up."

"Well, that's certainly true, isn't i-"

"Jackson," interrupted the voice of the show's producer, "hang on, we're just having a little trouble with the connection—"

Lily glanced up, catching Sam's eye across the studio. *Sorry*, he mouthed, gesturing to the monitors with a shrug; Lily feigned her disapproval, but winked.

"Okay, let's just wrap it up and take it to commercial," said the producer with a hint of panic, signaling for Jackson to finish Lily's introduction.

"Well, we're just having a bit of trouble here in the studio," Jackson said, "but we'll be right back after the break!" He paused, smile freezing in place for a moment, and then turned to Lily, letting his expression of amiability collapse. "Everyone here is a total goddamn disaster," he muttered to her, then rose to his feet, beckoning for makeup. "Can someone get me some concealer, please? My undereye bags are a fucking nightmare!"

Lily, meanwhile, departed to reach Sam, standing on tiptoe to brush her lips against his cheek. "Wanna meet me after?" she asked, gesturing over her shoulder to the frantic producer. "It appears they're suffering some sort of totally unexpected technological glitch."

Sam smiled. "Ramen?"

She sighed. "There are other foods, you know."

"Yeah, but I worry about sushi."

She rolled her eyes and he pulled her closer, kissing her firmly this time. "Just promise you'll pick something especially nutritious," he advised, "because tomorrow, we get back to work."

"We?" she asked, pleasantly surprised, and he nodded.

"We," he confirmed. "Or did you think I registered to vote just to sit around and do nothing?"

She opened her mouth to reply, but before she could, Jackson's producer was calling her back.

"See you after," she told Sam, departing with a wave, and then she rearranged herself on Jackson's sofa, adjusting her blazer.

"Ladies and gentlemen, welcome back! We're chatting this morning with Congresswoman-elect, Lily Nasser. Now Lily, you found out late last night that you took your district in a historic win, which seems to have equally puzzled and enraptured the country. What's your secret?"

Oh, a little this, a little that, she thought. Some fate, a smidge of luck, and a deeply unsexy amount of perseverance.

But then again, why kill the dream?

"Well, Jackson," said Lily, flashing him the smile of a humble, gracious politician who had learned that a little white lie never hurt anyone. "If I told you, what kind of secret would it be?"

THE IMMORTALITY PROJECT

ALTHOUGH NIKITA ALLEGRA ASHERMAN has been publicly dismissed from her job as Vice President of a large tech conglomerate, she firmly believes that the true motivation for her unceremonious sacking was the unintentional discovery of her employer's attempt to achieve immortality by virtue of unethical data collection. In an effort to reveal her boss's sinister plot, Nikita must uncover his co-conspirators and turn him over to the proper authorities.

Unfortunately, she may have misunderstood the true nature of his plan.

364

THE IMMORTALITY PROJECT

What follows herewith is a matter of legal documentation wherein I, Nikita Allegra Asherman, a probably heterosexual cisgender woman of sound body and mind who has consumed no more than three (5) improperly made martinis, will be recording the events of my pursuit of Article 1, Justice As A Result of Punitive And Immensely Not Cool Sacking From Previous Position As Vice President Of Well Known Software Behemoth Possessing Wildly Tyrannical Aims [REDACTED COMPANY NAME], as well as Article 2, Morally Sound Quest For Compensation With Which Any Reasonable Person Would Surely Agree Is Owed Due To Unlawful Fuckery By [REDACTED CEO NAME], Previous Employer and Massively Small-Penised Douche, and Article 3, Vengeance Of An Exceedingly Rational Nature, end quote.

Although I have every expectation that the man known forthwith and heretofore as The Insufferable Bouquet of Dicks will henceforth proceed to divest me of any credibility as a result of the aforementioned Weaponized Sacking, let it be known that I am not only a person of extreme and dare I say agonizing competence but also, importantly, a woman who is very much Not Having It, and therefore I anticipate what follows to be of equally agonizing clarity, send tweet.

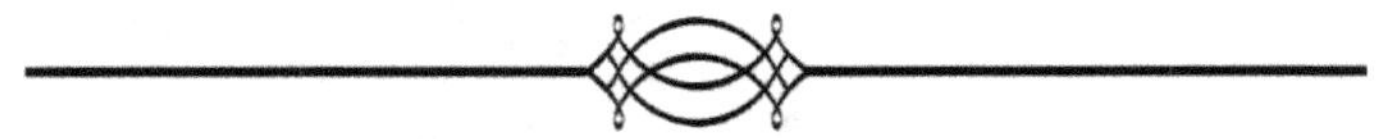

Am sober now, regrettably. Was not my aim and will continue to be a matter of avoidance.

As I was saying, this document will contain what I believe to be my life's most important work, which I am not undertaking for the purposes of myself alone but also for humanity. Seeing as I have devoted the past decade of my life to the accumulation of not only commercial accolades but also technical achievements for the good of [REDACTED COMPANY NAME], I have been granted the keenly unusual position of possessing quite a rolodex, otherwise known as a Little Black Book which is FILLED TO THE BRIM with the private lines belonging to some of the world's most influential and horniest tech CEOs. Oh yes [REDACTED CEO NAME] you Insufferable Bouquet of Dicks, you thought you'd stripped me of all your secrets, didn't you? I hope you're reading this now while you [REDACTED FOR GRAPHIC SEXUAL IMAGERY] yourself in your corner office, you patronizing blowhard. Yes, you may have kept me out of the room where the decisions were made and well done you for that, congratulations on being effectively the dumbest boy in school for the twentieth year running you massively top-heavy fuck! It follows that a man who needed my help to so much as ask nicely for your first round of private equity funding would believe that all secrets remain between two conspiratorial men with strippers sat blithely across their knees. Believe it or not [REDACTED CEO NAME], said stripper is at least ten times smarter than you are and, I have no doubt, astronomically better in bed, which is a fact of which your prissy team of sanguinary lawyers should be aware. Not because it's relevant to what will surely be the scandal of our lifetimes but because everyone looking at you should be acutely and better yet uncomfortably aware of your deficiencies. [LEGAL ANNOTATION: *uncomfortably noted.*]

Lest this take longer than the week I have very meticulously allotted for this effort in order to lure you into a sense of false security (at this very moment I can practically hear you saying to your old boy's club of equally Insufferable You Know Whats [LEGAL ANNOTATION: *here the author is referring once again to phalluses, although whether in the oft-repeated bouquet form or as individual units remains unclear*] that poor, poor Ash has slunk back to her very sad flat with her tail between her legs like a good little girl and wouldn't you know it, you always knew she wouldn't be a problem, she was always like that, you know, desperate for your approval, even in school, yes of course you were very good mates at university but even then you were aware in a sad, sympathetic sort of way that Nikita Asherman was indeed a very desperate sort of chum but never a *real* threat, she simply cares too much, it's not in her nature to be vindictive) and to you I say directly: Fuck right off and [REDACTED FOR GRAPHIC SEXUAL CONTENT, OBSCENE LANGUAGE, ANATOMICAL IMPOSSIBILITY, AND GENERAL INCOHERENCE].

To set the scene: in the early aughts, my inarguably sterling academic records will show my transfer from Yale University to Oxford University, where I would ultimately finish with double firsts in computer science and economics. During my time at Oxford, I would meet and become very close acquaintances with the Insufferable Bouquet of Dicks previously known as my employer, who at the time was a year above me in a similar program of study focused on what the Insufferable Bouquet [LEGAL ANNOTATION: *of dicks*] spoke of with incessant poeticism as "the language of algorithms," aka what every fucking computer science student was also studying, you Detestable Pighead Man. At the time I will admit to being a bit awed by him, as many others were, hence the subsequent founding of [REDACTED COMPANY NAME] in a brothel of a flat that he and I shared with our third founder, whom I will henceforth be referring to as The Weaselly Little Shit Who Owes Me A Literal Billion Dollars (I will abbreviate as Weasel) [LEGAL ANNOTATION: *this is appreciated*].

On a particularly sauced night over takeaway, Weasel, Bag of Dicks [LEGAL ANNOTATION: *'bag' appears to be interchangeable with the term 'bouquet' from this point on*], and I came up with the idea for a social networking platform which would form the basis for a mausoleum of personal data. I was aware of the unethical nature of such a venture but was also very hungry and needed urgently to pay rent. In our collective excitement, Bag of Dicks and I had extremely subpar sex during which I did not finish. Although we would later go on to receive a billion-dollar valuation within the year, Bag of Dicks would never satisfy me sexually despite nearly two decades to follow of similar encounters. In the event he claims this is untrue, believe me, it is not. I blame myself for faking orgasms and for accepting the position of Vice President rather than Chief Technical Officer in order to pacify our investors, whom I now suspect had not actually voiced this concern but rather, fulfilled an excuse presented to me privately by Bag of Dicks while I was distracted by the failing health of my mother (Sidenote: eat shit, [CEO NAME REDACTED]) in order to ensure I would never have full access to his private technological aims.

Which brings us to now, the day after I arrived at the office to find the door locked and my personal possessions boxed up and waiting for me in the corridor. This is, as I've mentioned, no doubt in response to my "sniffing around" (quoth Bag of Dicks) the fundamental misconduct to which we have now arrived:

The Immortality Project.

Surely it will not have escaped the attention of the lawyers I can only presume to be billing at crippling, exorbitant rates that the Bag of Dicks in question is a man of absurd and staggering means, with not only a tangible fortune but also an unprecedentedly high valuation that he would not possess without my assistance. [LEGAL ANNOTATION: *exaggerated verbiage and as yet undetermined conclusion aside, this is a valid summary of the pertinent facts*.] My aim as follows is to reveal to the world the insidious intentions of one Bag of Dicks and his Weasel, and in so doing, collect not precisely the amount I am owed (the money is not at issue although it would be well within my rights to make demands) [LEGAL ANNOTATION: *unconfirmed matter of subjectivity pending investigation*] but some degree of recompense in the form of indemnification to my reputation. This is a matter of restoration, not comeuppance.

Though if Bag of Dicks happens to eat a proverbial bag of dicks as a result of the following documentation, there will be no complaints from me.

Though I was locked out of the [REDACTED COMPANY NAME] server I helped design and therefore do not have access to my official contacts, I do still retain those personal connections I made as a result of being—and here a sigh—one of the ten most influential women in tech, which is an absolutely criminal thing to say when one considers that I ought to be CTO and am instead merely a secondary, perhaps even tertiary officer. For me to be named one of the ten most influential women in technology is made even more disappointing when one considers that the other nine women (and a half) are white, and five of them are simply the wives of the Influential Men in Tech.

All in all, this will undoubtedly require a libation.

Having paused to fetch a bottle of very good Sancerre that I will be billing the Bag of Dicks come six days from this moment [LEGAL ANNOTATION: *receipt for said bottle of wine has been inadvertently (?) adhered to this page of documentation by what appears to be some sort of soluble gummy candy*] I will now continue with my hypothesis, which is that Bag of Dicks and his Dick-Savoring Cronies (not a knock against anyone's sexuality by the way, as a consumer of dicks myself this is not inherently a matter of distaste but rather what I can only assume to be an apt descriptor given the blatant savoring of Bag of Dick's dick) have colluded in order to procure what I believe to be the biggest breach in history, *in re* personal data. It is my hypothesis, given a decade's worth of business development and the occasional immoral pillow talk when Dick was particularly insistent and I was especially weak [LEGAL ADDENDUM: *henceforth Bag of Dicks, formerly Bouquet of Dicks, becomes simply Dick, presumably for time*] that the company I founded with Weasel and Dick has been collecting personal data for the purposes of

1) charting human behavior

2) building an algorithm which will, in a sense, recreate human behavior and therefore allow the human mind, replicated by virtue of data extrapolation, to live eternally.

Anyone with insight into Dick's private life will confirm that his obsession with his legacy is incessant. It is a fixation, and one which I believe he would not have stopped pursuing even if he did already possess five fucking yachts. [LEGAL ADDENDUM: *list of personal assets currently accounts for eight.*] In order to prove my essential theory that Dick is seeking an algorithm which will allow him to live forever, I will undertake the following steps:

1. Suss out his most influential co-conspirators, which I suspect to be [CEO OF BIOCHEMICAL LAB AND PHARMACEUTICAL COMPANY, NAME REDACTED], [CEO AND FOUNDER OF SOFTWARE CONGLOMERATE, NAME REDACTED], [CEO OF ONLINE RETAILING COMPANY, NAME REDACTED], [CEO OF WEAPONS MANUFACTURING COMPANY, NAME REDACTED], and [CEO OF GENOMICS AND BIOTECH COMPANY, NAME REDACTED]. Henceforth they will be referred to as Idiot 1, Idiot 2, Jackass, Creepyfuck, and Shitbag.

2. Dick is small fries compared to the aforementioned crew of billionaire fungi. However his tech is very good (you'll remember I helped design it) so as much as it pains me to say it, Dick must be the brains and someone else will have to comprise the money. Once I have zeroed in on the source of the cash I will attempt to seduce and follow the breadcrumbs.

3. Once seduction has been complete and crumbs have been laid I will uncover the lynchpin of the operation. Thus far it is unclear where the project is based, though I assume it is a tax-sheltered island because billionaire fuckbois unimaginatively love islands and boats. Therefore I will travel to what is inevitably an island and infiltrate it to discover the source of The Immortality Project.

4. Once there, I will destroy it. I will destroy it with my bare hands, and then I will return to give Dick the following message: You

are a small man and worse than that you are a mortal one. You will die someday through no fault of mine—I will of course outlive you because I am a woman and this is what we do—but when you do, I want you to know that I could have saved you. Instead I sat in the sun with a beer in my hand and I laughed.

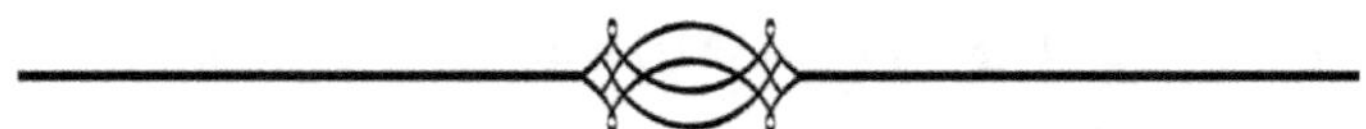

Am once again sober although not for long, ha ha. Have rung Idiot 1's private secretary (once lent her a tampon & now we are of course Best Friends) asking where he'll be and she has informed me he will be in a meeting, which means he will be in a disgusting " "gentlemen" " (double quotes for Extreme Skepticism)'s club.

It has occurred to me since awakening to a vicious sight (i.e. my face) that perhaps seduction is a method better outsourced. Will find accomplice and report back soon.

Have found a very excellent partner in crime in Saffron, which seems to me an odd choice for an escort name but I do not care which spices women happen to find desirous. Besides it is probably only one of many false names. [LEGAL ANNOTATION: *the aforementioned Saffron has not been found, so this is a very good point.*] Arrived with the intent to pay Saffron large amounts of money which she has accepted but also she agrees this entire thing is fucked and has promised to get Idiot 1 to spill the beans as a matter of solidarity primarily. She has also offered her services for

Jackass and Shitbag, both of whom are also frequenters of this Place For Disgusting Men, but says she will not be alone in a room with Creepyfuck. I tell her this is more than understandable and warn her that they may be very secretive about this, as it is not only illegal but also highly unethical and would probably get them all arrested if anyone knew. She has nodded very seriously so I think she understands what's at stake. I think possibly Saffron is some sort of mythical succubus but I do not mention this out of politeness. I do not know the politically correct term for such things.

Within one hour Saffron has fetched me from the back room to tell me that actually Idiot 1 is more of an idiot than I thought and coincidentally, Idiot 2 was with him. She admits she did drug them a bit to which I said that was not what I had in mind but she assured me they will be fine, there are no lasting side effects to her knowledge. I am aware this is legally very questionable [LEGAL ANNOTATION: *yes*] but this is how it is, and I can't hold Saffron's effectiveness against her. She tells me Idiot 1 and Idiot 2 claim the idea is theirs which means, in her expert opinion, it is not. Evidently whilst boasting of their prowess in both the bedroom ("Make sure to say they are explicitly bad at sex" says Saffron, paraphrased, who is currently watching me type this into my Notes app) and the boardroom, they were especially cagey about Creepyfuck.

This is bad news. Saffron looks sympathetic.

I do not like Creepyfuck, but it appears he will have to be my next call.

In practice for not calling him Creepyfuck to his face I will henceforth be referring to him by the name of Erik, which is not his real name (his real name is [REDACTED]) but rather the name of the Phantom of the Opera, who is indeed also a Creepyfuck no matter how tragic his backstory. If I slip up and call him Erik that will not be ideal but also it will be subtler.

Update: have carefully inebriated myself and watched a curation of sad film scenes on YouTube. Am now sufficiently in tears and will ring Erik. It is very important that he feels he is needed by me, a vulnerable woman with breasts. (The second part is the crucial bit.) Phone is ringing. Phone is ringing. Fuck, have not considered possibility of voicemail, shitfuckbuggerit what will I—

Update: Erik has answered the phone. Would love to see me, he says, feels terrible about what's happened to me, there has always been something between us, perhaps I would like to meet him in his home after his meeting which is running very late. I agree that I am very distressed and need to be comforted by a strong and virile man of obscene wealth. He says midnight will do.

Update: have rung Saffron for advice. She is truly an exceptional life coach.

Will update upon return.

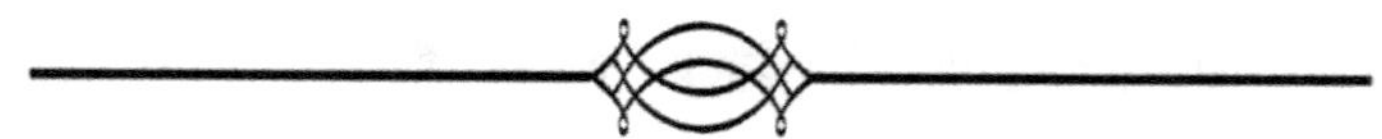

Things have gone slightly awry in that Erik now appears to be dead. I understand that this will look like my fault however it is not. I did have an unfortunate and unwilling spasm in response to his attempt to creepyfuck me but I am 70% sure this is not the cause of his death.

[LEGAL ANNOTATION: *the man known as Erik has since been autopsied. Cause of death is a blood clot, source unknown.*] One minute he was alive and creepy and the next he was dead and creepy. I am of course a disgruntled former tech employee being slandered by Dick for, quote, "hysteria related to my personal life" so this is obviously a problem. Pause while I ring Saffron.

Saffron has come to meet me. I regret to say that I have let her in using a corpse for biometric security measures. She says this is very bad and I agree, it does not look good. She reminds me again this is bad and I say yes Saffron I know and she says but it's so very bad, like, worse than she thought would happen and she had already considered many bad options. I agree that this is valid. Then she tells me I may as well snoop around before someone comes looking for him and I agree that this is another excellent point from Saffron. She covers him up with a sheet and then follows me to find Erik's phone and computer.

Whilst poking around through Erik's phone (facial recognition technology is excellent even when the face is immobilized and corpselike), Saffron finds the phone number from a friend she used to work the corners with, which I think (?) is a joke. She laughs so I'm pretty sure it's a joke. Anyway she is calling her friend now from Erik's phone, and then she begins speaking in another language. I am sort of a cultured and worldly transatlantic person so you'd think I would be able to recognize what they are speaking, but either because I am in shock from being 30% or less likely at fault for murder or because it's not a normal human language, I do not understand them. I look at my fingernails and think about Dick.

The night before he fired me he came to my flat in what I now realize was an effort to keep me away from my office, and potentially also to assuage his soon-to-be guilty conscience. He told me I had been his oldest and truest friend and that he wished he could be as good to me as I was to him. At the time I was quite sleepy and also a bit lonely, because working as much as I do means that men do not care to be deprioritized in my schedule. Dick was being Very Nice to me in the way that men sometimes manage to be from time to time. I wish now that I had not kissed him and instead stabbed him in the ribs.

Saffron has hung up the phone and informed me there is indeed an island. Her friend has been there, she says, and can give me the coordinates. I comment that I am unsure how I will pay for transportation to this island and Saffron hits a few buttons and says that Erik has now transferred a small fortune to my account. I say well this is going to make me look very guilty and Saffron agrees that it will. She tells me I should probably not come back and I say yes, probably not. She looks sad and so do I.

I ask Saffron if she wants to come with me and she says that will be fine, so now Saffron and I are going to the Caribbean. Will update later once I find a way out of the country, which I will have to do before Erik's maid service in the morning.

[LEGAL ANNOTATION: *the man called Erik was discovered three days later by his wife, who had just returned from a spontaneous shopping trip to Paris. The maid had been in but had not wanted to disturb him; she thought he was asleep and did not think it was polite to mention the smell.*]

Saffron has been an excellent investment as far as partners go. She knows many people, including several people at the airport who've helped us procure the private plane, and also someone else who has gotten us false papers. My name is listed as Cinnamon which Saffron seems to think is very funny and my picture is actually quite good. "Girl you got a face for passport photos" is Saffron's take on the subject.

We have arrived at the island (it isn't on a map but the coordinates are [REDACTED]) and there is no doubt that this is a haven for secretive billionaires. Most troubling is that Saffron and I are both not-white women who are not accompanied by a white man, which is quite a glaring error by us. I kick myself for not considering this in advance, but Saffron is very quick on her feet. She tells the staff we were sent by Erik as a gift for his very important guest and if we are not in his bed with our legs spread in the next fifteen minutes he will be very angry. They say which very important guest? and Saffron snaps that of course Erik didn't tell us who it was, which is again very clever and probably accurate. The staff seems to have heard this before, although they give me in particular a quizzical glance. Saffron says don't worry I'll have her makeup done by then. They nod in relief and relent, leading us to a jungle suite that can only be reached by boat. The whole thing reeks of fetishization and I want to hurl into the fake island canal. Miraculously I keep it down. Dicks. [LEGAL ANNOTATION: *for purposes of clarity this seems to be a cathartic exclamation, not a reference to any dick in particular.*]

It is immediately apparent to me, a person who is also very proficient in technology despite my burdensome ovaries, that there is something of massive technological significance on this island. A server, I suspect. There is a massive building that is clearly refrigerated and entrance is prohibited, and possibly impossible. There are no doors. I tell Saffron we have to find out what's in there and she agrees it looks "mad spooky," which I think means she agrees with me. We are transported to the VIP guest suite and inside it looks very Zen Monastic, which reminds me of Dick's flat. I have gone on at length to Saffron about Dick at this point, and have mocked his taste endlessly. There is minimalism and then there is blandness, I say, because the man is entirely devoid of sentiment or taste. He could live inside a mirror. She laughs and says honey, I know boys like that and it don't matter how much paper they got, they don't change. We conspire momentarily and she does my face so that I look like someone convincingly purchased for sex. She pokes my stomach lightly (this is not comfortable but it is also not offensive) and asks if I have had children, to which I say no, I haven't, I've just had a career for the last however many years and I haven't even been on a date in about six months. She asks me when I last had sex and I laugh until tears come out of my eyes. She says shh shh don't cry and I say I'm not crying, it's just really funny. She looks at me like I am very sad which might be true.

The door opens and the VIP is here so I will write more later.

Things have again gone awry. I should have known this would be Dick's special secret island suite because of course other rich men are more monarchical than monastic. I have narrowly leapt out of the window and into the surrounding canal, which thankfully was not very deep. I hear Dick say he thought there were two women so Saffron, very quick on her feet, says that he is a naughty boy who can have another toy when he finishes with his first one. My stomach roils at the thought of what comes next but then Saffron pokes her head out, spotting me, and tells me that she has once again used drugs. This is of course very helpful although the crimes do seem to be piling up more than I anticipated. [LEGAL ADDENDUM: *this is true.*]

Saffron tells me that's just how things go sometimes and to my dismay I suspect that she's right. The only thing that remains is to foil Dick's plan, and so I need to break into what I am positive now must be The Immortality Project's server. Saffron wants to come with me but I tell her someone has to keep an eye on Dick in case he wakes. She pouts but ultimately decides this is reasonable. We make margaritas and wait until the cover of dark, during which time Dick wakes once to ask why he's tied up. Saffron says doesn't naughty boy remember he's been very very bad. She is honestly a genius.

I am taking a moment to myself to reflect on the fact that Dick has stolen my life from me. Worse is that I let him do it. Why have I always cared for other people over myself? Why have I nurtured a bunch of meaningless stocks instead of my own desires? It occurs to me that at least if Dick lives forever he will do something with his life, even if that something is just being egregiously bad in bed with women who don't deserve him. If I could live forever, what would I do with the rest of my life? I've lived more in the last three days than in the entirety of my prior lifetime. If I died tomorrow nobody would even remember me. The most important thing in my life is to destroy Dick for what he stole from me, which for the record wasn't my job. Dick stole my whole life right out from under me. And I didn't even notice until after he'd already fit the whole thing into a cardboard box for me to find outside my office.

Initially I am not quite sure how I plan to get into the server room. As I said it does not have an entrance and I am not some sort of secret agent spy who can climb up the side of buildings. Once I realize that I will in all likelihood need Saffron's help again, I spend most of the night trying to properly diagram the server room so that we can devise a plan. [LEGAL ANNOTATION: *diagram has been filed in discovery*.] Eventually I realize the structure not only backs into the side of a mountain but disappears within it, which leads me to conclude it must be a cave. I decide the mountain will be our best method of entry, though I am not a proficient hiker and even less proficient at climbing.

I return to find that Dick is gone and that Saffron is waiting for me with our things. She says that Erik has been found dead and that Dick knows that Erik's last financial transfer was to me. He is livid and headed back home to tighten security surrounding what he called "The Project," which Saffron recognized as the very thing that had set all this in motion. She tells me we have to get out of here immediately. I say does she think we should try escaping into the remote mountains of a mysterious island? She says good idea girl, that sounds good.

Would kill for a bottle of Sancerre. Have been wandering around this mountain for hours looking for a way in. Saffron thinks if there's a hurdle we can't get over then we should go under. I don't know what that's a metaphor for but will report back.

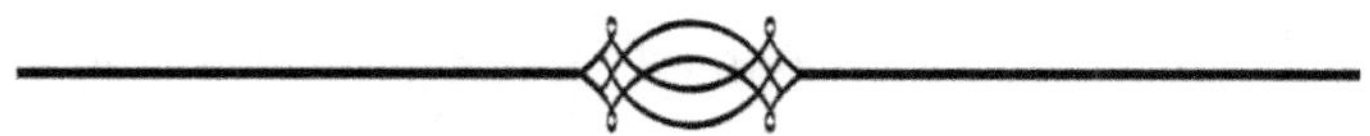

She meant literally.

Somehow Saffron was able to befriend some of the people who work on this island and they've helped us get the necessary scuba gear, though neither of us have any of the equally necessary scuba training. We are advised not to die, which we take under serious consideration.

One of the island staff who is almost certainly in love with Saffron runs over while we are practicing with our scuba gear. (I am not good at controlling my impulse to panic. Saffron is of course incredible.) The staffer, a slight but beautiful dark boy, tells us that the island's usual guests have ALL arranged to come soon and no one currently on the island is allowed out. They are worried that someone will try to breach the island's defenses and now we are essentially trapped. This would be disheartening to hear if I were not already being investigated for murder, which the beautiful dark boy tells Saffron in private as if he is concerned that I will murder her next. "Oh honey please," Saffron says loudly, "I know Death personally and she ain't as cute as this one." Neither the beautiful boy nor I have any idea what that means, but we are equally awed by it.

In any case, I am once again trapped without any choice of moving backwards, so I will have to progress with my plan of submergence into the server room, aka forwards.

Will report back or will be dead, TBD.

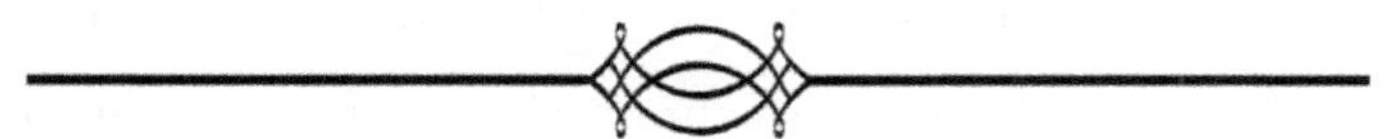

Have found an entrance into the server room. Beneath the surface of the island's various lakes was utter pitch blackness through which Saffron and I were forced to hold hands. I have never before been so set on remaining calm despite a thorough lack of inward tranquility. I considered, of course, the reward of seeing Dick lose everything, which was something of a North Star as far as meditational guidance.

After what felt like hours of swimming, our eyes gradually adjusted enough to avoid the jutting stalagmite from below, whereupon a glimpse of bluish something above the surface became visible. We swam towards it, approaching from beneath, and realized there was some light to be found, though not much. We broke through the surface and found ourselves inside a cave, which was illuminated not by the sun or the moon, but by a massive silver door.

Exhausted from swimming, Saffron and I drew ourselves up through the surface and collapsed on the banks of ashy, pebbled rock. It was exceedingly uncomfortable but the feeling of being alive was palpable and stark. I have recently come to realize that I did not fully expect to live through this, and thus I am overcome with gratitude to Saffron. I told her as much and she explained to me that a person like her doesn't concern themselves with the future. Things don't always get better, she says, sometimes they just stay the same and sometimes they get worse, and she didn't really expect to do anything or see anything and now she has. I reach across the jagged stones and hold her fingers tightly.

It infuriates me that Dick has wealth enough to ensure that a hundred million Saffrons never see another bad day and yet he clings to it like he deserves it more than anyone. I tell Saffron that if I do end up getting financial compensation—assuming I don't go to prison for murder [LEGAL ANNOTATION: *counts of second-degree murder against Nikita Allegra Asherman have been dismissed since the autopsy of the man known as Erik/Creepyfuck. She is now charged only with various amounts of theft, breaking and entering, and accessory to unlawful abduction*]—I'll give it all to her.

"Nah," she says, "we cool."

I have no idea what that means but I do think we should probably get this over with.

The silver door awaits.

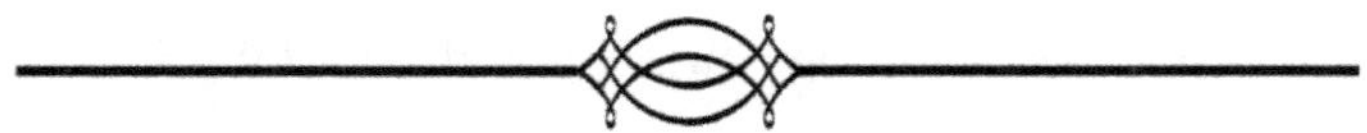

Can't write now. Did not expect this.

Am concerned Saffron may have drugged me. Will try again later.

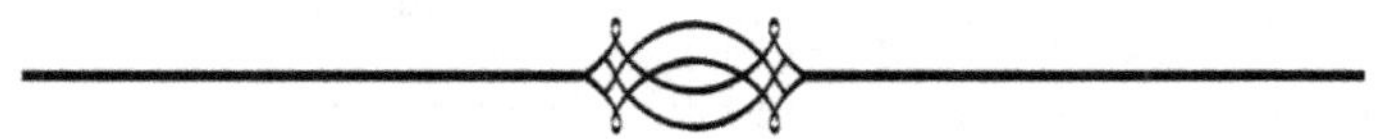

Saffron insists I have NOT been drugged and wants to know why I am not "aggressively" writing things down as usual. I say I don't know where to begin. She says begin at the beginning: we opened the door and it wasn't a server room like I said it would be, it was just a cave with a glittering pond and some kind of crazy-ass witch. I hiss to her that I don't think 'witch' is an appropriate term and then the witch interrupts to tell me that calling a thing by its name is not a problem, though she wishes I would call her (something that sounds like a dolphin shriek).

I need to eat something although I am afraid to. Will try again later.

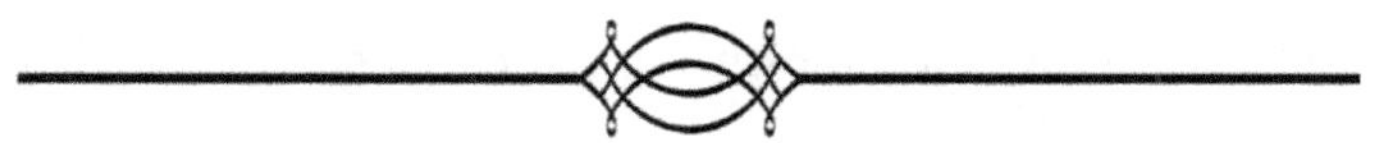

Either the stress of this week has finally gotten to me or there actually is some sort of mythical island witch here whose name I'd love to say but can't properly spell who is forcefully dictating to me the rest of her story. She was imprisoned here by men with wealth beyond imagination. They believe she is the mistress of the infamous Fountain of Youth, even though this is definitely a lake and not even remotely a fountain.

"I lied," she said, gesturing to her lake, which seems to be the reason she's been imprisoned. "It can cure a few things, you know, like—are you writing this down? Keep writing—arthritis and carpal tunnel. It's mostly a very effective anti-inflammatory because frankly my dear I am not convinced immortality is such a good idea, hm? Your kind is simply not fit to survive it."

I tell her this is disappointing news, not because I'm not fit for eternal life but because I was hoping to uncover enormous wrongdoing. She points out that she's been abducted and held against her will, which is a valid point, definitely, but I tell her this isn't something I can report to the authorities unless she'd like to press charges. She says no thank you that sounds tiresome. I tell her we could probably get her out since we did manage to break through the door that keeps her in (I am an ok hacker) [LEGAL ANNOTATION: *Nikita Allegra Asherman won four consecutive unsanctioned university hackathons before a certain Bag of Dicks rose to prominence in their program*] and she says that would be nice, thank you, and asks what I would like in return.

I ask if she means like a wish? And she says depends, maybe. Okay, yeah, sure, a wish.

For the first time I wonder what I would wish for if I could be granted only one thing. I am mostly a practical person, which is why I thought we were looking for an algorithm when it turns out that all the idiots and jackasses and dicks and shitbags were looking for a fairytale all along. I have never allowed myself to consider what I would do if I ever came across a bit of magic, nor would I have ever assumed any magic would willingly be used on my behalf. I think about money first, obviously, because I'll never get another job after this, but capitalism aside, that seems unnecessary. I can always lay brick or herd sheep or something even if I never code anything again in my life. If I never start another company then so be it; it's not like I ever really wanted power.

Love? Even if she could give me that, I think it would feel unearned.

So I say the first thing that comes to my tongue, which is: I wish that things were different. As in, I wish this were a different world, one less dominated by dicks and idiots and shitbags and more rewarding of Saffrons instead. I wish girls who didn't quite know their own power yet would not get swept away by boys who did. I wish a man could not claim all my success for his own, just as I wish he could not simply point at me and diminish me to nothing. I wish I had allowed myself to be a little more difficult a little bit sooner in my life, because it seems like only once I got angry did my life actually start to begin.

The witch whose name I can't pronounce tells me that of course this can be arranged, and for a moment her lake glitters, and she says go on, take a sip. I sigh and ask her if there was ever any immortality database like the one I suspected there was and she says she doesn't know, though this whole island reeks of greed and generally smelly vibes. Saffron, who has not made a wish yet, agrees.

Then the witch says, Drink.

So I drop to my knees and cup a little of her enchantment between my palms, letting it saturate my fingers. I bring the liquid to my lips, letting it seep in through the cracks, and then it cools my tongue.

In the moment it lingers before my throat, I think how strange it is to have been so lost for so long, and then behind me, I hear Saffron saying something, probably to the witch. I swallow just before the door behind us is wrenched open once again.

And then expectedly unexpected, we're found.

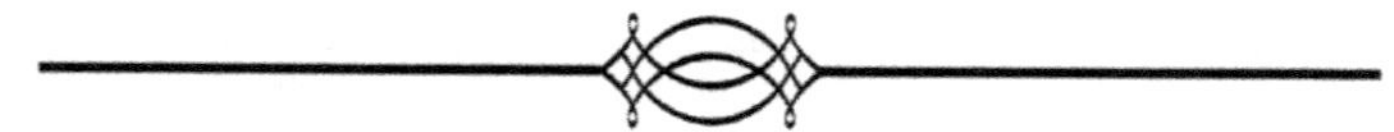

[LEGAL ANNOTATION:

Here the documentation provided by Nikita Allegra Asherman comes to an end. However, having spent a great amount of time poring over her personal notes and detecting what I believe to be an earnestness about her story, I have concluded this is not, as our client claims, an open-and-shut case of retaliatory employee dissatisfaction.

For example, the following was given to us by the man referred to by Ms. Asherman as "Dick":

I, Nikita Allegra Asherman, hereby confess to the murder of [ERIK] and the destruction of several billion dollars' worth of technological infrastructure. I am overcome with guilt and wish to say that [DICK] has been an invaluable support as a result of all this. I have been unwell for some time and have only now found the strength to seek treatment.

It is my belief that, given everything noted above, this statement could only have been written under extreme duress. It is true that Ms. Asherman was found unconscious on the floor of the island's server (her body heat, it is said, having destroyed the data in the files, thereby making it impossible to ascertain their original use) and therefore her state of mind may have been compromised. There is no proof that this "Saffron" character has ever existed, as there is no employee record at the club in question and the two CEOs named herein deny any knowledge of such a woman. Also, Ms. Asherman has herself confessed to profound intoxication. All of these facts do make her testimony somewhat open to interpretation.

However, I do not believe the story contained within these files to be, as our client claims they are, the delusion ramblings of a madwoman, nor do I think any of it is a lie. Perhaps that is because I saw his face when I told him these files existed. He does not know how they arrived on my desk, nor do I suspect that he should have.

Having turned over copies of this discovery, a full federal investigation is now underway. In my professional opinion as a qualified legal expert, I have reason to believe that the Dick in these files is indeed guilty of unlawful data collection. While the extent of his guilt will be put to a jury of his peers to determine, the gentleman referred to by Ms. Asherman as "Weasel" has already agreed to cooperate as a witness against Mr. Bag of Dicks, following an offer of immunity from the state. This, as Dick surely suspects by now, is what we in the industry call a smoking gun.

As to the matter of Ms. Asherman herself: I recently went to visit her in the rehabilitation center of her choosing, largely out of curiosity for the woman whose written thoughts I have been living in for several months. She seems lucid, and in my professional opinion, her involvement in her earlier crimes will likely be dismissed as a result of what can only be called a full psychotic break. I assured her that I would not allow my client, who will henceforth be billed as exorbitantly as she once suspected, to destroy what remains of her life or reputation. She will most likely face a punitive fine, true, but that can be paid from her compensation as a result of pain and suffering with regard to her unlawful termination. I assured her as gently as I possibly could that she has obviously been wronged, and I will see to it that the situation is rectified.

Having now turned over these files in full, I hereby withdraw myself from both the defense of my former client and the investigation against him as a whole. It is my opinion that he is indeed a bouquet of dicks, and that the company (in its more ethical capacity) would be better off in Ms. Asherman's hands, should she find herself restored enough to succeed him.

I will add only this, which is that while Ms. Asherman does not have any family, significant others, or close friends, she does appear to have a regular visitor. The name listed on the guest sign-in sheet belongs to the venture capitalist responsible for the restructuring of the five most profitable companies in the world, all of whom saw the arrest of their founders as a result of Ms. Asherman's investigation. This woman's name is, of course, not Saffron, although I do have to wonder if such a reference to the most legendary and expensive spice in the world is, as my former client protests, a delusion of Ms. Asherman's, or perhaps something cleverer and, indeed, far more satisfying an end.

As I am now recusing myself, I have nothing more to add, except to conclude this note to my former client with, per Ms. Asherman's wishes, her own words:

You are a small man, and worse than that, you are a mortal one. You will die someday through no fault of mine, but when you do, I want you to know that I could have saved you.

Instead, I sat in the sun with a beer in my hand and I laughed.

END ANNOTATION.]

ABOUT *the* AUTHOR

Olivie Blake is a lover and writer of stories, many of which involve the fantastic, the paranormal, or the supernatural, but not always. More often, her works revolve around what it means to be human (or not), and the endlessly interesting complexities of life and love.

Olivie has been published as the featured fiction contributor for Witch Way Magazine, as well as the writer for the graphic series *Alpha*, the anthologies *Fairytales of the Macabre*, *Midsummer Night Dreams*, and *The Lovers Grim*, and the novels *Masters of Death, Lovely Tangled Vices*, and *One For My Enemy*. She lives and works in Los Angeles, where she is generally tolerated by her rescue pit bull.